BORN AT DAWN

The Da'Valia Trilogy, Volume 1

Christina Davis

Cover design by: Ruxandra Tudorica of Methyss Art
www.methyss-art.com
Map design by: Jennifer Tedmon
Formatting by Polgarus Studio

To my dad, for a childhood full of magic.

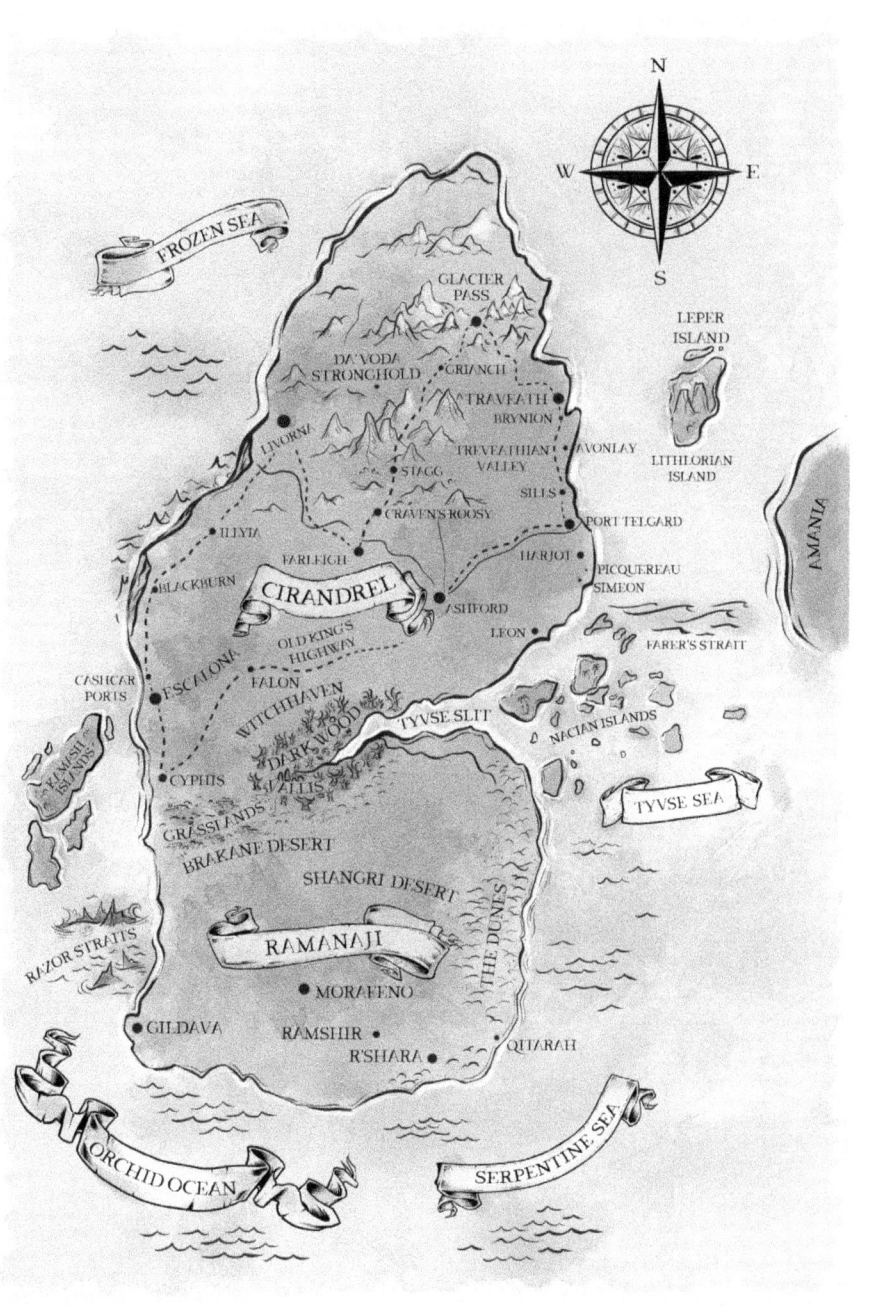

Chapter One

Fourth Fireside, 1631

We found something interesting in the archives today, and I think it's the key. The time has come so that what I write here must be done in secret. If we're right, which I suspect we are, I will be well-poised to win the title of donazhi when the summit arrives. We only need to prove what we've discovered is true before anyone else catches on.

— *Monazhi Da'Voda-Lira*

Second Vestive, 1650

Neva froze when the sound of footsteps approached the door, disturbing the steady hum of the howling wind. The tower quarters had been cold and empty when she climbed through the frosted window, and Flynn had assured her the duke would be engaged in festivities downstairs well into the night.

She held her breath, remaining crouched over the warded chest in the dark as she waited for the servant to continue past. The whisper of a lock pick and wrench scraping against the keyhole reached her, and her stomach dropped. After a moment, the door inched open, then closed with a barely perceivable *click*.

Neva silently backed against the study's stone wall. If the intruder lit a candle, she would be found out, so she murmured an incantation under her breath to call her favorite glamour to life. The telltale sting of invisibility washed over her as a man in black britches and a matching tunic strode into the study. The invisibility glamour was worth the gold she had paid, and the pain of having it stitched into her skin inch by inch, but it bit like poison ivy. She resisted scratching as the sensation faded.

A woven rug muffled the man's footfalls, and he squinted as he inspected his surroundings by moonlight, hesitating briefly when he passed the space where she stood, before continuing into the room. Her nose wrinkled. He smelled of spoiled milk.

Neva's enhanced sight allowed her to see the intense concentration on his clean-shaven face. His short blond hair was almost as light as her own, his hazel eyes were probing, and his nose was bent.

Neva stayed quiet as he moved around the desk and to the back of the room. There, he knelt in front of the warded chest.

Her teeth clenched and her hand inched toward the dagger strapped to her ankle.

A job like this rarely came along, and she was counting on it to make a name for herself. Not to mention that Flynn Abernathy, the most feared crime lord in Glacier Pass, had commissioned her. Anyone else after the same item was going against the Thieves' Code.

Neva could ambush the man. She didn't have the full power of a majila, a female Da'Valia, but she could do more than merely see in the dark. Da'Valia were fast, strong, brutal creatures. Eliminating this man from the realm of the living likely wouldn't cause them to hesitate, yet Neva did. Some said thieves were without honor, but she knew otherwise. Her father raised her to follow the Thieves' Code.

"You don't want to do that," she said, dropping her glamour and stepping away from the wall.

The man spun around as if startled but was nimble as he stepped away from the hidden prize and tossed an illuminator from his pocket.

The ball of magic exploded in a burst of yellow light before hovering near the ceiling in the center of the study. The temperature dropped to near-freezing, and Neva's breath traveled away from her in a fog. Illuminators temporarily revealed that which lay beneath both spells and darkness. Neva didn't know if the man had stolen this one, or paid for it with someone else's silver or blood.

Then, the taste of copper settled on her tongue. He had paid with blood.

He frowned and stood protectively in front of the chest as he looked her over. Neva was dressed differently than when she delivered firewood about the city during daylight hours. She had replaced her heavy fur jacket and traditional skirts with a costume of another kind. The black of her boots matched her fitted bodysuit, and a charcoal wrap covered her light blonde hair.

"Good evening, dove," he drawled, recovering smoothly. "Just who might you be?"

She noted with some relief this man's accent was foreign.

"Maybe that's what I should ask you," Neva replied. Anyone who had purchased an illuminator with blood was a serious threat.

"Allow me to introduce myself." He lowered into a slight bow, keeping his eyes on her all the while. "My name is Thatcher Sullivan. You may have heard of me."

"You're not supposed to be here," Neva said, her voice bitter and flat. His gallantry didn't fool her. He had made no indication he intended to stand down, and this job belonged to *her*.

"Ah." He nodded. "An astute observation, but, alas, here I am."

"You're breaking the Code."

A sneer flickered over his face. "I've been sent here by people who operate outside your Code."

A thought sparked in Neva's mind. His name was Sullivan, and his accent indicated he was from the west. Oh, she knew who he was all right. The Chameleon. Although she had never heard of him working this far north, he was notorious for taking contracts without local approval across Cirandrel.

It didn't matter who hired him. Someone went through the wrong channels. The thieving community could forgive that. But if Flynn discovered Thatcher was working in Glacier Pass, the crime lord would have the thief's head.

"I'll make you an offer," Neva said slowly. She wanted to keep the situation from escalating, if possible. "But only this once, so listen well. If you leave now, I won't tell Flynn. If you make me fight for this, you will regret it."

"So sorry, dove. I've promised some important people a certain item by the end of the night."

"Now, listen here —"

Neva made it two steps closer to the man before he flung another spell in her direction. This one knocked her off her feet, slamming her into the wall and then the hard floor. Against a human, the spell would have rendered its victim unconscious. Against a half-Da'Valia, it failed.

But Thatcher wasn't waiting to see if the magic worked. He was counting on it. By the time she regained her footing, he had used the lock pick and wrench from his pocket to open the chest.

He didn't notice her because he was so intent, but Neva was shaking with anger. She didn't think. She rushed him. Silent, fluid, nearly a blur. She slammed into him, and he flew into the opposite wall with a hard thud. Thatcher's body was still, his right arm at an awkward angle. The illuminator blinked out, sending the room back to darkness.

The noise from their scuffle made Neva cringe. She prayed the Guard hadn't heard. Perhaps she should have dealt with Thatcher another way, but there wasn't time to second-guess herself now.

She needed to return to her father's tavern quickly. The city's Watch checked in on those marked for thievery when something important went missing, so a solid alibi was crucial.

Neva refocused her attention on the treasure in front of her. The goblet appeared ordinary among three leather-wrapped scrolls and the biggest healing crystal she had ever seen, but she found herself drawn to it.

She didn't spare Thatcher's limp body another glance. Her hand wrapped around the modest metal. She lifted the item to put it in her bag, but unexpectedly, her muscles refused to respond. The stem warmed, and the goblet hummed as black oil bubbled up from inside.

She would have gasped and pulled away, but she couldn't. She couldn't move at all. She tried to rip her hand free again to no avail.

She watched helplessly as the liquid eddied, swirling to form miniature mountains. Their sizes doubled and tripled in a strange pattern until oil emerged from the cup without spilling.

The sharp smell of tar overwhelmed her as whispers started around the room. The noises flew from corner to corner, almost too low for her to interpret. What she heard, she didn't understand. An ancient dialect.

Oil swashed in the air like a small ocean in an unforgiving storm. It expanded, knocking scrolls off the desk and setting wall hangings askew until a building formed with perfect shape — larger than Neva's own body — with black oil-fire flickering around it. It was her family's tavern, where she lived with her father, aunt, and young cousins. People with silent screams upon their lips were running from the front door. Her father stumbled out, urging her cousins ahead. Flames licked at them as they scrambled away.

Held captive, Neva had no choice but to watch as a black wave obliterated the picture and an unfamiliar scene formed. She saw herself, unclothed and sickly, in the center of a grand room, surrounded by Da'Valia. She was slender with her mother's high cheekbones and her father's wide eyes, a blend of human and Da'Valia, and no match for the dozens of Da'Valia in the room — Da'Valia who rushed at her effigy in a single, unified effort.

Another wave crashed. Next, Neva saw horned figures locked in battle in a small camp. Da'Valia again. Their flowing forms fought with swords as they manifested pure, burning power in their attacks. She stood on a nearby hill. She didn't quite look the same, shaded beneath a hooded cloak, and she wore an unfamiliar necklace. In a flash, a blanket of flame ravaged over the bodies and tents, destroying everything.

A sick feeling rose in Neva's throat as she watched the visions before her. She felt renewed horror with every sight.

They were too detailed, too real.

Waves abruptly crashed in from every side, and the tar transformed into a cyclone, shrinking back into the goblet as whispers faded. But then another image struggled from the goblet. Another face, scarred and rugged. A male Da'Valia who had longer teeth and thick, protruding horns. His eyes held knowledge of death.

The face splintered, splashing down, returning to the goblet in a rush.

The magic rebelled upon being forced back into the goblet, sending out a shock wave. It pushed into her, tearing through her mind and knocking her body across the room.

Chapter Two

Eighth Fireside, 1631

Dhianz's Trishula is the greatest weapon ever created, so none of us expected this to be easy, but with our differences of opinion, we struggle to find our way forward.

Word has come that Trinizhi will arrive any day, and she'll want to be included. I would give anything to keep her from joining the hunt, but I can't let it seem as if I am afraid of her.

If we fail to substantiate our discovery before she gets here, she will become my greatest competition. No matter what happens, I won't let her win. It's obvious she would be a terrible leader from how she follows orders with disdain and lures beasties from other majilas for sport.

— Monazhi Da'Voda-Lira

Neva flew into the air and smacked back down on the hardwood floor, cracking the surface. She gasped as a bolt of pain tore through her shoulder. Her Da'Valia blood made her tolerance for pain higher, but a nasty bruise would blemish her skin before the end of the night.

She rolled over with a groan. Residue from the goblet's magic lined her mind, making her feel nauseous. She swallowed rising bile as she tried to ignore an alien heat that flushed over her skin.

Neva didn't know how long the goblet had held her captive. The time she spent staring at the strange visions could have been real or altered by magic. But she couldn't think about that now. She struggled to all fours. She needed to secure the piece and depart before the Guard arrived to investigate.

She swayed as she made it to her feet and yanked her gloves on before shoving the goblet into the black bag tied to her belt. She wouldn't touch the thing again for all the commissions in the realm.

Neva could hear the pounding footsteps of the Guard coming from the floor below. She spun around, looking for Thatcher, but the thief had disappeared along with the illuminator.

She shivered. The man was a ghost.

Neva pulled her dagger from her boot and slashed four marks on the top of the chest, imitating claw marks to ensure her thieving moniker, the Lynx, would get credit for the heist. They would whisper about the Lynx as one of the best thieves in the realm after this, she was sure of it. A quick smile flitted across her face, and then she was running back to the window in the sleeping quarter. Her escape.

She gripped the icy tower wall and pulled herself out. Frigid wind attempted to tear her away from the stone structure. She thanked Dhianz for her strength as she peered ten stories below, where stepping stones looked to be the size of marbles.

Neva was two grips down when a tall, black bearskin hat poked out of the window.

"Halt! …the Order…stop!" the guard shouted at her.

The wind carried away most of his words, but she wasn't about to slow down for anything. She could fight two guards, maybe three or four, with relative success. Her Da'Valia strength and knife-throwing skills, however, wouldn't be enough if they captured her. Breaching one of the House's towers was considered a harmful act toward King Stephan and the Order of Cirandrel. A second conviction mark and time in the stocks — or worse — would await her.

Neva looked down uneasily and let go of the stone structure. She fell ten feet before catching herself on another wood-lined ledge. Her vision clouded around the edges with the aftereffects of an ancient power. She slipped from the icy ledge before catching herself with her other hand.

Focus, she told herself. She took three deep breaths and her vision cleared.

She dropped, swinging to catch herself repeatedly while relying on lynx-like reflexes to keep her from plummeting to the ground below. She could only imagine the stern talk she would receive from her father were he to witness her methods. Her improvisation was dangerous. He had taught her better.

She could hear members of the Guard gathering beneath her in the ice garden.

Neva formulated a plan as she neared the third level of the tower. She was within firing range of an archer, and even with the heavy wind, a decent shot with a crossbow could easily find its mark. Neva altered her direction, kicking at a row of lethal icicles before she leaped onto the garden archway. The frozen spears plummeted, forcing the group of guards to scatter among the stubborn shrubs and frozen sculptures.

Neva fought to keep her balance on the icy archway. Guards shouted on the ground. Most of them were still in the garden when she reached the other end of the archway, but they were too close.

Focus, she ordered herself again. She tucked into a roll and hurled herself off the edge. With guards approaching fast on both sides, she pushed to her feet and sprinted away from the sound of music and merriment coming from the main hall. She couldn't leave by either of the gates now that the Guard was on alert, so she sped deeper into the House.

Temptation to use her invisibility spell nagged at her, but protocol dictated that the sooner the Guard lost sight of her, the sooner they would call for support from one of the House mages and alert the city's Watch. She needed to make it to the protection awaiting her on the city streets before that happened or else she faced failure.

Neva yanked the massive door to the library open and slid through, closing it and dropping the beam that usually acted as a weather barricade to lock it behind her. She heard the guards' shouts double, but she focused on finding the best escape. She raced past rows of towering bookshelves and through a side door as three more guards appeared at the opposite entrance.

Neva leaped down two flights of stairs. She went through any door that would open to her in an ever-changing route until she came to the library's archives. This was her way out.

She pulled down on a marble bust, a great thinker who had died centuries before, and a slit opened in the wall. Neva spun into the space, returning the statue to its original position as she passed.

She slowed as she descended into the bowels of the House in pitch darkness, navigating a maze of tunnels by memory. Neva's father, and her grandfather before him, had made use of these tunnels for similar escapes, and she counted theirs as a secret she was lucky to have. In her opinion, they were needlessly complex, but that was a feature that served her more than hindered her.

Finally, Neva came to the edge of House grounds, where manicured snow met the city's border above ground. Wishing there was another way to exit, she climbed out of a defunct sewer pocket, slithering through a grated opening surrounded by dirt and ice.

Topside, she laid still and flat against a snowbank until she was sure no one was around to take notice. She closed her eyes to call her invisibility glamour to life again, scratching a spot on her neck raw as the itchy burn traveled over her. Then she was up and moving again.

Several streets before her destination, Neva murmured words known by a select few of Flynn's subjects. The words were slow to work, but they cloaked her whenever she needed to disappear. After she triggered the magic, no human, dog, or mage could track her on the city's streets. The mage Flynn hired redrew the corresponding runes annually so the magic wouldn't weaken, and she never returned home from a job without calling on the protection.

But she didn't slow down. Neva was still breathing hard when she arrived at her father's tavern, a stone and timber building, which had a kitchen and dining room on the ground floor and rooms for her family and paying guests above. She entered through the kitchen. Soupy air rich with the aroma of garlic and thyme greeted her. Her aunt, Margret, tall and with enough gray streaks in her red hair to belie her youthful features, stirred a pot on the stovetop.

"Close the door quickly now," Margret called without turning around. The older woman's hazel eyes stared into the distance, as if she was thinking of another place and time. She did that sometimes, ever since her husband Abel passed.

Neva did as instructed and took the rear stairs to the privacy of her room. With a relieved sigh, she let her invisibility glamour drop and sank to the floor, burying her head in her hands.

Thieving was always a challenge — that was why she liked it — but her jobs were rarely so difficult. Flynn had better start offering her all the best jobs from here on out. Not only had she proved she could infiltrate the House of Trescony for a second time, but she had stolen from the duke's tower to boot.

Neva untied the bag from her belt and didn't hesitate to climb up on her bed and peel back the wallpaper in the corner of the room, a hand on the ceiling for balance. Deftly, she placed the black bag and her spelled glove inside the wall, smoothed back the wallpaper, and pulled away. She tried to ignore the nagging in her mind telling her something wasn't right — that the nausea, dizziness, and apparent fever she was experiencing meant something.

She lit a candle so she had light to work by as she activated her usual glamour spell to dull her skin and hair, and to hide the small, barely protruding horns atop her head. She wore the common glamour charm on a necklace, so it didn't hurt to apply or itch upon invocation, and it kept her hidden among humans who might otherwise notice her peculiar coloring. Together, Da'Valia had nothing to fear among humans, but one alone could be targeted as a source of evil, so her discretion was of the utmost importance. Only her family knew the true nature of her birth.

Neva donned a serving uniform without delay. A brown dress of heavy muslin was followed by a matching net for her hair and a wide leather bracelet to hide the embarrassing conviction mark on her right wrist. Two more mistakes and she'd be shipped off to Lithlorian Island to live out the rest of her days under the watch of the dragon wardens.

She cinched the dress in the front and looked in the mirror to make sure her hair covered the tips of her pointed ears. She stared at her foam-washed blue eyes, feeling like she should look different somehow. Her head pounded steadily, but she looked the same as always. Flashes of the goblet's visions her ran through her mind. They felt threatening, but she did not want to let fear overwhelm her. She would feel better if she worked through her worries.

"Neva!" Her father, the infamous Shaun Roberts, greeted her when she reached the bottom step. He grinned, and the action added life to wide blue eyes hooded by bushy copper brows. "It's busy tonight. Grab a pitcher of mead and help an old man, would you?"

Neva picked up two full jugs from the counter and called a smile to her face.

Shaun worked hard to keep the tavern going, but his age was catching up with him. Years of running over rooftops and escaping through sewers had taken their toll, manifesting in the form of lightly peppered hair and a limp in his leg. That limp was hindering his sizeable frame more in recent years. As a result, they needed her money from thieving to pay the healer's bills, to afford the boys' schooling, and to substitute the tavern's profits while snow closed the pass during Fireside. Flynn had fronted them half the coin needed to open, and they still owed him an uncomfortable amount.

"Course, Pa," she agreed as she pushed through the swinging door and entered the dining room, full of city goers and merriment: her alibi.

The scent of Margret's cooking disappeared as Neva stepped into a haze of sweet-smelling pipe smoke. The din of conversation overpowered the roaring fire in the tall stone hearth, and the room was awash in a warm orange glow from the burning wood. She turned to the first table to find several sheep herders who frequented the tavern.

"Nevazhi!" The table of herders welcomed her with her full name and a presentation of their empty mugs and coin.

"Gentlemen." She curtseyed and poured while talking about the weather and how the new year was treating them.

Neva stopped one of Flynn's runners by the door to pass along news of the Chameleon. Surely, Thatcher would obtain a disguise now that she had seen his face, but Neva wanted to give Flynn warning enough to protect his territory. He had kept steady commissions coming to her and, before that, her father. He deserved her respect and the warning, if he didn't already know about Thatcher's infringement. The crime lord had a canny way about him.

Her third table in, Neva found a familiar group mostly consisting of men she had grown up calling Uncle. All five of them were part of the same thieving ring as she and her father.

"Ne'er-do-wells." She lifted a jug, ready to fill their glasses. Fletcher shoved his mug down the table at her. He was usually the first to need a refill, and she obliged him.

"Look who it is, gents!" Morty stopped in the middle of embellishing a tale about the time he'd been mistaken for a legendary knight — a tale that they'd all heard no less than a dozen times — and edged his mug toward Neva.

"Morty," she said, sizing him up. "You look like you've seen better nights."

The older man's white hair stood in all directions, and his eye patch was crooked.

"Ah, a trained eye," he responded with good humor. "It's been a rough one. Now, you didn't happen to see anything interesting out on the streets tonight, did you lass?"

"Why, no," she said nonchalantly. "A few foreigners about, but nothing of much interest."

They didn't need to know about Thatcher. Flynn would deal with him soon enough.

Neva continued to pour as Archibald turned to Adam, the youngest of the group aside from her.

"Weren't you saying something had the Guard riled out there a moment ago, Adam?" Archibald's tone was dripping with false innocence, and he scratched his bald dome with a theatrical quizzicality.

"That I did, Archie." Adam raised an eyebrow, smug as usual, and leaned back. "Heard they were mighty upset about the duke's quarters being breached, but, like Neva says, just a lot of foreigners out tonight. No actual skill."

Adam Tate was older than her by several years, but that never stopped him from teasing her as they'd grown up. Unfortunately, Adam's wavy hair and dimpled chin ensured he got away with more than he should. He was broadly built, with lively, charismatic eyes and a catching smile. He was dangerous for more than his appearance, though. He was an excellent hunter and tracker, and he made a habit of picking up owed-favors around the city.

Neva cocked her wrist back and stopped pouring although his mug was half empty. She felt frustration tighten her throat. She had a reputation for not shying away from risky jobs. She couldn't, not if she wanted the Lynx to have a decent reputation — and decent pay. If Adam had observed the Guard coming from the House, the chance was good the men at the table knew where she had been.

"I guess I'd better save some mead for those foreigners then," she told him.

The thieves laughed. They knew Neva was the bigger risk-taker of the two. Adam was well-versed in the trade, but he lacked courage. He stole less now that his chief source of income came through selling weapons, and he had established himself well. His connections to Flynn and a brother-in-law who worked for the Glacier Arm shipping commissioner made sure of it.

But tonight, Neva had no inclination to let Adam get away with anything in front of the men who'd raised her — and they must have enjoyed watching her tease Adam back. Otherwise, Morty wouldn't have brought up the subject of her job.

"Heh, missy," her uncle Neil chuckled. "We know you can hold your own. Just be a mite careful with the travelers at your corner table."

Neil angled his shaggy head of hair, covertly indicating a dimly lit table in the back of the room. The group often relied on Neil's gut instinct, so she took his word of caution seriously. But Neva didn't turn to look. Instead, she gave a laugh and moved away from their table a step, leaving Adam's mug as the only less-than-full one.

"I've got to go refill, gents. Don't cause any trouble while I'm gone."

Instead of turning back to the kitchen, she spun around in the opposite direction, pointedly looking over the room as if she were searching for others who might want more to drink. She spotted two men in the corner booth. The one facing her looked familiar. He wore a black bard's robe, and she was certain he had sung at the tavern in the past year. As she remembered, he was genial enough.

But she couldn't make out the other guest because he wore a hooded cloak. She knew it was a man because she hadn't before met a woman of such remarkable size. He was impressive, even sitting down, yet mere bulk was not enough to justify Neil's words. He wouldn't have said anything unless the bard's companion warranted caution.

In the kitchen, Neva refilled the pitchers, and she steadied herself with a deep breath before approaching the table in the corner. The men seemed quiet enough, but trouble wore many guises.

"Welcome to Roberts' Tavern," she greeted them. "More mead, gents?"

She barely saw the swift smile the bard sent her from beneath his long beard before she turned to the other man. The first thing she noticed was he had ebony skin. Where his muscular chest peeked from his tunic, it looked as though it had been molded from coal. He tilted his head to look at her, and the light from the table lamp washed across his face.

She stalled for a second before she remembered to not act in any way that would insult the customer. His face was identical to the last image the goblet had shown her.

Before her sat a pureblood Da'Valia.

Chapter Three

Twelfth Fireside, 1631

Alizhi has said she will help me gain enough support for a motion to vote at the summit. Her alliad is powerful, so the others will listen, but she wants to mate again soon, so I won't be able to count on her for long.

— *Monazhi Da'Voda-Lira*

"More mead is always welcome!"

The bard's jolly demeanor did little to call Neva's attention. The Da'Valia didn't speak. He only stared, his black eyes lazy yet interested.

Neva filled the bard's cup, but she couldn't force her gaze from the Da'Valia in front of her. Although his hooded cloak blocked his horns from the customers, her view allowed her to see each was as wide as her wrist at the base, pointed on the end, and black. Instinct told her his ears were molded pointy like her own beneath his unshorn hair.

"And you?" Neva pushed the words out, trying to avoid staring at the scar stretching from below his eye to his jaw.

He was fearsome, yet something about him resonated with her. She had never seen a Da'Valia other than her mother, but she had heard the stories of the male warriors. Her mother's white skin had almost shone, but the males, the hilans, had not been born at dawn, according to the old stories. The hilans

16

had been born at midnight.

"Of course," the Da'Valia said, sliding his mug forward. His voice reminded her of a shepherd's horn, deep and echoing through the mountains.

"Have you heard any news from farther north these past months?" the bard asked as she poured.

Neva shook her head. The more northern regions were so remote only miners with gold fever ventured there. Fewer still ever returned.

"Very little comes to the Pass during Fireside," she said. "You would probably know of worthy things better than I."

She spoke with the bard, but every part of her was alert to the Da'Valia. Mentally, she thanked Neil for warning her. As far as her uncles knew, she was entirely human, but the Da'Valia's presence was intimidating enough.

The Da'Valia moved to pull his mug to him, but the edge of his hand tapped the ceramic, knocking it off the table. Faster than a human could track, Neva set down one of her pitchers and caught the mug by the bottom. She stopped its fall before a drop spilled. The action was pure reflex.

It happened so fast, the bard didn't take notice, but Neva was aware of the Da'Valia's unwavering gaze as she scooted the mug back into his hand. She hadn't taken her eyes off the bard, yet instinct told her the Da'Valia was looking at her. Silently, she cursed her reaction to his clumsiness. It would have been safer to let it drop to the floor and deal with the mess. She knew better than to show her speed in public, but she was rattled.

The bard paused in his story for another sip of mead, and the Da'Valia took advantage of the moment of silence.

"Nevazhi," he said.

"Aye?" she asked, keeping her eyes down, not wanting to look at him directly.

"I heard the customers call you that," he said, wrapping his hands around his mug. "It's an interesting name. How did you come by it?"

"Why, my mother gave it to me, of course," she said, forcing a chuckle. Polite, not giving anything away.

The silence that met her response dragged, forcing her to glance up. Her eyes locked with the Da'Valia's. Without meaning to, she held her breath. Maybe he didn't recognize her for what she truly was. Maybe he was just of odd character.

But his next words shattered her hope.

"Nevazhi is a name in my family as well," he told her.

"That's interesting," she spoke softly, ready to give her standard response. "But my mother was foreign. I suppose it's popular in other parts."

"No. It's not." The Da'Valia's voice took on a hard edge.

Neva stilled like a child found out for lying. She swallowed hard. The bard leaned forward, sensing something was amiss.

"Indeed," the bard said. "Nevazhi is an unusual name. I have not heard it in any of my travels, and I have walked to the far corners of the realm."

The Da'Valia kept his eyes on Neva's a moment longer.

"It's of no matter," he said to the bard, settling comfortably back into his seat. "Were she one of my people, she would not be able to deny who she is forever. Regardless, I'm sure the barmaid has more customers to attend."

Neva nearly bit her tongue to keep from engaging the Da'Valia further. What choice did she have? To accept it publicly would be to invite judgment, fear, and hostility from everyone in her life. Something he couldn't possibly understand.

"I should move on," Neva agreed instead, gesturing to the next table.

"Aye, of course!" the bard agreed, nodding.

Neva obtained their coin before moving to the next table. They stayed for more than an hour, and Neva felt the Da'Valia's eyes on her as they departed. As soon as the door closed behind them, she let out a lengthy breath. The Da'Valia had recognized her name and all but challenged her to admit her bloodlines. That scared her.

Neva stepped into the kitchen to collect herself. She had spent her entire life hiding the true nature of her blood, but for however long he was visiting Glacier Pass, the chances of her being found out were far greater.

"Neva?" Her father called as he walked into the room. He spotted her, and a frown splayed across his face. "Do you reckon he's here for the Trades?"

The trade social, dubbed the Trades by those in the city, only came around once a year, after the roads cleared following the dark days and nights of Fireside. Traders and metalworkers convened from around the realm for the event at the House of Trescony, allowing merchants to mix with nobles and strike deals for the rest of the dry season.

It would make sense the Da'Valia was visiting for the occasion. If strangers planned to be in the area during early Vestive, they usually made appearances. Especially if they had something to sell. Da'Valian mercenary services would fetch high prices.

"Perhaps," Neva replied. She took solace in the Da'Valia's scrutiny. It suggested he had been surprised to see her. Still, something in her bones told her it was too much of a coincidence he had been at her father's tavern.

"Are you all right?" Shaun asked.

Neva thought for a moment, remembering her mother teaching her to stunt her movements and conceal her natural grace when she was younger. She had practiced so much over the years that the guise was almost natural. She promised herself she wouldn't break from it again.

"I'm fine, Pa," she assured him. "Don't worry yourself."

"Since when am I supposed to not worry about you?"

Neva rested a hand on his arm.

"Since I'm fine," she lied. "That's when. I promise, there's no need."

Her father stared at her as if he wasn't sure he should believe her, so she smiled through the headache and willed herself to look convincing.

"He looked fearsome, didn't he?" she asked.

"Aye," Shaun agreed after a moment. "It's been a long time since I've seen one of those fellows. They look so different from the majilas. It's a marvel."

He got quiet, and Neva knew he was thinking of her mother.

"Let's go help Aunt Margret with the customers, shall we?" Neva asked, diverting the topic.

"Good idea." He fell back into the moment.

They worked until all patrons were gone, spills were cleaned, and tables were wiped down, so it was well past midnight before Neva rolled into the sunken middle of her mattress and closed her eyes. She felt dizzy with tiredness as she fell into darkness.

She was on the brink of sleep when icy fingers traced the back of her neck, sending a cold sensation down her spine. She gasped, her eyes flying open, and jerked away to where her bed met the wall.

A glowing presence at the foot of her bed had Neva flush against the headboard before she recognized the entity in front of her. Her heart pounded against her ribcage, and her throat constricted in shock and disbelief.

The Da'Valia's ethereal beauty — her wavy hair, arched cheekbones, and almond-shaped eyes — gained a silver hue with every moment. The spirit's lips moved without sound, and she appeared weak as she floated in a fading translucent form.

Neva could barely believe what she was seeing. She pinched the skin on her inner arm and winced.

How can this be real? Neva wondered in disbelief.

"Ma?" Neva finally mustered the courage to whisper the word, tears gathering in her eyes.

Monazhi raised her arm and pointed toward the door.

"What is it?" Neva looked at the door.

Monazhi continued to point.

"I don't…" Neva frowned. "I don't understand."

Monazhi dropped her hand, and a freezing gust kicked up around the room. Neva shivered and grabbed for her blanket, pulling it around her body.

Monazhi's stare pierced into her, sending a freezing burst through her head. The unnatural wind heightened, ripping the blanket out of her grasp and yanking her hair. The door rattled on its hinges and the armoire creaked.

Monazhi pointed at the door a final time. It flung open and crashed into the wall.

"*You are strong, powerful, and dangerous,*" Neva thought she heard an echo of her mother's voice drift to her as the room returned to darkness. "*You cannot remain.*"

Neva stayed shivering with frost coating the wall behind her for a long while before she tried to go back to sleep. *Strong, powerful, and dangerous,* her mother's words echoed in her head, a warning from the afterlife. It shouldn't have been possible. Everyone knew the dead could only visit those touched by Riska, the goddess of death. Neva had suspected something was terribly wrong before, now her suspicions were confirmed.

Neva awoke from a fitful sleep the next morning with her mother's ephemeral visit haunting her. When Neva was seven years old, her mother had disappeared after going off to fight rebels who were blocking incoming goods to the Pass during the Great War. They'd known it would be dangerous, but food supplies had dwindled, putting the city on the brink of famine. It had taken two weeks before a caravan brought her mother's frozen body back along with the other dead. Monazhi's skin had been so white, and it had looked the same last night.

The things Monazhi said echoed through Neva's mind as she rushed to get dressed before collecting her daily allotment of firewood. She found her leather pack on the floor near her armoire, not where she had left it. Exhaustion pulled at her, she still felt feverish, and she needed to talk with her father.

It was said to be bad luck to ignore a visit from the dead, and if there were any answers to be had, she hoped her father would be the one to provide them.

Neva found Shaun in the cellar, where he was busy distilling a fresh batch of brandy. Barrels of alcohol were stacked along the walls, and steam rose from his copper distillery equipment. He was wiping the sweat from his brow sporadically, and he had discarded his thick sheepskin jacket and the wool scarf Margret had knitted him during Fireside on the stairs. She skirted them as she made her way down. The sticky sweet smell of mead that always reminded her of her father and the tavern permeated the space.

"Carry that mead over here, would you, Neva?" he asked upon seeing her.

Shaun limped out from behind the equipment, leaning heavily on his cane. It must be a painful day. Some days, he only suffered a slight limp. Others, he needed the extra support to stay upright.

"Course," she replied, easily picking up a heavy crate of what would soon be potent brandy. "I need to talk to you about something."

She set the crate down next to him and took a seat atop a barrel.

"What's that?" he asked, checking a gauge.

"Ma." Neva said carefully. Monazhi was among the few things the two of them tried not to talk about. Shaun typically ended up looking depressed, and

Neva always ended up with more questions than answers. "I want to know what she didn't tell me."

"What she didn't tell you?" He turned to face her with his eyebrows raised.

"Aye."

Shaun's look of surprise faded to one of resignation. He wiped the nook of his arm across his sweaty forehead and took a seat on the barrel next to her.

"All right. What do you want to know?"

"Why would I be dangerous?" Neva had thought she had a firm grasp on who she was, but now she wasn't so sure.

He cleared his throat.

"What's bringing this on, lass? Did that Da'Valia say something to you?"

"I saw her," Neva said after a pause. She hadn't been sure she should tell her father, but she could only protect his feelings so much.

"Saw her?" he sounded confused.

"Ma came to me last night," Neva confirmed. Then, softly, she added, "she was beautiful."

"She came to you? …She must have done a spell before she died. I knew this day would come." He shook his head in lament, seeming to choose each word carefully. "It's important for you to know Mona only wanted the best for you. The Da'Valia are a fierce people, and your mother was afraid of how you would be treated, what with your mixed blood. We agreed it would be best if we kept you away from the clans for as long as possible — but every majila can wield a fearsome power, even a half-breed."

"But I don't, Pa," Neva pointed out. "You know as well as I do. I've had no powers beyond what's expected."

Even as she refuted the idea, she worried. Her cheeks were red, a rare sight, and she had felt feverish ever since touching the goblet. Something in her was changing.

"How do you know your strength and enhanced senses are the same powers all the other Da'Valia develop?" her father prodded her.

His words again gave her pause. She didn't know. She was only privy to information spread through rumors and gossip, and a few things her mother had told her during bedtime stories. It made her wonder exactly what they had kept from her. She deserved to know what her Da'Valia side could do, but if she could become dangerous, she wasn't sure she wanted it. She didn't think she could forgive herself if she hurt the people she loved.

"When a majila reaches the age, between thirteen and fifteen years old, she changes," Shaun explained as if he perceived Neva's thoughts. His eyebrows scrunched in concern as he looked at her. "In one moon's cycle, she becomes a different creature — far more powerful than any of the hedge witches or mages we have in the Pass. It is the curse Da'Valia blood bears, and only they can control such a change. You should have gone through this process years ago, but your mother couldn't stand the thought of you being raised in one of the clans.

"She wanted to protect you. She was one of the most powerful warlocks in her clan, and, like a mage, she could shape raw power into something magical, so she cast a spell to protect you from yourself. She told me only something with strength straight from the gods could break it."

Neva was quiet. Dread had slithered its way from her chest down her arms to the tips of her fingers, making them tingle.

Something with strength straight from the gods.

She'd begged Flynn for a job to prove herself, not a job that could get her and her family killed. Her hands curled to fists. She would be hard pressed not to throw the goblet at him when she saw him. As it was, she would have to wait until that evening to get rid of the thing, and their handoff couldn't come soon enough. She would have to pray Thatcher didn't find her before then. If a god had forged the goblet, she doubted a broken arm would stop him or whoever was paying him.

But the goblet and the visions it showed her weren't her only problems.

"I don't understand," she said finally, her voice tight with anger. "Why wouldn't you tell me? Didn't you think I had a right to know?"

Shaun looked down, rubbing his thumb over the calluses on the palm of his hand. "Because your mother's spell was meant to ensure the change would be kept at bay inside you. I hoped it forever would. That you could have a normal life."

Shaun's voice broke, and he stopped talking, clearly worn from their discussion. The lines around his eyes and silver in his red hair struck her. He seemed so weathered in this moment, and she realized he couldn't help her with Da'Valian matters. Only Da'Valia could.

A normal life. A simple idea of which she had often thought, although not too seriously. A husband eventually, high holidays to celebrate with her family, maybe children one day. She couldn't imagine how she would ever get there. She never let herself kiss the same boy twice, because getting that close to anyone would mean her secret was in danger. It was the same as concealing her prowess in knife-throwing tournaments and taking on solo jobs instead of working with those in her ring. Hiding who she was at every turn was vital, and now she had to worry about more than exposing herself. If she would put the people she loved at risk, then she couldn't stay. She didn't want to leave her family, but did she have a choice? Not really.

"I have to go to the Da'Valia," she told him. "You know that, don't you, Pa?"

The thought of seeking the Da'Valia made her nervous. But a part of her, which she usually kept buried, stirred. She had always yearned to know more about her mother's people, and that had seemed an impossibility until now.

Shaun nodded, seemingly resigned.

"Monazhi told me this day might come. I just had hoped it wouldn't come so soon. I wanted my little Lynx home and safe a while longer."

Neva wrapped her father in a tight hug. She couldn't imagine life away from her family, but she wouldn't remain if her power could hurt them.

Chapter Four

First Vestive, 1632

Frustration curdles my stomach like sour milk. We've wasted so much time trying to scry beyond the curtain hiding the Trishula. Athame, crystal, mirror... Our translation says we must pull aside the veil, but we might as well have to breach a fortress.

— Monazhi Da'Voda-Lira

The frosty air outside did much to reduce Neva's fever as she pushed her wooden cart over the cobbled streets of Glacier Pass. She shouted warnings to those in her way as she maneuvered through the throngs of workers to the Garin family's warehouse. Urgency pressed in on her to find the Da'Valia, but disappearing the day after a high-profile robbery was highly suspicious, so she went about her usual business. She wasn't the only marked thief who was an acquaintance of Flynn, but the Watch could point the duke in her direction as easily as the others. If she had to leave Glacier Pass to get the Da'Valia's help, she didn't want the Guard chasing after her.

Neva veered her cart to join the line for pickups, which wrapped around the large warehouse. Delivering firewood around the city was hard work, but it was also useful for reconnaissance, and it brought in extra coin for her family. She may have only finished primary school herself, but she'd paid for James' and Kendall's books last year.

She was struck by how comfortable she had become in her routine. She had never left the city in her life, and thoughts of packing up and leaving home overwhelmed her. Was she going to do this? How long it would take, and how soon she could return home? She didn't want the budding legend of the Lynx to wither in her absence.

The disconcerting sensation of someone watching her drew Neva out of her spiraling thoughts. She peered down alleys and through windows nearby as she inched forward, but she didn't see anyone aside from an unfamiliar waif limping down a side alley.

The tangy smell of pine washed over her as she entered the Garin's warehouse. The bays of chopped wood were significant, reaching well overhead. Neva chatted with her friend Mikel, a tall blond with pox marked skin and a wild beard, while they waited in line for their turns with the accountant, who managed the purse and ledger for the Garin family.

Mikel was still boasting about having bested her in an underground knife-throwing tournament the prior week. In reality, she had let Mikel win in the final round because she couldn't draw that much attention to herself. She attempted to be less than exceptional in everything she did — except for stealing under her Lynx identity. But she couldn't tell him that, so she suffered through his boasting and pretended to be upset about the loss.

Neva and Mikel paid for their wood upfront and parted ways to make their deliveries. The day moved swiftly, but by dinner time, Neva couldn't wait to make her way home, grab the goblet, and get it to Flynn.

Leaving the Dand District, a neighborhood of upper-class homes adjacent to House grounds, Neva spotted icicle shards near the base of the tower. She smiled. All things considered, she had evaded the Guard effectively the night before. She imagined them grumbling today about the Lynx's grand escape.

Once Neva arrived home, she changed from her fur jacket and heavy skirts into a nondescript, spun-olive shift, adding a gray bodice, matching skirt, and thick wool cape to complete the ensemble. The outfit was her usual garb for important visits. Uncomely and perfect for blending in with her surroundings.

Neva removed the goblet from its hiding place and tucked it into a small leather bag as dull as the rest of her clothing. She switched her usual glamour charm for another spelled necklace and invoked a cheap beauty glamour that hid her horns and darkened her complexion, turning her eyes brown. She rarely used this disguise, unless the situation called for it. Thatcher could be out there on the street waiting to jump her, so she felt better wearing it. Her bone structure was the same, but the first time her father had seen her with the glamour, he hadn't recognized her. If Thatcher was watching the tavern, he would never suspect her when she departed.

Neva left by the front door and made haste to a section of the city that housed the lower classes of the Pass. Cul Corner screamed depravity. When she reached Geary Street, many of the broken bodies surrounding her were badly in need of nourishment. Scents of cloves and opium seeped from buildings, and trash and sewage permeated the uneven cobbled streets. Neva was glad for the piles of snow covering most of it, because the stench would only heighten once Cravell, the warm season, arrived. Darkness cast over the city and the warmth of day would disappear soon, so out came the scarlet ladies, rowdy hands, and chronic drunks who were already deep in their cups and reeking of it.

Neva hurried past them all — even the ones she knew — and when she came to a familiar three-story building, she walked past that, too. She still had a feeling someone was watching her, so she doubled back before approaching the brothel.

The brothel was so old it leaned into its neighbor, but the madam made sure the girls inside were healthy, well-fed, and well-dressed. The strategy paid off, too, because the brothel had one of the best reputations in the city.

Happy girls meant more satisfied customers.

Some were so satisfied, they had made the brothel the base for their operations. Neva sighed. Actually, she supposed Flynn Abernathy was the only one to have done that.

Visitors frequently used the back door, so Neva was allowed inside after a brief knock.

A thin blonde woman stepped aside to allow her entry. As Amber moved, her black gown swished, seeming to sparkle in the receiving room. Amber's beauty had helped her earn both her position and Flynn's admiration over the years. Unfortunately, the woman's adoration for the crime lord was notably stronger than his for her.

"Alys." Amber's face became a mannered mask. Amber was one of the few who knew Neva in this glamour and the alias that went along with it. "I would be happy to show you upstairs. If you please, come with me."

Neva glanced in the open parlor rooms as they moved through the building. Despite the outside appearance of the brothel, framed paintings and window coverings decorated the walls, and the rooms nearly overflowed with red velvet furniture and pillows with intricate beading.

Neva and Amber climbed the stairs silently, but as soon as they were beyond hearing distance of the parlor rooms, Amber whispered to her.

"I'm glad you're here. Flynn has been acting strangely."

Neva frowned. She was ready to give Flynn a piece of her mind, but this sounded serious.

"What do you mean?"

"You'll see," Amber said, wringing her hands. "But I have some guests to entertain downstairs, so I'll leave you to it."

She knocked in a complicated pattern, opened Flynn's door, and ushered Neva through before hurrying away.

Flynn's headquarters was a corner room, so it had rows of windows offering an excellent view of the streets. Thick brown curtains shaded the windows today, which was unusual because Flynn often left them open to keep tabs on the guests. He was not above blackmail when the situation called for it.

Neva's eyes skirted over a desk with a bottle of her father's best brandy atop it, a card table, a tidy bed, and several wooden trunks likely holding everything from bought spells to weapons to she-didn't-want-to-know-what-else.

Neva said hello to Flynn's top man, Roger, who stood with his back against the wall next to the door. He was tall, fair-haired, and so quiet in a crowded room, she sometimes forgot he was there. His skin was weathered from the harsh conditions of Glacier Pass and tattered with scars from brawling. He acknowledged her with a nod, but he didn't speak.

As soon as Neva's gaze landed on Flynn, slumped in a green velvet chair in the far corner of the room, she knew Amber was right. Something was wrong.

Neva took in his appearance. His soft brown eyes were unfocused. His light hair was long and loose instead of tied back in its usual holder. The stubble along his chin indicated he hadn't shaved in a day or two. His black leather tunic and thick wool trousers didn't look wrinkled or stained, but something was wrong because Flynn wasn't smiling.

Throughout the years she had known Flynn, he was always quick to smile. She had seen him ram a brick into the head of a thief that challenged his position, smiling all the while. He smiled when he looked at Amber, when he ate, drank, planned. For all she knew, he smiled in his sleep.

But now his face was grim.

Chapter Five

Second Vestive, 1632

Benjamand has barely slept since Fireside, trying to figure out how to scry beyond the curtain hiding the second prong of Dhianz's Trishula, but he's finally done it! I can only think the spells hiding it must have weakened through the centuries. The gods have blessed us with the timing of this.

— *Monazhi Da'Voda-Lira*

"What's wrong?" Neva asked.

Flynn's unkempt appearance coupled with what she knew of the goblet had her checking the lock on the door. Typically, Neva dropped her disguise once she was in Flynn's headquarters. His security was so tight, not one person had gotten through in the past nine years of his reign. It helped that he had the ladies of the night at his back and regularly paid the authorities to look away, but this time, Neva chose to keep her glamour intact.

"They're watching me," Flynn said, unsteady and slumped in his chair.

"Who?" Neva asked.

"I don't know!" Flynn shouted, dragging his hands down his face.

Neva glanced to Roger and then to the covered windows. No one could see inside. She pressed her ear to the door and listened. Silence.

"There's no one here." Neva faced Flynn again.

"He's been in this state since this morning," Roger said from his post, keeping his distance.

"Has anyone else seen him like this?" Neva asked.

"I've been getting messages out through the runners," Roger said with a shake of his head. "He said to only let you in."

Neva approached the crime lord hesitantly. She stopped a few feet from Flynn so he couldn't cut her if he pulled a knife. A genuine fear had taken hold of him, and she didn't trust his state of mind.

"Flynn!" She nearly shouted to get his attention. His eyes snapped to her face, and she saw some recognition there. "Tell me what happened."

Flynn started to turn away, so she risked getting closer and put her hands on both sides of his head.

"Stay with me, Flynn," she looked into his eyes. "I'll help you. Just tell me what happened."

"I don't know. I don't — but they want it. They want the goblet."

"Why?"

"She said they needed it, and they put worms in my skin. There they are — there." Flynn held out his arm and pointed at it. "They want it, and they won't stop until they get it. They'll eat my heart!"

Neva looked down at his shaking arm. The tremors didn't stop her from tracking the other movements, the quivers under the skin. She called on her Da'Valia vision, which sharpened her sight and helped her see the faint glowing edges of magic. She blinked at the unusual heat flooding her eyes. She focused on Flynn and saw the worms glowing through. They wiggled as they ate through his flesh.

"Oh, gods," she whispered. A shudder washed down her spine.

"What is it?" Roger asked, keeping his distance still. "I see nothing."

"I think I can help him," Neva answered, not liking her idea but hoping it would work. She addressed Flynn, "Give me your knife."

Shaking, Flynn reached down, and a blade slipped from his sleeve. He almost caught it with the tips of his fingers, but it dropped. Neva released his face to sweep up the knife before it hit the floor. With her free hand, she dragged her hair out of the way. She didn't know who had put the creatures inside Flynn or what magic they had involved, but she would get them out.

"Hold him," she told Roger. "This is going to hurt."

Roger held back Flynn's upper body while Neva pinned his arm to the chair and stared hard as five of the squirming creatures climbed closer to Flynn's heart. She didn't want to think about the pain he was in, or the pain he would be in, if she didn't act.

She tightened her hold on his forearm, but that was the only warning he had before she slid the blade across his skin in short strokes, marring his flesh with deep slices. She dug her nails into each of the slits and squeezed out brown centipede creatures.

Flynn shouted a stream of expletives, sweat dripping down his face, and the centipedes dropped to the floor with muted thumps. Upon hitting the carpet, the creatures scattered. Neva slammed her heel down on two, and Roger jumped on the others until they were only bloody smudges.

Flynn slumped in his chair, unconscious, a waterfall of blood pooling on the floor. Neva hadn't thought this far ahead, so she ripped a cloth Roger tossed to her into long shreds. She tied the first around the lowest injury while Roger went to fetch Amber for hot water. Roger was like that. He always got things done, whether it was water or a bribe for one of the city's Watch.

Neva was wrapping a second strip around Flynn's arm when her fingers started to itch as if acid were eating her skin. Sweat broke out along her brow, and a flame of white power materialized on the tip of her finger. She didn't know what made her do it, but, as though some unseen force guided her, she touched the flame to the cuts.

Her finger slid over the sticky surfaces, and the wounds closed before her. She was sealing the last cut when Flynn stirred. His eyes fluttered and opened wide. In them, she saw her reflection, glowing silver around the edges as if raw power was cracking through her glamour. A look between awe and disbelief passed over Flynn's face.

"You just saved my life," he told her in a whisper.

Neva frowned and pulled away from the last of his wounds. She sucked in a breath, free of the compulsion. She stared at her hand, and the flame extinguished of its own accord.

Flynn straightened as Roger and Amber rushed through the door.

"Are you all right?" Amber rushed to Flynn, who was still pale but more lucid by bounds. The woman was careful to avoid the bloody mess.

"I'm fine, my darling," Flynn said with a smile.

Seeing the charm claim his face made Neva relax. He would be all right. She wasn't sure she could say the same for herself. She felt shaky, thinking about what she had done. She used the hand cloth to wipe the blood from her finger and tried not to think about losing control over her own body.

"It was a slight scare, my sweet," Flynn was talking to Amber. "Go back to work."

"Are you sure?" Amber gave Roger a frustrated look. "You haven't been out of your room in three days, Roger says you need help, yet now everything is fine?"

"Aye." The smile was still there, but a firmness entered Flynn's voice. It was enough to sway Amber. She rolled her eyes as if he perplexed her often and gave him a quick kiss before flouncing out of the room.

"We have got to get rid of this," Neva said, untying the sack with the goblet from her belt and tossing it onto the desk. She never wanted to see the thing again.

"Well done, little Lynx," Flynn said softly, and Neva liked to think she heard a hint of pride in his voice.

"That's it, then?" Roger asked. "The cause of all this trouble?"

"As long as we have it, they'll be after us," Flynn confirmed, coming to his feet. "If they already got so close… I need to move out now — right now. Every slither in my arm made it harder to stay sane."

A shudder rocked his body, as if the centipedes were still moving through his veins.

Flynn rubbed a hand over his arm, which appeared to be in far better shape than it should have been. The scars were faint and white, with only a tinge of pink in the center. They ought to have taken at least a month to heal, considering the depth to which Neva had cut. Somehow, she had done that. Cauterized the wounds. Stopped the bleeding. Healed him. She did not understand how, but that was something she would have to consider at another time.

Neva returned to the matter at hand.

"What about the Chameleon?" she asked.

Flynn looked to Roger, and the tall man shifted uncomfortably.

"He disappeared," Roger said. "Evaporated. The man's a ghost, I'd swear it."

"Really? I thought… Never mind." Neva realized she must have jumped to conclusions, thinking Thatcher was stalking her around the city. She eyed the goblet. She felt as if a weight had been lifted, but she still wanted it gone. She wouldn't feel safe until the goblet was well away from her and her family. "When are you going to turn it over?"

"We have a rendezvous planned," Flynn told her. "I'll head outside the city until then. No one will find me before I deliver it to my contacts. You'll get your commission as soon as I return."

It went unspoken that he would keep a sizable portion of her commission as reimbursement for the money he had lent her family. Their agreement was always the same. Seventy-five percent to pay off their debt, and the rest went to Neva directly.

"Thatcher aside, things did not go as planned at the House," Neva said pointedly. "The goblet is dangerous and more powerful than anything I've ever seen. As far as I'm concerned, your contact should pay you double what you agreed upon."

"And you'd like a cut, I presume?" Flynn asked with a raised eyebrow.

"Of course." Neva was firm. "Whoever hired you should have been forthright so I could have taken extra precautions."

She never would have infiltrated the House of Trescony alone if she'd known someone else was also after the goblet, and she never would have gone in at all if she had known what it would do.

"The idea does have merit." Flynn rubbed his arm again.

"Whatever you do, make sure your skin doesn't touch it," Neva warned him. "Keep it wrapped."

Perhaps the goblet might not affect him, but this wasn't a situation for unnecessary risks. She instructed Flynn to give her father her commission and informed him she might not be available for another assignment for some time.

"Not too long, I trust?" Flynn frowned.

"I don't expect so," Neva said, trying to sound reassuring. "Regardless, Pa will pay what we owe you, even if he must use the entire commission."

Flynn nodded, seemingly appeased, and swept up the goblet.

"You know the contingency plan," Flynn addressed Roger. "I may lie low for a week or so. Add a favor to be named to the books for the Roberts family while I'm gone."

"Consider it done."

Flynn gave Neva a look that she knew meant they would have a long chat when they next met. "Fare thee well, little Lynx."

He slipped a vial from his pocket and drank the liquid inside with a flourish. He grinned a moment before he disappeared with a strange sucking sound.

Neva shook her head at his casual use of such an expensive magic. What she wouldn't give for that escape route. Not that it didn't come with its own set of dangerous side effects. She had heard tell of those who appeared at their destinations with limbs missing. The dosage had to be exact.

Neva bid farewell to Roger and started home. As she stepped outside, she felt something warm and wet drip on her upper lip. She raised her hand and her fingers came away red. She pulled a kerchief from her sleeve to dab at her bloody nose.

Dread, which was becoming a familiar sensation lately, settled low in her belly. She swallowed around the lump in her throat. Neva had expected that being rid of the goblet would make her feel better, but now she was bleeding and fire had sprouted from her fingers like flame on a wick. Perhaps she was running out of time.

Neva awoke before the sun rose the following morning. She was hot and sweaty, even more than the morning before. Thin trails of smoke lifted in the air from her pillow, where she had tucked her hands. She jumped and swatted the pillow against her mattress until the smoke dissipated, then flipped it over and stared at the black streaks on the fabric.

"Oh, gods," she whispered, sinking onto her bed.

She was becoming dangerous like her mother's ghost and her father had warned her. Even though her power healed Flynn, it burned once it attached to something else. A wave of determination washed over her. She wouldn't let the vision of fire overtaking the tavern come to life if she could prevent it.

Neva started around her room, packing a few things she wanted to have with her when she left. Whether she could find the Da'Valia in Glacier Pass and persuade him to take her to his clan, she couldn't be sure. If she failed, she would have to leave and find her mother's people herself. Before the moon completed its cycle.

The Trades were that evening, and Neva knew it might be her last chance to find the Da'Valia who had visited the tavern. She had a plan to get inside House grounds, but she would need to be careful. All guards were sure to be on duty for such an important event, and any of them might recognize her from the other night.

Neva headed to the Garin warehouse and when she handed over her coin, she paid enough for two carts. She spent the rest of the morning hurrying through her normal delivery route so she could load her second cart before the workers shuttered the warehouse for the day. She arrived as they were dragging the doors closed. Panting, she ignored the disapproving look she received from the accountant. He could be as mad as he liked. She'd made it in time.

At the rear entrance to the House, Neva was pleasantly surprised she didn't need to give the guards on duty her story about delivering more firewood for the Trades. They waved her through with the line of bakers, musicians, and others there to serve and supply goods. Neva let out a slow breath of relief and went about delivering the firewood to the main hall, pretending she did so every day.

"Did Xavier tell you to put that there?" A buxom woman with her hands on her hips and a disapproving frown confronted Neva. The woman wore blue skirts and a bodice with the House emblem embroidered above her heart. A thin sheen of sweat lined the woman's forehead.

Neva had about a quarter of the wood unloaded and stacked beside the large stone hearth that was the focal point of the hall. She stopped with a log in her hands to see how much trouble she would be in.

"Aye," Neva lied, straightening.

"He never listens!" the woman said. "I told him three times we need the wood stacked on the other side to make room for the minstrels. You'll need to move it."

"Of course," Neva agreed readily, letting out a breath of relief.

"And be quick about it. The guests will be here before long."

"I'll have it done in no time," Neva promised.

The next moment, the woman was off to shout at a maid who was on a ladder, hanging fresh pinecone garlands above the entrance.

Once Neva completed her task, she took stock of her surroundings. The hall was still humming with a heady energy as servants prepared for that evening, but it was thinning out. She didn't have a House uniform and would be out of place if she remained. Neva ventured outside, pleased when she passed a man she assumed was Xavier pushing his own wheelbarrow of firewood toward the hall. She thanked the gods their timing hadn't matched.

Neva pushed her cart to the best hiding spot she could find, stashing it alongside the stables, and shoved her work gloves in a pocket. Even if someone noticed the cart, she doubted anyone would have time to move it. The House of Trescony controlled both the base and precious metal mines in the region, and it had a stockpile to trade now that Fireside was over. Hundreds of visitors were about to arrive.

Servants were igniting lanterns around the grounds, lighting walkways and illuminating ice sculptures. Although it wasn't dark yet, night fell quickly in the Pass. Its glacier namesake to the west made sure of that. Before long, a steady stream of well-dressed tradesmen, nobles, and their families strolled through on their way to the festivities.

Neva nestled in the dark corner of a covered walkway junction. The walkways connected the stables and many buildings on the back of the House property to the main hall. She evaluated the attendees as they passed. Years of thievery had trained her to identify an easy mark as much as whom to avoid.

As soon as she spotted the bard who had been with the Da'Valia at her father's tavern, she held her breath, waiting to see who would follow.

A large, ebony-skinned Da'Valia appeared. He was handsome, lean, and dressed in a decorative suit with a broadsword sheathed at his hip. His military air was undiminished by his gracefulness. With an angular jaw and exotic sliver-black eyes, he looked much like the Da'Valia whom Neva had met the other night, but this Da'Valia had no scar on his more-refined face. He might have been larger, too; his horns made him nearly as tall as the corridor ceiling.

His eyes met hers and Neva felt her heart jump in her chest. She pretended it didn't speed up when he stopped and told the bard he would wait there for his traveling companion.

Neva watched the Da'Valia lean against the corner across from her, sinking into the shadows in a manner similar to hers. His wolf fur-lined cape flowed in tandem with his movements. He appeared to be about a decade older than her, and he ignored her as he pulled a pipe from his jacket and lit it with a spark of black flame from his finger.

Neva mustered her courage, but before she could utter a word, he spoke.

"So, you are her," the Da'Valia stated, his eyes drilling into her.

His stare was so intense, she wished he would look away.

"I'm not sure I know what you mean," she told him, amazed she sounded so calm.

"Nevazhi, the half-breed pretending to be human and without power."

The frequency of guests traveling to the Trades was dwindling, but another noble couple hurried past once they noticed the Da'Valia in the corner. Neva ignored them and went to stand next to him. Soon, they were alone.

"But I do have power," she told him.

He puffed on his pipe slowly.

"Bryand told me," he said, giving her the name of the other Da'Valia she had met. "But our speed can barely count as our power."

"No." She shook her head. "That's not what I meant."

She held out her hand and remembered what the flame had felt like with Flynn. In an instant, a white fire sparked to life. The Da'Valia looked moderately surprised at her words, but at the sight of fire licking the air above her palm, a concerned expression washed over his face.

The other Da'Valia, Bryand, appeared from the walkway. Neva jumped involuntarily when he grabbed her arm above the elbow, digging in his fingers.

"Put it out," he ordered her.

Neva looked at her hand and concentrated. The flames inched lower, sputtered, but then they filled out again. She focused all of her attention to no avail. She looked at Bryand, a speck of fear in her eyes and a lump in her throat.

"I can't."

Chapter Six

Third Vestive, 1632

The blood sacrifices have been difficult. It's draining to lose so much blood, but it's worth it. We should discover the exact location in our next few attempts. I never thought I would see our race earn redemption in my lifetime, but now I feel anything is possible.

— *Monazhi Da'Voda-Lira*

The flame pushed to Neva's wrist. By all rights, her skin should have blistered and burned, but it didn't. Neva tried to stifle the power, but she couldn't make it recede.

"Oh, for the sake of Dhianz!" The larger Da'Valia pushed Bryand aside and yanked her to him.

Her pulse fluttered at the contact, and she held her breath. His skin appeared impossibly dark in contrast to her own. She didn't know why that thought stuck with her.

The Da'Valia dropped his pipe, scattering ash across the floor, and pulled out a silver bracelet from within his cape. He slapped the icy metal band over her wrist, an automatic clasp locking so it fit snugly around her skin. A chill pierced her flesh and the fire extinguished. Neva instantaneously became cooler than she had been in the past two days. Her fever was gone.

Neva's eyes watered before the sharp sting emitting from the metal disappeared. Her tolerance for pain was high, but the bracelet hurt.

The Da'Valia turned to each other, and the larger of the two started talking first. Their dialect was foreign to Glacier Pass, but Neva had learned the Da'Valian language from her mother. Although some words were difficult to make out because she hadn't heard them in so long, Neva could understand what they were saying.

"I thought you said she wasn't with power!"

Neva felt the larger Da'Valia's fury fill the hallway, pressing in on her.

"She wasn't!" Bryand shouted right back. "I don't know what happened. Just calm down."

The other Da'Valia bit off a flurry of words so fast in their delivery Neva lost their meaning.

"Stop!" Neva shouted at them in the common tongue. Their fighting wouldn't help her cause. "I need your help."

Bryand looked at her. The other Da'Valia ignored them both, bending down to pick up the pipe he had dropped. He cleared it out, allowing the remaining ash and dried leaves to flutter to the floor, and slid it into a pocket.

"Pray listen," Neva pleaded. "I don't know what is happening to me. Yesterday, fire fell from my fingers, and it happened again this morning."

"Yesterday," Bryand repeated the word as if he had an unpleasant taste in his mouth. He looked at his companion and said, "We have twenty-one days before the next full moon."

The large Da'Valia trained his eyes on her again, and she thought she saw a flicker of recognition there. The bracelet on her wrist animated, tightening. A stabbing pulse emanated from the metal. She saw her arm and gasped. A dark gray was spreading from the bracelet as her hand reddened with blood.

"Astiand!" Bryand shoved the other Da'Valia against the stone wall.

Astiand blinked as if startled from a trance, and the pain stopped. He ripped away from Bryand and walked to Neva, lifting her chin with a finger so she would meet his gaze. A shiver ran down her spine at his nearness.

"You can't stay here," Astiand said. "The city would see chaos should you remain. We're leaving tomorrow at dawn. Be here to meet us, and don't be late. I'll make sure the guards will be expecting you."

Astiand looked pointedly at Bryand and left through a shadowed archway.

Bryand waited until the sound of Astiand's footsteps disappeared before turning to face Neva.

"He can hold back your power with the shacklay now and will keep it in check," Bryand told her. "By the laws of the clans, we will take you to your firérite, but we have other priorities, and you've just become a terrible inconvenience. You had better watch your step."

Neva tried to focus on his words, but it was difficult. Her arm throbbed and the gray bruise still stained her skin. The ache was only now beginning to dull.

"Do you understand?" Bryand's voice broke through to her.

They made eye contact, and he cursed.

In her mind, she screamed at him. No, she didn't understand. She didn't understand Astiand's sour attitude, her own emerging powers, or what the piece of metal circling her wrist meant, but she fought to remain calm.

"Until he takes it off, he's the only one who will be able to keep your power from releasing of its own accord," Bryand informed her. "Make sure you're here to meet us, and you'll be less likely to rile him. Now, excuse me. I have business to attend."

He walked off toward the Trades.

Neva watched him leave and then looked at her hands. They were trembling. She clasped them together. What had she gotten herself into?

Neva thought about her encounter with the Da'Valia as she walked home. It hadn't gone well, but it could have gone much worse. After pushing her cart around the city twice, her back was sore and she moved slower than she usually did. She realized if she was meeting the Da'Valia in the morning, she had precious few hours left with her family. She wanted to tell her father she forgave him for not telling her the truth all these years, give Margret a hug, and ask the boys how school was going. She had never spent more than a night away from them.

Shouts littered the air as Neva got closer to the tavern. Smoke assailed her senses, and all other thoughts fled in an instant.

"No, no, no," Neva said desperately, already knowing what she would find ahead.

As she turned the corner and the tavern came into view, Neva spotted her father pushing her two young cousins out of the burning building. Kendall was coughing, rubbing at his eyes with two fists. James was crying. Flames shot out of the windows, and the wind whipped billowing smoke away from the roof. It was the exact image the goblet had shown her.

She abandoned her cart and ran, weaving through a gathering crowd.

Neva darted toward the building while most people were running away. She recognized several regulars, but she couldn't see if Margret had escaped the budding inferno. Neva looked around for her aunt but didn't see her.

Neva was by her father's side in an instant.

"Did everyone make it out? Aunt Margret?"

"I couldn't find her!" he shouted, bent over, coughing.

Without hesitating, Neva rushed up the steps and through the open door, fighting to see past the smoke. The dining room had cleared out. She pushed into the kitchen, which was also empty, and jerked away from the flames leaping off a burning wall as she darted up the stairs. An intense heat pierced her shoulder, but she barely noticed.

Neva checked her aunt's room, which was nearly engulfed, and shouted for her with no response. Neva checked her father's room, her cousins', and her own in succession, instinctually snatching the pack she had prepared that morning.

There was only the basement to go, where every barrel of alcohol could fuel the fire. With incredible speed, Neva vaulted down the stairs and jumped over a fallen ceiling beam to access the basement. She barely allowed her feet to touch the heated steps as she descended.

She landed in a solid crouch in the cellar. Flames raked the walls. Smoke stung her lungs and made her eyes water as she tried to peer through.

Neva glanced at the stacks of barrels as she rushed to a lumpy form, clad in dark brown wool on the ground. The fire was growing along the wooden stairs, only inches away from the collection of potent alcohol. Neva barely looked at her aunt before slinging her body over her shoulder.

Flames now danced around the barrels. Neva turned away from the alcohol as the first barrel caught fire, exploding in a shower of burning droplets. The heat of it rained around her, but she ignored it and raced over the fallen beam toward the stairs that led to the kitchen.

The step beneath her snapped in half as she reached the doorway. Her feet dropped. Neva pushed Margret's body into the kitchen and grabbed a hold of the edge of the wall. Her stomach hit the floor, scraping as her fingers instinctively wrapped around the hot wood. She was wearing her work gloves, but the searing heat still shocked her, and she couldn't stop herself from letting go. She dropped again and caught herself with one hand, feet dangling. She flung her other arm up and pulled herself back into the kitchen as a second barrel exploded, igniting a chain of blasts from the stack.

In a blur, Neva scooped up her aunt's limp body. Catapulted by inhuman strength and the explosion behind them, Neva sprang out the back door.

The ground shook where they landed, and Neva covered Margret's body until the scorching air of the blast dissipated around them. The pack Neva had grabbed from her room protected much of her back, but some splinters and glass stabbed through, drawing blood in small patches.

Neva winced at the discomfort as she sat up and checked to see if Margret was still breathing. She was, but it was shallow. The stench of smoke washed off Margret's body and heat radiated from the building behind them.

Neva dragged Margret a few feet farther to cleaner air.

"Healer!" Neva shouted, looking around. "I need a healer!"

Neva's voice was raw from the smoke, but she kept screaming for help. It was a moment before anyone in the crowd along the side of the house heard her above the roar of the fire. Then, she saw two young women jump to attention and scatter, and, before long, an elderly man hobbled over with a healer's bag.

Neva backed away. She was ill equipped to help in matters of medicine.

"This is bad," the healer said, his head pressed to Margret's chest. "I'll do my best, but I cannot promise she'll make it."

Oh, gods, Neva thought.

"Do whatever you can," Neva told him. She would worry about paying for it later.

Neva looked around for her father and saw him sitting down, one hand on his leg, across the street. The grimace on his face made it appear like he was in pain. More from watching the building burn than his aging limbs, she would bet. This place and an honest life had been her father's dream for her entire life. Watching its destruction was akin to losing a friend.

Crews of city folk had switched their efforts from trying to douse the fire to preventing the flames from spreading. Half of the tavern had crumpled in when the explosion demolished the foundation, and as Neva studied the structure, she could imagine how the erect half could easily fall outwards. The heat coming from the building was so intense that snow on the nearby street had already melted into a muddy mess.

Neva jogged over to where her father and cousins sat across the street.

"You made it out," her father said. His shoulders drooped as if he'd been holding his breath until now.

"Aye. Are you boys all right?" Neva asked her cousins, checking them over for injuries or burns.

"Is Ma alive?" James asked. Moist tracks from crying were clear on both his cheeks, and his short red hair was wild. Kendall remained silent and tearless.

"A healer is with your ma in the back," Neva replied. She turned to her father, who was now speaking with authorities. "We should go if you …" She ran out of words. She was out of breath.

Her father nodded at whatever the Watch was telling him and looked at her sadly.

"Aye," he said to Neva. "We should be with her."

He thanked the authorities and called her cousins, who obediently followed, slow and scared.

Neva stood over the twins protectively until they were told they could go to their mother.

The healer had propped Margret against the porch of a neighboring building. Her eyes were closed, and her skin was more pale than usual. The healer was rubbing a strong salve on her chest to help her breathe.

"How did this happen?" Neva asked Shaun. The extent of the damage was staggering.

Her father put an arm around Margret.

"It took over the tavern with a will of its own," he said gruffly.

"What do you mean?" Neva asked, leaning closer.

"It was witchcraft."

Chapter Seven

Seventh Vestive, 1632

Trinizhi is too cunning for her own good. She snooped until she learned the prongs of the Trishula are in Cirandrel. Luckily, she doesn't know where exactly, because we've only just figured it out ourselves! We've drenched more maps in blood than I care to count, but the scrying crystal landed on Glacier Pass tonight, and now we know where we must go. We will leave soon to travel north again. Thank the gods Fireside is over.

— Monazhi Da'Voda-Lira

"What else happened?" Neva wanted the entire story. Her father wasn't one to make wild accusations.

"Foreigners were asking about a goblet," he said. "A woman. A beautiful woman."

A woman. Not Thatcher. Despite the heat from the fire, a chill washed over Neva. Then pure anger. She spun around, taking stock of their surroundings again. This time, she eyed the individuals in the crowd with suspicion. None of them were paying attention to Neva and her family. Their focus was locked on the spectacle of the burning building.

But someone was still searching for the goblet, and whoever it was had been willing to go after her family when Flynn survived the cursed centipede creatures. Her father didn't know what her most recent commission had been, but if the goblet was the cause of the fire as she suspected, she was to blame. She hadn't covered her tracks well enough.

Somewhere, she had slipped up, now her family was suffering for it.

"It's my fault," Neva whispered, barely able to say the words.

"Your fault?" Shaun asked.

Neva swallowed hard and raised guilt-ridden eyes to meet his.

"The Lynx?" Shaun asked in a whisper, leaning toward her. He would have heard of the tower heist by now, and she could see he was connecting the dots as he studied her face.

Neva nodded, biting her lip. She wondered how long it would take her to forget the fear on her cousins' faces, or the image of Margret in a heap on the floor of the basement. She should never have accepted the commission without a lookout. She had allowed her need for hiding her true nature and her desire for making a name for herself overrule her better judgment.

Shaun said nothing else. He didn't have to. His fear and disappointment was obvious to her, and she could feel it pierce her chest. She had failed him and failed her family.

"Neva. Shaun. You're all right."

The voice surprised her from behind, pulling her away from her thoughts. It was Adam.

"Come on." He wrapped an arm around her, which was unexpected yet comforting, and held a hand out to her father. "We should get you all somewhere else. Clean up. There's nothing more we can do here."

Roger, who arrived a few steps behind Adam, scooped up Margret. Neva tried to make sense of her feelings as she let their friends lead her family to a scantily furnished apartment above a nearby grocery. One of Flynn's safe houses. She wasn't sure if she might cry, or if the smoke had scratched her eyes as well as her lungs.

Leaving her family now no longer felt right. But the Da'Valia earlier had alluded to her rising powers, and hadn't she caused enough damage? Neva swallowed hard, knowing the answer. She could only take comfort in knowing Flynn's people would take care of her family after she left in the morning.

Roger brought Margret and the boys to a bedroom with the healer in tow.

Neil, who followed them from the tavern with Neva's cart, started pouring cups of brandy in the kitchen. Neva watched them get situated for a moment before heading into the apartment's only other room.

She sighed, sitting on the bed on the floor. She reeked of smoke. She slowly slid the pack from her back and pulled off her jacket, her face twisting when the material pulled on the splinters of glass and wood embedded in her skin.

Neva lit a candle atop the dresser and fought to see through the tears clouding her eyes as she started pulling the splinters from her side.

The door squeaked, and she glanced up to find Adam standing in the doorway.

"What is it?" She hastily wiped her tears away.

"Your father is wondering if you will join us for a drink," Adam said, studying her in the dim light.

"I'll be right there," she responded, pulling a shard of glass from her shoulder. Her father would need to mourn the loss the best way any of them knew. With a cup of brandy, reminiscing with friends.

"Actually," Neva winced mid-sentence, "would you send the healer in, if he isn't too busy with Margret?"

"I'll see if he can leave her yet," Adam said.

He disappeared from the doorway, and Neva tried not to pay attention to the ragged splinter sticking out of her waist, oozing blood. Before long, she looked up again to find Adam had returned with a clean cloth, a bowl of steaming water, and a jar of salve.

"He wanted to stay with your aunt to monitor her breathing," Adam explained. "Just lay on the bed, and I'll take care of it."

Neva didn't know what expression was on her face, but it apparently said she had little confidence in his ability to tend wounds.

"Lie down. It's not like I've never done this before," Adam said. "I've had my share of close calls."

The thieves in the Rings often tended each other until they could find a trusted healer. Neva had heard tell of Adam and their friends surviving several dire situations, so he had probably triaged wounds before. Plus, she didn't have much time to argue. She wanted to speak with her father to support him as much as she could before her dawn departure. She owed him that.

"Fine." Neva stood and untied the bodice of her overdress. Her shift would have to be cut away.

Adam averted his eyes until she lay on her stomach, successfully shielding her front. Her dress crumpled to the floor, revealing her shift, which was soaked in patches of blood. Neva didn't mind Adam seeing her in such a potentially embarrassing state of undress. They'd known each other so long it shouldn't matter.

"Gods, Neva." Adam brought the candle over. "How are you moving around still?"

Neva didn't respond. Her body was predisposed to numb pain, but she was sure he wouldn't want to know the truth of her ancestry.

"Just cut it off." She closed her eyes and turned her head to the side.

Adam placed the healer's bundle next to her on the bed. He sliced her shift in a careful movement and peeled the material to the sides. Drying blood made the fabric stick in places as he worked, but his hands were efficient, cleaning the wounds and covering them with salve.

Neva let her mind wander. Her thoughts instantly went to the goblet's visions. The first had come true. Did that mean the others would as well? She was leaving with the Da'Valia, and if they attacked her as she had seen in the second vision, she didn't know what she would do.

Her thoughts blanked as Adam finished tending to the last cut on her lower back. His hand stayed touching her skin, and he was silent. Her eyes slid to his, and she felt something she hadn't expected to feel with Adam. Ever.

It was new and a little frightening, and entirely too human for her tastes.

"I'm glad you're all right, Neva," he said. Then, after a pause, "I heard you were talking to a Da'Valia at the House earlier?"

How did he always know what she was up to? But then she supposed she had been rather conspicuous. Anyone speaking with a Da'Valia alone and out in the open would be.

She wanted to look away from him, but she found it was impossible.

"I'm leaving," Neva said. "I have to go with them."

He cocked his head to the side, his gaze sliding to the bracelet around her wrist and then her face.

"What?" she asked defensively. She was incredibly aware of his scrutiny, and of his proximity.

"Nothing," he mused. "It's just…"

Neva waited for him to finish the thought.

"I never looked so closely at your coloring before." Adam's hand lifted to her cheek and hovered. "You're lighter than others of the Pass."

"Adam." A familiar annoyance creeped into her tone as she tried to ignore the uncomfortable feeling pooling in the bottom of her stomach. Adam hadn't paid her this kind of attention her entire life, and she wasn't sure what to think of it.

"Stay," he said abruptly, taking her hand in his. "I have a big job coming up, and you could work it with me. We could take care of your family together."

Neva opened her mouth, then closed it. She would be lying if she said she hadn't carried a torch for Adam once, but she had put an end to those feelings. She'd had to, because she could never tell him the truth about what she was. She finally looked away.

"I can't," she said. It wasn't a fair answer, but it was all she could bring herself to say.

"Right," he said, letting out a sigh. "I suppose I should have known that would be your answer, but I couldn't have you leave without trying to give you a reason to stay, could I?"

Adam stood up awkwardly and moved to the dresser, where he took out a tunic and a set of trousers that had been made with the warm weather of Cravell in mind. Gently, he placed them next to her.

"I'll let your father know you'll be out in a moment," he said.

"I'm sorry," she whispered, thinking things might have been different if she weren't part Da'Valia, if she could have been honest with him. But her mother had trained her well.

The only sign he heard her lament was a slight hitch in his step as he continued out of the room.

Neva sighed and pulled herself off the bed to begin mechanically getting dressed. Really, Adam should be the least of her worries, but he'd surprised her tonight. She shook her head. Maybe in another life.

Neva tried not to dwell on leaving as she joined her father and uncles at the table. A fire roared in the room's small stove and it was slowly warming. Her father counted on her, so she worked hard to be a voice of reason as the men debated about what her father, aunt, and cousins should do next.

Despite years of hard work going up in flames, Neva's father was insistent on rebuilding. Determination was a trait they shared, so she angled the conversation to include securing funds and finding laborers over the dry season. As for funds, James, the eldest twin, would bring in a small, steady flow of coin by taking over her delivery route, and Flynn had made an official record of owing Neva a favor. He wouldn't be happy about lending the Roberts family more coin for another tavern, but he was a man of his word.

Neva left the conversation late in the night and napped for a few hours before her father woke her for her dawn meeting. She dragged herself out of bed and changed into clothes from her pack. Her wool pants and hefty sheepskin jacket would do plenty to protect her from the harsh northern conditions. Rummaging around in the borrowed room's dresser, she found a traditional blue bodice and orange skirts with heavy furs for insulation. She wasn't sure how long their journey would take, so she shoved the clothing and an extra pair of stockings in her pack so she would have another outfit.

Neva found Neil and Adam asleep at the table, where they had succumbed to the lull of liquor in the infant morning. She grabbed three biscuits, deducing Roger had departed during her nap. She devoured her breakfast before waking her cousins, whispering goodbye and kissing her aunt on the forehead. Margret was still pale, and the healer looked worried at her bedside. The old man had not slept.

"I'll return as soon as I can," Neva told her father in the main room.

"Just stay safe, my lass." He wrapped her in a tight hug. "Never forget you have people who love you here."

"I won't."

Neva soaked up the feeling of being safe in his arms before sliding out the door. She stepped into the dark morning with her pack slung carefully over her shoulder so it didn't irritate her wounds. The freezing air pierced her lungs before she adjusted her headscarf to cover her mouth.

Neva moved quietly, the only sound being her booted feet crunching a thin layer of frost. She walked past the charred skeleton of the tavern and wiped away tears as she watched the last of the smoke drift away. A foreign resolve to do something she never would have dared before rose inside her. The prospect of seeking a Da'Valian clan was intimidating, but she had Astiand's shacklay around her wrist, and her home was gone. She couldn't turn back now.

Neva arrived at the House moments before the sun peeked over the ridge. The guards at the front gate barely spared her a second glance after they found her name on their list of approved visitors. She hurried to the stables, which were already buzzing with activity. While the merchants and nobles slept off stupors from the Trades, their servants were in a rush, preparing wagons and steeds. She was just a body in the crowd.

Bryand and Astiand came down the steps from the main structures. They had changed from their decorated elegance the night before into traveling clothes with fitted fronts reminiscent of soldiers' uniforms. They were a sight to behold, a defined force of darkness in the morning light. Both wore swords at their hips and strode with a bleak air about them.

That Da'Valia essence was not unlike death itself. These Da'Valia could bring pain to those who opposed them. They moved with a gracefulness Neva usually had to work to conceal. She took the scant time before they reached her to study them, wondering if she was making the right choice by going with them.

Astiand was taller by about three inches, although both hilans were over six feet. Astiand's complexion was darker, and he was slimmer. She could tell he would be the more savage of the two in situations where brutality would be a virtue. He was also far more attractive.

Bryand was less refined, with shaggier hair and the scar. His eyes were like his companion's — haunted and calculating. Bryand's nose twitched, and Astiand's dark silver orbs fixed on Neva as they approached her.

"Let's go," Bryand said.

Astiand walked straight to the staging area without stopping.

Bryand talked with the stable hands while Astiand stood to the side, glowering at anything that moved near him. He didn't speak.

Soon, Neva and Astiand climbed inside a compact coach led by four horses. The contraption was made of stained wood and dark metal, and it looked speedy because of its size. Bryand climbed up to the front bench to drive.

Neva looked out the window as they rolled slowly out of the House gates. She had never left Glacier Pass before. It was strange to know she might not walk these streets again for some time.

"Sit back. There's nothing to see," Astiand grumbled, leaning his head back on the cushioned seat.

He was obviously tired and irritated. The look should have been intimidating on him, but it reminded her of a pouting child instead. A large, handsome pouting child.

Neva did as he ordered. But as they passed the impressive stone wall, leaving the city streets behind them, she stole one last glance at Glacier Pass, imprinting the image of her home upon her memory. She allowed herself a slight smile. Astiand hadn't noticed her pull the curtain aside again. His head bounced softly as he slept.

Chapter Eight

Tenth Vestive, 1632

Benjamand has given us the name of a man who will help us. If we can obtain Dhianz's Mouth, the second prong of the Trishula, before the summit, it should be enough to sway the clans in my favor. However, we must do so before Trinizhi gets ahead of us and tries to steal it away. She's determined enough to try. I've never seen another majila so hungry for power.

— *Monazhi Da'Voda-Lira*

They accelerated once they were on the main highway, heading southwest. Man was no match for the ruthless orchestra of nature, but the Order's troops kept the Old King's Highway well-groomed after Fireside. They did so in part because they regularly moved between all the houses, and the House of Trescony added the incentive of coin to make sure merchants could partake in the Trades.

Neva held onto the wall of the carriage to keep herself from falling this way and that. An hour later, she convinced herself they were making good time. The strength of her conviction was directly proportional to the queasiness in her stomach. Another hour into the ride and her nausea had grown into a roiling discomfort. Chills climbed her neck, making her want to toss back up the biscuits she had eaten.

She was staring at the corner of the ceiling, concentrating on calming her stomach, when Astiand's eyes cracked open. He stretched in the compact space, his muscular frame overwhelming.

Neva tried to ignore him.

"Are you all right," he asked, assessing her greenish complexion and white knuckles.

"Do I look all right?" she ground out the words, her concentration shattered. She was going to throw up. She could feel it.

"I'll teach you a trick I learned on the battlefield long ago," he said. A burst of cold shot from the shacklay up her arm and then was gone.

"Ouch." Neva rubbed her arm. "How is that helpful?"

But her stomach wasn't as bothersome as before.

"Da'Valia can use pain to focus our minds," Astiand said. "See if you can use it to control your nausea. I'd prefer to not travel the rest of the way with the smell of your spew."

Neva glared at Astiand, but she tried to heed his words. Even as the pain disappeared, she pushed the memory of it to the forefront of her mind to block her stomach's rebellion. Amazingly, it worked.

Astiand sat back in his seat and pulled aside the curtain covering a window.

"We should stop soon," he said.

Neva stared out the window in wonderment. Sparkling blue sky and clouds flew by as the scenery changed much faster than it should have. She had never been far from Glacier Pass, but this view was unlike anything she could have imagined. Laced with the aura of magic.

"What is that?" Neva asked, inching closer to the window before Astiand dropped the curtain, blocking her view.

"Pardon?" he responded with purposeful obstinacy.

Neva waved her hand at the window.

"That!" she exclaimed. "You know what I mean. That isn't normal."

"This carriage isn't exactly normal — by your standards, anyway," he informed her. "Thanks to expert Da'Valia craftsmanship and steeds."

Neva frowned. She had seen the carriage before they'd left the Pass. It'd been well-designed, sturdy, but nothing to write home about.

"Look at the horses when we stop. You'll see what I mean."

Before long, the carriage halted by a worn tavern by the highway. Neva climbed out after Astiand and studied their stop. The words "Grianch Inn" were carved into a wood sign hanging over a porch. Grianch was a popular stopover for those traveling to and from Glacier Pass, which also meant a day-long trip had taken mere hours. Neva inspected the horses while her companions handed the reins to the innkeeper. The sleek, black animals looked normal enough, steam flowing off them in the cold. Except for one thing. The horses' eyes were a distinct, glowing red.

Even out of the carriage, Neva's stomach was in no mood for food, so she declined everything but water. After Astiand and Bryand ate a hearty breakfast of meat pies with pickled vegetables and paid their bills, the Da'Valia led her back outside. They surprised her when they started walking behind the carriage inn toward a grove of trees.

"Where are we going?" she asked them, her practiced human walk ill matched to their gliding gaits.

Astiand didn't respond, and Bryand made a shushing noise.

Neva closed her mouth.

"Ow!" An adolescent girl's voice came from around the corner of a blacksmith's station. "Stop it. You're hurting me!"

The sound of a body being knocked into the wooden structure followed.

Neva turned toward the noise, but Astiand and Bryand had already changed their direction, brushing past her in an instant. She followed them hurriedly and didn't like what she saw. Two red-headed adolescents were behind the smithy. The boy, the taller of the two, had the plump girl against the wall and was rummaging through the pockets of her smock.

"Shut up, and tell me where you put it."

"Is there a problem here?" Astiand growled.

Startled, the boy spun around, wild and ready for a fight. His eyes grew wide as they landed on the Da'Valia headed toward him. He took a hasty step away from the girl, and the sun glinted off something shiny in his grasp.

Astiand stopped inches away from the boy, staring down from his higher vantage while Bryand waited nearby.

"Is that your sister?" Astiand asked.

A silence followed.

"Answer me!" Astiand pulled the hilt of his sword a few inches so the shaft showed, causing the boy to yelp and his skin redden almost enough to shade his freckles.

"Y-yes, sir. Yes. She is." The boy took another step back.

"Let me tell you something, boy," Astiand spoke low and close to the youth's face. "You'll have plenty of enemies in your lifetime, I assure it. Leave your blood alone. One day, you may find they're the only ones who will save you."

Astiand pried the gold piece out of the boy's fingers and flicked it to Bryand, who caught it and held it out to the girl. She wiped tears from her wide blue eyes and hesitantly reached forward to snatch the coin before running away, her red curls flying out behind her. Only once she was out of view did Astiand step back from the boy.

"Get out of my sight."

The boy scrambled across uneven snow and through the back door of the smithy, knocking his shoulder against the building in his haste.

"Satisfied?" Bryand sounded resigned, as if he was used to such actions from Astiand.

Neva hid a smile, thinking it was a good thing Astiand had intervened. Otherwise, she would have put the fear of the gods into the boy herself.

"It had to be done," Astiand responded.

"By you?"

Astiand shrugged.

"We'll be late." Bryand said, and they started walking again.

At the end of the municipality, they turned toward the woods and entered a secluded grove of pines, their feet crunching in the snow. They stopped and Bryand swore as he and Astiand surveyed the damage. Neva sidled next to them on a narrow patch of ground between two trees. She looked past Bryand's shoulder and saw the cause of his curse.

A man's body lay in the center of the grove, his throat slashed and a puddle of blood seeping into the surrounding leaves and snow. A light breeze ruffled his long blond hair, but there was little other movement within the circle.

Neva forced herself to keep breathing steadily. There was something too familiar about that lifeless form.

Bryand moved in a speedy circular path around the grove, checking their surroundings, and Astiand jumped into action toward the road. Neva knew Bryand was looking to make sure the area was secure, but she couldn't stop herself from rushing forward. She reached the body and found her fears confirmed.

There was no smile on Flynn's face now. His features were frozen in death.

The leaves on the ground were messed and strewn. Flynn had fought against his killers, but the cut across his throat was clean.

Neva made quick work of checking Flynn for the goblet, blocking her actions from Bryand with her body.

"Move aside," Bryand's voice boomed from above her.

Neva fell away.

"He's dead." She stated the obvious in the hope he wouldn't notice how long she had lingered. If he thought she was in a state of shock, he was less likely to ask questions about her interest. And in truth, she was in shock. Flynn had been so alive the last time she had seen him, now he was so still. Even his eyes were frozen in place, and from their direction, Neva knew his killers must have stood where she was now.

The implications of his death astounded her. Her father might not rebuild, Amber would be devastated, and the thieving community would take a crushing blow. Roger would be next in line for Flynn's old position — if challengers didn't make him fight too hard to keep it. With Adam to help him as one of the best arms dealers in the city, Roger had a good chance.

But the goblet was gone, and that surfaced above Neva's many concerns.

Bryand was rifling through Flynn's empty pockets and pack when Astiand returned with wind-swept hair.

"Is it here?" Astiand asked.

"No," Bryand responded, straightening. "They must have taken it."

Astiand swung around with a roar and punched a fist into a large pine. It shuddered in the ground. Pine needles and snow showered down. Neva's wrist ached, and she didn't have to look down to know the shacklay was working its magic. She was grateful she was standing with Bryand between her and Astiand. A screen between her and the embodiment of absolute rage.

"Their tracks disappeared at the highway," Astiand said, his voice reverberating with frustration. "There's no way for us to tell which way they went."

"The body is still slightly warm," Bryand said. "They could've left even after we arrived."

"If it was the Da'Foha," Astiand thought aloud, "they would have traveled south, and if it was the Da'Xana, they would have headed east. It could have been either of them, but it was more likely the Da'Xana. They've been watching closer."

Neva frowned, trying to keep up with their conversation. Understanding their rapid display of Da'Valian was harder for her than she would have hoped. She assumed they were speaking of the goblet and knew they talked about other Da'Valia clans.

"There is a chance they don't know what they have." Bryand sounded hopeful.

Astiand tossed aside the suggestion. "Even if they don't know, it wouldn't take the Da'Xana long to find out."

Neva stood silently as they debated. She knew little about the Da'Valia, mostly rumors and the few stories her mother had shared with her. Scholars could trace alliances and broken promises among the groups through accounts of human battles and wars for hundreds of years. When the Da'Valia were driven out of the desert centuries before, feuds eventually led to their fracture. As a result, the reclusive Da'Valia clans had emerged, five in all.

The Da'Xana were the safe keepers of ancient scriptures and texts pertaining to the Da'Valia and their god. Stories of the Da'Xana's grand white fortress built in the cliffs of Picquereau were the stuff of legends. The Da'Foha clan was from the Brakane Desert. The Da'Bruna and the Da'Foha, they said, stayed with the old ways. Rumors said they ate their dead.

"In the worst case, the Da'Xana have it, so I'll head east," Bryand said. "If it's the Da'Foha, we have more time before they discover what they possess.

I'll report back as soon as I know something."

"If we each follow one trail, we'd have a better chance of getting it back."

"If we split up, she," Bryand motioned to Neva, "won't make it to the firérite in time, and we'll have to answer to the clan."

"We'll be answering to the donazhi in any case," Astiand said, driving home a point Neva had no trouble comprehending. Each clan had a donazhi, a majila ruler similar to a queen, although hers was not an inherited title. Neva was beginning to understand the Da'Valia had been charged with obtaining the goblet for her.

"You put the shacklay on her, and now you have to follow through," Bryand told him. "To ignore the promise of guardianship is to forsake Dhianz and the laws we follow in his honor."

"Fine," Astiand threw up his arm in a motion Neva was sure pained him after he had hit the tree with such force. "Don't waste any more time. Return as soon as you are able."

Bryand set off at a run. He didn't wait for Astiand to finish talking before he cleared the edge of the grove.

Neva watched Astiand drag his unblemished hand through his hair.

"Let's go," he said. He started walking back to the carriage without waiting to see if she would follow.

Neva knelt to Flynn's body and drew the sign of peaceful passing on his forehead, saying a quick prayer to Riska. He likely wouldn't get a proper burial for some time because the ground would be frozen for weeks still, and she didn't want his spirit stopped from descending to the Underworld.

"You will have to abandon your human nature if you want to survive the clan," Astiand warned her with an impatient look over his shoulder.

Neva slid the necklace she snagged from Flynn's neck into a pocket. If she had not felt some loyalty to Amber, she wouldn't have risked infuriating Astiand further by taking the time to grab the keepsake. And if she had not felt some loyalty to the man who had given her steady work for so many years, she wouldn't have bothered to risk the time for the blessing, either. But around Astiand, she couldn't help but think maybe she did need to embrace her Da'Valia side — for the sake of self-preservation.

Chapter Nine

First Cravell, 1632

Benjamand's human is not what I expected. Shaun Roberts, he calls himself.
If I am honest, he drove me mad at first, always insisting we do things his way,
but there's a reason we're paying him so well. I've learned he is a skilled thief
and an honorable man. He makes me think about things I shouldn't even
consider. He will help us seal away the Mouth, and nothing more.

— Monazhi Da'Voda-Lira

If Bryand's driving left something to be desired, Astiand's were more sorely in need. Neva braced herself, trying to arrange her body so the jostling wouldn't irritate the cuts riddling her back as they wound through the mountains to Stagg. They were down to two horses instead of four, since Bryand had rushed off with the other steeds, so they were covering less distance. When they did finally halt in front of a two-story inn after dark, Astiand tossed a coin to a youngster on the street with orders to tend to the horses and keep his silence.

Neva watched the silver flicker in the lamplight and a memory nagged at the back of her mind. Astiand had flicked a gold piece to Bryand earlier. The gold piece that had belonged to a peasant girl in a pass-over town. Why hadn't Neva noticed, or thought to say something earlier? She didn't know who had the goblet, but they had enough funds to secure Thatcher's services and get him to Glacier Pass just after Fireside. Both those things required money. Lots of money. If only she had thought of it earlier, they might have been able to question the youths and send Bryand after the goblet in a more promising direction.

Neva followed Astiand inside, knowing she couldn't say anything. Pointing out the clue now would stir his anger, and she didn't want to raise questions about her line of work. The fewer specifics Astiand knew, the better.

After paying for their rooms, they trudged up the stairs. The innkeeper followed with a tray of food that smelled of fresh-baked bread, an aged cheese, salted meat, and dried fruits. The man's wife remained downstairs, obviously too nervous to serve a Da'Valia. Neva saw the woman at the reception desk wringing her hands and staring after Neva with a concerned expression. Neva supposed she and Astiand looked like a strange pair. A young woman and a monstrous Da'Valia. Neva waved in an attempt to ease the woman's fear.

In Astiand's room, Neva sat at a two-person table under the window and thanked the innkeeper for the meal, relieved to be out of the carriage.

"For your discretion, and your wife's." Astiand pressed a coin into the innkeeper's hand before closing the door.

"His discretion?" Neva asked as Astiand shrugged out of his coat, revealing an expensive silk shirt.

"The last thing we need is villagers getting worked up about a Da'Valia and his pretty prisoner," Astiand said, placing his coat on the end of the bed before joining her.

"If only they knew I begged to come along," Neva said wryly, covering her surprise. *Did he just call me pretty?* Her comment earned a quick bark of laughter from Astiand.

Neva fidgeted in her chair. The cuts on her back were a steady source of discomfort. She focused on that to overcome her lingering nausea and was pleased when her appetite came roaring back.

Once Astiand joined her, she downed half her mead. She was starving, and she had worked up a thirst during their travels. Luckily, drinking mead wasn't unlike drinking water for her. She ran warm, so she burned through it quicker. She promptly started on her bread, and Astiand did the same.

"You said your mother was one of us," Astiand said between bites.

Neva nodded, still chewing. She wasn't about to share specific details unless he asked her directly. Unfortunately, Astiand perceived this and rephrased.

"What was her name? What clan was she of?"

Neva swallowed and washed it down with the rest of her mead.

"Her name was Monazhi Da'Voda-Lira," she answered. Unsure she wanted to give up information without getting anything in return, she asked, "have you heard of her?"

Astiand shook his head. His gaze avoided hers, making her think he was hiding something. He pulled a flask from his pocket and splashed a generous portion of some clear liquid into his cup. He held the container out to her, and she poured it into her own mug.

"Never?" She returned the container.

"But our clan, the Da'Voda, is fairly large," Astiand said. "And I would have been young during your mother's time."

Neva frowned. She didn't like the way he refused to look at her when he spoke. She took a swig of her new beverage and grimaced.

"Gods, what is that?" she asked.

Astiand smiled at her reaction, but it wasn't exactly friendly.

"My family's concoction. The Da'Valia call it hagave."

"Oh," she said. "It's good."

Flattery seemed like the best course of action, even if it wasn't truthful. Neva took another couple of sips to make her point, trying not to wince at the sharp taste and lingering burn. She thought she spied a hint of a smile playing on his lips.

"Brandy is the drink of choice in my family," she explained.

"Your human family," Astiand said. He sounded puzzled, as if he was trying to work something out.

"The only one I've ever known," Neva said defensively.

"So… you didn't come into your power until when?" Astiand asked after a pause.

Neva sighed.

"The day before I met you. The day I met Bryand."

They ate in silence for a while.

"You half-breeds go against our laws." He said with a frown. "The latest I can remember seeing a majila come into her power was the age of fourteen. You're older than that, if I am not mistaken."

"A bit," she agreed. She looked him full in the face. She wasn't sure precisely what it was, but he didn't seem so fearsome right now.

"Us hilans come into it earlier and easier," he told her. "I think I was seven."

"What can I expect?" she asked. "When we return to your clan, I mean."

"I can't say," he mused, a change coming over him as if he had remembered something. "Your timing is horrible, and your status doesn't allow me to talk about the firérite. We live and die by these strict rules."

He shrugged, as if the answers he would have shared otherwise were of little importance. Any hint of his openness moments before was gone. Frustration crept into her fingers, drawing her hands into fists. What about returning to his clan would cause him to clam up like that?

"What can you tell me, then?" she asked. Hearing her own voice, she wasn't so sure she had a good hold on her emotions.

Astiand shrugged and rubbed the space between his eyes.

"Nothing."

"Fine." Neva gritted her teeth and threw down her napkin. "If you'll excuse me."

Neva was up from her chair and out of Astiand's room before he could acknowledge her departure. Her steps were off-kilter, her tongue felt loose, and her temper was unchecked as she entered her room. The hagave was different from the other liquors she had tried. She would need to remember to be careful drinking it. She didn't want to say anything she would later regret.

Further, she resolved to pester him about the Da'Valia and bring him to the same point of annoyance he so easily brought her. Maybe then she would get a satisfactory response or two.

And she did.

The next day, she prodded him with questions. At breakfast in Stagg. At lunch in Craven's Roosy. At dinner in Farleigh. And then again before they went to sleep. It became a ritual for the duration of their trip. It was childish of her, but she had nothing to lose. Her strategy would either work, or it wouldn't.

"Is this some game to you?" he finally asked her as they huddled beside a campfire in a mountainous region north of Livorna. The terrain had grown challenging as they deviated from the Old King's Highway to less well-traveled roads. Snow covered the trees and ground, and few animals roamed. Likely, many were still in hibernation.

Neva swallowed a drink from her waterskin and took a deep breath. The air was thin here, but it was clean, too. It hadn't been muddied by thousands of chimneys and the metal forgeries, but merely her and Astiand's modest campfire.

Astiand left his gaze fixed on her, awaiting an answer. His displeasure was thick.

"It's not as if a half-breed like me could use anything you tell," she pointed out.

"You do realize there are things a Da'Voda could meet death for sharing?"

"I —" She stopped. She had realized nothing of the sort.

"Other things might warrant lashings or beatings," Astiand said. "We take our oaths seriously."

"Then…" She swallowed hard. She was testing uneven ground. "Can't you tell me something about them that wouldn't warrant such harsh punishment?"

"No." Astiand said it as if it were final, but she had other ideas.

"No inner secrets," she rushed to reassure him. "But I've heard stories. Is everything they say about you true?"

Astiand grinned. It transformed his face for the merest of moments, and she realized it was the first time she had seen him smile sincerely — and he looked like he would say something.

"More than you would think," he told her.

Neva waited, watching the light from the fire flicker across his face and dance in his dark silver eyes. Their pull was enthralling, so she diverted her gaze to the sky.

"I'll tell you what." He leaned forward in a cross-legged position. "You drop your glamour, and I'll set you straight on one of the more popular misconceptions."

Neva's gaze flew from the stars to Astiand's face again. She didn't know why, but his proposal surprised her. He was getting something in return, so she wasn't sure she was winning her own game. Still, she was looking for information.

She closed her eyes reluctantly and released the clasp on the chain around her neck, snapping the spell. It was a miraculous feeling. She hadn't appeared as herself since leaving Glacier Pass. Her parents had raised her to side with caution, yet she felt safe to show herself here. She hadn't seen a human since morning.

In a slight shimmer, her hair brightened until it shone in the firelight. Her skin lost some of its human coloring and whitened to match the silvery snow around them. She opened her eyes, still a clouded blue, and ran her fingers through her hair, pulling the strands away from her horns and pointed ears. Neva rolled over on Bryand's sleeping mat, which she had adopted for the past several nights, so she was on her side across from Astiand.

"Your turn," she dared him.

Astiand's eyes dragged over her, and Neva forgot to breathe as they lingered here and there. Even with a blanket covering her, his gaze made her feel self-conscious. When he reached her face, his wicked smile was back. For the slightest moment, she had thought she saw the being beneath his cool exterior, but now it was gone.

"You should be proud of who you are," he said, seeming to pick up on her vulnerability.

"Easy for you to say," Neva retorted, unnerved. "You've never had to hide who you are."

"Do not pretend to know me," Astiand said quietly.

Neva opened her mouth to respond, but something made her hesitate. She did not want to jump to conclusions about him as easily as he did about her.

"I would not presume," she said. "Now, wasn't there something you were going to tell me?"

"Aye, I'm true to my word." Astiand said. "Do you know why Dhianz cursed us?"

Neva's mother raised her with the knowledge that Dhianz, the god of war, was their creator. He had brought the Da'Valia into being through a blending of potent magic and his own blood, but Neva did not know why he had then cursed them. She shook her head.

"Her name was S'donzhi, and she was the most beautiful and powerful majila who ever lived. A fierce warlock." Astiand settled back against his pack. "She caught the attention of Dhianz and his half-brother Goj and the brothers took our form for a time, both attempting to seduce her. Dhianz, of course, won. Every battle heated the passion between them. She became his mistress and gave him a son born not of his blood but of his seed. They named him Ferrand.

"Soon after, a division grew between the gods, and our world became their gameboard. Amid a glorious battle, Dhianz was captivated by death, as he so often is, and he turned to Riska, spurning S'donzhi. Determined to fight, S'donzhi gave the boy to Goj for safekeeping."

"No," Neva gasped. Goj was the vengeful god of trickery, and in all the stories she had heard, he most enjoyed molding children into dark creatures, or killing them.

"Aye," Astiand said gravely. "Goj tortured the young boy until Dhianz withdrew his influence from the war. Afterwards, Goj refused to give the boy back. He cut off his head, arms, and legs — burnt them and scattered the ash in the wind so no one could repair him. Bitter at having been slighted, furious at having been tricked, and grieving the loss of her son, S'donzhi stole Dhianz's precious Trishula with the intent to fetch Ferrand from the Underworld. She had nothing left to lose, and channeling her wrath, she fractured the barrier between this realm and the next. But, ultimately, Dhianz and Riska prevented her from infiltrating the realm of the dead, and that only infuriated her more.

"S'donzhi dismantled the Trishula, separating Dhianz's Eye, Mouth, and Hand — tools of such strength they had never before left the safekeeping of the gods. She used her great power to hide them so he might never find them again. Dhianz was crazed. In a fit of unrivaled rage, he disowned his half-brother, killed S'donzhi, and cursed the Da'Valia. He never returned to the heavens, and he has dwelled in the Underworld since."

"That's terrible," Neva whispered. "It sounds as if nobody won."

"Certainly not our people," Astiand agreed. "For centuries, every majila born to the clans has been cursed with a dangerous power, and they cannot control that power without the balance instilled by the firérite or the shacklay. We've lost too many majilas to count to the brutal process of the firérite, so even now, we pray and await the day when he will forgive S'donzhi's sins and no longer hold us in contempt."

Neva bit her lip, thinking. The story triggered memories of Monazhi telling her stories on stormy nights. Monazhi's tales had left out some gruesome details Astiand was only too interested in sharing, but Neva remembered her mother's soft voice as she spoke of Dhianz's Mouth, which the dragons captured at the beginning of the Great War; of his Eye, which had disappeared without a trace several hundred years ago; and of his Hand, which was placed within a strong majila without her consent or knowledge so none could detect it.

"Why do I have a feeling you're leaving something out?" She wanted to know if he would tell her more.

"I am leaving a great many things out," he told her, adding wood to the fire. "There is much more to the story, but not to why we honor Dhianz."

Neva grinned, satisfied. She had finally learned something from him. If other Da'Valia were as tight-lipped with information as Astiand, she would have to hold her own secrets close, as he did in the story's telling.

Chapter Ten

First Cravell, 1632

*I could scream my frustration. Trinizhi followed us into the city tonight
and wrecked our plan. The dragon absconded with the Mouth to Lithlorian
Island, and she orchestrated it. I don't know the details of her deal, but I
consider this to be the ultimate betrayal to our people. There's no chance now
we might retrieve it before the summit.*

*I regret us working largely in secret. Who would believe me if I called her
out? What honorable donazhi would grant a kilstroke based on hearsay?*

*To make matters worse, she broke the human. Now his leg is mangled, and
I cannot say whether he will live. For some reason, this weighs on me more
than it should.*

— Monazhi Da'Voda-Lira

In the carriage the next day, Neva could only think of being among
Da'Valia by nightfall. The scene the goblet had shown her set warning
bells clamoring in her mind. She tried not to think of them attacking her
and spent a good deal of time studying her boots as a result.

Despite all the time she had spent inside the Da'Valia contraption,
camping on the rugged mountain sides had taken a toll. Dried snow slush and
dirt clung to her shoes. She was sorely in need of a thorough scrubbing. Her

wounds from the fire were the only clean parts she had left, and that was merely because she was meticulous about avoiding infection. She had learned that lesson when Morty lost his eye following a knife fight in Cul Corner.

Neva tried to imagine the goings-on back home. By now, her Ring must suspect something foul had befallen Flynn, even if they had not yet learned of his demise. Her mind wandered, speculating about her family and friends, and she eventually let the steady rumble of the carriage lull her to sleep.

Shouts outside roused Neva as the carriage slowed near midday. She fumbled to grab her pack in a groggy haze as Astiand directed the carriage into the Da'Voda stables. They came to a stop, and she stepped out, eager to see the stronghold. The miasma of hay and manure was the same as any other stable, but what differed was the horses peering back at her with shining red eyes — and they were unabashed in meeting her gaze. That was different. Livestock typically avoided her.

The horses were not the only foreign creatures. Two stable hands that passed by were distinctly Da'Valia, as was the large hilan with whom Astiand was talking. The stables were constructed of black bricks with doors and lofts of black-painted wood. The stark contrast was almost as striking as the full-blooded Da'Valia themselves. Neva couldn't stop staring.

"Come," Astiand said, already striding down the rows of stalls.

Neva followed him out into the afternoon light. She blinked, adjusting to the change in brightness. She tried to keep up with Astiand, but her attention was constantly being pulled in all directions.

They walked on a white cobblestone street with light brick buildings covered in snow on each side. Black shingled roofs arched elegantly toward the blue sky with thin trails of smoke wandering from the chimneys. The beauty astounded her. The Da'Valia had constructed every building with the artistry and care that graced the House of Trescony.

Looking down several streets, Neva realized not one of them bore resemblance to Cul Corner. Mercenary work paid well. Despite years of practice, but she would have difficulty determining which of these buildings housed better wares.

Behind the stables, majilas fought in a practice yard. They used long staves to attack each other, flowing white forms clad in pearly clothing. Most of their horns were longer than hers by several inches but shorter than Astiand's or Bryand's.

Neva spotted children, still without their ivory or ebony horns, flopping into the snowbanks against the stables in what appeared to be the end of a mock battle. Across the street, a group of Da'Valia looked up from a dice game in a courtyard. A long-haired hilan nodded to Astiand before joining the other dark creatures to stare at her. She had seen more intimidating-looking humans, but these were battle-proven Da'Valia. They could kill the hoodlums and hooligans in Cul Corner for using weighted dice in minutes if they desired. Neva looked away and walked with as much confidence as she could muster.

"In here," Astiand soon directed her through a decorative cast iron gate that led to a large, two-story home.

They traipsed through a yard smothered by mounds of snow. At the end of the icy walkway, they entered an arched doorway, met with heated elegance and soft lighting.

For its utilitarian owner, the house's decorations were unusual, an impression of refined wealth. Some people came into money and purchased according to trends. But old money showed in everything from construction of the sweeping staircase to rugs that depicted ancient battles and legends. Hints of a desert land were reflected in the intricate beaded tapestries and ceramics the color of sand.

Astiand didn't stop moving once they were inside. He ascended a sweeping staircase, shouting for an attendant in Da'Valian. Neva closed the door behind her, the size of the handle dwarfing her hand. They followed the grand staircase to the second floor. Astiand opened the first door in a long hallway.

"You may use this room," he said.

Astiand rifled through two drawers of an ornate dresser while she looked around. The room had a plush bed she yearned to collapse upon and a tall oval mirror hanging across from the shuttered window. The space looked comfortable, although not recently used. A layer of dust covered the top of the dresser, and a stale rose smell suggested no one had opened the window for a long time.

Astiand tossed her a bundle of silky clothing, leaving a drawer open with items hanging out.

"Make that fit," he said, seemingly unsure of what to do with a female's clothing. "You'll have a little more than an hour to wash and change."

"Very well," Neva said, a nervous thrill running through her.

"Remember, I'm bringing you in front of the donazhi tonight," he told her, moving to open the door across the hall, revealing a washroom. "It's unlikely you will need to speak, but if you're called upon, you must do so with respect and decorum."

Neva nodded and nearly jumped when a figure in a brown robe brushed by her.

"Miland, make sure the water is hot for Neva," Astiand ordered.

Astiand's last instructions floated to her from over his shoulder as he strode to a room at the end of the hallway. He slammed the door behind him in his haste. To say he appeared tense would have been an understatement.

Neva studied the back of the servant, who was filling the bath with water from a pump, another impressive luxury. Miland wore his hood drawn, so all she could see was his profile. She judged him to be about six feet tall, wider than both Astiand and Bryand, and also more muscular.

"If you would just knock twice when you're done, I would be grateful," Neva told him.

She didn't want to watch him work, so she started toward her room. She had never been waited on before. In all her life, she had always been the one doing the serving. She felt incredibly uncomfortable.

In quick order, two knocks sounded on the door. Neva gathered the bundle Astiand had given her and slipped into the washroom. She began cleaning her hair immediately after seeing her reflection. Even in her non-glamoured state, it was dulled by fine coat of dust, and she smelled of campfire smoke. She took her time soaking in the large tub, letting the grime slide into the water. Once she finished, she felt rejuvenated.

The outfit Astiand gave her was a white combination of a top and pants that shone like a pearl under light. At first glance, she thought the pants were a long, flowing skirt, but she discovered they were designed for effortless movement. The top was also different from what she was accustomed to: there were no lacings or clasps. She shimmied into the circular wrap and pulled a longer sash over her shoulder before securing it with a tan leather belt around her waist. The top left her arms bare and diamonds of skin showing on the sides of her waist.

She was not accustomed to showing as much skin as the majilas she'd seen earlier, but she didn't have time to find an alternate solution. Neva found matching slippers in the closet. They were too tight but not so much that she couldn't walk in them. She resented Astiand's order to make the clothes fit. If that were within her ability, she would.

Neva wove her hair into a simple braid, allowing it to part to reveal her budding horns. She studied the full length of her reflection in the mirror. The pants-skirt was about half an inch too short, but overall, she looked Da'Valian. She took a steadying breath before leaving her room to go downstairs in search of food.

"Excuse me —" she stopped when she spotted the hooded servant in the entryway. She had been about to ask where she might find something to eat but halted when she spotted what was beneath the rim of his cloak. Someone had sheared off the Da'Valia's horns. The sight was so shockingly disturbing that moments passed before she composed herself enough to look him in the face.

"Who did this to you?" she asked in a horrified whisper.

The Da'Valia didn't respond. His thick eyebrows shadowed midnight eyes that harbored anguish. The rest of his muscular stature and clean-shaven appearance didn't match the tortured look, but Neva thought his soul was a scarred one. In Glacier Pass, humans reserved robes such as his for temple priests or priestesses. But here, she had the feeling they meant something else entirely.

"Miland!" Astiand's voice cut through the air like a sword.

Astiand stood on the stairs, garbed in fine clothing not unlike what he had worn to the Trades. A dark green sash was strung from shoulder to hip, and his hair was loose but still damp from washing.

"Nevazhi will need a cape with a crest on it. Quickly." Astiand strode down, stopping on the last step so he towered over Neva. "Miland does not speak, so you're wasting your time if you're trying to get him to talk."

"Who did that to him?" Neva asked.

"There are prices on many things among the Da'Valia, dishonor to our donazhi among them," Astiand said, a fierceness overtaking his features.

"But his horns were cut off." The distress in Neva's voice was real. She had always been told the Da'Valia were ruthless, but seeing it was different.

Astiand shrugged one shoulder, fingers tapping a pattern on the hilt of his sword.

"You must disarm your adversaries to maintain power. The donazhi knew this and used this. If you are to be among us, you would do well to remember that."

Miland returned with a green velvet cape draped over his arm. He handed it to Neva while Astiand yanked open the front door. Neva hooked the clasp above her bosom, below the lump in her throat.

If the donazhi had done that to Miland — to one of their own — what fate might await her?

Chapter Eleven

First Cravell, 1632

*I've delivered the human to a talented group of healers at the House of
Trescony and paid them in gold. Still, I cannot bring myself to return to the
clans yet. The temptation to denounce Trinizhi is l strong.*

*Alizhi and Benjamand plan to return to the Da'Xana clan, and it will
be the first time we've not been together since Alizhi and I came to the
fortress at Picquereau. Alizhi and Benjamand warned me it may not be
safe to remain alone among humans, so I've purchased a human glamour
to hide behind. If that fails, I will have to rely on my coin, my power, and
my dagger for protection.*

— Monazhi Da'Voda-Lira

Neva and Astiand didn't have to walk far. Beyond the homes, they passed a temple atop a nearby hill and arrived at a pentagonal building occupying a vast expanse of land. It had one level, topped with a dome roof covered in hard sheets of snow, and five-story bell towers stood at each of the five corners. Lines of thick icicles hung along the trim, sparkling and dripping in the early evening sun.

In front of Neva and Astiand, three majilas entered the building through a wide, arching doorway that sloped to a point.

"Follow me," Astiand ordered.

Neva missed a step and slid in behind Astiand while glad for his cover. She pulled her cloak tightly around her.

Inside the auditorium, Da'Valia stood in groups. Intricate rugs decorated a granite floor, and incense infused the air. Everyone carried weapons, truly the warrior race Dhianz created them to be. Chatter dimmed as Astiand approached a seating area to the left. Matching sections descended from the other walls, separated by balustrades, and drums larger than Neva's own body were positioned in each corner. Each section sported a cathedra, elevated above chairs arranged in stadium style. Astiand lowered himself into one such seat, and a young hilan and an otima, a holy servant of Dhianz, occupied the others. That left two more empty.

Following another of Astiand's orders, Neva sat nearby. Her stomach grumbled from nerves and hunger, but she focused on her surroundings. She was inspecting wooden pillars carved with geometric patterns. They brandished candles that illuminated the dome ceiling.

Neva recognized the donazhi immediately when the matriarch arrived. The donazhi's outfit was much like Neva's but far more richly constructed, lined with silver threads and small amber stones.

The donazhi's tall, willowy form flowed to an ivory throne, which was raised above the seating area next to Astiand's. When she faced the room of Da'Valia, they hurried to find chairs. The children lowered themselves to the floor as near to the walls as they could get. With all the bodies organized, Neva spotted a circular dance floor of stained wood set in the middle of the room. She didn't pay much attention to it, sliding her gaze back to the donazhi.

The majila was striking. Two swords were positioned diagonally across her back, and a headpiece with what must have been a hundred black jet stones in a silver setting rested on her head. Her horns were pure white, smooth, and curved to points. Her face was round, framed by silver-blonde locks pinned low and to the side at the base of her skull. Cherub lips were icy and unsmiling, as were white-silver tigress eyes, separated by a thin, curved nose. Faint lines on her forehead suggested that the donazhi was at least twice Neva's age, maybe a decade older than Astiand.

"Let the matters of this forum be brought forth," the donazhi said, her voice chilling.

Astiand stood and addressed the room.

"Astiand Da'Voda-Cuchilla, at the donazhi's service." He bowed. "I have returned from the northern ice city this day to report that our dealings with the humans went well. An order for twenty in service to the Kamash Islands was approved and signed for early Cravell. An order for fifteen in service to the Cashcar Ports was approved and signed for late Vestive. Deals for two teams for mid-Cravell bridal transports were also agreed upon."

He bowed again and sat. Fresh whispers circulated at the news. Neva judged Bryand and Astiand had been busy during the Trades to procure so many assignments.

The donazhi kept her face an immovable mask.

"Well done," she said. "But what say you of Bryand Da'Voda-Solatta?"

Astiand stood and bowed again.

"Alas, Donazhi," he addressed her directly now. "Bryand Da'Voda-Solatta stayed behind to finish arrangements for the mid-Cravell bridals and to witness signings. I would still be with him, if it wasn't for a matter of the firérite."

Astiand stressed his words when he spoke of Bryand finishing arrangements, but Neva barely had time to analyze the lie before she felt the donazhi's eyes on her.

"And what, pray tell, is the firérite you bring forth?"

Astiand sent a shot of cold pain up Neva's arm from the shacklay. She flinched and stood.

"Nevazhi Roberts of Glacier Pass, daughter of Monazhi Da'Voda-Lira. A half-breed." Astiand identified her, his voice amplified by the acoustics of the room's construction.

Whispers started around them at a ferocious pace, and Neva knew at once he had lied when he had said he did not recognize her mother's name. Neva kept herself from glancing back at him in her anger. She wouldn't give him the satisfaction of knowing how much his deceit perturbed her.

Neva instead stared at the donazhi, who appeared colder than she had before. Neva felt a tickle of fear climb her spine. Why was the donazhi not looking at her now?

"She has invoked the Rule of Rhianzhi," Astiand added, almost as an afterthought.

Had she? Neva wasn't aware she had done any such thing.

"Of course." The donazhi waited for the room to quiet. "Of course, we will honor our ancestors and grant the Lira offspring a proper firérite. If her begetting was foul, we will have this, at least, be honorable. I assume you will be her proctor, Astiand? That is your shacklay on her wrist, is it not?"

Astiand bowed his head in answer.

"Very well." The donazhi connected her steely white stare to Neva again. "Your firérite will commence at nightfall tomorrow."

As Neva had seen Astiand do, she lowered her head. In agreement or submission, she couldn't be sure. Maybe it was both.

A majila slightly younger than Neva stepped to the center of the room and onto the circular hardwood floor. Her eyes were a creamy silver, her nose boney, and her skin was a bright white. Her outfit was a beige wrap. The weapon at her side a sword. She addressed the donazhi and Astiand together, bowing.

"Lindzhi Da'Voda-Lira, at the service of this clan." Lindzhi spoke each word as if she threw a rock with it, and for Neva, she might as well have. Da'Voda-Lira was her mother's family name. This majila was likely a close relative, cousin or other.

"I request," Lindzhi continued, "the blessing of the great Dhianz and the Da'Voda to invoke the kilstroke with the ward of Da'Voda-Cuchilla. In doing this, I seek to restore my family's honor.

"Long-ago, my cousin Monazhi broke one of our most sacred laws and besmirched our family name. I ask now only for the privilege to discard the filth she brought upon the world, to once again bask in the glory of our great god's shadow."

An angry heat flushed across Neva's face at the majila's speech, and, this time, Neva looked back at Astiand. If she wasn't mistaken, she was being called out for a kilstroke, a fight to the death. It was the stuff of legends in human cities.

The donazhi gave Lindzhi a considering look.

"What say you, Astiand?" the donazhi asked.

"Of course, I would honor tradition and hand my ward over to participate in a kilstroke." He spoke without hesitation. "But might I suggest we postpone such an event until after Nevazhi's firérite so the mighty Dhianz would be honored with better-matched opponents? The brutality of a kilstroke might be hindered by uncontrolled power. I, for one, would not rush to insult our ancestors with a mockery of their most sacred dance."

For once, Neva found herself grateful for something Astiand had to say.

During Astiand's speech, the Da'Valia in the fifth raised chair had remained silent, only a witness to the night's proceedings. Now, the young Da'Valia stood and bowed. His skin was smooth, the darkest black, he kept his hair in short and loose curls, and large horns punctuated his high forehead. Straight brows hooded his soft eyes.

Neva didn't know why she hadn't noticed this Da'Valia before. He was surely the most gorgeous creature she had ever seen. He was about Astiand's same height and build, but a coarse sensuality accented his stance. She was sure he could simply breathe and be beautiful.

"Arroyand Da'Voda-Esava, at the donazhi's service." His voice was deep. "I would but humbly agree with Astiand were it not for the length of time Lindzhi Da'Voda-Lira and her family has suffered from the disgrace her cousin wrought. Our loyalty to Dhianz would be better shown with a timely kilstroke than one balanced to the ever-elusive idea of perfection. Presenting our god with the opportunity to pass a final judgment on this long-past betrayal now must surely hold more merit."

The hilan retook his seat.

"I have seldom dismissed a request for a kilstroke," the donazhi said. "And I have postponed such events even less frequently. The great Dhianz and this clan would be most honored to allow Lindzhi Da'Voda-Lira and Nevazhi Roberts of Glacier Pass to invoke the kilstroke this night."

Scattered whispers started around the auditorium, and Neva tried not to let them worry her as bile rose in her throat. She would be outmatched in a kilstroke. She had a vague idea of how to defend herself with the array of weapons the Da'Valia wore as if they were statements of fashion, and she had no experience going against others with her same strength and finesse. The only advantage she had was a background packed with years of fighting dirty against the other pickpockets who often sought to skim from the smaller purse cutters.

But it had to be. The Da'Valia would not let her out of this, and she had promised her father she would return to Glacier Pass. She intended to follow through on that pledge.

"Donazhi, of course you speak with sagacity," Astiand said. "Let the kilstroke commence."

Ominous drums started from the five corners of the auditorium. Astiand motioned for Neva to follow him and walked to the circular floor in the center of the room. The level wooden platform they headed toward was the dance floor, just not the kind Neva had assumed.

"When it comes to it, kill her. Otherwise, she will end you," Astiand said to Neva in a warning tone.

The room was already in a frenzy, with Da'Valia wagering bets, compiling purses, and rearranging for optimum seating.

Astiand stopped at the fighting area with the otima between them and Lindzhi.

"What weapon say you, Nevazhi Roberts of Glacier Pass?" Up close, the otima did not look like the majilas in the room. It was as though the otima was caught between hilan and majila, power and anti-power, near to androgynous. Dark eyes were set high in a white face, small breasts were at competition with muscular arms, and black hair framed white skin. The faint scent of molding citrus wafted to Neva.

Neva opened her mouth, but she found herself at a loss for words. She wasn't expecting a choice of weapons. She hadn't been expecting a choice in anything.

"Daggers," Neva said finally.

Astiand nodded as if satisfied and backed away.

"With honor, Neva." He gave her the final warning before returning to his seat.

"Daggers!" The otima repeated Neva's choice loudly.

Lindzhi's lips set in a line of grim satisfaction. She discarded her sword, handing it off to a nearby child. The young hilan gave a toothy grin and returned excitedly to his seat.

Two attending otimas appeared and knelt, holding matching sets of daggers. Lindzhi grabbed one pair and Neva took the other. As soon as their hands touched the metal, the otima began reciting a rite from memory, asking Dhianz for his blessing over the kilstroke. Lindzhi walked to one side of the circle and Neva took a place across from her while watching how the majila moved. Her cousin was light on her feet.

The otima finished the rite and addressed Neva and Lindzhi.

"Skill only. No shows of power. No spells. If you step out of the circle, your life is forfeit. Begin when the floor changes to black. Fight with honor."

"Die with pleasure," Lindzhi responded, her eyes locked on Neva.

The otima knelt and drew a charcoal rune on the edge of the floor. As they completed the symbol, magic crept from the marking, charring the wood.

Neva's mouth went dry as the smoke inched out to cover more than half of the kilstroke floor. She held the shining daggers with ease but refrained from flipping them to test their weight. To do so would reveal she could throw — something she wished to keep to herself until the kilstroke began. If she did throw and missed, she would be a weapon short.

Once the smoke reached the far side of the ring, Neva jumped in and circled with Lindzhi. The drums pounded in the background, but the sound barely registered with Neva.

Lindzhi ran forward on a high note of the melody, sweeping one blade down and one blade up, aiming for Neva's midsection. In a blur, Neva blocked the strokes, and they began the dance.

Lindzhi was a voracious opponent. They slid, attacked, and parried, their blades sparking as metal hit metal. Each jarring clash sent bone-creaking vibrations through Neva's hands. A human's bones would have shattered on impact, but she was stronger. If Lindzhi expected a half-breed to be an easy mark, Neva aimed to disappoint.

Lindzhi lunged at her from the side, airborne and kicking at Neva's head.

Neva ducked and twisted, but the movement wasn't enough to avoid Lindzhi's other foot. It met her collarbone with a bruising force, knocking her aside.

Neva landed near the edge of the ring, but not outside it, and she was up again before Lindzhi charged. One knife slashed toward Neva's throat, followed by the other dagger. Neva struck back, locking their blades together. Neva slammed her head into Lindzhi's skull, shoving their bodies back toward the center of the circle.

Neva couldn't and didn't stop a grin from creeping across her face as they fought. She felt exhilarated and determined. She was made for this.

Neva avoided being tripped up twice, jumping back from her opponent's kicks. She caught a descending blade with an awkward block that sent both daggers flying out of the circle. Children seated on the ground nearby jumped aside to avoid the weapons.

Neva regained her footing for only a moment before Lindzhi knocked her down. The majila threw her body atop Neva and angled her blade toward Neva's neck.

Neva caught Lindzhi's wrist with one hand, channeling all of her strength to keep the knife from cutting her throat. Her grip was wracked with an icy pain from Astiand's bracelet.

A scream tore from Neva as a spasm ran through her hand. It forced her to let go of Lindzhi's wrist. Neva ripped her other hand free from Lindzhi's weight, relinquishing the dagger she had held there to grab one of Lindzhi's horns and yank. Her cousin yelped, dropping her remaining dagger so it slid away, and put all her energy into forcing Neva's hand off her horn.

Neva barely registered she was angry — both at Astiand invoking the shacklay and at Lindzhi's calling her out — before she focused her rage.

Neva let go of Lindzhi's horn and sent her frustration into every blow she landed on Lindzhi's head until the majila pulled back and rolled away. They circled again. Neva rushed at Lindzhi, but her anger had somewhat clouded her judgment, and the full-blooded Da'Valia was ready for her attack.

Lindzhi flipped Neva onto the hard, black floor. It vibrated with so much force nearby pillars shook. Neva thanked Dhianz her spine hadn't snapped.

Lindzhi was a blur as she leapt onto Neva, straddling her back. The majila reached a firm hand forward, sliding it through Neva's hair, securely digging her fingers in under Neva's eyebrows. Neva could only see stars because of the pressure.

"Die with pleasure, half-breed," Lindzhi whispered, ready to tear her head back.

Chapter Twelve

Second Cravell, 1632

Alizhi has mated. I've lost one potential aliado to the Da'Roha, and two
of my political allies have left me because of Trinizhi's treachery. My status is
faltering further as I linger, and I fear that by the summit her support will
outweigh my own.

— *Monazhi Da'Voda-Lira*

Neva pushed down with all of her might, driven by the will to live. She flipped Lindzhi over with a desperate lash of energy and a guttural scream. The impact of Lindzhi's body rattled through the black wood and to the foundation of the building. A strange crunch sounded as several of the majila's bones snapped. An already unstable pillar of candles toppled over. It broke into the circle, knocking Lindzhi to the side and spraying a stream of hot wax across her neck.

A battle fever rushed through Neva's blood. But more than that, she had felt something deep inside her flare to life. Not just Da'Valia instincts, but a rage that made everything else outside the kilstroke circle disappear. Dhianz had created her for battle, and it absorbed her.

Lindzhi grunted in pain and shoved the pillar away. Smoke curled in its wake as it rolled away. She turned to face Neva, but it was too late. Neva jumped through the air, striking down on Lindzhi's chest with a blow that shoved her back to the ground. Neva stamped her foot on the majila's throat.

"You first," Neva said, pushing down with all of her weight, crushing Lindzhi's windpipe. "Cousin."

Neva spat out the title and watched as Lindzhi dragged in her last breaths.

The kilstroke floor faded back to its base color. Slowly, Neva registered the fight was over. She blinked at the still gaze of her cousin's corpse, bent to close the majila's eyelids, and stood to stare at the auditorium of Da'Valia watching her. She had never felt more alive, and at the same time, she never wanted to feel this way again. She was trapped in a nightmare.

A low growl began around the room. The sound increased, transforming into cheers and shouts. Coins were paid out to those who'd wagered on the underdog, and some Da'Valia filtered out of the auditorium. Before Neva knew it, a group of young hilans surrounded her in congratulation.

The child Lindzhi had handed her sword to approached to return the item to Neva, but she waved him off, telling him it was his now. The thought of taking the sword made her nauseous. She didn't want any reminders of what she had done.

The Da'Valia Arroyand, who approached with a much older hilan, provided a welcome distraction. Neva surmised the elder was near the age of fifty, by far the oldest in the room. Da'Valia had notoriously short life spans because of their mercenary lifestyles, so his age was remarkable.

"Be gone!" the elder shouted at the unaligned hilans surrounding her. "Predictable beasties. Pouncing on any majila who hasn't risen yet."

He scowled at them before turning to Neva. He pulled the loose strands of hair from her face and inspected her horns without introduction. His actions were so unexpected, she didn't even try to pull away.

"Well, I'll say one thing for you," Arroyand drawled. He stood with a confidence and ease that said he was better than everyone else, or at least he thought he was. "You know how to make an impression."

The elder frowned and backed away, seemingly finished with his inspection.

"Impression, maybe, but she'll never be more than a middel," the elder said.

At his words, several of the young hilans walked away, but more than a few stayed near.

"Ah, well, the beasties will be disappointed," Arroyand allowed, nodding thoughtfully. Then, with an amiable smile, he addressed Neva directly. "We ambitious fellows are always on the lookout for a power worth aligning with, but don't worry about a lower status. Half-breeds almost never reach toppel, and the majilas that do can be real bitches."

Neva didn't realize she had been so tense until his words set her at ease. She didn't know what she had expected following the kilstroke, but this definitely wasn't it. Arroyand, although he seemed too overtly sexual for her tastes, was also strangely charming.

"'Ambitious fellows' is putting it lightly." The elder hemmed.

"You might have a point, but my ambition also means I get to do this —" Arroyand reached out a muscular arm and pulled Neva to him by her belt. He lifted her fist into the air with a grip slightly too tight to be comfortable.

"With honor and with pleasure!" he roared.

Cheers renewed as Arroyand slid a dagger from the sheath at his waist and notched a sliver out of Neva's belt. His ease with the blade said he was comfortable with small weapons. Intuition told her his familiarity with the dagger was from cutting something softer than leather. Flesh, perhaps. She suppressed a shiver.

"We do this to remember those we send on, and to keep count," he said. "Wear it with pride."

A warm hand grabbed the back of Neva's neck, pulling her away from Arroyand. She turned to find Astiand.

"I guess this means you're keeping the belt," Astiand said.

Neva felt an angry heat come over her.

"No thanks to you." She would not easily forget his use of the shacklay during the kilstroke. "I suppose you would have had me die tonight."

"Tonight or any other. All things in good time," Astiand said wryly. His eyes captured hers. "Truly, you're lucky I stopped you from unleashing your power. Your life would have been forfeit. Instead, you won. Dhianz has ruled that your mother's act of dishonor is forgiven."

Neva opened her mouth to give him a piece of her mind, but she stopped. Was that true? Had she been about to use her power? She didn't know what to think.

"What's her measure?" Astiand moved his attention to Arroyand.

"She'll ascend to middel," Arroyand responded. "Although, it'll be middel with Lindzhi's holdings so she'll fetch some interest, obviously."

"What do you mean?" Neva asked. "What holdings?"

"Your victory secures more than a notch on your belt," Arroyand explained. "That little whelp had some possessions you will enjoy by the laws of the kilstroke."

Neva frowned in distaste.

"I think I'd rather not."

"You must take responsibility for them at some point." Astiand waved for Arroyand to follow him. "It appears we are being beckoned. Behave while we speak with the donazhi."

Neva watched them walk away and turned back to her dwindling group of admirers. As soon as she spied Arroyand and Astiand leaving through a door behind the donazhi's throne, Neva asked directions to the latrine and escaped her unfamiliar company.

She made her way around the outside of the building and angled to a rear corner, far from the view of the Da'Valia filing out of the building. She peeked in a window. She had seen Astiand and Arroyand head to the corner bell tower with the donazhi, but they had apparently not stayed on the ground level.

Something was going on, and Neva wanted to know what it was. Astiand lied about Bryand in front of the clan. There had to be a reason.

Neva would have climbed to the second-story window, but the Da'Valia architecture was plastered smooth, so she had to work instead with the trim, carefully reaching around the icicles. By the time she reached the edge of the window, she had to race to catch up with the conversation.

"… Just know I've made note of it," the donazhi's muted voice traveled through the glass.

"I would never seek to defy you. You know I take our agreement seriously," Astiand said.

"Well, now that's covered," Arroyand interrupted, playing with the edge of the donazhi's wrap as if he would like to slide it off her shoulder. "Where is Bryand, really? And the goblet?"

Astiand told them of finding Flynn with his throat slashed, losing the goblet, and concocting an impromptu plan.

"How much does she know?" The donazhi's voice was unfriendly.

"Nevazhi? Nothing. Only that we were supposed to take possession of an object and it wasn't there. It's pointless to worry about the half-breed anyway. You could dispose of her in your sleep."

"Fine. Inform me immediately if either of you hears from Bryand."

"Should we dispatch a convoy?" Arroyand asked. "If he needs assistance, it would give us an advantage."

"Aye. Arrange it quietly. We've kept them from asking questions so far, and we don't want that to change."

Neva sensed the conversation was ending, so she abandoned the window. She didn't have to wait long before Astiand joined her outside the main door. He didn't acknowledge her before he began down the hill. Neva was accustomed to his long stride now, and she didn't have trouble matching it. Neither of them spoke.

She took notice, though, that the notches on his belt left few areas free of markings. She tried to calculate his kills but gave up past a hundred. Besides, she didn't have a clear view of his other side. She could, however, see his purse. It looked suspiciously fuller than it had when they arrived at the auditorium.

An unexpected thought shocked Neva. There was only one reason she could fathom for his purse to double in the past hour. It made little sense for him to throw the fight with the shacklay if he had bet on her, so perhaps he had been telling the truth earlier. Her gut told her he had hidden motives, but maybe she shouldn't fault his use of the shacklay this one time.

After dinner, Astiand requested she meet him in the parlor. Miland had already set out a tray of hagave, and Astiand lit a fire in the hearth with a flick of his wrist. Black flame dropped into the stone fireplace with a whoosh. Light flickered to all corners of the room, tinting the steel blue walls green and illuminating the tapestry of the Battle of Olgor. Astiand lounged in the chair, so Neva moved to the edge of the couch next to him.

Astiand studied her as she fidgeted with her glass. She was used to his long stares, but his intensity still made her want to squirm.

Astiand swirled his hagave and took a drink, then another, seemingly in a dark mood. Neva tried to keep up, finishing her cup of hagave before she remembered she hadn't intended to drink so much after how tipsy she got the last time.

"Because I'm your proctor for the firérite, I will allow you to ask me questions." Astiand spoke as if he had a sour taste in his mouth. He refilled her glass.

"What kind of questions?" She ignored the drink.

"Just ask." He sounded frustrated. "I can't and won't answer them all, but this is part of the rite of passage. Only I can speak to you about the firérite. How about I give you three for free?"

Neva would have bargained for more, but she didn't want to push her luck.

"What part does middel play here?" she asked. The elder had said she would be one.

Astiand leaned forward in his chair.

"Toppel is the highest level of power, middel is one step lower, and lowel is at the bottom of the tier. For us, that means different things. Middel for a majila is above toppel for a hilan. It's all relative to alliads. Not to mention the variables — our effectiveness on the battlefield also bears much weight in political matters.

"The donazhi is always a toppel majila, usually with a cohort circle of toppel hilans. Sometimes middel, but hardly ever. It would lower the circle's status to allow lesser hilans. All unaligned hilans are looking for more power to align with. It allows us to pull on your power in battle, or in magic craft in the case of warlocks."

Neva let that information register before she asked her next question. If

Astiand, Arroyand, and Bryand were in the donazhi's circle, they all would, essentially, work for her. They wouldn't act against the donazhi because it would only hurt themselves. And now she knew: if she was middel, she would have some standing despite the disgrace of her birth.

"How does the firérite work?"

"That I mostly can't tell you." Astiand shrugged. "The process is unique for every majila. Some are done in a few days, some are done in a few weeks. Middels, usually a week. When you're done, you'll have control over your power, and I'll take the shacklay off because you won't need me to ground you anymore. You would have to learn to apply your power outside of battle — if you want to. But you will be able to harness your power and direct it to your will, which is the point of the entire process."

Neva nodded, looking at the raging fire. She vividly remembered her mother whispering spells under her breath while working in the garden, but Neva had never thought she could work magic, to manipulate and mold god-given power that way. And really, she wasn't sure she wanted to. Unless… if she could make her own spells for her thieving jobs, she would save a significant amount of coin. Coin that could help her father rebuild.

"Will I be free to leave?" She had saved this question for last because she wasn't sure she would like the answer.

"None of us will keep you here, but you may not want to go. Certain attributes of yours may change. Your horns, for instance. But my guess is you'll also identify with us more. You may not feel as human as you once did."

Neva downed her refilled hagave glass. As she had suspected, she didn't like his answer. She already felt too much Da'Valia in her at times. Like in the kilstroke circle. She had never killed anyone before, but tonight, she had not thought twice. Now, in the aftermath, it felt wrong, and she wished she could take it back.

She leaned forward and dared a fourth inquiry, feeling particularly bold.

"When did those grow in?" She looked pointedly at his horns.

Astiand stared at her in response. He knew she was trying to get more information than they had agreed.

Neva's face was flushed, and she couldn't stop her hand from reaching out and touching the smooth black edge of one horn. She noted the ridges lining the base like tree rings. The horn was as hard as any animal's, but its smooth luster reflected the firelight in a display that mesmerized her.

A tingle ran up her arm on contact. It was pleasant, but it had an electric edge to it that made her stop moving. She didn't want anything to go wrong before the firérite. For all she knew, she might catch his hair on fire. That image in her mind made her want to giggle, but the laughter dissipated in her throat as she looked to Astiand's face. He seemed relaxed — almost at peace, save for his enthralling steely eyes, which locked with hers.

She felt confident. If she had been thinking clearly, she would have blamed the hagave, but at the moment, everything was a little foggy.

Neva focused on the horn again. It was so different from hers, both in color and texture. She studied the back edge, which was slightly convex, and ran her finger over it. His eyes closed. He didn't look as annoyed as when he had been answering her questions, but he didn't look happy, either.

"I didn't mean to," she said. "I — are you tired?"

She clasped her hands in her lap. He remained calm, as if hagave had no effect on him.

"No. I'm not tired at all. How long have you had these?"

He brushed a lock of her hair to the side. The ridges of her own horns were barely protruding, ivory, and about an inch long, if that.

"A few years."

His thumb brushed the side of a horn, and her breath caught as sparks of heat washed down her face. It wasn't unpleasant. Not at all.

"What …" The question died in her throat as he ran his finger over the off-white gloss again.

Each movement sent tingles like the ones that had shot through her arm, but stronger and somehow enjoyable. It was as if she was touching some other power that wanted to connect. The attraction surprised her.

Neva felt warm, and the way he was looking at her now caused her gaze to slide to his lips.

"Our horns store our power," he told her softly, "when another touches them with their power, there is a mixing of strengths. We can use it for alliads or fun, or to defeat our enemies, so you must always protect them. No matter what happens."

Chapter Thirteen

Second Cravell, 1632

My chances are withering, and this time I have no one to blame but myself. I told myself I would stay only until Shaun was removed from Riska's door, but I remained too long. If anyone finds out I've mated with a human, all possibilities are lost. Oh, Dhianz, what have I done? Forgive me for this egregious affront.

— Monazhi Da'Voda-Lira

"Wait." Neva's voice stirred herself from the trance. Astiand lowered his hands at a fraction of normal speed and then hurried to scoop up his glass and finish his drink. Neva pulled away.

"You should go to sleep now," he said. "Tomorrow, you'll need your energy."

He set the cup back, and they were both quiet for a moment.

Neva managed to stand, unsteadily, and heard herself penetrate the silence, bidding him goodnight. She was proud of herself, of being able to keep myriad emotions from her voice when they were rampant beneath her skin.

"There is no pleasure without pain among the Da'Valia," his voice carried after her. "Know that."

Neva stopped in the doorway. She couldn't name the determination that bloomed inside her, but it was fueled by hagave. She strode back to him, halting when her pants brushed his legs, and she leaned down, steadying herself by holding onto his shoulder and a chair arm.

She hoped she looked imposing.

"You act heartless, but you're not, are you?" Neva looked deep into those dark silver eyes. Then she was kissing him.

Neva leaned down, rested her hands on his shoulders, and pressed her lips to his. His restraint prompted her to close her eyes and increase her efforts. He was holding back. He always was. Keeping things from her. Lying to cover the truth. She wanted to know who he was beneath the austere exterior.

A moment passed before he surprised her. He didn't touch her with his hands, but his mouth met her demands. Heat flared where their skin met. Passion swept through her, stealing air, and Neva drew back to catch her breath.

"You can't tell me that wasn't pleasure," she managed to say, her mind swimming. "And you'll have to try harder if you want to convince me that I'm such a burden to you. Your purse says differently, after all."

She marched out of the room, not giving him the chance to have the last word.

Infant shadows of dusk washed over the village as Neva followed Miland to her firérite. She was once again led to the building on the hill, but instead of taking a seat in the auditorium, Miland directed her through a series of turns in underground hallways. The temperature dropped the farther they went, and they eventually stopped at an imposing black door. He rapped on the wood, and it opened to reveal a willowy majila with her hair wound in braids about her head like a wreath.

"Come in." The majila stepped aside to allow Neva entry.

Miland disappeared as the door shut behind Neva, and she was left to stare at a room of Da'Valia, most of whom were female. Neva recognized a few from the night before, but one Da'Valia stood out: the otima. Smelling of rotten oranges, they took Neva's hand in greeting and brought her to sit on a cushion in the center of the room. The floor and walls comprised black slate tiles. As bodies parted to make way for her, Neva noticed Astiand in a raised chair in the rear, perfunctorily illuminated by a flickering lantern. Neva tried to push his presence from her mind. Instead, she focused on another young majila in the room. The majila must have been no more than twelve years old. Her cheeks still held the chubbiness of childhood, and her figure had only hints of the hips and breasts that would eventually emerge.

"Ellazhi Da'Voda-Ostra and Nevazhi Roberts of Glacier Pass, welcome to your firérites. May Dhianz bless you and grant you a balanced power." The otima's hands were raised, palms up, as they spoke.

Neva gave a weak smile to Ellazhi. At least neither of them would be alone in this.

The otima began a long chant that sent a fog-like magic spinning around Neva's body and limbs. The damp substance didn't burn like Da'Valia power did, and she shivered at the ghostly touch.

Two majilas brushed Neva's hair, and another loosened her sash. Meanwhile, on the other side of the room, their movements were mimicked by those attending Ellazhi. Next, the attendants disrobed Neva. Neva twisted her wrist when they removed the leather bracelet covering her conviction mark, hoping no one would notice the small tattoo, but she saw one of Astiand's eyebrows raise the barest amount. Neva felt a blush creep up from her bosom and regretted it. The only item she still wore was Astiand's bracelet. She tried with all of her will to ignore his gaze. She wanted to get this over with so she could go home.

The majilas rubbed a sharp smelling balm into her skin and braided her hair into a tight design. They rubbed the balm into her scalp and face, too, and the substance left trails of coolness in its wake. The chill was seeping deeper into her skin when someone handed her cracked pepper cakes and a mug of hagave. She accepted both with thanks. The pepper cakes were salted, and she drank the alcohol a little too readily, hoping it would help wash her palate and calm her nerves. Immediately, she began coughing.

Neva wiped her mouth and handed the cup back. She tried swallowing and found the pepper cakes had washed away her sense of taste. The hagave traveled through her system, and she felt a burning by the time it reached the middle of her chest. It worked into her blood at a frightening speed, clashing with the coolness of the ointment.

A tingling started in the tips of her fingers. Neva looked down to find miniature white flames sliding up her arms. They danced harmlessly across her chest and down her legs.

"Stand up!" the otima ordered her with urgency.

Neva stood, but not quickly enough. The cushion she was sitting on burst into flames. Power encased her body and inched up her throat, over her mouth, coating her nose, suffocating her until she could no longer hold her lips shut. She opened her mouth to breathe, and the flames slid in like a rising tide. She coughed and choked, scratching at her neck.

Out of the corner of her eye, she spied a dark inky stain on her skin as it crept from under the shacklay to douse the flames. With the smoke came a familiar icy pain, but then the black stain disappeared. Its appearance had been enough to remind Neva of Astiand's instruction: focus on pain as a method of control. She recalled the feeling of her wounds from the fire, the sting of the shacklay, and Lindzhi slamming her into the wood of the kilstroke circle. Neva used her newfound concentration to fight back the flames. She took in a little more air, but her mind already felt fuzzy.

"You are ready," the otima whispered to her and gestured for her to step forward.

They entered a black stone tunnel full of glinting eyes. Neva and Ellazhi were surrounded by Da'Valia who splashed them with slushy, half-frozen water from buckets as they walked. Da'Valia slapped Neva with sticks and riding crops, raising welts and splitting her skin. She couldn't help but flinch at the assaults, but she remained silent and held her head high. She didn't want them to think her weak. Ellazhi did the same.

The fuzziness in Neva's mind did not recess. It grew until her vision was almost completely clouded. The otima continued to guide her forward, and then they disappeared.

Neva stopped walking. She could barely make out the other Da'Valia. Ellazhi had been with her, but now the young one was gone, too. Neva's heart was beating fast, as if it wished to climb out of her chest. The sharp slaps and splashes stopped, and the figures around her faded as she lost her vision completely.

Blackness coated the world around her as she realized she could no longer hear her madly beating heart. She could only feel its movement inside her ribcage. She had no sense of taste, smell, or sound. Her incapacitated existence was nothing short of terrifying.

The droplets of water coating her body moved, each an icicle drawing on her skin, sliding into her newly opened cuts and nestling there like small shards of glass. Neva felt a scream well in her throat and held it back.

The only thing she knew of her surroundings was the shards as they worked their way deeper, cutting and grinding into her fat and muscles. She stood, doubled over, as she tried to fight through the pain. Then the shards hit bone, and she fell to the floor, unable to curse her ancestry or plead for Dhianz's forgiveness. She tried not to make any noise, but soon she couldn't stop the low keening that emerged from her. Not long after, she could do nothing but scream.

The uneven ground was cold. Jagged rocks only added to the tortuous sensations assailing her. The shards continued to cut through her until there was no *her* left. She was bone and flesh and pain to the core. She was sweating and shaking. The agony persisted until she could no longer withstand it. Her mind buckled, and she lost consciousness.

Minutes later, she awoke, and the pain began again. The cycle continued until she didn't know when and where she was. Each stabbing shard that moved through her skin, veins, organs, and eyes ripped a section of her soul apart from the whole. Each time she passed out, she awoke with pieces missing. Slowly, she forgot her life before the present, what Glacier Pass looked like, her father's face, her name. Did she need a name, or was she merely pain itself? They were becoming one and the same.

Eventually, she wasn't sure if she had been laying on the floor for days or weeks. Everything in her stomach had been cast out.

The pain still came in waves, one overlapping the other so it was never absent yet still heightened at times. In her mind, washes of reds and oranges coursed through her until she felt like rock had replaced every part of her, down to her toenails. The waves slowly leveled until they flowed in a steady stream.

She finally opened her eyes without suffering, stood without falling, and found a cool stone wall that supported her weight. Her vision was still weak, but she could see.

Liquid flames coated her body once again, but this time, she blocked them from her face and throat with only a little concentration.

In her agony, she had become the pain, become the power. Her body had transformed into a sturdy harness. She no longer needed to control the flame — she was the flame. She was Da'Valia. Her name came back to her then. Nevazhi, a Da'Valian name.

Neva felt her way along the stone wall until she came to a door. She brought it halfway open before the metal handle melted. Wild power sprang from her and engulfed the door as she shimmied through the opening.

Hilans stared at her. There must have been at least thirty of them in the well-lit, grandiose room. Neva froze, unsure of what to do, too worn to make a coherent decision.

Astiand strode forward from the middle of the startled group.

"Get the otima!" he shouted to no one in particular.

Five hilans nearest the door fled upon the order.

Astiand stood far enough away that she couldn't burn him, but close enough so he could reach her in a single bound. His expression was a mystery in her dimmed sight. With a start, she realized the rest of the hilans also stayed back.

"How do you feel, Neva?" Astiand asked.

She swallowed to dampen her raw throat, but her vocal cords felt hot and clogged.

"I can't see well." As the coarse words emerged, fire poured from her lips. The dense white heat that had suffocated her earlier pounced on the opportunity to resurface.

It gushed from her in a rushing stream. She choked on it. The flame flew into the room and at the group of hilans surrounding her. The Da'Valia closest to her crouched and dodged. They used their power to deflect and override hers to extinguish it, but wild strands escaped them and climbed the walls.

Neva shut her mouth, covering it with both hands. She held the flame at bay until her body rebelled, searching for breath. She gasped for air and more fire slid from her lips. The shacklay, still on her wrist, emanated only wisps of blackness. Instead of climbing her arm as it had done before, the anti-magic was overwhelmed. The pain from the shacklay meant little in her mind. It bothered her, but it didn't constrain her power as it had done before.

Beads of sweat dripped down the sides of Astiand's face as streams of Neva's power burned through the room, despite the hilans' best efforts.

On some level, Neva knew she was out of control. Too much power rebelled from within her, but she couldn't do anything about it. The concentration that worked only moments before no longer produced the same effect.

The otima arrived through a side door in a burst of action. As soon as they appeared, the hilans in the room rushed at Neva with grim determination. Neva's flame shot out again and knocked several of them back, but more than a few made it close enough to push her into the stone wall. Instinctively, she fought them.

The hilans piled on her until they could hold her down by her arms, legs, and hair. It was the second vision from the goblet, but she didn't remember that. She only knew the present. Fear gripped her and made her struggle more.

Quickly, Astiand moved in front of her. He shoved a burst of magic through the shacklay. The anti-magic rocketed through Neva, turning her skin to charcoal briefly and pushing her power aside. The otima grabbed Neva's head at the same time, tilting it back and shoving a small vial to her lips.

A stringent liquid forced its way down Neva's throat, and the otima and Astiand jumped away.

The concoction burned its way through Neva, spreading into her chest. Her mind blurred again, and her vision recessed at twice the rate it had before. Someone — Astiand or the otima — cut her, running sharp blades down the center of her chest and arms so blood flowed anew.

It was the start of the firérite all over again. Only this time, spit and droplets of water didn't work their way into her wounds. There was only the liquid flame, dancing round the room in a torrent of heat and light. As the contents of the vial worked, quieting all of her senses except for touch, her power returned to her.

The pain she had felt before was terrible, but the burst of flames working into her skin through the three shallow cuts was one thousand times worse. It was shards of glass mixed with blistering heat. It shot to her core in a matter of moments, and she wished she could pass out again.

Hands dragged her back to the firérite room, and their touch was so soft they felt like everything good in the world, gone all too quickly.

The pain worked its way into her head. Her black vision turned red and her skull split. It broke apart and the horns atop her head were joined by another, smaller set. Pain continued to wrack her body for what seemed like an eternity.

Her ability to breathe stopped and started erratically as a tearing feeling bombarded her heart. She was ripped from the inside out. Eventually, her mind cleared, and she was so hollowed out that she no longer felt human. No human could have survived this. But she had. She was alive. She had survived.

Neva focused on that singular truth as the ability to form lucid thoughts returned.

It was some time before she could gather enough energy to crawl to the door. By then, her vision had returned, but all she could see was large shapes in the dark. She was so drained, she couldn't stand. It took her full concentration to leave the firérite room.

She collapsed on a carpeted floor. Its hard bristles felt kind to her abused skin. Her mind struggled to reassemble in a coherent collection of thoughts. She wanted to cry in relief at the absence of pain, but there were no tears left in her.

Two pairs of hands lifted her up and laid her on a couch. Finally, she closed her eyes and slept.

Chapter Fourteen

Third Cravell, 1632

I must return to my people. These past few weeks have been… everything. I feel more alive than I've ever felt before. I don't want to return to Picquereau, yet I must. I only need to muster the courage to tell Shaun first.

— *Monazhi Da'Voda-Lira*

A stream of light filtered through Neva's window and inched across her face, stirring her from a deep slumber. She turned her head, blinked several times, and a moment passed before she could make out the bright morning sun coming through her window. Slowly, the smell of old roses and dust registered, and she recognized the room Astiand had allotted her in his home. She sat up, struggling with the effort.

"You may want to wait before moving around much." Astiand's deep voice sounded from beside her.

Neva let out a slow breath before carefully reclining upon the thick feather mattress. She closed her eyes and tried to relax her body.

Astiand was unshaven and unkempt, as if he hadn't slept in some time. He wore a dress shirt, but the material was wrinkled. Two cups were on the small bedside stand next to him. She recognized one as being half full of hagave, but the other liquid was unfamiliar and deep green in color.

"Astiand," she said his name, testing it in her mouth. The noise that emerged was hoarse and raspy.

"Aye?"

"Is it over?" she asked.

"Over?" he murmured her question. "It isn't as over as much as it has just begun, unfortunately."

Neva felt her eyes prickle with the onset of tears, but she was dehydrated, and there was not enough of the salty fluid left in her. She licked her dried lips to no avail and reached for Astiand's mystery cup, but her arm was too weak to complete the task.

She didn't know how much more of the firérite she could withstand. She desperately wanted Astiand to tell her the firérite was done.

Astiand held the mug to her mouth.

"Wash away that frown," he ordered her in a soft tone.

Neva swallowed and felt almost immediately more alert. Her muscles relaxed. Her mind sharpened and homed in on Astiand. Something was different about him. He was being too nice.

"What's happened?" she asked, her voice sounding slightly more like its usual self.

"You're done with the firérite, if that's what you mean," he responded, placing the mug on the table.

The anxiety in her chest dissipated and relief took its place.

"But..." he trailed off.

"What?"

"Take a look." Astiand handed her a small, circular mirror from his pocket.

Neva stared at her reflection. Her skin was white and dry. Her eyes were bloodshot and red around the edges. She tilted the glass up and spied her horns.

Four horns curled up and back along her skull.

The two she'd had since puberty had grown several inches during the firérite until they matched Astiand's in length, and two smaller horns had emerged between them. The sight was enough incentive for her to rise to her knees so she could look in the large mirror on the wall.

She appeared so ... wrong.

Her hands moved to her hair on impulse. Her fingers worked to undo the braids holding her hair tight next to her skull. As the designs unfolded in crimped strands, clumps of skin and hair fell out, replaced by new horns.

"Your firérite lasted eight days," Astiand told her. "Which is normal. The donazhi's was twelve. But what wasn't normal was you awoke during it. Do you remember?"

Neva sank back onto the pillows and raised her eyes to his. Her mind was sharper than it had been when she first awoke, but she still had to concentrate to pull back her memories of the firérite. Slowly, she nodded.

"I remember, I had flame coating my skin," Neva said. "The pain was so much lighter, but it was still there. They attacked me. And then you and the otima gave me something to drink and took me back into that room."

"That has never happened before. *This* has never happened before," he touched a finger to one of her new horns, sending a tingling jolt down her spine.

With the tingle came a bit of dread.

"What does it mean?" she asked.

"It means you are truly Da'Valia now, powers and all," Astiand said. "You are entitled to one week of rest, here, away from the Da'Voda. Every majila requires at least that time to rejuvenate, and you won't be treated any differently. Beyond that, no one knows exactly."

Astiand ruffled his disheveled hair as if the action would help sort his thoughts.

"When will you take this off?" Neva raised her hand to show him the shacklay.

"I will leave the shacklay on as a precaution," he said.

"But my firérite is over. You said so." Neva frowned. "Can't you take it off?"

"I'd prefer to leave it on," Astiand replied. "As your guardian, I suggest you trust it's for the best."

Neva felt uneasy to know things had gone awry during her rite of passage, and Astiand was not instilling confidence in her by insisting she continue to wear the shacklay.

"I'll probably never need to invoke it again," Astiand said as if that should assuage her fears.

"Probably?" Neva asked.

"Probably," Astiand said more firmly.

Neva refrained from rolling her eyes. Barely.

"What about the other one — Ellazhi?" Neva asked after the young majila who had been sent into the firérite with her.

Astiand hesitated.

"Her firérite did not go well," he said. "You will not see her again."

"What do you mean?" Neva pushed herself up again.

"Dhianz's curse," he said solemnly. "The firérite was too much for her, as it often is for majilas. Her mind could not cope."

Neva shook her head. She didn't want to believe it. Ellazhi had been so young. A child, really.

"So she... what? What is her fate?"

"It's unlikely she will heal," Astiand said. The haunted look that entered his eyes made her think he had personal experience with losing someone this way. "Dhianz's curse means majilas might perish in the firérite. Others lose their minds. Their fates might as well be the same. Few ever recover enough to participate fully in clan life again.

"But don't concern yourself with those who are lost. There are more important things to consider. You will be subject to the same protocol as all other majilas who have survived their firérites. I don't know how much thought you've given to where you will go from here, but with your firérite and the power I believe you can now harness, there are certain implications."

"Implications?" Neva caught his attention as he turned away. She rested her hand on his arm, light but insistent.

"The donazhi has been the strongest toppel among the Da'Voda for many years. She has her own agendas throughout the realm, but some Da'Voda are starting to think you might have been chosen by Dhianz for something significant. Your unique ascension will not go unnoticed — by her or any hilan in this clan."

Astiand slid his hand over hers and let it rest there for a moment before he stood and stepped back.

"I know this has been quite the ordeal for you, but I need some rest. I will send Miland up with the protocols so you can better understand what to expect."

Astiand left, and Neva let her thoughts roam. Ellazhi's fate weighed on her mind. Neva's memories of the firérite became clearer as she drank more of the green liquid. Although she missed her family fiercely, she was glad they couldn't see her like this. She glanced down at the nightgown covering her. She didn't remember putting it on and wondered if Astiand had done the honor. She preferred not to dwell on it.

Neva spent a few hours reading the scroll of protocols Miland delivered until she could no longer focus. She slept again and re-awoke to continue the endeavor. She understood bits of protocol from watching the donazhi's clan gathering before the firérite. Conversely, there was much she had never fathomed. Hilans were expected to form alliads shortly after a majila's firérite, typically within a year or two. Most majilas would secure at least one aliado, but usually two or three. Additional members meant additional strength, and that meant better standing for the group.

The scroll didn't include all the protocols among the Da'Voda, but it had all of those concerning a firérite and forming alliads. Neva wasn't sure she wanted to stay among the Da'Voda forever, but the thought of returning home now made her uneasy, and she didn't want to remain ignorant of their ways. A nagging feeling was telling her she shouldn't return to Glacier Pass until she was more comfortable with her newfound power. She was more leery of the last vision the goblet showed her now the second vision had come true. Maybe it was best she stay away from humans for a time.

Miland returned in the evening with a full dinner tray. She knew from studying the protocol that eating too much wouldn't be safe. After the firérite and weeks of an empty stomach, any substance would shock her system, and a large amount would have dangerous consequences. She accepted the tray anyway just as Astiand entered her room.

Astiand's hair was damp from washing and he had shaved, yet he strode into the bedroom with a brooding air about him.

"Did you finish reading it?" he asked her.

Neva was relieved to see his surly self had returned. She second-guessed his intentions more when he was good-tempered.

"I'm almost done," she said.

"Well, be quick about it," Astiand ordered. "That week I told you about is being shortened."

Astiand had her attention.

"Why? What's changed?" she asked.

Neva straightened and the tray on her lap shook, catching Astiand's attention. He stared at the food as he answered her.

"The donazhi has requested an audience with you in two days' time. I have apprised her of the ordeal during your firérite and told her about your horns. She is eager to meet with you."

Astiand stopped speaking abruptly, shooting Miland a look.

"That's your dinner?" Astiand asked Neva.

"Yes, but I —" Neva had been about to tell him she wouldn't eat much, but before she could, Astiand had grabbed Miland by the front of his robes and pulled him out of his seat. The shacklay tightened around her wrist.

"You know the protocol," Astiand growled at Miland. "She cannot eat so much."

"Leave him alone!" Neva said. "He didn't do anything wrong."

"Do you want to kill her?" Astiand asked Miland, ignoring Neva's interruption. "If you do something like this again, I'll send you to Arroyand's residence for a week."

Miland's dark skin faded several shades lighter, but he remained silent. With a sound of disgust, Astiand stormed out of the room.

"That overbearing brute!" Neva said as vehemently as she could. But she had heard his words, and she had read the scroll. Too much food could kill her in this state.

Miland watched Neva as she rubbed her arm, where the sting from the shacklay was slowly dissipating.

"The shacklay is not a terribly refined magic, and it's tied to strong emotions," Miland told her knowingly. "An abrupt change in Astiand's mood might activate the magic."

Neva did a double-take. She opened her mouth, then closed it and acted as if she wasn't surprised Miland could talk. She had started to think it wasn't a choice but that he had lost the ability when his horns were taken.

"He must be the moodiest male I've met in my entire life," Neva grumbled after recovering from her surprise.

"The donazhi is pressuring Astiand," Miland replied. "She often does. Still, I've never seen him so protective over another, not in a long time."

"Well, he sure has a terrible way of showing it," Neva said. Her frustration was simmering.

"I'll not argue that," Miland said. "I want you to know, I saw you read the protocol about the reprieve following the firérite. I didn't think you would try to eat everything I brought. I only sought to provide an assortment to choose from."

"You have my thanks," Neva said. Miland seemed sincere, and she felt special because he'd chosen to break his silence with her.

"I'm not sure you quite grasp how things work here," he said. "But we pay for the sins of our parents and our own. Astiand has only escaped payment because he plays the game well, but with the risks he takes, it's only a matter of time before our donazhi cuts him down, too."

Something in Miland's voice told her he was speaking from experience.

"Miland, what happened to you?"

He stared at her with those sad eyes.

"In a game with many skilled players, the unskilled suffer the worst. I was never so skilled." He shook his head as if to clear it. "I'll bring you a fresh tray and draw you a bath."

With that, he departed.

Neva's mind wandered. If the donazhi held so much power over Astiand, Neva didn't want his shacklay on her arm to help them control her. She moved it around absentmindedly before she inspected it, searching for any weak spot she might exploit, but she couldn't find any. The clasp had disappeared.

She would get it off eventually. She knew that much.

The next day, the elder who had inspected Neva after the kilstroke visited. He introduced himself as Oliand Da'Voda-Dejada while Astiand walked them to the basement, a stone-walled room used to store and maintain weapons. She should have figured Astiand would stock his home with a private weaponry.

When Neva was alone with Oliand, she asked the elder the question that was most nagging her.

"You said I would rise to middel, but, with everything that happened, is that what I am now?" Neva asked.

"No," Oliand said. "I lied."

Oliand directed her to take a seat so he could access her horns. He pulled her hair away from the area he was inspecting. Carefully, he poked one with the tip of his finger.

Neva felt a flurry of power shock her mind on contact.

"Ow," she said, annoyed. "If you don't mind my asking, why would you lie?"

Oliand pulled away.

"Has anyone explained to you what it means to us that you are a half-breed?" he asked.

She gave a short laugh.

"No one tells me anything if they don't have to."

"Knowing your guardian, I'm sure he thought that was best." Oliand walked across the room, brushing back his loose sleeves. "We can talk later. Right now, I want you to stop or deflect any power I send your way, however you want. Try to stop it when it comes at you. Ready?"

Oliand's power erupted in the air in front of him, a pure night-sky flame aimed directly at her. She jumped off her seat to avoid the first shot and rolled to evade the second. The first shot hit the chair she had been sitting on, and the other slammed into the stone wall behind her.

"Don't run from it!" a frustrated Oliand grumbled. "Fight it!"

On the directive, Neva ignored the instinct to flee and faced the fire. She lashed out with her power, stopping the bursts Oliand threw at her. He switched from single, large bursts to smaller, pointed attacks, but she managed them with relative ease. Close to a half hour after Oliand started testing her defenses, his flames were twice the size of her body, and she found she could control them better when she aimed with her hand. Oliand had instructed her to extinguish the flame or divert it. She threw up some shields, but she found it easier to smother his power and order it out of being the way the hilans had in the middle of her firérite.

The elder was breathing heavily and small beads of sweat trickled down his forehead before he called for a break in their session. Neva was only slightly out of breath, as if she had been racing her cousins to the licorice stand. She and Oliand sat at a table in the corner of the room and shared a pitcher of water.

"So, what does it mean that I'm a half-breed?" she asked, taking advantage of the silence.

"Oh, that. I suppose you ought to know. You won't have heard of the cardinal taboos. Those who commit them are usually executed or excommunicated from the clans," Oliand spoke matter-of-factly. "One is forsaking our maker. Second is cutting off another's horns without a conviction. Last is mixing our blood with that of any other peoples, but especially a weaker race such as humans. Those who do, or the products of their mating, are symbols of what our law most abhors."

"So my mother…" Neva trailed off. Monazhi must have been brave to fall in love with Neva's father.

"Ah, your mother," Oliand mused. "A smart one, but not too wise if you ask me. She abandoned her better judgment when she mated with a human. You're lucky to have invoked the Rule of Rhianzhi and won your kilstroke."

"You knew my mother?" Neva asked. "What was she like when she was here?"

"Of course, I knew your mother," Oliand said. "Everyone knew Monazhi. She was an exceptional warlock, and an adversary of our esteemed donazhi before she rose to power."

Neva swallowed hard, thinking of Miland's warning about paying for your parents' sins. She hadn't realized the danger upon her arrival. The whispers around the auditorium from the night of the kilstroke made more sense now. But why had Astiand lied about knowing Neva's mother? What was he hiding?

"Enough talk," Oliand announced. "It's time to test your attacks."

Chapter Fifteen

Third Cravell, 1632

Benjamand sent word that Trinizhi is hunting the Eye. If she succeeds, I fear our doom. Her heart is not one of a leader. Her mind may be cunning, but she is self-serving and full of malintent. With even one prong of the Trishula, her reign would extend beyond the Da'Voda to all the clans. Its promise is too great for the other clans to deny. Redemption would mean so much to any majila nearing the change, to anyone who has ever lost someone in a firérite, to all of us.

I leave Glacier Pass on the morrow.

— Monazhi Da'Voda-Lira

Oliand warned Neva her attacks would be larger than his in scale, so to avoid destroying Astiand's home, they went to a snow-covered field on the edge of the village. There, they switched roles, and it was her turn to wage a mock attack.

The first burst she channeled was immense, as if years of disuse made the force more rebellious — except the burst was direct and perfectly controlled.

Neva shoved all of her resentment over her birth marking her as a symbol of taboo into the second burst. She threw all her years of loneliness into the next blast. Why could she never be herself? Oliand deflected the flame harmlessly into the ground or off into the sky.

Into the fourth, she sent the pain of the firérite. The fifth, everything she wanted to understand but didn't. The sixth, losing her mother. As they continued, she no longer felt burdened by the resentments. They carried on until Oliand tired of putting out the flames.

For more than an hour, she had drawn from the reservoir of power she could now picture clearly in her mind. She collected from the surface of the pool, neglecting that thing deeper, that thing she wasn't sure Oliand could avoid, deflect, or overpower. It stirred and stretched like a cat, but she forced it back down. Still, the blasts she manifested were impressive. Some children had watched the show from along the tree line. By the time Neva and Oliand finished, most of the snow on the field had melted.

"I am not sorry I deceived you before, Nevazhi," Oliand told her as they walked back to Astiand's home. "But I apologize nonetheless. Just trust it was for your own good. You are indeed a toppel. The beasties would probably go mad for you whether or not your blood was tainted."

Neva nodded. She could only imagine how much more horrible the Da'Voda, their donazhi in particular, would have made her firérite if they had known a half-breed would ascend so high. His lie might have been a blessing.

Back at Astiand's house, Neva removed her shoes, bid Oliand farewell, and made her way upstairs. At the top of the second flight, she paused and crouched where the staircase leveled to listen to the conversation below.

"I'm glad you came to me," Oliand told Astiand. "I don't usually test majilas after they come into their power, but this is something I've never seen before. She's a toppel only because there's no better word. Given the peculiar nature of her firérite, many of us are wondering if the gods don't have something important planned for her. You should expect the rumors to grow once the clan knows her power level."

Neva missed what Oliand said next as she registered that information. She hadn't really believed Astiand when he said her unique firérite was drawing attention, and she didn't believe what Oliand said now. It seemed far-fetched that the gods would pay her any attention. She was no chosen one.

"In all my years, I've seen nothing like her," Oliand told Astiand. "It may be safest to keep the shacklay on her until we know what we're dealing with, or it may be unnecessary. I'll leave that up to you and the donazhi."

Neva swallowed hard. Even a Da'Valian elder couldn't say whether she could still be a danger to others. She felt uncomfortable in her own skin knowing that she hadn't really unleashed in the field with Oliand.

More than anything, Neva wanted to go home, but knowing what she did now, she couldn't convince herself it would be safe for her family.

Astiand handed Oliand several coins and showed him to the door. Neva picked herself up. She was still stiff from the firérite, but she made it to her room before Astiand could catch her spying.

"Did you finish reading the protocol?" Astiand asked her over a rather bland dinner of boiled chicken, potatoes, and greens. His voice nearly echoed in the grand dining room. It was far too large for two people.

Neva swallowed a sip of hagave to wash down a bite before answering.

"Aye. I gave the scroll to Miland so he could return it to your library."

"Good. You are meeting with the donazhi tomorrow evening. Everything you do reflects on me. I'd like you to keep that in mind."

Her formal meeting with the donazhi. She could hardly forget, especially not now that she knew her mother and the donazhi had been at odds.

Neva took several more bites, trying to pretend she didn't notice Astiand was now ignoring her. Her effort did not last. If he wasn't going to volunteer information, the only way to learn anything new was to nudge bits and pieces from him. She sensed the donazhi was off-limits, but she could still encourage him to talk about other things.

"You haven't mentioned Bryand," she said.

Astiand looked up, surprised.

"Pardon?"

"Any word from Bryand?" she rephrased.

Astiand leaned back in his seat and picked up his cup.

"I expect him to return in the next few days."

"Did he find your g —" Neva stopped herself short of saying 'goblet.' "— missing object?"

"I won't know until he returns," Astiand spoke as he studied her. "It strikes me, though, you watch closer than I thought."

Her stomach clenched, but she forced another bite of food down. She had nearly tipped her hand. Her mind scrambled.

"Watch?" she asked. "I was just asking after him. I would have expected him to be back already. I mean, you both said he would have to track down other Da'Valia. How long could that take?"

Astiand continued scrutinizing her, and she realized she did not sound as nonchalant as she would have hoped. A human, she could fool. Astiand considered things differently, as if he were searching for secrets incessantly.

"I wouldn't indulge too much curiosity about the matter," he instructed. "The donazhi does not take kindly to other toppel majilas getting close to her aliados."

"I'm close to you," Neva said.

"I was your proctor," Astiand said.

"I live in your house."

"Out of necessity."

"We kissed," Neva pushed again, immediately kicking herself. It hadn't happened again, so undoubtedly, it was a one-time thing.

"Actually, you kissed me," Astiand reminded her.

Oh gods. Why did I bring it up? Neva blushed at the memory. Fighting with Astiand was frustrating, and entertaining if she was doing the provoking, but kissing him had been altogether different. Kissing him had been a rush that rivaled stealing from the House of Trescony.

"It was the hagave." She struggled to sound convincing.

He raised an eyebrow at her.

Neva tossed her napkin down on the table, muttering under her breath. "I could spend my life fighting you, but I'd still never win, would I?"

"Probably not, no." His tone said he was enjoying their exchange.

Neva stood to leave the room.

"Good night," she said, forcing a polite expression. She wouldn't allow her mild frustration to become anything more.

"Good night," he returned.

She bit her tongue and let him have the last word. This time.

The following morning, much to Neva's relief, her muscles no longer strained with simple movements, and the cuts she had suffered in the fire and the firérite were close to smooth again. If she couldn't have a week of reprieve before meeting one-on-one with the donazhi, at least she didn't feel as if her firérite had just ended.

Thanks to reading the protocol, Neva knew what was expected of her. She would be diplomatic and Da'Valian and everything she needed to be for her meeting with the donazhi.

Neva spent a little time looking in the mirror, marveling at the new set of horns atop her head. She missed Margret helping braid her hair early in the mornings and being able to hug James and Kendall when they went off to bed at night.

Neva dressed in a gray wrap and pants from the dresser in her room. Not for the first time, she wondered who these clothes had belonged to before she started using them. Neva followed a solitary breakfast with a quick walk to learn the lay of the clan's holdings. She noticed every Da'Valia she passed steered away. The donazhi wouldn't express her opinion until after their meeting, so the Da'Voda chose to show no interest or favor.

Neva couldn't fault them for it. Back home, she knew when to keep her head down, too. Most notably when the Watch Commissioner had failed to please the duke, or when the Watch Patrol had a new quota to meet.

Inside Astiand's again, Neva wandered until she came to the library, which was placed to the rear of the first floor. Mahogany shelves sported books on three of the walls, and a fern-green couch sat beneath an enormous glass window that allowed natural sunlight to brighten the room. A long mahogany table stood in the center of the space with four stands atop it and four old and ornate scrolls atop them.

Neva picked up a scroll, mindful of the soft, yellowing material and taking care to touch only the brass handles. She couldn't make out some words because the cursive differed from the printing her mother had taught her, but the content she could comprehend was so interesting she didn't want to return it to its resting place. She read about the creation of the Da'Valia, when the great Dhianz poured his own blood and will into a mighty spell nearly one thousand years before in a prelude to one of the greatest battles among men.

She was in the middle of calculating exactly how many years might have passed since the Da'Valia's creation when Miland interrupted her. His access to power may have been severed with the gelding of his horns, but he still moved stealthily.

"You shouldn't have touched that," he told her. "Astiand is meticulous about his scrolls, especially that one. It's a copy of one the Da'Xana have in their archives, rare and precious."

"I'll put it back." Neva returned the scroll to its prior resting place. She took an extra moment to make sure it settled in exactly the way she had found it. She thought Astiand's penchant for ancient history was interesting.

"You might find the book in Astiand's safe to be better reading," Miland said in hushed tones. "If you can get to it."

Neva frowned after him as he escaped the library, her interest piqued. A challenge was just what she needed to get her mind off her meeting with the donazhi. Neva stilled and listened for any movement in the house to reassure herself she was alone. It was silent aside from Miland's retreating footsteps.

Neva began inspecting her surroundings with more purpose. In her experience, people locked away their valuables in the last place they expected someone would look. The library only had two such locations, but she already knew the wall behind the painting of Dhianz in his centurion form was too thin to hold a safe, and lifting the tapestry adjacent yielded nothing. She skipped the parlor. No one ever hid anything of value in their parlor.

Neva bit her lip, thinking. What was the last place Astiand thought someone would look? She grinned and her blood quickened as she hurried for the stairs. Astiand would return shortly, but she had free rein of the house until he did.

Neva wasted no time, bounding up the stairs and pushing open the door to his room. She studied the chest in the corner first, looking for the telltale glow of a magic ward around the edges and lock, but she found nothing of note.

Slowly, Neva turned and scrutinized her surroundings. She had been so sure Astiand was the type to hide his valuables where he slept. After all, it was what she did. But his walls were irritatingly devoid of decoration, and too thin to boot. The armoire across from the bed looked like it might crush her if she tried to move it, so she doubted he had a safe behind it. She wouldn't insult what she knew of him by looking under his bed, either.

Neva sighed in frustration and moved toward the door, thinking the armory was her next best bet. Her heart quickened as a floorboard gave a gentle moan. The safe was underfoot. The sound registered at the same time as another from downstairs. Astiand slammed the front door behind him and shouted for Miland. Neva darted into the hall and slid into her own room as Astiand crested the top of the stairs.

She left her bedroom door ajar, knowing he would hear the click if she closed it behind her, and bent to touch the floor in one of her favorite stretches.

"Nevazhi, we should be leaving shortly," Astiand stopped outside her room and nudged her door open with the toe of his boot.

She paused and straightened as if surprised to see him. "Already?"

"Almost," he said. "Miland will bring you a change of clothes more suitable for the occasion."

"Very well," Neva agreed, hoping she didn't sound as out of breath as she felt.

Astiand nodded and headed toward his bedroom. He paused at the threshold, and Neva tensed. Had he noticed her scent? The dust that had been disturbed? After a moment, he stepped inside and closed his door behind him. Neva flopped onto her bed with a long sigh of relief.

The outfit Miland delivered to Neva was similar to the one she wore in the kilstroke, except it fit her precisely, covered her arms, and had a lovely peach tone to it. She frowned, not sure whether she liked Astiand having his own ideas about what she should wear, especially when she thought the tone would bring out the human color of her cheeks. But he knew more about the clan, and he knew more about the donazhi.

"I will return in an hour," Astiand told her as they climbed the hill to the auditorium. "Mind the protocols."

"I read them," Neva replied.

"And now is the time to mind them." Astiand reiterated annoyingly. He left her at the entrance.

Neva rolled her eyes at his back, took a deep breath, and walked inside. About twenty chairs were set in rows. Almost all were occupied by young hilans, and she recognized a few from the night of the kilstroke. She was an anomaly with four horns, but according to the protocols, the size of a Da'Valia's horns was indicative of their power level. And that meant that … every single hilan in the audience was toppel.

Two chairs were set in front of the others, so she removed her cloak and draped it over her arm before lowering herself onto the less ornate one. She didn't have to wait long for the donazhi to arrive.

The grand doors burst open, pushed by a magnificent shot of white flame, followed by the donazhi. She glided into the room, not sparing the young hilans a glance. Silver threads painted her beaded wrap and pants, and her jet stone headdress perfectly framed her white face. She took her seat gracefully and crossed her hands in her lap.

Even in such a pose, her sword — on her hip today — was at easy reach.

Neva ignored the human inclination to run, and she stood to address the regal majila.

"Nevazhi Roberts, at the donazhi's service," she spoke with her head lowered before connecting her eyes to the donazhi's.

Then, she sat again.

The donazhi held Neva's gaze with silver-white irises so bright they seemed to flicker.

"As determined by winning the kilstroke against your cousin, Lindzhi Da'Voda-Lira, Dhianz has allowed you a place in our clan. As donazhi, I am reserved the duty to evaluate new clan members. What say you?"

"I accept your evaluation," Neva said, knowing she had no other choice.

She couldn't go home, not yet. She needed to stay here until she could be sure she wouldn't be dangerous to her family and friends.

Neva hadn't finished speaking when she felt herself being mesmerized, sucked into the donazhi's eyes. Those silver-white pools swirled in never-ending spirals, drawing Neva into a landscape of the donazhi's making.

Neva blinked through the vertigo. When her eyes focused again, she was in a completely different room. On some level, she was aware the donazhi hadn't transported them to this unfamiliar place, yet there Neva sat in a world made of ice. The floor was a crosshatch of ice slabs, and a thick layer of frost coated her chair. The chill in the air felt real.

"Where are we?" Neva asked.

The donazhi smiled, and the wide expanse was as cold as the air on Neva's skin. Maybe that was where Astiand learned it.

"As one of Dhianz's chosen, I have a special power under my command. This is a place of my making. I bring everyone I need answers from here, to my own personal landscape."

"I see." Neva watched her breath travel away from her in a fog and noticed dense swirls of mist creeping along the frozen floor, playing with the splayed bottoms of the donazhi's pants. It looked real. There could be no question of who ruled here.

"Our laws dictate that I must ask two questions of you before you may be inducted into our clan," the donazhi spoke with purpose and finesse.

Induction into the clan. The idea was so far from anything she thought she would ever do, but it was for the best. If she stayed here, she couldn't hurt the people she cared about.

"First, will you accept Dhianz as our one creator, as the being whose will of battle you shall follow in honor of our existence?"

Neva took a moment before answering. Dhianz had created the Da'Valia. It was a fact her mother had taught her since birth, a truth she could no more deny than the horns atop her head. Would she follow his will to incite conflict? Wasn't that what she had always done? Stealing from one fellow for another? In her own way, creating discontent and distrust had always been a part of who she was.

"I, Nevazhi Roberts, accept Dhianz as our one creator, as the being whose will of battle I shall follow in honor of our existence." This choice was a simple one, as if the donazhi had asked whether Neva wished to continue breathing.

"And do you agree to abide by the laws of the Da'Voda and to keep with our agreements with other clans?"

Neva allowed herself a pause under the watchful gaze of the donazhi. Neva had never agreed to follow the law before. Her Ring back home would think her compliance was a funny joke. But she was certain she could. She didn't need to be the Lynx among Da'Voda. And she was certain she would remain far enough away from other clans to avoid interference with political arrangements. If that was all she needed to do to be a part of her mother's people — to know finally what it was like to belong somewhere, despite being different — then she would fulfill such a promise.

"I, Nevazhi Roberts, agree to abide by the laws of the Da'Voda and to keep with its agreements with other clans."

She answered exactly as the protocol directed. Astiand would be proud.

The donazhi seemed satisfied. She reclined a little, draping her arms over the ice of her chair.

"Those are the questions I am required by our laws to ask you, but I also wonder, Nevazhi, what did your mother tell you of our people?"

There it was. Neva bit her lip, feeling uncomfortable. She had already answered what she was required to, so this was what the donazhi wanted to know? About her mother? What if Neva didn't want to respond? The few memories she had of her mother were ones she cherished, and she wasn't sure she wanted to share them.

Enough silence passed so the donazhi became perturbed.

"Nevazhi, you are in a world I have created. If you choose not to answer, I will make you answer."

The donazhi's words sent the barest of shivers down Neva's spine, but that didn't stop defiance from solidifying her resolve.

"With all respect, Donazhi, if I choose not to answer, I believe there is little you might do about it." As Neva spoke, she felt her power rise to the surface. She realized she was doing the exact opposite of what Astiand had instructed her to do. She backpedaled. "But I will answer because my mother did not tell me much. She told me only children's tales and stories of the great Dhianz. Beyond that, she shared nothing. I didn't know about the firérite until I met your aliados. I believe… I believe she thought she was protecting me."

The donazhi's eyes flickered with a harsh intensity as Neva stumbled at the end of her speech, but Neva's apprehension at the look was gone in the following moment.

"Very well," the donazhi said. "I am pleased to offer you a place here among the Da'Voda."

"I accept," Neva said, surprised to feel proud to be part of the clan, officially, and thinking she would have to follow Astiand's advice and hide her human nature to survive it. If she was lucky, she would make them all forget she was a half-breed.

"Good," the donazhi said. "You're too much of a jewel to let one of the other clans get their hands on you."

Abruptly, the ice slab beneath their feet cracked with a great boom. The ice splintered, and the room melted away.

In the auditorium again and in front of the audience of hilans, the donazhi rose from her seat and walked to stand behind Neva. The donazhi looked out at the hilans and stroked a hand through Neva's hair, sweeping it to the side.

"As donazhi of the Da'Voda, as a Da'Valia leader chosen by the great Dhianz, I welcome you to your people, Nevazhi Da'Voda-Roberts."

As the donazhi spoke the last, edged syllable of her scripted greeting, she used a flame from her finger to burn the symbol of the Da'Voda on the back of Neva's neck. Neva avoided flinching, but she thought the donazhi let the power burn more than necessary.

Neva rose to face the crowd. The hilans, who had watched quietly, lowered their heads in the smallest possible acknowledgment. By being there, they were declaring their interest in a potential alliad, but in front of the donazhi, they still did not show overt favor. Or perhaps some were only in attendance to see the outcome? Neva couldn't be sure.

The hilans' attention was diverted when the doors to the auditorium were flung open and Bryand tumbled in, falling to the floor in a heap. The donazhi and the hilans jumped into action.

Neva hurried after them. The donazhi crouched on the floor and wiped blood and sweat away from Bryand's forehead. He was unconscious. Neva spotted a bandage on his wrist, two on his right lower leg, and one blood-seeped gauze ligature wrapped around a small weapon still embedded in his chest.

The donazhi took Bryand's horns in her hands. Her eyes shut with concentration, and a strange glowing pulse emitted from them.

Without thinking, Neva stepped toward Bryand, reaching for him. She had cauterized Flynn's bloody wounds with her power once, and she was more powerful now. Perhaps she could help.

"Stay back." A toppel with a row of knives sheathed in a rig on his chest blocked her movement with an outstretched arm.

Neva jerked to a stop.

"Why? Can't I help?"

"By the looks of him, Bryand has been messing with some powerful magic," another hilan, this one with a pox-scarred face, murmured. "You'd need years of magical training to be of any use."

A Da'Valian healer, with his black hair held in a tail at the base of his skull, rushed in from outside. An assistant followed, carrying a healer's bag. The healer took one look at the donazhi's position at Bryand's head and moved around to the hilan's feet. It wasn't long before Astiand and Arroyand followed through the door in a blur. Both hilans bent on a knee next to their donazhi. She opened her eyes at their presence.

"Carry him to the north tower," she addressed Astiand and Arroyand first, and then the crowd. "Someone find the prime otima. Now!"

Several hilans hurried away in search of the prime otima, but Neva remained unmoving and worried for Bryand. She had seen no one survive who was so close to death.

Chapter Sixteen

Fifth Cravell, 1632

*More rumors are circulating about Trinizhi tracking down the Eye. I
cannot say if they are true, and the summit is approaching. I cannot allow
Trinizhi to assume our donazhi's position. I fear the consequences would be
too great, especially with the state of things. King Charles was never popular,
but now nobles are choosing sides. Dhianz will decide, but I predict war will
be upon us soon.*

— Monazhi Da'Voda-Lira

"Nevazhi?"

A hilan more than a head taller than Neva approached her after the crowd had dissipated and she had made her way outside. The air was heavy with fog and small droplets stuck to her cloak. From the smell of it, Vestive rains would not be far behind.

The hilan's face was thin, vaguely familiar, with a soft chin and boney nose. His coloring was lighter than Astiand or Bryand, and his horns smaller. He looked to be around her own age, maybe a year or two older, and he carried an ivory box at his side. Neva was fairly certain the hilan was middel or lowel, which meant he wasn't likely seeking an alliad. All the other hilans in the audience had been toppels.

"And you are?" Neva asked, knowing full well her horns confirmed who she was.

"Jorand Da'Voda-Lira." He walked beside her.

"You're a relative of Lindzhi's?" Neva asked, recognizing his name.

"Her brother, which also means you and I are cousins," Jorand said.

"I see." Neva averted her gaze. Her eyes landed on the dark green of his modest uniform and stuck there.

"May I bend your ear on your walk home?" he asked.

"Certainly," she replied apprehensively, thinking how he must hate her. She didn't have a sibling of her own, but she was close with James and Kendall. She would be livid if anyone so much as touched one of them.

"You didn't attend Lindzhi's funeral, so what you probably don't know is you dealt my sister the death she wanted," Jorand said.

The abrupt start to their conversation made Neva mentally cringe. She hadn't attended Lindzhi's funeral, it was true. But she wasn't sure it would have been the right thing to do, her firérite — which had taken priority — aside.

"I'm not sure she would agree," Neva said. "I saw the look in Lindzhi's eyes when we were in that circle. She challenged an uninitiated half-breed, and she intended to win."

Jorand nodded, seemingly unfazed by the topic.

"Be sure she would have enjoyed the glory of killing you and the good standing it would have brought her, but the truth is she was always seeking notoriety, no matter the cost," he said. "In that hall, every eye was on her, and, in death, she will be remembered as your first kill."

"Is that supposed to be flattering?" Neva couldn't see what he was getting at.

"No, no. Of course not." Jorand's steps faltered. "What I mean, cousin, is you're something special. None of us knows exactly why yet, but we can recognize greatness when we are confronted with it."

He said 'cousin' deliberately, as if to make her feel at ease. It didn't work, exactly, but she understood the intent and appreciated it. She relaxed a little. Jorand didn't seem that bad. Sincere, actually.

"I just — what I mean to say is Lindzhi's device to redeem our family name worked, even if you were the one who managed it and not her," Jorand said. "I just want you to know I won't fault you for taking this. You've earned it, and she would have wanted you to have it."

Neva eyed the box he held out to her as they came to a stop in front of Astiand's home.

"I was expecting you to secure her holdings sooner, but I realize we must do some things differently from humans."

"I'll say." Neva reluctantly relieved him of the heavy box, and he surprised her again when he started unbuckling a sword and sheath from around his waist. She hadn't noticed he was wearing two swords beneath his cape. He held the sword out to her, and she swallowed hard.

Stealing from the living was one thing, but inheriting the belongings of someone she had killed was another. She had fought to get away occasionally over the years — once against the city's Watch, which had ended with one of their men injured and Neva's wrist marked — but she had never killed for someone else's property. To do so seemed dishonorable. There was no skill in it, and it went against the Code by which her father had raised her.

She accepted the black leather sheath from him and admired the swirling designs on the hilt. The sword was much heavier than the small blades she was accustomed to. Neva pulled the hilt to show the blade. Scratches whispered of battles long past, and the edge was dull.

"This sword was passed down from our ancestors who escaped the desert," Jorand said. "It's not as ornate as Lindzhi's other blade, but it should go to the next majila in our family line. It ties to our blood."

"Does it?" Neva asked. She set down the box, pulled the blade free, and swiped it through the air.

The sword's weight was unfamiliar to her, yet, if she was honest with herself, she wanted it. She wanted something that connected her to her Da'Valian bloodlines. She looked up at Jorand and found him staring at her.

"Do you know how to use it?" He eyed her awkward grip.

"No," she admitted, lowering the sword and lamenting she was off to a terrible start convincing the Da'Voda she was one of them. "Swordplay wasn't a skill I ever learned."

"The sword is basic," Jorand pointed out. "Our knowledge of weaponry is a matter of pride. If you don't know it, that will reflect on the Da'Voda and our family."

Neva was silent. He was also saying her lack of skill would reflect poorly on Lindzhi's memory. She didn't think he meant to insult her, but his underlying disapproval was obvious.

"Maybe I'll learn to fight," she mused, bending down to retrieve the box, which was practically radiating protective magic. The spell was like a living thing unto itself. It met her skin, searched, and recessed. She was familiar with this type of lock, and it had deemed her worthy to open the box. That was something for which she usually had to pay. A quick flick of the latch popped the top.

"Ambition was her obsession and eventually her downfall," Jorand said sadly.

The box was full of coins glinting faintly in the dim light. Neva did a quick calculation. The amount of currency in front of her had to be an accumulation of many years of payments. She could easily fund her father's rebuilding efforts and still have coin left over.

"This is a lot," Neva said, feeling a little breathless. She couldn't imagine how many commissions she would have to accept, or how many decades she would have to deliver firewood, to earn such an amount, but a stone settled in the bottom of her stomach.

"Lindzhi only took the most dangerous contracts because they were lucrative and prestigious," Jorand said by way of explanation.

I'll say, Neva thought. She felt uncomfortable with him there, although handing over the profits from his sister's holdings seemed straightforward for him. She wondered how many family members he had lost.

Anyone Jorand would have lost was a relative of hers, but she wouldn't ever have the chance to know them.

With a snap, she shut the box.

"Jorand, you have my thanks," Neva said. "I promise you, I will respect your sister's memory."

"I appreciate that." He held her gaze a moment before switching the subject. "Are you hungry?"

"Aye." Neva realized she was.

"Come with me. We'll find something to eat, and I want to introduce you to someone."

Neva couldn't think of a reason not to follow along. If her guess was right, Astiand would be with the donazhi and Bryand for some time, which meant she had no one watching over her. She could go where she wished for the first time in a long while.

Neva placed the box and the sword in her room and followed Jorand on a lengthy walk through the Da'Valia township to the opposite end, which was speckled with businesses instead of houses. They came to a well-lit tavern that stretched back until it disappeared into the forest along the border of the village.

Three hilans stood on the wrap-around porch. Neva felt their eyes boring into her back as she and Jorand entered. Inside, small candleholders hung from the ceiling, strung from the center of the room in an arrangement of circular lines. The design was familiar: its twin marred her neck. The donazhi's brand itched as Neva thought of it.

"We should grab that table." Jorand motioned to a line of booths of which one empty table remained.

Neva moved toward it, dancing around a group of inebriated majilas to avoid getting in their way as they flirted across the room. Neva took a seat, and Jorand joined her a few seconds later. She watched a rowdy bunch of mercenaries over Jorand's shoulder as they bashed their mugs together before downing their drinks.

Their actions were familiar to the veteran barmaid, but what wasn't normal was the midnight sky gliding like speckled smoke around the floor. Nor were the flirtatious smoke-like strings of power the majilas sent through the air to a group of hilans against the far wall. Nor was the bar, which was manned by a hilan and a majila and was alight with a strange yellow glow. If Neva narrowed her eyes, she could see the faint outline of magic covering it.

"What is this place?" Neva asked.

"They call it the Tiger's Eye."

"It's..." She searched for the right word. "Miraculous."

Jorand laughed. It made him seem more distinguished and sure of himself. "I'm glad you like it." He humored her.

Neva was reminiscing about the last time she served at her father's inn when a barmaid appeared at their table. Jorand ordered dinner and junipero beverages for both of them.

Neva tried to pay attention to Jorand again after the majila left them, but she found it was difficult to pull her gaze away from their surroundings. She watched one of the hilans reach out and grab a smoke-like tendril of a majila's power. The majila raised her glass with a laugh, toasted her friends, and walked over to him, swaying her hips provocatively.

"It must be so different among humans," Jorand guessed, appearing to enjoy her enthrallment.

"What are they doing?" Neva pointed toward the group of majilas, a cluster of white in their dark surroundings.

"Casting." Jorand replied. "When a majila is interested in forming an alliad or flirting, or other things, she sends out a cast. If a hilan returns the interest, he may accept the lure. It is a very public action since the rest of us can see which majila the lure is coming from."

The barmaid returned and deftly placed a platter on their table. Neva ate the breaded stew with an enthusiasm she didn't know she had. The flavors played on her tongue, and the junipero drink was fresh and minty.

"I see you're enjoying the food," Jorand commented, grinning at her delight.

Neva swallowed and smiled.

"I am. The food at Astiand's isn't nearly as flavorful."

"That sounds about right. Astiand joined our forces young. He wouldn't have developed finer tastes while he was living on rations during the Great War."

"He fought in the Great War?"

The Great War had lasted more than a decade, eventually giving way to King Stephan and the Order of Cirandrel's rule. It was unsurprising Astiand had fought, but that meant he would have been a few years younger than Neva when he joined the ranks.

"That was back when he and Bryand earned their scars and names enough to catch the donazhi's attention. Probably about your age now. She's always been drawn to the fresh beasties."

"And who isn't?" A bulky middel hilan with a majila on his arm swaggered up to their table. "A young thing now and then can't do any harm!"

Ego oozed from the hilan. He didn't have to work to call attention to himself. His character demanded it. Neva laughed as the majila punched his arm with little restraint. She was smaller but forceful, and the action spelled out the order to behave.

"Mind if we join your table, Jorand? I would hate for Nevazhi of Glacier Pass to be saddled with only your company tonight." The hilan recovered from his beating with ease and nodded to Neva. He was tall with a round face and thick stature. His green uniform was a copy of the one the Jorand wore. His hair was loose and long, but not compared to the majila, whose white locks fell to below her elbows.

"What he means," the majila interjected, "is he was on assignment earlier today, and he wants to know what came of your meeting with our donazhi."

Jorand moved to the other side of the table next to Neva to make room for the couple.

"I'm Roland Da'Voda-Punya." The bulky hilan introduced himself as he scooted onto the bench after his companion. "Pray tell, how was your meeting with our esteemed leader?"

"Ah-hem." The majila cleared her throat, flinging her hair over her shoulder. "And I am Kelizhi Da'Voda-Gamonda. Don't tell him a thing. It'll be much more fun to watch him suffer in ignorance."

"Punya and Gamonda work the patrols with me," Jorand filled Neva in, calling his friends by their last names. "We've been spending a lot of time walking the Da'Voda border."

When Neva asked about their work, the three informed her the donazhi believed their location to be so remote as to only need sentries near the main road, water sources, and at the lookout towers on the peaks of surrounding mountains, unless there was an alert. That left the whole of their border to be checked by patrol teams. A thorough sweep, they told her, usually took a day or two.

Before long, Roland directed the conversation back to Neva's meeting with the donazhi, interrogating her about the donazhi's landscape. Neva pulled her hair to the side and bent her neck so they could see the crisp burn on her skin.

"She's one of us!" Roland's booming voice demanded attention from several nearby tables, despite the steady flow of chatter. "We've got the Power from Glacier Pass! A Da'Voda! We need drinks!"

He jumped up and went to the bar, leaving Kelizhi laughing on the bench seat.

"It would have been fun to keep him guessing," she informed Neva in a stage whisper. "But this will be an adventure, too."

Roland returned with two pitchers — one of hagave and one of junipero — and Neva learned how Da'Voda soldiers celebrated what they considered good news. Da'Valia she didn't know slapped her hard on the back several times. Roland returned to the bar for more drinks twice within the hour, and, before long, Neva lost track of time. Eventually, the pub was so crowded Roland decided it was no longer worth the effort to make it to the bar to get refills.

"To the great Dhianz!" Roland began another toast in a lengthy series with the last of their pitchers. "May he know how much we appreciate the diversion he is to our donazhi — as ruthless and temperamental as she is. This way, our patrols are shorter and our pockets filled with the fruits of our excursions!"

Neva's jaw dropped before she laughed at the words and drank with the others. She was getting the feeling Miland was not alone, and the Da'Voda suffered through their donazhi's rule more than Neva had first thought. Neva would bet the donazhi would take offense to someone calling her temperamental, but Neva hadn't been this carefree in as long as she could remember. She was cautious, aware she would be sandwiched in a room of ferocious Da'Valia if anything went wrong, but politics were not at play here as with Astiand or the donazhi.

The hilan manning the bar climbed atop the counter and rang a brass bell with three sharp pulls. Speech among the patrons faltered and bodies started moving. Coin exchanged hands to close out bills.

"Come on." Roland stood and waved for her to follow. "It's nearing midnight, and you'll want to get a decent seat."

"A decent seat for what?" Neva was confused, and a little tipsy. "Where are we going?"

"We're going into the Tiger's Eye," he said with a wink.

Chapter Seventeen

Fifth Cravell, 1632

I have an idea. It is dangerous but intriguing. Dare I?

— *Monazhi Da'Voda-Lira*

The group descended a circular flight of stairs underground. Neva hung back with Jorand while Roland and Kelizhi navigated a path through the stream of bodies. Neva realized the pub portion of the Tiger's Eye was only part of the establishment as she looked over a railing and down. A steady magical glow illuminated a giant circular pit of orange dirt three flights from ground level.

Da'Valia arranged themselves around the edges of the pit on stone seats. With Roland's shouts and shoves leading the way, they procured seats within the first few rows. The stone was hard and cool, and the air was thick with heat from so many bodies.

Neva found herself next to a slightly older toppel majila. Unlike the other Da'Voda in the room, the majila was a picture of sobriety. Her black wrap did little to shroud her toned, thin stature, and her shrewd eyes and set mouth added to her somber demeanor. The toppel had a black leather whip with a metal tip at her waist, but no other weapon was visible.

"Great Dhianz!" Neva heard Jorand mutter when he saw who sat on the other side of her.

The majila eyed them critically.

"Neva," an uninhibited Jorand whispered, leaning back so Neva's body blocked the majila's view of his face. "You're sitting next to the master at arms."

"Jorand Da'Voda-Lira!" The majila's voice snapped him to attention with a commanding tone. "Don't think I can't hear every word you say."

Jorand straightened as if a rod was tied to his back. He leaned forward to talk over Neva.

"Of course not, Master Vivizhi. Wouldn't think of it."

The master at arms seemed like she was about to say something else, but the crowd of Da'Voda was on its feet. The hilan who had been tending the bar raised his hands in the center of the ring.

"Tonight, we have a special selection of beasties!" he announced. "A group of Da'Voda about to join with the Da'Roha and go searching for their own places among the clans!"

Five hilans, with their smooth chests exposed and dressed only in white linen pants, entered the pit from a side gate. They formed a line for introductions.

"Tonight, you will choose one of these young beasties to challenge our reigning champion. But first — three times undefeated — I am pleased to welcome Laurand Da'Voda-Steila to the ring!"

Applause rocked the earth as the hilan called Laurand jumped into the pit from the first row of seats. He ripped off his shirt and let out an animal roar, causing more of a reaction from the audience.

The announcer turned to the line of beasties and requested the audience's approval for each candidate. The applause doubled and Da'Valia roared when the announcer pointed to the last hilan in line. Roland, Kelizhi, Jorand, and the master at arms increased their cheers, so Neva did the same.

The final fighter was a toppel. Neva could tell he was lethal. He should have appeared bulky at his height and weight, but his toned muscles make him athletic and imposing instead. He didn't make a spectacle of himself as Laurand did. Rather, he stood so still he might well have been a statue. A flicker of intelligence and hunger for the fight sparked behind his eyes. He was attractive and also alluring in a way Neva had never seen before.

"We have a match! Laurand Da'Voda-Steila against our challenger, Emiliand Da'Voda-Riga!"

The line of rejected hilans filed out of the pit as the announcer called for everyone to place their bets. Jorand stuttered as he wagered against Vivizhi that Laurand would come away the victor, and Roland bet everyone within shouting distance that Emiliand would win.

In short order, the crowd settled down. The announcer traded places with the majila who had tended bar earlier. She sauntered to the middle of the pit, and the fighters stood opposite each other against the earthen walls.

She raised one hand until the crowd was nearly silent.

"No holds barred!" she shouted.

With a blast of power, her body shot up through the air to latch onto a catwalk near the ceiling.

Neva had barely a moment to marvel at the theatrics before her attention was called back to the pit, where black streaks ran together as the hilans fought to keep up with each other's blows.

Quickly, Neva could see the difference in their fighting styles. Where Laurand was fond of charging and asserting himself instinctually, Emiliand seemed almost methodical, as if he knew the consequences and benefits to every blow, block, or duck before it happened.

Their fighting was different from the kilstroke. There was still an element of honor because of the respect of the crowd, but there was no real dignity in some of the techniques. The hilans used dirty tricks to trip each other up and shoved their power into potentially fatal moves.

Emiliand was the better fighter and his superiority seemed to infuriate Laurand. The reigning champion sent a spiral gust of burning power straight at Emiliand to gain an advantage.

That was a mistake.

Emiliand rolled on the floor of the pit, orange grime coating his chest and back in his effort to escape the twister. He threw up both hands as it passed, and a dark silver flame shot out to overtake the spiral. Laurand fought to bring the twister back to him, but it was too late. Emiliand's power won.

Emiliand sent the twister spinning for Laurand, and it enveloped the hilan's body. Neva gasped along with others in the crowd. Laurand used his power as a shield to keep it from burning him to a crisp, but he couldn't stop it from lifting him and slamming him into the wall. The twister exploded in a burst of dark fire, and Laurand fell, his head striking the hard earth. He stilled, unconscious.

With a high-pitched scream, the majila plummeted from the catwalk. A blast of her power slowed her to a stop so her landing was smooth. She grabbed Emiliand's arm and lifted it into the air.

"Our champion!" she shouted.

Neva clapped with the others. She only half expected the growls amid the cheering. It would take some time before she became accustomed to that. Still, she couldn't stop a small smile as she watched Emiliand. He acknowledged the Da'Voda congratulating him and accepted a towel from the hilan announcer with thanks.

"I'm going to congratulate our beastie," Kelizhi said to Roland. "Are you coming?"

"Of course, I'm coming!" Roland shouted at her from the end of their seating area. "Just give a poor soldier a chance to collect on some debts, will you?"

"Hurry up!" she shouted back.

Jorand slapped a coin into Vivizhi's palm before she departed, and he turned to Neva after he double checked the majila was out of earshot.

"The master at arms is one of the most formidable majilas in the clan." The scent of liquor tainted Jorand's breath. "I would have been nerve-wracked sitting in your seat."

He beckoned Neva to follow him down the steps.

"They'll be along," he said, motioning toward Roland and Kelizhi, who was not-so-patiently waiting for her aliado with her arms crossed. "I want to get down to the pit before Riga leaves."

They reached the bottom of the steps, and Jorand vaulted over the short wall around the pit. Neva followed despite a glare and a shout from the hilan announcer.

The gaggle of majilas Neva watched in the bar earlier had surrounded

Emiliand, admiring his scars. When they saw Jorand and Neva approaching, they abandoned their conquest and left the ring. One of the middel majilas threw an annoyed look over her shoulder.

"Well done out there." Jorand slapped Emiliand on the back.

Emiliand turned to face them, slinging a towel around his neck. He smiled when he saw Jorand and returned the slap.

Neva wasn't sure if it was the fight or his natural complexion, but Emiliand's skin tone had a distinct gray to it she had not seen in any of the other Da'Valia. His power, too, had a silver hue to the black. There was something about him that drew her. Whether it was because of his skill in the fight or his humble demeanor, or his muscular physique, she couldn't say.

His eyes were lighter than most and sparkled with a friendly spirit. As soon as those eyes focused on her, they turned calculating. It was a look to which Neva was becoming accustomed. It seemed many of the Da'Voda she met were trying to figure out what they could get from her. But almost as quickly as the look was there, it disappeared and he replaced it with a hand held out to her.

Neva took his hand in her own and was surprised to receive a handshake in return. No one had shaken her hand since arriving at the Da'Voda enclave.

"I heard that's how humans meet," Emiliand said, smiling at the shock she was certain still painted her face.

"Well, you heard correctly," was all she could think to say.

"Riga, this is Nevazhi," Jorand introduced her. "Nevazhi, this is the person I told you I wanted you to meet."

They exchanged Da'Valian formalities, and Neva complimented Emiliand on his win before Jorand inserted his own agenda.

"Riga, I'm hoping you can help my cousin."

"Rumors have already spread about Nevazhi of Glacier Pass," Emiliand said with good humor and a pointed look at her horns. "But I have not heard of why you would need my help."

His gaze turned direct, and Neva felt her face turn red. Jorand knew she needed weapons training. They had discussed it earlier in the night, but admitting as much to a stranger, especially a fighter of Emiliand's caliber, was embarrassing. Unfortunately, she didn't see any way out of it.

"I'm looking to learn how to fight," Neva admitted, resigned to Jorand's agenda.

"What's to learn?" Emiliand asked. "Aiming for nerves will get you answers, aiming to kill will speed things up, and forgetting to aim will get you dead."

Neva recognized the old saying from soldiers who occasionally stayed at her father's inn. They were words to live and die by in war, but they alone wouldn't help her.

"No, Riga," Jorand tried to explain. "She knows nothing!"

Neva couldn't help rolling her eyes to the expansive ceiling. Couldn't her mother have shown more foresight and given her some education in this matter? If Neva hadn't chosen to keep company with street rats, thieves, and cutthroats, she probably wouldn't have learned her knife skills either, seeing as her father never liked her participating in knife-throwing tournaments. He was always worried someone would notice her throws were too fast, her aim at greater distances too good.

"All right, Jorand." Neva wrapped an arm around her cousin's shoulders in a joking manner. "That's enough!"

"Riga! I knew you'd win!" An ecstatic Kelizhi arrived with Roland in tow. He chimed in with his own congratulations, distractedly counting his handful of coins.

Neva was glad for their interruption. She found it difficult to pull her gaze away from Emiliand's — a fact made worse by her embarrassment over her own shortcomings.

Before too long, the group started the lengthy climb up the stairs. They collected their coats and capes from the pub and stepped outside into the early morning air.

Roland and Kelizhi parted one way, and Emiliand and Jorand offered to accompany Neva home in the other direction. She accepted their escort because, while she was fairly certain she could find her way back to Astiand's on her own, she didn't mind the company.

"I'll leave for the Da'Roha at the end of the month," Emiliand explained to Jorand as they walked. A light rain began to fall. "Should be weather fit for travel."

Neva recognized the name of the Da'Valia clan. Toppel and middel hilans often traveled with the nomadic Da'Roha group to other enclaves in search of strong majilas with which to align. Jorand interrogated his friend with a series of questions, and Neva tried not to be too interested in the answers. She was certain she failed miserably by the time they reached Astiand's home. It sounded as if Emiliand had an adventure ahead of him. Not only did the Da'Roha travel to the other clans, but they were also an army for hire.

"Good night, cousin." Jorand wished her well, propping himself up on the ornate fence marking the border of Astiand's yard.

Neva realized she liked Jorand. Not only was he sincere, but he didn't hold a grudge. She reasoned she had Dhianz's judgment in the kilstroke to thank for that.

"We will see you tomorrow, then?" Emiliand asked her.

"Tomorrow?"

"At the north practice yards," Emiliand said, his eyes searching out hers. "For the afternoon sessions. It's the best place to learn how to fight."

"Oh, yes. Of — of course. At the practice yards." Neva hated how she stumbled over her words.

"At the practice yards!" A still-woozy Jorand yelled.

Neva rushed to shush him. She was still shaking her head as she crept inside the house. Much to her relief, Miland was asleep. She could hear his rhythmic snores coming from the servant's room behind the kitchen. She spied Astiand's open bedroom door and realized the master of the house had not yet returned. She was rather relieved, imagining that meant Bryand was still alive.

Her hand hovered over the handle to her own door. She was tired, but she couldn't count on another chance to explore Astiand's room anytime soon. This was likely one of the best opportunities she would get.

Neva had made a serious promise to the donazhi earlier. Doing what she wanted now would violate that promise, but if she thought she knew anything about Astiand, it was that he wouldn't take her to the donazhi if he discovered her trespass. Her actions would reflect poorly on his guardianship. He would deal with her himself, and taking him on didn't sound all that bad when she thought about kissing him before her firérite.

Her mind made up, Neva grabbed her pack from her room and hurried to the end of the hall. She yanked back the ornate rug covering the floorboards in Astiand's room and stifled a sneeze in the crook of her arm as dust ballooned around her. She tested the boards until she found the one that had creaked under her weight.

Neva got down on her knees and dug her nails between the loose board and its neighbor to pry it out. Freeing the board, she smiled. The glow of protective magic coated the spindle on the safe Astiand had stored there.

Nimbly, she removed her spelled glove from the pack and pulled it on, putting her ear against the safe. The glove was good for only one use, but she hadn't needed it in the duke's tower thanks to the Chameleon's illuminator. She might as well use it now. She turned the spindle handle until she heard the faintest pin drop, spun it in the other direction, and repeated the process until the magic of the safe initiated. The spell felt for Astiand yet found nothing unsatisfactory about the glove.

My thanks for the glove, Flynn, Neva thought to his spirit as the door released with a satisfying pop.

Careful not to disrupt the other contents of the safe, Neva withdrew the sole book inside. The brown leather cover was worn and had the initials MDL in the bottom corner. Neva's breath caught in her throat. Was this what she thought it was? She opened the book, her hands shaking. The room was dark, but she saw enough to know Miland had been acting in her interest when he had given her this tip.

Her suspicion confirmed, she closed the book with a snap, put Astiand's safe back in order, and made with haste to her bedroom.

There, she lit a lamp and opened the book again. She couldn't stop herself from stroking the first page lovingly. She would have recognized her mother's handwriting anywhere. It looked the same on the pages of the diary as it had on a slate years ago, when she first learned the Da'Valian alphabet from Monazhi.

This was her mother's personal journal, and perhaps she was violating her mother's private thoughts by reading it, but she felt a deeper need to know the woman who was taken from her too soon. Especially now.

Neva was curious how Astiand had come to possess such a treasure, but that didn't matter because she had it now. He would confront her if, or when, he noticed the book was missing, and she would fight him to keep it. She bit her lip, thinking it was a good thing she was going to the practice yards later.

Neva flipped to the first page and started reading. Her mother's diary began after her own firérite, and Neva was excited to see where it would go. She read of her mother's own evaluation, exhilaration at being a toppel, and some experiences entertaining potential aliados. Monazhi, as a warlock, had been a devoted student of magic and history. She had once fallen into her own landscape with a friend, indicating she had been chosen by Dhianz and would be a potential donazhi. Neva was impressed.

Unable to stop reading, Neva continued into the late morning, giving into slumber near midday. Bleary-eyed, she had enough wherewithal to slide the book under the pillow tucked beneath her head before sleep claimed her.

Miland woke Neva when he brought her a tray of food mere hours later, causing her to open her eyes and instantly despise the light streaming through the window.

"My thanks," Neva told Miland sleepily. "Did Astiand return yet?"

He shook his head and pulled open the drapes.

Neva covered her eyes in response and eagerly accepted the tonic Miland handed her next.

"Have you heard anything about Bryand?" Neva asked between sips.

Again, Miland shook his head.

"You know, I know you can talk," Neva pointed out. "You don't have to play this game with me."

Miland stared at her.

Neva frowned back. She thought Miland was on her side, but that didn't mean she understood his peculiarities or his motivations. She took her time getting out of bed, reading a little more of her mother's diary before washing and dressing for the day.

Monazhi wrote of contemplating her first alliad with a toppel who might help her follow in the footprints of her donazhi. She wrote of planning a trip to the Da'Xana with her mentor, a warlock whom Monazhi adored. Alizhi. Neva committed the name to memory. Perhaps the majila was still alive.

Neva dressed in a brown uniform she found in a drawer. It didn't fit perfectly, much like the other clothes she found in Astiand's home, but it was functional. She wanted to be prepared to get dirty since she was going to the practice yards.

Neva vaguely remembered walking past a training area when she first arrived, but that was toward the east if her memory was correct. She headed north instead and found the walk to the practice yards was a quick one.

"Emiliand! Roland!" Neva greeted her new friends when she arrived. She scanned the troops for her cousin but failed to find him.

"Oh, please, not so loud," Roland begged her, rubbing his head.

His hair had knotted in several places while he slept, and he had made no effort to straighten the mess.

Emiliand grinned, keeping an eye on the action in the yards. Three rectangular yards sat side by side: one for archery on the far side, one for short-range weapons in the middle, and one for grappling where they stood.

This was where the soldiers trained, Emiliand explained to her, a ring of pride in his voice. The east and south yards were for optional workouts where Da'Valia often went to spar, whether or not they were engaged in active service, and the west yards were for horseback bouts as they were nearer to the stables. Neva asked after Jorand and discovered he had missed the morning call and was mucking the stables as punishment.

"Attention!" Emiliand shouted unexpectedly in their discourse.

As Neva watched, everyone in the yards stopped, turned, and ducked their heads to the white majila dressed in pure black who was striding across the concourse. She walked with purpose, a metal-tipped whip at her hip, hair tied tight behind her head in a long single braid. Neva couldn't help but recognize the master at arms.

The majila stopped and inclined her own head. At once, everyone jumped back into action. The Master of Arms walked directly to Emiliand, Roland, and Neva.

"Riga, what's the progress here?"

Emiliand recited his report. At the end, he motioned toward Neva.

"Master at Arms, Vivizhi Da'Voda-Mourda, you have heard of Nevazhi Da'Voda-Roberts, formerly of Glacier Pass. She is here to learn from us."

Neva smiled hesitantly at the other majila, not sure how she would be received.

Vivizhi looked her up and down and then finally lowered her head in greeting, but only slightly. This was her territory.

"It is an honor," she said. "But Gaband, I am sure, would be better suited to help you train."

"Gaband?" Neva wasn't being turned away or welcomed, but she was being redirected.

"The weapons masters would be willing to help you choose a specialty," Vivizhi said. "I saw you in the kilstroke. Daggers might suit, and they are Gaband's forte."

"What you saw there is near to everything I know," Neva admitted. "With maybe a little luck thrown in."

Interest sparked in Vivizhi's eyes.

"*Near* to everything, or everything?" she demanded.

"Near." Neva's admission was weak. She had used all of her tricks to stay alive in the kilstroke circle. The only skill she hadn't used was throwing.

The master at arms looked her up and down.

"I see. Come with me."

Chapter Eighteen

Fifth Cravell, 1632

*I sought out Benjamand to research what I think is possible. S'donzhi
controlled the Trishula, and she was mortal. Perhaps I can as well. He's
promised to find what he can. I just hope he can do it in time.*

— *Monazhi Da'Voda-Lira*

Neva moved at double speed to catch up with Vivizhi. The majila strode purposefully along the edge of the practice fields, her gaze homing in on the soldiers as they drilled and scrimmaged. Her critical eye raked over the trainees as well as the strategically placed instructors. Neva got the feeling Vivizhi was taking notes about the performances of both in her head.

Shouts from the short-range sparring area accompanied the loud, steady clacks from quarterstaves and wooden practice swords. To Neva, it looked much like the Order's practice yards at the House of Trescony, but the speed and force of each blow was tripled and the clacking amplified because of it.

"I'm not subversive," Vivizhi's voice was whisper-low. "I want you to understand that."

"Of course." Neva cleared her throat sharply, surprised by this unexpected start.

"I serve our donazhi every day, and I do it with honor." The master at arms kept her voice hushed so the noise of the yards drowned out her words beyond Neva's ears. If anyone hoped to overhear their conversation, they would meet with disappointment. "But that also means I know what methods she prefers and how she thinks. You'll need to know how to fight. Whether you will be an ally or a foe in the end doesn't matter. Whether you will fight for the clan or aim to become the donazhi's successor does matter."

"I don't want to be the donazhi here," Neva rushed to reassure. "And I'm not full-blooded, so I doubt it would be permitted. Besides, I met your donazhi yesterday, and she seems... rooted."

Vivizhi nodded her approval to the hilan in charge of the archery range as she listened. Her eyes still roved.

"I'm sure, but her reign makes us wary," Vivizhi said. "We never had to worry over the sins of our parents before, you know. Those punishments began when the donazhi isolated challengers of her authority, and now she uses it as a tactic of fear.

"My point is Dhianz wouldn't have blessed you with such great power unless you were meant for something. Whatever the gods have in store for you, it would only dishonor our creator if you were to head toward such a destiny unprepared for battle."

Neva let a silence fall, wondering if she was being tested. Vivizhi's straightforward manner seemed honest enough, and Neva thought she could trust this majila, but she couldn't be sure.

"What exactly do you think my power has to do with the donazhi?" Neva asked.

Vivizhi looked at her unnervingly.

"You've sat with her, and she knows the extent of your power now. She will seek to use you when she needs you, and she'll seek to stifle your development — diplomatically — when she can. And then if you become a political threat, she will figure out a way to get rid of you. So, you see, your power has a lot to do with the donazhi."

That settled Neva's mind. If this were a test, the donazhi surely would have employed another to approach her. This majila subscribed to particularly cynical opinions of the matriarch.

"Will you teach me how to fight, then?" Neva asked.

"At night," Vivizhi said. "In the indoor training facility. Emiliand will bring you, and none of us will ever speak of it."

Neva felt a rush of excitement wash over her. She was tired of being unsure what to expect, of fearing the Da'Valia around her. She was confident she could harness more power than the donazhi, but she wasn't sure how much that would count for in a fight. Neva could dedicate herself to learning the art of combat in honor of her mother, her bloodlines, and the life she had taken. Jorand would be satisfied. She would do this for them as well as herself.

"No one else can know," Vivizhi made clear. "Especially Astiand."

Neva noticed a change come over Vivizhi's features. It was soft, hard, and nostalgic all at the same time. The expression was akin to the look Amber used to wear when she thought Flynn wasn't paying attention.

"You know Astiand," Neva surmised, emphasizing the word 'know.'

"I knew him, once," Vivizhi corrected. "Long before he became our donazhi's aliado, but he's your guardian. He's too close to the donazhi for him to know what we're doing. We must be cautious."

The master at arms offered no more information, but Neva understood the need for secrecy.

"He won't discover us," Neva said. "I'll make sure of it."

Vivizhi nodded, seeming satisfied, and dismissed her.

Neva made her way to where Roland and Emiliand grappled, and she whispered with Emiliand about meeting later as the afternoon practice cleared out of the yards. Once Roland and Kelizhi finished their training regimen, Neva walked with them a while. Kelizhi entertained them with battle stories until they parted. She had been personally involved in a few mercenary dealings. Neva suspected she embellished the retellings, but Neva didn't mind. It reminded her of her uncles and how an easy job became a narrow escape with death on the line when they recounted their missions over a mug of warm brandy.

Inside Astiand's home once again, Neva went in search of Miland. He hadn't been speaking to her earlier, but after failing to find information about Bryand during her excursion, she wanted something to satisfy her curiosity.

When she found the servant, he was closing Astiand's bedroom door behind him.

"He's back?" she asked.

Miland only looked at her.

Neva brushed past him and charged into the bedroom.

"What happened with Bryand? Is he all right?"

Astiand was halfway into his bed, a sheet barely covering the lower section of his nude body. His eyes appeared sunken with dark half-moons under them. He quickly recovered from her surprise entrance and lowered his sculpted form onto the mattress. He moved slowly, as if the smallest movement grated on his skin.

"Bryand will be fine." Astiand seemed perturbed, as usual.

"Oh. Well, what happened?" Neva was curious — and trying to present a brave front to cover the embarrassment threatening to climb her cheeks. She hadn't expected Astiand to be naked.

Astiand took his time to answer her. The silence between them became awkward.

Finally he said, "You can go ask him yourself. He'll be staying here until he has mended."

Neva stared at Astiand, waiting expectantly, trying not to notice the sheet protecting his lower half inching down. Her efforts fell short, and she cleared her throat, shuffling her feet.

"He's in the next room." Astiand waved a hand at the wall. "Go bother him for a while, if you don't mind. I haven't slept in too long."

Neva could only imagine what magic the donazhi and her alliad had been using to heal Bryand, so she decided she wouldn't prod Astiand further. For now, she wanted to see Bryand with her own eyes.

She spun to leave but paused before closing the door behind her.

"I'm glad you're home," she told him.

It seemed odd after his harsh treatment. Ridiculous, even. But somehow, it was true. She knew too few people here. She told herself that had something to do with it. And having the last word didn't hurt.

Instead of barging in on Bryand — aware he may be in a similar state of undress as Astiand — Neva knocked lightly, calling his name. She expected Bryand would be easier to handle than Astiand because Bryand had less of an effect on her. Maybe she could wrangle some answers from him.

He called her in, and the temperature of the room shocked her. The fireplace roared, and waves of heat warmed the space. As she suspected, Bryand appeared to be in a matching state of undress to Astiand. Bryand, though, had several layers of bed coverings pulled up to his chest. Beads of sweat collected across his brow, yet he shivered.

"Bryand." His name fell from her lips in an unintended hush.

Where Astiand appeared haggard, Bryand looked like the donazhi had brought him back from the edge of death. His usually dark complexion was a frighteningly light shade.

He did a double take upon seeing her.

"Great Dhianz," his throat sounded dry.

Neva tried to smile, and her hand went to her horns. They still felt odd to her touch, and she had spent enough time looking in the mirror to know the sight was shocking.

"It was unexpected," she answered his unasked question with a shrug.

"I don't doubt it. Amazing."

Neva went to his side and took his hand. As warm as the room was, his skin was hotter.

"What happened to you?" Worry strained her voice.

"I made a bad decision. That's all."

"It doesn't look like that's the half of it." Neva released his hand and lifted a cup of healing tonic from the bedside stand to his lips. "Where did you go?"

She listened as Bryand walked her through an adventurous three weeks. He'd headed east for the Da'Xana in search of the stolen object, barely stopping to eat. When he arrived at the coastal clan's grand fortress on the cliffs of Picquereau, he moved about in secret. Because of his suspicions, he had to bypass the clan's protection spells and infiltrate the enclave without announcing his arrival. The clans met only once a year and rarely worked together. A long-standing distrust between the clans meant if anyone identified him as a Da'Voda, it would have undermined the fragile relationship the donazhi had carefully constructed with years of diplomacy. Inside the clan's walls, his search was fruitless.

Which meant the Da'Foha must have the goblet — Neva filled in that blank herself.

"As I left the enclave," Bryand told her, "I didn't expect their attack. I barely made it out, and it's taken me this long to get back here. A convoy the donazhi sent after me made that possible. If they hadn't discovered me, I wouldn't have managed to complete the journey on my own."

"Did they know who you were — the Da'Xana, I mean? Did they recognize you as the donazhi's aliado?"

"You've been learning a lot I see," Bryand said. "It was dark. I'm confident the space between us was enough so they couldn't discern who I was." Bryand took the cup of healing tonic from her and finished the last of it. Moisture lined his brow, and his lips were cracked and dry.

"Now, what's happened here?" Bryand asked.

Neva told him almost everything. Her mother's diary and her meeting with Vivizhi were the exceptions. He attempted to look at her belt when she mentioned the kilstroke. She glazed over most of her firérite because she didn't want to conjure the painful memories, and she ended her story with becoming a Da'Voda.

Bryand congratulated her, and she tried to ignore the sense it wasn't exactly heartfelt. She blamed her mixed blood. She took the mug from him when he started shivering more and turned their conversation to another topic.

"So, have you devised a strategy?" Neva referred to the situation with the goblet, and he knew it.

"I imagine the donazhi will sleep for a few days and then plan. Healing the damage from the Da'Xana's warlocks was no simple task."

"I can see that. I don't mean to pry, but what is so important to the donazhi that this other clan would want?" Neva asked.

"I assume you've already asked Astiand, and he declined to share any information with you?" Bryand asked knowingly.

Actually, she hadn't dared to ask Astiand directly because he always seemed suspicious of her. He deflected questions, skirting the topic time and time again.

Bryand tried to sigh and ended up coughing instead.

"A magical item of little consequence," he said once recovered. "Astiand is correct about many things, this being one of them. Just because you're a part of the clan now doesn't mean you're privy to business conducted between our alliad."

"Of course not," Neva said, forcing a pretend smile. "I won't bother you about it again."

She left to allow Bryand a more peaceful rest. He, at least, didn't know how much she was aware of the donazhi's dealings.

Neva wished she could understand all the circumstances of the donazhi's infatuation with the goblet. Still, Neva knew more than the donazhi's alliad would ever suspect. She had held the goblet and been subjected to its power. The memory still pulled at her, especially because the first two visions came true. As for the last... She didn't want to become that Da'Valia.

If the donazhi recovered the goblet, would it show her Neva on a hill about to unleash a wave of death? Or would it show the donazhi another set of equally dangerous prophecies? Such a tool would be more fearsome in the wrong hands, and judging by Miland's horns, the donazhi's hands would be the wrong ones.

Neva returned to her room to read her mother's journal. Monazhi had thrived among the Da'Voda, and Neva suspected she could learn something from her mother's writings. The journal continued with a journey to the Da'Xana along the coast. Monazhi and her warlock mentor, Alizhi, traveled with a squad of Da'Valia soldiers. Once with the other clan, the majilas worked in the grand libraries, where they learned from the largest collection of clan histories in existence.

Monazhi did not directly address the purpose of her visit — in fact, she stayed a perceivable distance from mentioning any political matters at all — but Neva suspected her mother was meant to align with a powerful Da'Xana hilan to strengthen clan relations. Monazhi alluded frequently to a war brewing. A war Neva knew would be the Great War.

Meanwhile, Monazhi was permitted to scour the Da'Xana's library. Monazhi and her mentor studied detailed indexes and texts, lingering on all details about Dhianz and his endeavors, but ultimately never found what they were looking for. In her free time, Monazhi made friends with many of the Da'Xana and reacquainted herself with a former Da'Voda hilans. She would frequently take trips during the day to discover foreign coastal terrain or visit nearby cities, and she would read at night.

The descriptions Monazhi had penned rivaled some of the most romantic settings Neva's mind could fathom. The Tyvse Sea lapping at the white sands of Cirandrel, with water stretching into the distance as far as the eye could see. The Da'Xana's ancient fortress, which appeared to grow out of the cliffs themselves. Sunsets the color of exotic fruits. Sea creatures that could emerge from water to walk on land. Reading about them made her want to see them as her mother had.

When afternoon shadows overtook her room, Neva closed the leather-bound book. She had enough time to eat a small meal before Emiliand would escort her to meet Vivizhi. Neva made her way downstairs and dined with Miland. Both Astiand and Bryand remained resting in their rooms. Miland chose not to talk during dinner, and she couldn't find the strength to carry a one-sided conversation, so the silence continued. She felt like a stranger in the house.

After their meal, Neva lifted her cape off a hook by the door and ventured outside to wait for Emiliand out of sight from the house. His hair was damp from washing and curled near his collar when he arrived. He was dressed in a cleaner version of the same green soldier uniform she had seen him in earlier.

"Ready?" he asked.

"As ready as I'll ever be."

Chapter Nineteen

Sixth Cravell, 1632

I can't believe I never noticed it before. Benjamand and I were poring over the texts again by candlelight tonight and I caught him looking at me. He wore the same expression I wear when I look at Shaun. I wonder if Benjamand would become Da'Voda for me... It would strengthen my standing entering the summit. I am proud of my studies as a warlock, but he is truly exceptional.

At the same time, when I close my eyes to think of who I want to be my first aliado, all I can see is Shaun.

— Monazhi Da'Voda-Lira

They started with survival.

Neva was fairly certain years of keeping to the shadows had honed her self-preservation, but she quickly learned she was wrong. Among humans, she could hold her own: deflect, avoid, and evade. Against Da'Valia, the skills she had gained as a thief were substandard, and Vivizhi wanted to make sure she knew it.

"First, we will make sure you can avoid dying," Vivizhi greeted Neva when she and Emiliand walked into the training room.

Neva noticed the floor had a little give to it, thanks to mats atop the wood, but the walls consisted of jagged rectangular stone and some kind of magic. The magic explained the taste of silver on her tongue, and why Vivizhi's voice didn't echo.

Neva agreed immediately to Vivizhi's approach. She would have preferred to learn to attack, but she would not argue when the master at arms had agreed to help her.

"Good." Vivizhi said in a calm tone. "Now duck."

Neva dropped and rolled without question. The lesson had already begun.

Emiliand's fist flew through the air where her head had been a second before, and his other arm reached around her middle. He shoved her to the ground. The exchange happened so quickly, her mind struggled to catch up. She froze beneath the pin, her breath knocked from her.

"Again," Vivizhi said. "This time, try to avoid the attack."

Emiliand offered her a hand up. She took it, and without warning, he dove for her lower body. She managed to jump back, but he held onto her. Neva shoved off the floor and spun around his body, pulling away until he had to let go or break his wrist. Again, he aimed to knock her legs from under her.

"Move back," Vivizhi shouted.

Neva responded, moving until she felt a stone wall behind her. Emiliand sprang at her from a crouched position, forcing her lunge to the side. He kept attacking until he had moved her to the corner of the room, trapping her. Then, his arm was at her throat, her head shoved against the wall.

"Never allow yourself to be cornered," Vivizhi instructed, showing her a few tricks to break away and how to reach back to temporarily blind her opponent. "Always be aware of your opponent's intentions. Try to anticipate his moves."

Emiliand attacked her for several more hours. They stopped for water breaks only twice. Vivizhi corrected Neva the entire night: her stances, her rolls, and her blocks. Nothing was exactly as it should be. Neva noted each of the alterations with stony concentration. Still, she was slammed into the walls and floor, Emiliand stopping before killing blows more times than she could count. She was resilient enough and Emiliand was careful enough so no serious injuries ensued, but she couldn't pretend she didn't feel it.

For their last scrimmage of the night, Neva was forced to use every technique Vivizhi had tried to teach her. She faked her direction and read the intent in Emiliand's movements.

Emiliand flipped her on the training mat one last time, but she slid her body down and twisted. His hand would have pinned her throat, but it slammed into her eye instead. She thought briefly how she would need to return the favor. *He is too good looking anyway,* she thought, concentrating on seeing through her other eye.

Emiliand faltered and in the moment he was off balance, Neva pushed off the ground. She rolled over him, jutting her knee between his legs and her arm across his throat. Clumsy, but effective.

They froze.

"Good!" Vivizhi said.

Neva panted. She couldn't believe she had done it. Emiliand met her eyes and smiled, apparently thinking along the same thought. In a real-life situation, his fisted hand might have held a blade and she would have lost, but she had thwarted his attack. Slowly, Neva peeled herself off him and offered him a hand up.

"We'll make a Da'Valia out of you in no time," he joked, standing.

"We'll see," Vivizhi said coolly. "We still have more work to do."

"My thanks to both of you," Neva told them. Her confidence that she could prove herself to the Da'Valia was growing. She felt better about her time among the Da'Voda already, satisfied she was honoring the ways of her ancestors. She liked to think Monazhi would have approved of her daughter's progress, even if she couldn't teach Neva herself.

Vivizhi nodded curtly.

"Why don't you see her home?" the master at arms instructed Emiliand. "And go a round-about way in case anyone is paying attention."

Emiliand lowered his head in answer, and they watched Vivizhi leave. A short while later, Neva and Emiliand made their way outside.

"Let's go this way," Emiliand directed her down a side street.

Neva followed, watching Emiliand out of the corner of her eye. He was nothing short of elegant when he moved, and his slightly gray coloring added a mystique about him that none of the other Da'Valia had.

"You're different, aren't you?" she asked curiously.

Emiliand slowed his flowing gait.

"Different how?"

"Different how I'm different," she said. "It's in your coloring. It's in the way you move, the way you fight. You're not like everyone else here."

"No. I'm not." His shoulders tensed.

They stopped in front of Astiand's house. Neva would not pry anymore. As easy as Emiliand was to be around, she didn't want to overstep some boundary.

Before she turned up the walk, he surprised her by speaking again.

"I don't talk about it much," he said. "You've seen how it is here."

Immediately, she was regretful.

"I didn't mean to pry," she said.

"It's all right. Like yours, my mother mated with someone from another race. Speaking of it is not recommended." He let out a slow breath as if deciding how much he wanted to tell her. "She fell in love with a Colavalia. Have you heard of them?"

Neva slowly shook her head. A memory in the back of her mind tickled. A story she had heard once about the creatures that dwelled in the Dark Wood? She couldn't remember exactly.

"The Colavalia are another breed Dhianz created after S'donzhi betrayed him. He made them like he made the Da'Valia, but he gave them a specific purpose."

"And what was that?" Neva asked.

"To guard the entrance to the Underworld." Emiliand said. "They were a gift for Riska."

"And the clan didn't cast out your mother?" Neva asked, surprised.

"She was Da'Bruna," Emiliand explained. "She fled and came here, probably the best place to be if you've dishonored the Da'Bruna. She won a kilstroke to earn a place among the Da'Voda, but she died in childbirth."

Neva's gorge rose at the dramatic tale as if she could feel his pain as her own.

"That must have been difficult," Neva said. Growing up without a mother was hard, but the way he spoke made Neva think he blamed himself for his mother's death, and that was an impossibly heavy burden.

"There's no need for apologies, but you're right. It was hard. Alas, I am a better fighter for my mixed blood, and that's something they respect around here."

Neva nodded thoughtfully, feeling like she knew him better.

"Again tomorrow?" Emiliand asked her.

"Again tomorrow," she confirmed.

"Make sure you put something on that eye," he told her. "Otherwise it will be black by morning."

Neva felt the tender skin around her eye and winced. He was right. She watched him walk toward the barracks and gave an awkward wave when he glanced back. In the few steps it took her to reach the front door, she tried to think of a plausible excuse for a black eye.

Inside, she discovered she needn't have bothered.

She heard Miland's breathing from his room. It was even and shallow. The rest of the house was quiet. The hilans were asleep.

Neva silently removed her cloak. She was draping it over a hook next to the door when a voice startled her from behind.

"Who was that?"

Astiand's growl forced her hand to cover her throat in shock as she spun around. She hadn't seen him before, but there he was, standing in the doorway to the parlor, which had an excellent view of the street.

"Pardon?" she asked, covering her surprise.

He seemed as large as ever, filling the doorway with his own broad frame. His muscled chest was exposed by the deep V of his collar, and he wore black linen slacks. His expression was one of annoyance, but it had a distinct edge to it. That anger ever present around him.

He didn't repeat his question.

Neva swallowed.

"Emiliand Da'Voda-Riga. He was —"

"He's a foot soldier," Astiand interrupted her.

"But he's —"

"That means he's below you."

Neva frowned. She had been about to point out Emiliand led sessions at the practice yards. She had to wonder what had gotten into Astiand. She usually found him frustrating, and now he was getting territorial.

"In case you haven't noticed, equals are difficult to come by these days." She motioned to her horns.

"The donazhi wouldn't approve of you hanging around a foot soldier."

"We're both toppel," Neva pointed out. "Maybe he's a foot soldier because he isn't an aliado yet."

"I don't like him." The tone Astiand used said Emiliand was becoming dangerous territory, but Neva ignored it. She would keep training with him whether or not Astiand approved.

"Well, you don't have to deal with him, then." She tried to be reasonable.

"I am your guardian, and that means I do," he said.

"Then maybe I shouldn't stay here anymore!" Neva kept her voice hushed for the benefit of Miland and Bryand, but it emerged in a raised whisper. The shacklay sparked to life.

"Can't you see I'm trying to keep you safe?" Astiand asked. "Have some sense."

"I have my cousin's holdings," Neva replied defiantly. "Anytime you want me gone, I'll leave."

The words sounded bitter and ungrateful. Astiand dropped his hand from the doorframe and laughed sharply.

"That's out of the question," he said.

"That's not what you said before my firérite. You said I would be able to go where I wished."

"Things have changed. I have my orders, and she wants you here for the foreseeable future."

Neva clenched her teeth. That was how the donazhi would play this? Neva could practically see her choices for the future being ripped away from her. Did the donazhi think she would go along with such oppression without standing up for herself? Probably that was exactly what the donazhi thought.

"She doesn't get to decide where I go," Neva said.

"Oh, but she does." Astiand said. "Do not dare to defy her."

Neva let her shoulders droop. "All right. Fine."

Astiand eyed her.

"Fine?"

"Fine. You get it your way, but don't expect me to like it."

Neva shoved him out of her path and stomped to her room. She shut and locked the door and tried to control her breathing. She wanted to hit something.

She had realized while Astiand was talking that Vivizhi had been correct. The donazhi would stifle Neva's development and seek to influence Neva if she could. Keeping Neva under Astiand's roof was probably the most effective way for the donazhi to do that.

But Neva had meant what she said. She didn't have to like it.

She stayed in her room the following day save to relieve herself. Her firérite put enough stress on her body to delay her monthly cycle, but now nature was catching up with her, and that only put her in a worse mood where the donazhi's domineering aliado was concerned.

Neva accepted the trays of food Miland brought to her door, but mostly avoided stepping beyond its threshold. If they wanted to keep her where they could control her, she would let them think that's what they were doing.

Near dusk, Neva climbed out her window. The sloping architecture of Astiand's home was more difficult to traverse than the familiar rooftops of Glacier Pass, but she managed it without too much trouble.

Neva went to head off Emiliand, calling on her old invisibility spell to avoid being spotted. All she needed now was Astiand to accuse her of roaming the streets while she was supposed to be in her room. Should anyone mention seeing her to Astiand or the donazhi, she imagined some form of punishment would be called for. She fought the desire to scratch as she walked, but ultimately gave in to quell the sting.

Neva found Emiliand before he turned down the road to Astiand's house. She whispered quietly in Emiliand's ear and pushed on his elbow to direct him away.

Emiliand spun full circle, taking time to study his surroundings. He eyed a group of three younger Da'Valia wandering past.

"That's a handy trick," he said of her invisibility.

"Expensive, too," she whispered, remembering how long she had saved to pay the elderly, opium-addicted mage in Cul Corner to sew it into her skin. Invisibility wasn't like her other glamours. It was practically a part of her and it didn't fade with time, making it far more valuable.

When no other Da'Valia were within earshot, Neva explained it would be better if they weren't seen together. Emiliand gave a barely perceptible nod, following along. She imagined neither of them wanted to bring trouble to Vivizhi, or themselves.

They made their way to the training building, and once there, it was more of the same. Emiliand attacked and Neva fought back. She managed to land a few good blows and occasionally succeeded in staying 'alive,' but she never won.

Halfway through the night, Vivizhi told Emiliand to throw power behind his punches. He didn't take it lightly.

Shots of deflected power flew around the room. Neva was impressed to see the walls absorb the energy, adding to their own strength, but a sharp pain cutting into her side brought her back to the task at hand, and she started throwing blocks up around herself.

Her moves were much more instinctive than when Oliand had tested her. Then, she had concentrated on trying to show the elder what he wanted to see. Now, she acted on impulse. Her power was strong enough so if the aim of her deflections was on target, she had nothing to worry about from Emiliand's power. Like with Oliand, she could overtake them and extinguish them with a flick of the wrist. Unfortunately, the bursts of power were in addition to his physical attacks, not instead of them. Her attention was divided as she fought to focus on both aspects and all of Vivizhi's rules.

"Do you braid your own hair?" Vivizhi asked her as they stopped for a drink.

"I do," Neva confirmed. Tonight, it was in a single braid down her back.

"Good." Vivizhi showed Neva how to weave a shield of power. Lines of fire erupted in front of the master at arms, and she intertwined them to form a shield about the size of her own body in the air. "You feel your power on the surface of your skin, don't you?"

Neva thought and nodded. If she concentrated, she could sense the barest amount surfacing in her pores, surrounding her.

"It's a natural barrier of protection," Vivizhi told her. "For a toppel, the natural barrier will protect against a graze or even a punch backed with power. Those will still hurt, but they wouldn't do nearly as much damage as you might think. Now, *this* takes more concentration, but it will hold against a barrage."

Vivizhi knotted the edges of her shield and demonstrated different poses with it. Neva watched her with a steadfast concentration. She copied Vivizhi's movements and managed a rudimentary braided shield. It took more energy to maintain, but none of the shots Emiliand launched broke through. She looked forward to practicing more intricate weaves.

By the end of the night, Neva and Emiliand were both bloody and exhausted. Neva had learned fighting while calling upon her power took more energy, and while Da'Valia stamina was noteworthy, it wasn't endless. That deeper well of power stirred, and she had to work to push it down.

Neva collapsed into a cross-legged sitting position on the mat by the door, and Emiliand joined her. Her arms and legs were already sore.

"Where do we need to close you up?" Vivizhi asked with a practical air, carrying a pitcher of water into the room.

To Neva's surprise, Vivizhi knelt and cleaned Neva's broken flesh and then used power to seal the wounds. As flame sprouted from the majila's fingertips, Neva's mind went back to a time that seemed so long ago. She recalled healing Flynn and how Adam had tended to her cuts from the fire. Her thoughts drifted to her family.

Clenching her teeth as Vivizhi seared her flesh, Neva pushed the memories away. If she didn't think about home, maybe she wouldn't miss it.

Luckily, Vivizhi wasn't done yet with the day's lessons. She provided a welcome distraction as she explained how to close the wounds with optimal cleanliness on a battlefield. Emiliand's knuckles were in particularly bad shape, so Vivizhi's demonstration moved to him next.

"If there's running water around, you'll want to wash it out. Make sure the wound is as clean as it might be. You don't want to seal infection in."

Vivizhi talked as she worked. She also explained how their power had two basic purposes: to destroy and to heal. It could be molded and shaped into spells with years of magical training, but to commit one's life to that endeavor, she said, was not what their god had intended. Blunt force and healing were.

"I cauterized cuts once," Neva mentioned, leaving out it had been unintended. "But I was told I couldn't help when Bryand came back wounded."

Vivizhi gave a less-than-delicate snort. "That's not surprising. Whatever our donazhi has him involved in, it's also guaranteed to be beyond your skill. I wasn't exaggerating when I said channeling power into proper magic takes years of study."

"Not to mention, he's in an alliad," Emiliand pointed out. "It's bad form to invade on that."

Emiliand's comment ended their conversation, but their group continued sparring as the nights wore on. Emiliand was far more practiced than Neva and he won all the bouts, but her determination was steadfast. She refused to let ignorance or fear of the donazhi stifle her. She was aware the donazhi would put a stop to Neva's lessons if they became known, and worry occupied her mind while she waited for sleep to carry her away from the aches of her body.

Soon, Vivizhi allowed Emiliand to use practice weapons. It was always some new wooden replica: a knife, a sword, or a mace. Disarming Emiliand was Neva's primary goal. Slowly, the nights blended together.

During the days, Neva avoided leaving her room and seeing Astiand as much as possible. This was in part because she was still too angry to see him and because if he spent too much time studying her, he'd notice the small scars quickly accumulating.

Each morning, she soaked in a tub Miland filled for her. She wasn't sure if he suspected her activities, but she trusted him to keep his silence. While she sat by Bryand's bedside later in the day, she would occasionally sneak a sip of his healing tonic. It eased the tightness in her muscles and helped her retain movement.

The tonic was working wonders for Bryand as well, and he was looking better every day. Astiand started to take up some of his time to discuss the donazhi's matters. They talked some strategy but mostly waited for word from a convoy about the location of the goblet. Neva knew this because she had a habit of putting her ear to the wall.

When Astiand wasn't there, she would fill Bryand in on whatever gossip Jorand or Emiliand had passed on. In return, Bryand answered most of her questions about alliads and the clans. His outlook was notably cynical and reminded her a little of Vivizhi. He even once called the clans damaged, although Neva diplomatically overlooked the comment. Since the donazhi was in charge of the Da'Voda, Neva didn't think it was a smart discussion to engage with one of the donazhi's aliados.

Neva spent hours with Vivizhi and Emiliand in the training facility after dark, so her talks with Bryand helped make her presence in the house known. Neva didn't see any signs Astiand suspected her nighttime activities. He continued to refuse to let her move out on her own, and Neva still refused to look him in the face unless it was to argue her point.

"Our alliad commitments are voluntary, but that doesn't mean we always like what we do for them," Bryand told her one afternoon. "An alliad is a sacred, life-long commitment. For that reason — and a variety of others — we compromise. We're aligned with the donazhi, so we work for common goals. Because she's the donazhi, those goals are dictated entirely by her.

"She picked us at the end of the Great War, when we were both eighteen years old. It was an honor, and it still is, but our alliad with her is different from others because of her position and standing. Even the smallest public slight is unacceptable — and because she's the donazhi, anything is punishable if she deems it fit."

Neva sucked in a breath, trying to think impartially.

"Are you saying he wouldn't keep me here, otherwise?" she asked.

"The way you rile him?" Bryand asked, jokingly. More seriously, he said, "I've known him a long time, but I've never seen him look at another majila the way he looks at you when he thinks no one will notice."

Neva opened her mouth to ask exactly how Astiand looked at her when she wasn't paying attention, but she didn't get the chance. A knock sounded on the door downstairs.

In all the time Neva had been living in Astiand's home, no one other than Oliand had visited.

"She's here," Bryand said in a matter-of-fact manner.

"Who?" Neva asked.

"The donazhi."

Chapter Twenty

Sixth Cravell, 1632

Some part of me didn't truly think it would be possible, but our research suggests otherwise. I've decided to do it. I will call the Hand into myself. Should Trinizhi get the Eye, as her supporters say she will, I will force her to share the prestige. Mayhap then I can save the clans from her greed and ill-intent.

If Benjamand's translation is correct, the incantations alone will take several days. Then there's the blood sacrifice… This will take everything I have, but it must be done.

— Monazhi Da'Voda-Lira

"Toss me my shirt?" Bryand asked Neva, scooting to the edge of the bed.

Neva grabbed his silk tunic and threw it to him as she slid into the hallway to give him some privacy. She crept forward to look over the banister as Miland moved to the side of the entryway. The donazhi's cloak swirled around her, caught in the wind at the threshold of the house. Neva wasn't surprised Bryand was correct about who their guest was. Maybe it was some part of their alliad that allowed them to attune to each other. She pondered whether he could always sense where the donazhi was, and if so, was it mutual?

Miland accepted the donazhi's cape and then turned to Arroyand, who followed through the doorway.

Arroyand's motions were purposeful and slow. He slinked more than walked. In comparison, Miland's actions appeared disjointed. The servant took Arroyand's cape, but the other Da'Valia held onto the material so Miland couldn't immediately move away.

"It's been too long, Miland," Arroyand spoke softly. He raised his hand and caressed Miland's cheek in what should have been a loving manner. Instead, it sent a shudder down Neva's spine.

She had heard the rumors about him. Emiliand mentioned a soldier showing up for practice with knife cuts on her arms and half her face a blue-purple as if someone had beaten her. Arroyand, they said, enjoyed bringing pain to others in the bedroom, and he was undiscriminating about who he slept with, unless it might interfere with his relationship with the donazhi.

Miland bowed his head so Neva couldn't see his face as he backed away from Arroyand. Neva glanced at the donazhi and saw the majila's silver-white eyes staring back at her. Neva felt a wave of resentment, but the donazhi didn't appear to notice. A graceful smile played on the donazhi's lips.

"Nevazhi! Come down and join us." The donazhi's voice was pleasant enough, but Neva knew it was an act.

Neva was as close to a prisoner in this house as she could get without being behind bars, and that was by the donazhi's decree. The donazhi's friendly demeanor only made Neva more apprehensive of her. Nevertheless, Neva complied. She was turning to descend the stairs when Bryand breezed by her, leaving her to follow in his wake.

"Tell me this isn't the first time you've been out of bed." Arroyand eyed Bryand's haphazard, unshaven appearance.

Bryand responded by staring down the other Da'Valia.

"I've been keeping limber," Bryand said finally. "But the Da'Xana warlocks were using more than your standard peacetime spells. I suppose that's the least of what we can expect when we foster distrust among the clans."

"Let me look at you," the donazhi said to Bryand, ignoring the hilans' exchange.

The donazhi grazed the stubble on his chin with her fingers and smiled again. She seemed to recognize something in him that was invisible to the rest.

"Strong again. You should be out of this house in no time."

"That is my hope."

"And let me look at you." The donazhi turned to Neva.

Unprepared, Neva held still under the donazhi's probing eyes. Silence stretched. Neva trusted whatever the donazhi was looking for, she couldn't see. Bryand might have been an easy read for her, but Neva and the donazhi didn't share a special connection.

"How are you getting along here, Nevazhi?" the donazhi asked, her gaze hinging on Neva's eye, which was almost healed.

"Quite well, Donazhi," Neva bowed her head. "My thanks for your inquiry." Despite the utter falsity of the response, Neva managed to keep a ring of truth to her words.

"She hates it here, actually," Astiand drawled from the direction of the sitting room.

They all turned to look at him, and he shrugged as if it didn't matter.

"I think she finds us too beastly for her tastes."

Neva watched the donazhi's eyes narrow, looking from Astiand back to her.

Actually, Neva was certain everyone under Astiand's roof was conscious not to be too beastly — as he put it — around her. Except for Astiand himself, that was. Bryand and Miland behaved as if they didn't want to frighten her away most of the time. She wondered fleetingly what their reactions would be if they ever discovered her training sessions with Vivizhi and Emiliand.

"Hm. Well, sometimes you're all too beastly for my tastes, too," the donazhi said without humor. She directed her words at her alliad. Behind the comment, though, Neva sensed a thoughtfulness that made her want to analyze Astiand's statement more thoroughly.

"Oh, my love, don't say that," Arroyand wrapped his arms around the donazhi's waist and pulled her to him so he could touch his lips to one of her horns. "It's not like beastliness tastes bad."

"What brings you here?" Astiand asked, ignoring the display of affection.

The donazhi stepped away from Arroyand. He dropped his arms to his sides without indication of defeat.

"We need to convene," the donazhi said.

"Very well," Astiand said, leading the donazhi and Arroyand to the parlor.

Bryand paused, still beside Neva.

"This is a matter of our alliad, so you'll have to find something else to do for a while," Bryand said.

It sounded almost like an apology.

Neva watched him close the door to the parlor. She stole a quick look at Miland. The servant stared back at her.

"Who are we trying to fool?" Neva muttered to him. "It's not like you're going to tell anyone if I eavesdrop, now are you?"

He didn't answer, which was as she had expected.

Neva moved silently down the hall and pressed her ear against the wall. The Da'Valia in the room hadn't declared themselves as enemies in so many words, but Neva was determined to be well-informed when they made their intentions clear, and she couldn't get any nearer without following them inside the room. A meeting between a donazhi and her aliados may be akin to sacred, but Neva would not let that deter her.

As Neva listened, she worked out each of the voices. Astiand's always had a hard edge to it, Bryand's was incredibly deep, and Arroyand drawled out his words slowly. However, it was the donazhi who had come for a discourse.

"Jasand and Hanazhi have returned from the last convoy," the donazhi said. "They believe the Da'Foha have the piece. We will need to procure it from them."

An uneasy silence filled the room.

"Do they know what they have?" Astiand's voice was more grim than usual.

"No." The donazhi was certain. "They know it's important, and they know we want it, but they don't know what it is."

Neva blanched at her memories of the goblet. Stealing it had been the most exciting and terrible event of her life until coming to the Da'Voda.

"And they have a Vodou witch," the donazhi added.

"So they're trying to figure it out," Bryand said.

"If they have a witch, it won't take long," Astiand interjected. The shacklay animated. "They might already know."

"They don't know," the donazhi said. "They wouldn't keep her around otherwise."

"So we'll send a unit to arrange a compromise," Arroyand said. "Contribute a hefty amount of gold, and even though they don't like us, they'll still make the deal. We're not talking about the Da'Bruna."

"What if that doesn't work?" Astiand asked.

"It has to work," Bryand said.

The donazhi was quiet, so Astiand filled the silence.

"No, it doesn't necessarily have to work. We must be missing something. Why, for instance, would the Da'Foha come so far from the desert? Where did Hanazhi find them?"

"They are camping in the woods beyond the wall around Glacier Pass," the donazhi answered.

"You see? You don't find that suspicious?" Astiand asked. "If the Da'Foha were on a contract before stumbling upon the piece, they would still have orders to return to their clan. There's another strategy at play here. Gold isn't going to make a difference, not if they've set their minds to something collectively."

Neva thought back to Flynn's frozen face in the grove where they'd found his body, his veins crawling with insects before that, and the fire laying waste to her family's tavern. No, gold wasn't going to make a difference. Not at all.

"What are you suggesting?" the donazhi asked.

"You know exactly what I'm thinking," Astiand replied.

"That's ludicrous." The donazhi sounded like she was becoming angry. "They can't know what we're trying to do."

"Can't they?" Astiand challenged.

"That would mean one of us has broken this alliad," Bryand interjected.

"I know what it would mean," Astiand snapped coolly.

"Well, we're all still here, aren't we?" Arroyand threw plain reasoning in the mix. "We're undeniably loyal, so if what you are suggesting is true, someone else must know."

"No one else knows." The donazhi spoke as if her word was final.

"You're not weighing all the options," Astiand accused. "That puts us all in danger."

"It's not possible," the donazhi said, still firm.

"Are you here to discuss or dictate, Trinizhi?" Astiand asked. "You had better decide."

So the donazhi had a name. Trinizhi. Neva could picture the donazhi's glare in her mind.

"I want a unit sent out by the end of the week," the donazhi said definitively.

"A group of beasties is leaving to meet up with the Da'Roha," Bryand said thoughtfully. "It would be inconspicuous enough to head out at the same time. Otherwise, we may have to involve others."

"We're not involving anyone else," Trinizhi said. Astiand had forced Trinizhi into the role of dictator, and she was rising to fill it. "Not yet, anyway. I want Bryand to go with Hanazhi and Jasand to negotiate. If we send any more, the other clans might become interested, and the last thing we need now is Shaundrazhi or Perzhi getting curious."

"I have to disagree," Arroyand interjected.

Neva wished she could see Trinizhi's face.

"I think I should go, too," Arroyand continued. "We'll leave Jasand here if you're worried about word spreading, but Bryand hasn't had experience with Vodou witches, and I have."

Trinizhi was quiet.

"He's right." The voice was Astiand's. "Vodou witches can be dangerous unless you know their tricks. Sending Bryand in without that knowledge wouldn't be smart. Unless you want me to go, Arroyand's our best chance of success."

"You're staying put," Trinizhi told him. "I need you here to watch over the half-breed. Her mother was a thorn in my side, and I'm counting on you to keep her from following in Monazhi's footsteps. Arroyand and Bryand, go quietly with Hanazhi. Jasand can stay. We need this taken care of."

Neva's eyes narrowed. The extent to which the donazhi was attempting to control her was more than a little aggravating. This information made Neva even more pleased that she had liberated her mother's journal from Astiand's safe. From what she had read, Monazhi had been a committed researcher, and she'd had agreeable relationships with Da'Valia from other clans, but Neva didn't think those were the footsteps the donazhi referred to now. What else had her mother done to cause such trouble for the donazhi?

Neva sensed the discussion was coming to a close, so she abandoned her post and made her way upstairs. She wanted to make sure Trinizhi saw her on the second floor when the donazhi departed. Neva didn't have to wait long and was able to make a point of her location by waving goodbye. It might have been a useless effort; they all looked preoccupied.

Once the visitors left, Neva addressed Astiand as he climbed the stairs.

"You told her I find it too beastly here?" Neva demanded.

He scowled at her, but she didn't wait to hear the response she was sure he had ready. She didn't want to hear more of his opinion. This was the perfect charade to see her back to her room for the rest of the night without question. She spun on her heel and slammed her door behind her.

Her mood was turning dark. Maybe it was her Da'Valia side coming to light, but she felt a swelling desire to fight.

Neva paced her room until the day gave way to night. She couldn't focus enough to read her mother's journal. She yearned to be back in the training room with Vivizhi and Emiliand, to be learning vital techniques that would help her avoid making a fool of herself among a race raised with weapons in their cribs. She needed to keep busy, and she was itching to hit something.

Under a blanket of darkness once again, she slid out her window and scaled down the building.

"I want to try this with weapons today," she told Vivizhi when they met in the training room.

Vivizhi looked at her critically, as she always did, and gave a curt nod. Maybe Vivizhi sensed the turmoil of her emotions. Neva couldn't know for sure, but she didn't care, either. She just wanted to hit something. Let her Da'Valia side loose before bottling it back up.

"Emiliand?" Vivizhi checked with Neva's sparring partner.

He stretched on the mats and didn't look their way when he replied.

"I think she's ready," was all he said.

Chapter Twenty-One

Sixth Cravell, 1632

We've done it! The summoning took three days and I can barely lift my quill. I am so very tired, but otherwise, I feel no different. I expect change will come in time.

— *Monazhi Da'Voda-Lira*

Neva and Emiliand circled each other at first, spelled practice weapons still sheathed. She had carved daggers from Vivizhi strapped at her waist, but she didn't see any blades on him. He had agreed to her request, though, so she didn't doubt he had them close at hand. She was ready for whatever he would draw.

Neva was counting on his physical strength and his skill, but she wasn't counting on what happened next.

She felt him *push* on her mind. It was unlike anything she'd ever felt before. He infiltrated her thoughts with a sliver of smoke-like power she could sense but not see.

"You're still standing wrong," Emiliand said in her mind. *"Widen your stance."*

Neva was thrown off guard, and he attacked as if to prove his point. Her arms moved at a ferocious speed to block his hits, but he was right. Her stance was off, and he didn't allow her a second to collect herself.

"Get out of my head!" Her mind latched onto the string he had used to connect them and shoved the demand at him. She didn't know how he was doing this, and she didn't like it.

She jumped back, narrowly avoiding his fist colliding with her face. His kick missed her knee and hit her thigh instead as she twisted away.

"Why? Afraid of what I'll see?" Emiliand asked.

She didn't respond with a thought this time. Instead, she jumped back, landing on the balls of her feet and shoving out a wave of power. It blasted into the room, knocking Emiliand to the floor while his natural shield protected him. The wall absorbed the blast.

"Look at this." He poked around her thoughts. *"Always hiding who you really are."*

He tossed two orbs of power at her while he regained his footing. She extinguished one easily and deflected the other. He knew it took more than dual attacks to distract her after all their time practicing together.

"I said get out!" Neva shouted. It was easy to scream in her mind when she would have otherwise kept her silence.

"Pretending to be human among thieves, and pretending to be Da'Valian around us?" Emiliand asked.

Neva ignored Emiliand's words and sprang at him. He ducked and rolled out of the way as she had expected him to do. As she flew through the air, she pulled her daggers and twisted to follow his momentum. She would not let him put any space between them.

"How long have you been living in fear of what you are?" Emiliand's taunts were starting to infuriate her.

Neva slashed at his midsection, and then he had his own knife in his hand. *Clack. Clack. Clack.* Their weapons clashed. She wished she could ignore his taunts, but it would have been easier if he wasn't dropping them in her mind. She shoved power through her daggers to make each blow stronger, pleased that their magic worked in a similar manner to the walls. Her thoughts raced as her body acted and reacted instinctively.

How could she not be afraid of herself? Oliand had tested her, but she had no real way of knowing how strong she was. She still hadn't dared to let loose that thing that dwelled deeper in her. What if the last vision the goblet showed her came true? What if she could massacre a battlefield in one fell swoop? She was dangerous, and she had a feeling no one else suspected how much.

"How else am I supposed to be?" Neva shouted, slicing a long scratch up Emiliand's forearm with a side strike. *"I am an abomination!"*

Her voice sounded loud in the room, echoing off the walls. Out of the corner of her eye, she saw Vivizhi stiffen. The majila had been unaware of the silent conversation between her and Emiliand.

"Fine! You're right. So just because you changed in the firérite, you've lost who you once were?" Emiliand spoke as he dodged a series of kicks. "I guess we should all stay away from you in case you decide to kill us, then?"

Neva felt a growl rise in her throat and the unfamiliar sound gave her enough pause for Emiliand to knock her down. They rolled together on the floor mats, his hands trying to control hers.

"Maybe you should!" Neva said with a shove.

Emiliand barely moved as she struggled against his grip.

"The donazhi knows it! Astiand knows it!" she shouted at him. "So why are you still here? Why are you still around me?"

Neva felt tears well, and she dropped her head onto the mat in defeat. She looked into Emiliand's eyes, searching for a reason, for any explanation in which she wasn't so dangerous to others.

"Because," he gazed back at her. *"We're meant to be together. We're meant to align. Can't you feel that?* We have a connection, Neva."

She shook her head, denying the words. Her thoughts raced back to when she first met him. She had felt drawn to him, been embarrassed by the inexplicable attraction that never wavered although she tried to forget it. Theirs was a kindred connection, and she didn't want to think he might be in danger because of it.

"No," she whispered the lie between them, feeling tears trickle down the sides of her face.

"You don't mean that."

"There is no connection between us." She held her breath. She didn't want to believe him.

He was silent and still. Then, he picked himself up and left the room.

Neva rolled onto her side and curled her legs as she watched him walk out. He wasn't just angry. She had hurt him. It made her heart feel as heavy as a lead weight. If turning him away was the right thing to do, why did it hurt this much?

Vivizhi came to her side.

"You cannot push him away forever."

Neva swallowed hard. She could try. The fewer people she was close to, the less likely she would hurt them. The less likely they would die by her side.

"You need to know that what the donazhi and Astiand are doing, watching you, it's not because they're afraid of how destructive you might be," Vivizhi told her. "It's because she anticipates it, and she wants to use you. We were created for battle. Each of us is a weapon, but what you are is special. An alliad with Emiliand would help see you through it. He doesn't want to use you. He would rather be used by you."

Vivizhi's point didn't sit well with Neva because she wasn't sure she wanted to do anything of the sort. Maybe it would be better to have a friend in this, but she didn't think she could afford that luxury if it meant losing him in the end.

"I can feel it, Vivizhi." Neva was surprised by how level her own voice sounded, free of the torrential emotions raging through her. "I can feel I'll drag him down with me."

"None of us will live forever, Neva." Vivizhi was less kind, more annoyed now. "Isn't it better that we have someone to fight for? Half the Da'Valia in this clan would step onto a battlefield for you tomorrow and give their lives because we can see you're meant for something bigger."

"That's not what I want." Neva sat up. Was this supposed to be comforting? That if she asked, she could motivate the clan to go willingly to their deaths?

"I know it's not." Vivizhi's voice softened. "But there are those of us who believe in you, even if you don't believe in yourself just yet. Emiliand especially. Can you tell me — honestly — you can ignore that?"

Vivizhi triggered a memory. Neva thought again how Emiliand had shaken her hand in greeting after his match in the Tiger's Eye. How he had immediately invited her to the practice fields when she let it be known she wanted to learn to fight. He had accepted her easily — both sides, the human and the Da'Valia. He believed in her. And he accepted her. She could count the people who had embraced her knowing the truth of who she was on one hand, and they were all blood relations.

"What if I have to ignore it?" Neva asked, dismayed Vivizhi's argument was so reasonable. "What if I don't have another choice because they are watching me and aligning with anyone might be too much of a threat for them to ignore, even if it is with another half-breed?"

Vivizhi spoke slowly and with purpose. "You may certainly choose to give up simply because you're afraid, but I don't think that's what you want. I think you're a fighter, Nevazhi. I think you can deny the Da'Valia blood running through your veins no more than you can deny the desire that has brought you here each night. Are you so willing to give in to cowardice?"

Neva felt the answer swell in her chest. Neither her mother nor her father raised her to be faint of heart. She could not honor them by doing so.

"No," Neva said.

"Then you have to make this right."

Vivizhi was correct, and Neva knew it. She nodded.

"Just tell me what I have to do," Neva said.

"We'll find him at the Tiger's Eye," Vivizhi said. "I'll meet you there."

Some faces in the pub were familiar, but many were unknown, vigilant as Neva walked past. While Vivizhi had gone ahead so they wouldn't arrive together, Neva had taken a few extra moments to clean up. She had worked herself into a tangle of nerves in the meantime, but she felt better about entering the public house not looking like she had been crying.

Neva spotted Emiliand at the bar immediately. He was standing with Roland, Jorand, and several others from the Da'Voda ranks. She thought she had seen him looking her way when she walked through the door, but he wasn't looking at her now. She wanted to march up to him and pull him aside so she could explain — she had so much to apologize for — but her nerves prevented her.

She saw Vivizhi in a booth along the wall and went to join her, walking past Emiliand as the beasties started up a raunchy version of an old ballad. Neva tried but found it impossible to catch his eye as she passed.

"You're going to have to cast for him," Vivizhi said as Neva sat down. The master at arms spoke in a tone low enough that it would be difficult for others to overhear.

Vivizhi ordered drinks while that information sank in. Once the barmaid left, Neva turned to Vivizhi.

"You cannot be serious," Neva hissed.

"And why can't I be?" The brow Vivizhi raised looked dangerous.

"Because it's…" Neva searched for the right word. "It's so public."

"That's the point," Vivizhi informed her. "Trust me. I know Emiliand. What better way is there for you to show you're not afraid of yourself or of him — or of what anyone else thinks?"

"But I don't know how." An uncomfortable heat climbed Neva's neck. She didn't want to ruin this. She could imagine the eruption of laughter at her obvious inadequacy and the wrath she would face when Astiand found out about her casting.

Vivizhi frowned at her and tossed a coin to the barmaid, who had returned with two mugs of hagave. Vivizhi took a sip of hers, and Neva did the same. The liquid burned down her throat.

"You know in theory, yes?" Vivizhi asked her.

Neva nodded. Jorand had explained it to her.

"It's the same as a young girl who flirts. She's never done it before, but she approaches him and smiles. It's innate."

Innate. Right. Neva thought.

Vivizhi looked at her, waiting, but Neva stared back helplessly. She didn't know how to begin.

With a sigh, Vivizhi said, "It might help if you visualize it."

Neva took another sip of hagave knowing the drink's false bravado wouldn't hit her system before she attempted this thing. She set the mug on the table and focused on Emiliand across the room. She could see his face as he laughed with the other beasties, and she resented it. If he would look at her, it would make this so much easier.

She frowned, sat straighter, and called on her power. Raising a finger, she imagined what she wanted to happen and sent a smoke-like string of power swirling outwards, looping around the crowded floor and across the bar.

Jorand saw the cast first. He looked surprised as he spotted it, hovering above Emiliand's shoulder. He followed the line until he spotted Neva and realization dawned. Jorand grinned at her.

Neva was grateful for the support, but she hesitated before dropping the line onto Emiliand's skin, unsure.

Jorand kept quiet, but Roland nudged Emiliand with his elbow as soon as he saw the cast.

Emiliand glanced over his shoulder. His eyes landed on the wisp of power, still hovering, and skipped to find her face. She couldn't say what he saw there. A room full of eyes bore into her, analyzing every bit of this exchange. The most powerful majila they'd ever seen was casting for a toppel hilan who happened to be their best fighter.

Emiliand's gaze traced the power from where it flowed from her body to the air before him. He reached up and plucked the line before swirling it around his index finger. Roland gave an exaggerated whistle as Emiliand headed for her table.

The line shortened as he approached until, finally, he took her hand in his and it extinguished.

"Excuse me, won't you?" Vivizhi asked them, rising.

Emiliand dropped Neva's hand and slid into the vacant seat across from her. All traces of the cast were gone, but it had served its purpose.

"You were right," she blurted out as soon as Vivizhi excused herself.

He clenched his jaw, but he didn't speak, so she rushed forward.

"I've spent so much time lying about who I am that it's hard to be honest with myself," she lowered her voice. "The truth is I'm afraid. I wasn't brought up to know your ways, and ever since I got here, I've been looking over my shoulder half the time and looking at myself in the mirror the other half because I don't know where the real threat will come from."

He seemed unmoved. He probably knew as much, but she needed to say it. In this moment, she wanted nothing more than to be a majila worthy of him.

"And the truth is," she said again, gathering her courage. "The only thing that has made me feel safe is being with you and training with you. Your friendship isn't something I want to lose."

By the time she finished speaking, Neva's voice had become a low whisper. Her eyes had strayed to inspect the lines in the wood table, now she dragged them back to Emiliand.

"I've been waiting for a toppel I could align with for years," he murmured. "It's not something I take lightly."

"I know that," she agreed.

"For an alliad to work, the majila has to be responsible. I cannot align with you if you have to sneak out to be with me."

"I know that, too."

"Are you willing to commit to it?" Emiliand asked. "Are you willing to wait for me?"

Neva let out a slow breath to release the tension in her chest. If he could ask her that, they could make this work. Still, a frown creased her brow.

"Wait for you?"

"Neva, I'm leaving for the Da'Roha in a few days' time."

"But…" she faltered. Her stomach hollowing.

"I have a contract for one year of service," Emiliand reminded her. "It's a matter of honor."

"A year," she repeated. His honor was one of the things she most liked about him, but a year was a long time. A lot of things could happen. A lot of things could change.

His eyes caressed her face.

"I'm not going to align with anyone else, Neva. It will be you."

The promise rang true.

"I trust you." And she realized she did as she said the words. Of course she did. "And I'm willing to wait."

She might be extending her time under the donazhi's watchful eye by agreeing to this, but she could endure.

"Good." He relaxed in his seat.

The chatter in the bar had dimmed during their exchange, but now it started back up. Those near their table were reiterating there was an alliad forming between Roberts and Riga. From the corner of her eye, Neva spied Vivizhi slipping out the door.

"Before, what you said..." Neva swallowed hard. "It was true, but I couldn't help it. I can't help being afraid."

"Neva," his protest fell on deaf ears.

"Maybe I'm just too human. I don't know. How is it you know more about me than I do? How did you know what I was thi —"

"Neva." His interruption was sharp and serious, and she realized she was starting to ramble in a very public place.

"Let's continue this conversation elsewhere," Emiliand suggested.

"Of course," Neva agreed. She had many questions.

They crossed half the room before Neva saw him standing near the door. Arroyand had a toppel majila on one arm and a middel on the other. Neva hadn't seen him while casting or talking with Emiliand, but his would have been just a face in the crowd. It was obvious from the look in his eyes he had witnessed their exchange. Smoothly, Arroyand rearranged his expression into one oozing superiority.

"Nevazhi, what a pleasant surprise to find you here," he drawled. "Chaunzhi, Elzhi, would you excuse me for a moment."

He didn't say it like a question, moving his arms so each majila rolled off. One of them glared at Neva with creamy, dangerous eyes as she flitted away. The other majila rolled her body back to Arroyand, slinging an arm over his shoulders and pressing her boney body against his.

"But when will I get to see you again?" she moaned, obviously inebriated.

"When I say." Arroyand's eyes never strayed from Neva. The majila pouted but let one of her friends pull her away.

"Arroyand." Neva finished walking to the donazhi's aliado, and crossed her arms in front of her.

"I would love to accompany you home, my dear," he said, as sincere as ever.

"I'd rather you not," Neva told him standoffishly.

"And I wasn't really asking."

"Neva, perhaps it would be best if Arroyand did accompany you," Emiliand interjected. "I've got a few loose ends to tie up before I leave at the end of the week."

Neva could see Arroyand responding. He stood taller. Neva raised an eyebrow at Emiliand, but his gaze never moved from Arroyand.

"I'll come find you tomorrow," Emiliand dropped the words into her mind. *"It looks like you'll have to answer for this now."*

"Fine. Leave me to the donazhi's watch dogs."

"Only because I taught you how to fight them off," he reminded her.

Arroyand offered Neva his arm.

Chapter Twenty-Two

Ninth Cravell, 1632

I fear that all is lost. I've been sick for weeks. Mayhap the power I spent and the blood I lost was too much. My belly revolts and my head fills with pain. I want to do nothing but sleep. Something is wrong, and I fear Riska is approaching my door at this moment. Mayhap my power and the spell were not enough to control the Hand. I can feel it, somewhere inside of me, but I've no access to it.

— Monazhi Da'Voda-Lira

Neva ran through what felt like a hundred scenarios in her head as Arroyand led her back to Astiand's home, yet she knew when they got there, whatever played out would be scripted unto itself. She had made a choice tonight, and every night during the past few weeks, and she would have to answer for that.

Neva's instincts screamed at her as Arroyand knocked. They told her to flee the impending confrontation, but her Da'Valia half knew better. Her blood steamed like it was trapped inside a kettle over an open flame. It waited to burst forth screaming.

Miland's eyes went wide when he saw them standing at the door. Arroyand's hand maintained a steady hold on her arm.

"Take us to him," Arroyand ordered.

Miland motioned for them to enter and led them to the basement. Her heart quickened. She would have preferred any other room in the house.

There were no rich tapestries or elegant artifacts in the basement, only impenetrable stone and a collection of deadly weapons.

Neva heard Astiand rummaging through a pile of tools and blades before she saw him there at the worktable with a sharpening stone set upon it. A cup of hagave sat next to the sharpening stone, forgotten. He wore a loose shirt and a distracted look. She guessed he had been working in the subterranean room for some time.

"Astiand," Arroyand called his attention.

Astiand stood and turned upon hearing his name, and Miland took his leave of them.

"Look what I discovered at the Tiger's Eye," Arroyand purred.

Neva gathered her courage to step out from Arroyand's shadow. She raised her eyes to meet Astiand's. She could practically see his annoyance smoldering behind a stoic front.

Arroyand made a show of dropping her hand.

"I found her casting for a beastie. Surname Riga."

Astiand remained unresponsive, and it seemed to give Arroyand pause. If Arroyand was anything like her, Neva knew he must be wondering why he wasn't getting the reaction he had anticipated.

"Don't you think the donazhi will be interested to hear of it?" Arroyand prodded.

"Maybe." Astiand shrugged one shoulder. "But then I did tell our Nevazhi here that since the donazhi accepted her into the clan, she should get to know some locals."

Neva nearly gasped at the blatant lie, but she caught herself. Arroyand looked puzzled.

"I didn't expect her to frequent such an unsavory establishment as the Tiger's Eye." Astiand continued with his façade. "Shows her poor character, I suppose."

"Hm." Arroyand frowned, then smiled. "Well, at least I've delivered her from keeping bad company, eh?"

Neva glared at him.

"You know the way out, don't you, Arroyand?" Astiand gestured toward the stairs bluntly.

"Right." Arroyand turned to her. "Nevazhi, anytime you wish to socialize with the locals, remember you can always cast in my direction."

He lowered his head gracefully before heading up the stairs. Neva watched him go through slitted eyes.

As soon as he closed the door, Neva turned to Astiand.

"Astiand, I am —"

She had been about to apologize, but the livid expression on his face stopped her.

"Don't say anything. Not a single word."

If clouds could have rolled in with his voice, thunder would have echoed off the walls. She stilled, waiting for the storm to break.

Astiand looked like he was concentrating on something, so she focused on listening to Arroyand as he moved through the house. Miland was showing the hilan to the door. Neva could still hear his footsteps, ever so faintly, disappearing down the walk.

Then, he was gone.

In an instant, Astiand was lording over her, mere inches separating them.

"I told you to stay away from him!" Astiand said.

"I —"

"You really don't sense any danger in mingling with this Riga under the donazhi's rule?" The shacklay tightened and a familiar sting worked its way up her arm.

"I can take care of myself," Neva refuted, ignoring the little voice that told her he was right. They'd been so careful about keeping their training sessions under wraps. Until tonight.

"I'm not so sure you can," Astiand ground out. "She is tracking your every move. One day, your antics will force her to act."

"Let her," Neva retorted. "I'm tired of your ridiculous edict that I can't see Emiliand. If that's what the donazhi demanded, Arroyand wouldn't have believed you so easily just now. So I'm calling your bluff, Astiand."

She backed up instinctively, aware that the stairs were too far away for her to reach in a single bound and that the weapons on the wall behind him were a fool's dream. Astiand would undoubtedly prevent her from going for either, so she stopped where she was and glared at him.

"You think this is a bluff?" Incredulity entered his voice. "Do you think threatening a donazhi is a game of some sort?"

The pain climbing her arm was becoming distracting.

"Stop with the shacklay," she ordered.

Astiand looked surprised and the pain disappeared. His expression softened as he took another step toward her. He was so close, she could feel the heat radiating from his body. She licked her lips nervously. The tension between them was heightening, and she felt like they were on a precipice.

"You called my bluff," Astiand said. In a breath, his energy seemed to morph from frustration to a new emotion: desire. "That makes it my play."

No man had ever gazed at her quite how Astiand did now. It stole her breath and resurfaced the vivid memory of their kiss. It made her want to wrap her hands around his horns and share their power. It made her forget the shacklay and every other reason to be mad at him.

"No matter what I do" — he raised his hand and gently caressed her neck — "you may soon be the death of me, Nevazhi."

The way he said her name sent a delicious shiver through her. Astiand leaned in and halted, his lips less than an inch away from hers. She could almost taste him.

Neva was completely frozen now, waiting. They stayed like that, a growl building in his throat until he crushed her mouth with his, and, finally, she could taste him. His tongue invaded her mouth, sure and strong with a tinge of hagave.

Her thoughts fled, and the apprehension she felt a moment before became a distant memory.

The hand on her neck turned into a rough caress that traveled down her front and grazed the skin of her abdomen. His lips played on hers, teasing and enticing with a heady energy.

Her blood answered. It sang for him in a way that would have frightened her if she hadn't been paying all of her attention to the feel of his skin on hers.

He curled his fingers through hers and pulled her hand above them, so she remained at his mercy.

Vaguely, Neva recalled kissing Astiand before.

That had been nothing compared to this.

Before, he had been restrained and reluctant. Now, he was uninhibited and intent. He deepened his kiss. She closed her eyes and met his tongue with hers. He uncurled his fingers and slid them through her hair until they came to rest by the base of an outer horn. She mimicked the motion, aware of every strand of his shaggy mane that grazed her palm.

Astiand stroked one of her outer horns. She shuddered as heat washed over her and pooled low in her belly. She was only aware of feeling, and feeling too much. She wanted to be closer to this hilan. To this Da'Valia whose power was only a small part of him. To this hilan who was bound to the donazhi.

Gods. If Astiand thought Trinizhi would be mad about Neva consorting with Emiliand, Neva couldn't imagine how livid the donazhi would be if she saw them now.

His lips left hers and traveled to her neck, blazing a trail of tingling awareness. He sucked her earlobe into his mouth. Sparks of pain flashed from the shacklay with irregularity, but it wasn't uncomfortable anymore. It was perfect.

Neva's fingers skimmed the smooth surface of Astiand's horn and she felt his body stiffen for a moment. Then, his lips were back to coaxing hers. A current of power flowed from Neva to him and back again as they kept contact through their horns. It burned and hurt, and she didn't want it to end.

This might be wrong. It might incite Trinizhi. It might destroy Neva's shaky relationship with Emiliand. But all she could concentrate on was Astiand. He lifted her with one arm, and she wrapped her legs around his waist.

She held onto him as if her life depended on it.

Eventually, he turned their bodies to the stairs and leaned her against the hard stone. He kissed her again and again, working her wrap loose. She traced his top lip with her tongue, and their breaths mingled.

"Astiand!"

Above her, Astiand turned to stone, looking at the Da'Valia coming down the staircase. It took Neva a moment to realize the voice meant they were no longer alone.

"You bloody idiot!"

Neva registered it was Bryand standing a step above her head, a moment before the hilan's foot lashed out, connecting with Astiand's chest and sending him flying across the room.

"Nevazhi," Bryand reached down, taking her arm. "Get up. Come on."

She was halfway turned toward the scarred hilan when she heard Astiand growl from behind her. A dangerous sound. She hesitated, disoriented.

"I'll settle this with him." Bryand straightened her wrap, feeding it through her belt. "Get back to your room."

Bryand lifted her up a step and pushed her toward the door. Her feet faltered at the threshold. Maybe she should turn back. She had been a part of this, too, so whatever Bryand had to say, maybe he should say it in front of her.

"I said I would settle it. Leave now, Neva." Bryand's eyes were trained on Astiand's, and they didn't stray as he addressed her.

Neither did Astiand's, she realized. This was between them.

She closed the door behind her.

Chapter Twenty-Three

Ninth Cravell, 1632

I can only imagine how much more powerful S'donzhi must have been to direct this force. It is impossible.

— *Monazhi Da'Voda-Lira*

Neva could still smell Astiand on her skin. She attempted to go to sleep, but every time she closed her eyes, she pictured him and imagined the incredible heat they'd had between them — not to mention she could feel the tremors and hear the clamors sounding from the basement, where a Da'Valia fight raged. She was left alone to imagine the Bryand's anger and Astiand's frustration clashing. It was more than an hour before the walls stopped shaking. Finally, she slept.

As Neva went about dressing in the morning, she couldn't help but stare at her reflection. Her black eye from training with Vivizhi and Emiliand was almost gone, but she found new red lines across her back from where Astiand had reclined her against the stone steps in the cellar. Somehow, she didn't mind the marks. They were proof she hadn't imagined it all. Proof Astiand couldn't hate her completely.

At breakfast, Neva felt her cheeks flush as Astiand entered the dining room. He took a seat as far away from her as possible. He sported several fresh bruises from the night before, and Neva could have sworn she spied bloody residue near his collar. Bryand, who sat next to Neva, appeared to be as healthy as she had ever seen him — entirely healed from his run-in with the Da'Xana.

Astiand swallowed three bites of eggs, almost without chewing, before tossing his napkin on the table and leaving the room.

Neva fought to rein in her emotions as she looked at the crumpled linen. She realized with dismay that she didn't understand Astiand any better after last night, even after what they'd shared.

"He lost his mind last night," Bryand told her. "It won't happen again."

They lapsed into silence. Neva was grateful Bryand didn't attempt more conversation, but the silence in the house overwhelmed her by midday. Astiand departed shortly after breakfast, and Neva exiled herself to her room once again. It wasn't as much a show as it had been the past few weeks. Her angst was all too real. Too human. What Bryand said bothered her. What if she did want it to happen again? She wished she could braid a shield around her heart.

Neva rested on her bed and eyed the thin painted planks in the ceiling. She ran through the night before in her mind. How had so much changed so quickly? She wanted to see Emiliand again. With him, at least things were clearer. They understood each other in a way she had never experienced with anyone before.

Then what were you doing with him? Her mind shifted again to Astiand.

Feeling, she thought. She had been feeling. And whether she liked it or not, that was what she always did around Astiand. He spoke to her blood in a way not unlike Emiliand. Simply more potent — incredibly potent.

Neva groaned and banged her head against her pillow. She winced when the bruised knot on her scalp hit the headboard, and the bolt of pain reminded her more of the night before. She sincerely hoped Astiand was as equally confused about the encounter. She nearly leaped out of bed when a knock sounded at the front door.

Neva found Emiliand waiting for her in the foyer, and she smiled at him to calm her nerves. She needed to tell him about what had happened between her and Astiand.

"You survived," Emiliand greeted her.

Neva glanced quickly at Miland, who stood next to the door. She wanted to get Emiliand out of Astiand's house as soon as possible. Before her guardian returned.

"Make sure you're back before sunset," Bryand said, moving lazily down the stairs.

Neva turned to look at him. Bryand gave her a slight nod. She wasn't sure he approved of her companion any more than Astiand did, but he had her back. She took the cape Miland handed her and addressed the scarred Da'Valia with her thanks. Moments later, Neva and Emiliand headed toward the main stables.

"Vivizhi gave me the day to check our boundaries," he explained to her. "I thought you might help me?"

Her throat clogged, nerves on edge.

"What do we need to do?" Neva asked, but her mind was not on the topic at hand. Why couldn't she address what she needed to tell him?

"The donazhi wants the perimeter patrols tested," Emiliand explained. "Something about not wanting our soldiers to become relaxed in a time of peace. All we need to do is go outside the boundary and attempt to infiltrate."

Neva nodded, thinking of Bryand's miraculous escape from the Da'Xana. She supposed that because Bryand breached the Da'Xana's fortress, Trinizhi wanted to make sure the same couldn't be done to the Da'Voda enclave, especially because Bryand had made it out alive.

"It's nothing the Lynx can't handle," Emiliand added casually.

Neva stiffened and then looked around hurriedly to make sure no one was within hearing range.

"Emiliand, you can't tell anyone," she hissed at him.

"No?" he asked innocently. His playful mockery reminded her she knew his greatest secret, too. Neither of them would talk.

"You're good for a laugh," she said, rolling her eyes. "How long have you known?"

"Since you showed up in the Lynx's favorite disguise," Emiliand said.

"My glamour," Neva realized. She thought about that for a moment. "It's impossible to keep a secret from you, isn't it?"

"Not impossible," he denied. "Just very, very difficult."

"Hm." Neva crossed her arms. Perhaps that was for the best.

"So, do you want to talk about it?" Emiliand asked her abruptly.

"Talk about what?" she stalled.

He waited.

"It wasn't what I expected," she tried to explain. "At first, Astiand was angry... really angry. But that turned into something *else*."

Neva looked at him as she stressed the word so he would understand her meaning.

He did.

He stopped walking under the shade of a tree.

"So did you...?"

"No!" Neva rushed to defend herself.

"Why not?"

It was such a Da'Valian question.

"Bryand arrived unexpectedly," Neva admitted.

Emiliand waited gravely.

"And gave him a thrashing," Neva added.

"Good — that saves me the trouble," he said darkly. Then, a slow grin spread across his face. "I wish I could have seen Bryand take him on."

Neva slapped him on the shoulder, relieved by his perverse glee. It went a long way toward making her feel at ease.

"I wasn't sure how you would react," she confessed.

"Well, I don't like it," he said. His smile slowly turned to a frown. "It's dangerous to be so close to an aliado of the donazhi, and you're living with two of them, but it's your choice."

Neva was quiet as they resumed walking. Living with Astiand wasn't her choice any more than the shacklay around her wrist, but that wasn't what Emiliand was talking about.

"What we have is about power," he told her, trying to clear the air between them. "And sometimes, mating comes with sharing power, especially in alliads."

She was afraid her cheeks were as red as they felt. Yesterday, he had been a friend and sparring partner. Today, they were discussing delicate matters.

"I know," she said weakly.

"Right now, that is separate for us," Emiliand continued. "Maybe someday that will change, but until then, we don't have to make this —" he grabbed her hand and held it "— be about anything more. All right?"

They came to a stop in front of the stables, and she faced him. It still amazed her how attuned he was to others, even for someone who could read minds. She was again at ease, and she rather liked the feel of her hand in his.

"Agreed," she said.

"Good," Emiliand said. "But for the record, I would prefer it if you stayed away from Astiand as much as possible. The donazhi isn't as forgiving as some."

Neva knew he was right, yet it was difficult to hear. She trusted Bryand to keep his silence, but she worried what might happen if the donazhi discovered the attraction between her and Astiand.

"An alliad can't be broken, can it?" Neva asked, half-certain of the answer.

"Only by death," Emiliand confirmed.

Emiliand supplied Neva with one of the patrol horses. Neva was unaccustomed to riding, but he made sure she mounted correctly and had her heels down in the stirrups before they set out into the mountainous forest.

Her bruises and sore muscles weren't too uncomfortable to start, but riding the beast didn't help. She was grateful for the crisp air of Vestive, and the impressive trees provided a distraction. The trunks were more than twice as big as the pines at home. She could only wonder at how long they had been rooted in the earth. The branches were so long and thick, they still held piles of snow atop them. As the afternoon warmed, the snow melted into teardrops and cascaded in the wind.

Neva and Emiliand climbed for an hour before stopping atop a ridge where they tethered the horses to a post beside a quartz column. She listened to the animals scurrying away through the undergrowth as they passed.

"You know," Emiliand started their conversation up again. "I didn't go to your initiation."

Neva did know. She was sure she would have remembered seeing him there with the other beasties.

"I didn't go because if you were everything they said you were, I didn't want to meet you. After waiting so long to find a toppel I could align with, I didn't want to meet you knowing I would be leaving so soon."

His seriousness sat with her. What he wasn't saying directly was now he had found her, he was committed. It reminded her of something Vivizhi had told her.

"Vivizhi said something that's been troubling me," Neva confided. "She said she could tell whatever the gods have intended for me was important enough to die for, that many would be willing to do so, and that you were one of the willing."

"I would not waste my life for any trivial matter," he said softly, sensing the depth of her concern. "Vivizhi tends to see things in black and white. All or nothing."

Neva nodded, but she couldn't shake how unnerved she was.

"If it makes you feel better, I promise not to die for you," Emiliand said.

Neva was instantly and incredibly relieved. She looked down. She felt self-important to request anything from him.

"You didn't think you could get rid of me voluntarily, did you?" He nudged her with his elbow.

It would have been funnier, she thought, if she hadn't been so afraid.

"I don't know," she murmured wryly. "I'm not a mind-reader."

He didn't say anything, grinning.

"Speaking of which," Neva said, "I'd appreciate it if you could explain that to me."

He laughed. "I suppose I could," he started. "Vivizhi is the only other Da'Voda who knows what I can do. She recognized my talent in the ring many years ago, and she wanted to know how I always won.

"See, what's different about the Colavalia is they always win. No soul has ever broken through their guard. They are what prevents the living from visiting the dead and what keeps the dead from returning to this realm. Dhianz made sure Riska's guards were well-equipped."

Neva had heard about the Colavalia in a bard's song before, but the details were foggy, and she never imagined the fantastical creatures in the Dark Wood were real.

"So, it's in your blood?" Neva's curiosity piqued.

"I have no proof, but it must be from my father's side," Emiliand said. "It's the only explanation that fits."

"And no one else has guessed?" Neva asked.

"I've been careful," he replied. "When you can see inside the minds of others, especially our donazhi's, it makes one wish to be very discreet. Vivizhi was different, though. She answers to the donazhi because she thinks that's what is needed, but she has Dhianz's desires at heart. She's honorable, and she understands strategy. I could see that."

"Have you ever met the Colavalia?" Neva asked. "I mean, what about your father?"

Emiliand shrugged uncomfortably.

"Lots of Da'Valia are orphans," he deflected.

"But you're only part Da'Valia." Neva immediately wished she could take back the words. Many Da'Valia were orphaned young, and in that way, Emiliand fit in. But were Neva in his position, she would always wonder if she had a father out there somewhere who didn't know she existed. Or worse. A father who did know and didn't want her.

"Are you always listening?" she asked.

What remained of Emiliand's smile faded.

"I rarely let myself go as far into another's thoughts as I did last night, so, no, I'm not listening to your thoughts now."

For someone who wasn't reading her mind, he perceived the real question with an uncanny finesse.

"But you could if you wanted to?" Neva asked. "I mean, how does such a thing work?"

After years with only Vivizhi to confide in, Emiliand seemed eager to explain. He preferred to focus on one mind and didn't like crowds. He could hear anyone's thoughts, no matter how powerful they were, unless he was drinking. Alcohol dampened the ability. And although he hadn't dared to practice, he felt confident that he could link more than one mind together.

Emiliand tiptoed around all the toppel majilas and hilans. Some things, he said, no one wants to know.

He paused as Neva shook her head, experiencing the strangest sensation.

"What is it?" he asked.

"It's just... I always had to hide who I was," Neva said, meeting his eyes. "I thought I was alone in that for a long time. Until now."

Chapter Twenty-Four

Tenth Cravell, 1632

I was wrong. So very, very wrong. It's taken me some time to admit this and to accept what I've done. I called the Hand unto myself, but it went into it. Into the child I carry.

Benjamand's translation didn't carry the true essence of the spell. S'donzhi didn't sacrifice blood to the gods. She sacrificed a life.

I didn't know. I didn't suspect… but it's been far too long since I've bled, and I cannot deny the flutters in my belly. I cannot deny I feel the Hand within me, but it is beyond my reach.

None of this should have happened, and the fear I feel in this moment is greater than any I have ever known. May Dhianz forgive me. May he grant me mercy and be my guide in this dark hour.

— Monazhi Da'Voda-Lira

"We will cross to the other side." Emiliand motioned across a vast break in the mountain. A river down the steep mountainside below them rushed away snow melt. The trees and bushes were no longer plentiful here, among giant boulders and rocks preventing sunlight from ever reaching the ground.

"This patrol team is in charge of the northern face, from there," he pointed to one ridge and then another, "to there."

They weren't directly in the middle, but they were close.

"What's our approach?" Neva asked.

"We'll stay together until the river. I'll head back in this direction and you can try to cross. Don't forget what Vivizhi taught you about evasion, and you should be fine.

"They've had more experience with firefights, but you should be able to block what they throw at you. Wait for their attack. Standard orders are for capture. Remember, their weak spots are our weak spots, too."

Neva took another look over the edge and into the ravine. This would be a challenge. Fortunately, that was exactly what she needed to get her mind off Astiand.

Neva and Emiliand worked their way down the cliff face, sticking to the afternoon shadows to remain undetected. Emiliand directed her with hand signals, but she wasn't trained as a soldier, so could only interpret a few. She stayed close to him.

They were almost halfway down when Emiliand slowed.

"They know we're here," he said, a ring of urgency to his voice.

He sped up, and Neva followed his cue, scaling quicker. They jumped now, from boulders to shadows down the mountainside. Finally, at the base of the cliff, they came to a stop behind an enormous stone.

"They're waiting for us to cross in the open," Emiliand said. "Are you ready?"

Neva gave a quick nod and wiped her hands on her pants.

They sprang apart and scaled the mountain at full speed. For Emiliand, that was incredibly fast, and for Neva, it was only slightly slower. Emiliand headed up river and Neva turned down. She jumped as her foot hit the edge of the icy water. She flew through the air, twisting her body mid-leap to avoid the shots of power the soldiers directed at her. Landing in a crouch, Neva skidded atop a damp boulder in the middle of the river, exposed.

She spotted Kelizhi, perched on the side of the ravine, halfway up the opposing face. Jorand was directly in front of her and deftly channeling flaming shots of power. He might not have been toppel, but he made up for it with skill and speed. Neva braided her power into a shield to block his barrage and then sent a burning wave at him, knocking him off his feet. Still, Neva moved, turning and altering her speed to avoid Kelizhi's more pointed attacks.

Neva reached the other side of the river and jumped across three boulders in a matter of seconds, dropping behind a line of rock to shield her from Kelizhi's view. Neva's landing jarred her bones, but she made it stick soundlessly. As long as she was behind the line of rocks, neither Jorand nor Kelizhi would know where to send another attack.

Neva calculated the best routes.

Just like the old days, she thought. Outnumbered but not outdone. Not yet, anyway.

Jorand had recovered, and she could hear him as he climbed. She didn't like being between him and Kelizhi, but Neva couldn't help it.

Neva counted to three and jumped from her hiding place, her braided shield her only protection. Kelizhi had moved farther up the ravine, but her sharp shots still came from the same direction, so Neva avoided them easily.

Neva shoved two more attacks in Jorand's direction. He blocked one too late and was sent flying back to the river's edge, far enough away so his power would burn out before reaching her. Kelizhi had a talent for distance, so Neva had to keep fighting the majila's attacks until she worked her way up the mountain.

Neva glanced up, ignoring the blast that exploded on a rock next to her as she arrived at the same plane as Kelizhi. Neva was nearing the tree line. If she made it that far, she could reach the top of the ravine.

While Neva was looking ahead, she missed Kelizhi changing the direction of her attack. Instead of sending shots of power at Neva, Kelizhi targeted the edge of the cliff at its apex.

Less than ten shots shattered enough of the stone so the cliff fractured and splintered off. Rocks of all sizes tumbled down the ravine. Neva gave Kelizhi an annoyed look and sent dual blasts of power in her direction. The majila captured the first and buckled under the weight of the second as it pushed her and her defenses to the ground.

Neva charged up the ravine, toward the trees. Her shield was taking too much energy, so she dropped it, locking her eyes on the rocks falling in her direction. Emiliand had been telling her the truth when he said the patrol team wasn't cleared for killing on sight, but Kelizhi was doing plenty to capture her.

Neva could have run back and ducked behind the line of rock again where the stone avalanche couldn't reach her, but, thanks to Vivizhi's training, she knew that was where the patrol team wanted her to go to trap her between their forces.

She ascended in leaps, blasting apart the rocks that neared her so nothing remained in her path. Finally, she flung herself into the shadows of the trees and ran for the ridge Emiliand had marked as her destination.

She broke free of the tree line at a dead run, and a sharp blow slammed into her chest.

She smacked hard onto the ground, and a heavy wooden stave came to rest on her throat.

Neva blinked at the Da'Valia in charge of the weapon. The afternoon sun glared down at them, obscuring Neva's view, but she could see enough. She had been defeated. She dropped her head back to the ground with a groan, realizing how artfully Kelizhi had driven her to the soldier above her. Neva had been too preoccupied with Kelizhi and Jorand to recognize the additional threat. Word would travel, but Neva was glad Vivizhi hadn't been there to witness her failure.

It took a moment before Neva found her breath again. Her chest stung from the force of the blow.

"Hanazhi!" Neva recognized Emiliand's voice from somewhere in the trees.

"Hanazhi, you can let her go." He got closer. "She was helping me with a border check."

The quarterstaff disappeared, and a hand appeared to help her up. Once righted, Neva took a better look at the majila who had brought her down.

Hanazhi didn't look like many other Da'Valia. She had a striking red coloring to her hair and horns. She wore the Da'Voda's standard starched green military uniform, but it looked wrong on her, as if she was meant to wear better things.

"We suspected we were going to be tested," Hanazhi said gruffly. "Didn't think we'd have the Power from Glacier Pass to contend with."

"You contended all right," Neva said, rubbing her chest. *You knocked me on my ass.*

Emiliand arrived with Roland and another majila whom he introduced as Mazhi. Mazhi was of the quiet variety, a middel by judge of her horns, and serious. She was older by more than ten years, Neva guessed.

Roland filled Mazhi's silence with enough enthusiasm, and she didn't seem to mind.

"Nevazhi!" Roland greeted her. He was still a little out of breath. "Astiand let you live?"

"Apparently," she said wryly.

"I thought when Arroyand showed up you were done for," Roland continued.

"Thanks," Neva said dryly, hiding that she had assumed the same.

Roland gave a toothy smile, catching his breath, then turned to Emiliand, wanting to know more about the donazhi's order for the border test. Emiliand filled them in as they waited for Jorand and Kelizhi to join them. As Emiliand talked, Neva marveled at how Bryand might have infiltrated the Da'Xana alone. He must have been skilled to accomplish such a feat undetected until his departure.

"I knew I had you there," Roland was telling Emiliand when Jorand and Kelizhi reappeared.

Kelizhi rolled her eyes appropriately, walking up behind him.

"Did you really, Roland, or did you make Mazhi do your work for you, as usual?" Kelizhi asked.

Neva spied a modest smile from Mazhi.

Kelizhi screeched as Roland picked her up and slung her over his shoulder.

"Put me down!" Kelizhi made the furious request several more times before he agreed.

The soldiers quizzed Emiliand about the details of his service with the Da'Roha as they walked back to the horses, crossing a rope and wood bridge upstream.

"So what are you going to do?" Jorand asked Emiliand. They both were sweating heavily and Jorand was wiping his brow with a handkerchief. "I mean, we've had you your whole life, so we're glad to be rid of you, but Neva has had you — what — one sunrise?"

"She doesn't have me yet," Emiliand pointed out, puffing his chest. "She has to wait a year for that privilege, once I've finished my service with the Da'Roha."

"I'm holding my breath in anticipation of calling you my own," Neva said, playfully mocking his peacock display.

Her tone was sarcastic, but as Emiliand looked back at her, they both realized her words were true. Emiliand glanced at the sky before dropping back to swing his arm across her shoulders.

"See?" Emiliand said to Roland. "Who wouldn't want to align with this?"

They all laughed.

The walk back was the best time Neva had with Emiliand before he left for the Da'Roha. She committed it to memory, unsure what he would encounter during their time apart. The Da'Roha jumped from one conflict to another. Although she tried not to, she dwelled on what the next year could hold for him even more than she worried over her own future.

"I got you something," Emiliand told Neva after their last training session together a few nights later. They had stopped to part ways at the road that would lead her back to Astiand's home. A light wind flickered the power Emiliand ignited in his palm. The dark flame illuminated a silver necklace with a charm in the shape of a flaming sun nestled in a circle of intricate knots. He held the delicate chain out to her.

"You bought me a necklace," Neva stated.

The gesture felt so intimate. No one had ever bought her jewelry before — probably because she would never have allowed them to do so.

"Spelled," Emiliand said. "So I can find you in a year's time, no matter where you are."

Neva opened her mouth, then closed it. She had been troubled by the fear that something would change when they were apart, or that she would move on from the enclave by the time his service was complete. Emiliand must have seen it in her mind, and his keepsake was the perfect answer.

"I don't have anything for you," Neva admitted, wishing she had thought of it.

"You could give me a kiss," Emiliand said mischievously. "To remember you by."

He was only partly joking, and Neva knew it, but she couldn't deny she had thought about kissing him as they trained together and wondered what it would be like. A year seemed like a long time not to find out.

Before she lost her nerve, Neva took the necklace and pressed her lips against his softly. She pulled away.

"Read my mind," Neva told him, looking deep into his eyes. Back home, she never let herself get this close to anyone. This meant something to her. *"Enough to remember me by?"*

"More than enough," Emiliand said. "Here, let me do the honor."

Emiliand took the necklace and fastened the chain behind her neck. She shivered at the touch of his fingers on the sensitive skin.

"Good night, Neva," he whispered in her ear.

She closed her eyes hard. This was goodbye.

"Farewell, Emiliand," Neva whispered back.

When she turned around, he was gone.

Emiliand and the other beasties set out on the same day Bryand and Arroyand left. The donazhi's aliados departed with a small contingent of trusted soldiers to track down the Da'Foha, saying they were escorting the beasties to the Da'Roha. Whether the Da'Voda believed the story, Neva couldn't say.

Astiand continued to avoid Neva as if she carried a plague, which was fine with her because it gave her more time to continue working with Vivizhi without arousing his suspicions. He was rarely home, spending more time out of the house than inside of it.

But Vivizhi was often busy, and with Emiliand gone and Astiand keeping his distance, Neva had to admit she felt lonely. She didn't even have Bryand there to visit. Trying not to dwell, Neva continued reading her mother's journal. She liked her mother's problems better than her own for one reason: She knew how Monazhi's story ended.

Finally, Neva was forced to come to a stop. The journal had concluded with her mother still among the Da'Xana, searching through abbreviated histories. Neva gave a heavy sigh when she flipped the last page. She felt like she was losing her mother all over again.

Neva thought about her father. She missed him, too. She felt alone among the Da'Voda now more than ever. Neva felt a prickling behind her eyes as a blanket of melancholy wrapped around her.

She rested her hand on the leather-bound journal, trying to remember the details of her mother's face and failing. The picture in her mind was so basic, it could have represented almost any majila.

Neva felt tears well, and she couldn't stop them from falling.

One dropped on an open page, smearing the ink. Neva rubbed it with her thumb, but that only made it worse. Another tear fell. She wiped this one more carefully. Still, the letters bled into a puddle.

She frowned as the ink spread and separated, slowly forming a new set of characters, more words, a sentence, and then two. Against her will, her power flared, and the journal absorbed the flame. Neva dried her eyes in haste and looked at the book in wonder.

There was more to her mother's story.

Neva had tried to ignore the part of her mind still questioning why Astiand had the book under his roof. Now, her curiosity was rekindled. The journal had something more to tell her, but the partial words that appeared on the page were difficult to make out, and they had no meaning without their counterparts.

Neva jumped off her bed and snuck across the hall to the washroom. Miland always kept a basin of water set out. She wet a cloth and ran it over the pages with one hand while holding a small flame next to the book in her other palm. The spelled journal responded to the water and absorbed her power, revealing new words upon the pages.

Neva marveled at her mother's spell. No one in their right mind would put liquid near a manuscript, nor hold an open flame next to the fragile paper.

Page by page, Neva coated the sheets. By the time she was halfway through, her hands were shaking with excitement. When she finished, she checked to make sure the hall was empty before returning to her room.

For hours, Neva sat engrossed by the window. Revelations upon revelations had her mind in a whirlwind. Oliand had said the donazhi and Monazhi were adversaries, but now Neva stared at Trinizhi's name and a chill scurried down her back like a parade of mice claws. Adversaries had been too weak a word. They had been enemies.

Neva frowned as she read of Dhianz's Mouth, Eye, and Hand. They were supposed to be akin to myths, hidden from the gods. If they were real and attainable, that could mean the redemption of their people. But Monazhi couldn't have been right. If Neva's mother had found any of the prongs of the Trishula… Something would have had to have gone terribly wrong for that knowledge to have been lost.

Or hidden? Neva rushed to continue reading and was given pause when her father's name caught her attention. It was infinitely odd to read about her father through her mother's eyes.

Neva's throat constricted. For as long as she could remember, her father's leg had been a source of pain and hardship, and now she knew, without doubt, who was responsible for that burden. It was Trinizhi, who Neva had allowed to mark her neck, to brand her as a Da'Voda answerable to none other.

She felt sick. Why hadn't her father said anything? But she forced herself to continue reading. She thought she knew the ending to this story, of her mother finding and falling in love with her father, but she had a sinking feeling as the journal progressed, as if she should have known there was more to it all along.

"Great Dhianz," Neva finally said aloud.

She was the Hand? Her mother had sacrificed her to the gods? What did that mean? Oh, how wrong the Da'Valia had been. She wasn't chosen by the gods. She had been *sacrificed to them.*

Neva closed the journal, stunned. She felt oddly removed from the story, as if she wasn't the half-breed child that took her mother by surprise, as if she might still be able to tell herself she was somehow human.

But the truth was, she couldn't. She had access to more power than any other Da'Valia, and she had a double set of horns to prove it.

Gooseflesh rose on her arms. She wasn't like her mother. Neva didn't just sense the power of the Hand within her — it was there for the taking. She could use it. She felt certain. She hadn't dared to do so, but instinct told her if she dug into the deep recesses of her mind and beckoned it, the power of the Hand would answer her call.

She was Dhianz's Hand.

She swallowed, her mouth dry. This was a secret she must keep at all costs.

Neva committed the details of her mother's journal to memory and burned the book so they might remain lost. She was keeping many things from Trinizhi and Astiand, and Neva feared it might be only a matter of time before they caught on. Her heart was in her throat when Astiand sought her out in the library at midday a few days later. They were destined for a confrontation as soon as he discovered the book was missing from his safe, and tension now rose every time they were in the same room together.

"The donazhi wants to see you," Astiand told her, leaning against the doorframe, his brow furrowed. Pipe smoke billowed around him before fading. "Now."

He looked similar to when she first saw him, Neva thought, remembering him at the House of Trescony on the donazhi's business. His movements with his pipe were slow and purposeful, and she wondered if he did that to control the undercurrent of nervous energy she sensed in him.

"Why?" Neva asked. She relaxed upon confirming he didn't know about the journal, but had the donazhi somehow discovered what it contained?

"I'm not sure." Astiand's frown deepened. Knowing him as well as she did, he didn't like being kept in the dark. "Something unexpected."

"Is it…" Neva didn't know how to ask if the donazhi had found out about their moment of passion. She almost hoped that was it, as long as the donazhi didn't know Neva harbored the Hand.

Astiand frowned at her harder.

"No. Let's go."

"Should I change?" she asked, looking down at her inelegant garb. She was wearing one of the simplest uniforms she had found in her room. It was comfortable but a couple inches too short around her ankles.

"We will not keep her waiting," he said, tossing Neva a cape.

Neva slung the cape over her shoulders as they stepped outside, wondering if he was always in a foul mood where the donazhi was concerned. The sense of urgency around Astiand was putting her on edge. The other times she had gone before the donazhi, he had made sure she was presentable.

Astiand escorted her, as always, to the meeting room of which Trinizhi seemed so fond. Neva suspected Trinizhi chose the room because its grandiose design served to intimidate. The donazhi was sitting on her elevated throne with soldiers guarding her on both sides.

"Nevazhi." Trinizhi's piercing eyes locked on Neva as soon as she and Astiand stepped foot inside the door.

As they approached the throne, their footsteps echoed in the space. Neva noticed Trinizhi's mouth was set in a grim line, and although the donazhi didn't have many wrinkles, she was dangerously close to developing a line between her eyebrows.

"I'm hoping you can help me with something," Trinizhi spoke coolly.

Neva could practically feel tension radiating off Astiand next to her. She could only imagine his response if she angered Trinizhi. Neva would have to be careful here for more reasons than one.

"Of course, Donazhi," Neva said, adjusting to the hostile environment.

"I believe I have something of yours," Trinizhi said. Her hands gripped the arms of her cathedra.

Neva looked up to see Trinizhi gesture to a soldier, who opened the door in the corner of the room. Two soldiers carried in a body — unconscious, bound, and gagged — and dropped it on the floor in front of Neva.

It was human.

Chapter Twenty-Five

Eleventh Cravell, 1632

*Even with the lines of power in my family, I worry the Hand would be
too much for a half-breed to control. I worry it would burn this child from
the inside out.*

*Benjamand owes me nothing — he knows now what transpired between me
and Shaun — but he will help me protect my child. The rest is up to me.*

*I will keep this baby far from Trinizhi and her scheming, and from all the
clans. Not that they would have anything to do with me once it becomes
apparent I have, indeed, mixed our blood with that of humans.*

— Monazhi Da'Voda-Lira

Neva kept her facial features tranquil despite the horror rising inside
her. Her eyes raked over the body in front of her while she tried to
look disinterested. She wasn't sure what Trinizhi's next play would
be, but Neva knew enough to infer she was in big trouble.

Adam, how did you find me? Neva wondered as she looked him over. It was
true Adam was an excellent tracker, but the Da'Voda enclave was hidden in a
remote location for a reason. They valued their autonomy and the natural
defense of seclusion. No wonder the donazhi looked so furious.

Adam was bound and gagged, but he was breathing, Neva discovered with relief. His hair was longer than she remembered, and rugged stubble lined his jaw. She deduced some form of magic must have knocked him out because he didn't have a mark on him. That, she imagined, would change.

"I'm not sure what you want me to say," Neva said slowly.

"Well, is it yours?" Trinizhi asked.

If anyone else had posed the question, Neva's answer would have been 'no.' Adam wasn't hers in a sense of ownership. But this question had more stacked behind it. This was a matter of responsibility, and although she didn't know what she was taking responsibility for, she knew how she needed to respond. Adam's life may well be on the line.

"Aye," Neva said finally. "He is mine. He was helping tend my family after I left home."

"And do you know why it would come here?" Trinizhi asked.

"No, Donazhi," Neva said.

"Would you care to venture a guess?" Trinizhi suggested.

"No, Donazhi," Neva replied again.

Trinizhi set her smooth jaw in a hard line.

"It is my duty then. Nevazhi Da'Voda-Roberts, you will receive one hundred lashings at dawn for this violation of clan laws."

Neva sucked in a breath, preparing to defend herself. Astiand's shacklay tightened in warning.

"Unless…" Trinizhi cocked her head to the side, tapping a fingernail on the arm of her throne. "Unless you would rather the human received the punishment directly? I would be willing to issue such a directive; although, I doubt it would survive."

"No." Neva wasn't about to allow Adam's death. "I will gladly bear his punishment, if you think that's what he deserves."

"If?" Trinizhi's voice bordered on disgust. "It most certainly is. Are you aware of the threat your human poses to the clan?"

"Threat?" Neva did a double take. Adam was hardly a threat to the Da'Voda. She tried desperately to think of something to placate the donazhi. "He's weak and unimportant."

"I am counting on that. I sincerely hope your human will not be missed,

Nevazhi." Trinizhi's face was set in an angelic mask as she addressed the guards next. "Lock him in the dungeon."

The soldiers moved to pick up Adam.

"Wait! Please, don't." Neva took a step forward to gain Trinizhi's attention again.

"Do not test me," the donazhi's words were halting and laced with ice. "We protect the location of our stronghold for a reason. I cannot allow your human to leave."

The soldiers continued without pause, hefting Adam and carrying him out.

"But whatever he knows, he's not going to tell anyone!" Neva protested. "I'll make sure of it."

Trinizhi wasn't listening.

"Astiand, control your ward so I don't have to," the donazhi said. "I'm counting on you to make sure she arrives here before the sun rises tomorrow. Her punishment will be carried out in front of the troops' morning gathering and I will reassure my people of our seclusion."

Astiand took Neva's hand and gently pulled her to his side. It was the first time he had touched her since that night in the basement.

"Get out of here, now," he said. "It's already done."

"But —"

"Now!" He didn't shout, but he said the order with such authority that she obeyed.

Neva spun around and hurried from the building. Free from its walls and Trinizhi's sight, she ran to find the soldiers who took Adam. She couldn't let them do this.

She found them carrying him not far from the bottom of the hill. Adam was rousing in their arms.

"Adam!" she shouted.

She was close enough to see he would have responded if he could have. His eyes darted around frantically. Old self-doubt cringed deep within her. She knew what he would see when he looked at her. Would he recognize her?

"Please," she said as she placed her body in front of the soldiers, walking backwards as they continued on. "Please, let him go. He didn't do anything!"

One of the soldiers pushed her. She stumbled back, still close enough she could see the fear register in Adam's eyes.

"We don't answer to you," the soldier said gruffly. "If you have an issue, take it to the donazhi."

Neva's steps faltered. Panting, she watched the soldiers carry Adam away.

"Don't fear, Adam," she said, raising her voice so he could hear her. "I'll fix this."

She just wished she knew how.

"She ordered them to lock him up!" Neva couldn't keep the raw emotion from her voice as she barged into Astiand's home to find Miland in the foyer. He stood there silently for a moment, looking at her. She saw a kindness in his dark eyes but found it impossible to focus on that.

"Trinizhi threw Adam in the dungeon!" Neva paced, the door still open behind her. She knew she couldn't seek out Trinizhi. To do so would be to invite more punishment, either unto herself or Adam. And it wasn't practical to harass the Da'Voda soldiers. They had their orders. But she needed to talk with Adam, to see why he had come all this way. What could be going on back home that would bring Adam to track her down and put himself in harm's way?

"Can you help me?" Neva asked Miland.

He closed the door and inclined his head, turning toward the kitchen for her to follow. There, she filled him in on what had happened and then allowed herself to take a breath, waiting to see what he would say, if he would say anything. He moved methodically around the space, retrieving a red apple from a large canvas sack in the pantry and slicing it into slivers for them to share.

"Your friend will be stripped of all weapons and assigned a cell in the dungeons before you may request a visit," Miland said in his raspy voice.

"How long will that take?" Neva asked.

"At least an hour," Miland said. "You must bide your time until then."

As he leaned on the wood-top counter across from her, she realized this was the first time they had conversed on the same level. He was usually tending to one of Astiand's demands, but a mutual respect had grown between her and Miland. Neva felt certain she could depend on him.

"Can I ask you a question," Neva swallowed, her gaze unintentionally straying to his sheared horns, "and have you answer, truthfully?"

"I will not share with you the details of my gelding," Miland said as if he expected her to broach the subject again. "The punishment they dealt me is my own to suffer."

"It's not that!" Neva exclaimed. "I wanted to ask you how you knew about my mother's journal."

Miland held her gaze.

"It was in Astiand's library for years," Miland told her. "For a period, he would pore over it for nights on end. I believe there is something in your mother's writings of importance to the donazhi and her aliados. The night you arrived here, Astiand moved the book from the library to his safe."

Neva was quiet for a moment. Astiand's resolve to keep her removed from details of her mother's life was infuriating. But what was more significant, if he had spent so long reading the journal, he might have been looking for the hidden entries she had discovered. It made sense. If everything her mother wrote was true, Trinizhi did not give up easily.

Neva felt determination come over her. Determination to get away from him and Trinizhi. Determination to keep the Hand far from their evil plotting.

"I'll leave tonight," she said, finally. "We will disappear."

As she spoke, Neva realized she was surer than ever. She was escaping with Adam. Before the donazhi could use Neva for her own agenda. Before the donazhi delivered her punishment for Adam's trespass.

Monazhi hadn't been able to trust the Da'Valia. Neva couldn't believe it had taken her so long to see she couldn't trust them either.

"Leave?" Miland asked. "Where will you go?"

"I don't know." Neva thought, formulating a plan. "I need to talk with

Adam and find out why he's come. I'll escort him safely back to Glacier Pass and I'll get as far away as possible, so even if the donazhi or Astiand wishes to find me, they won't be able to."

"You will have to cover your tracks."

"I will," Neva said. Adam could help her.

"You will need to move quickly."

"I will," Neva said again, a little perturbed.

"Even with the human?"

This would be harder with Adam involved. Neva couldn't deny it.

"I'm afraid this will be more difficult than you might anticipate," Miland said reasonably. "Your value cannot be underestimated. If either the donazhi or Astiand senses your mind, they will stop you before you've begun."

Miland polished off the last of the apple slices and waited for her reaction.

"You're right," she said finally.

Vivizhi had warned her that the donazhi might seek to use Neva's power for her own gain, and Trinizhi would be furious at the additional breach in security. Neva would have to be careful to make sure the donazhi and her alliad never found her. If they did, her punishment wouldn't only consist of lashings at dawn.

Neva knew one thing for certain: she couldn't do this alone.

"Will you help me?" she asked Miland for the second time.

"I already am," he rasped.

"All right. Then here's what we are going to do…" Neva laid out a course of action and Miland changed it where necessary. At the end of the hour, they set out to visit Adam and apprise him of her plan.

The walk to the dungeon, which was built at the base of one of the hills on the outskirts of the mountain village, was quick and silent other than the crunching of gravel beneath their feet. Neva was glad to have Miland at her side.

They arrived at the entrance to the dungeon, where stone walls arched from the ground to well overhead to protect an entry chamber from the weather. Inside the space was a raised portcullis and two soldiers standing guard. Neva approached them and requested to talk with Adam. After signing in, a guard led her and Miland into dark tunnels adorned by skulls of the Da'Voda.

The soldier dealt many deaths in his life. The essence of it almost rolled off him like an invisible fog. More visible were the markings on his belt, indicating numerous kills. He marched them deeper into the caves. Shadows washed over them as they made their first turn into the tunnels, passing cell doors made of massive slabs of black stone. Neva couldn't tell if the stone doors were originally that color, or if everything down here was merely coated in earthen grime. Oil lamps posted at regular intervals along the wall provided substandard sources of light. The air was stale and moist, and as cold as the height of Fireside.

"You don't have long, so be quick about it," the guard ordered as he placed his hand upon one of the black stone doors.

Neva narrowed her eyes and watched the telltale glow of magic pulsate around his hand before he pulled it open. She tucked that information away. She would use it later.

A stench so foul it made her want to throw up wafted from the cell. Neva switched to breathing through her mouth, but the reek of excrement and decay had already singed her nostrils. She ducked to enter the cell, leaving Miland outside with the guard. Neva called upon her human glamour, fidgeting with the charm on its chain around her neck once again. Adam had seen her true appearance for a moment earlier, but she would bet he would be more at ease if she appeared as her old self. And if she was honest, she would be more comfortable with it, too.

The door slammed behind her, sending the dungeon into a pitch black. She blinked and waited a moment for her eyesight to adjust. A figure slouched against the wall.

"Adam?" she called.

He jerked in response, and Neva rushed to his side. She nearly slid on the slick substance covering the rocky floor.

"Adam, are you all right?" Neva crouched next to him and pulled at his shoulder so he was facing her.

He appeared to be in good condition.

"Neva!" Adam exclaimed. "Thank the gods. You don't know how glad I am to see you."

He wrapped her in a hug. She froze, and her mind rushed to catch up. It felt strange to be touched by a human. Why did it feel so strange? Had she changed so much so a simple hug didn't seem natural anymore? She pushed the thoughts away and returned the embrace. For just for a moment, she let herself be human. Then, she pulled back.

"Can you get me out of here?" Adam asked, the chains around his ankles clanking as he sat up.

"I will. Both of us are going to get out of here."

"Good. Your father… Gods, Neva, your family needs you right now."

"You'll have to tell me about them later — once we have you out of this place," Neva said. "I only have a short time before the guard will ask me to leave, so I have to do this."

Neva knelt and blasted each of the manacles around his ankles with raw power. The metal held, so she attempted it again and again until the screws broke and the cuffs finally fell away. Adam watched her as she worked, and she avoided looking at him, not wanting to see the fear she knew she would see. Once she finished, she held her breath to see if the guard had become suspicious. No noise came from the other side of the door.

"I will return later tonight," Neva told Adam, watching the door. "Be ready to go, because we're going to have to run fast."

"I'd follow you out of here right now if you'd let me," Adam told her.

"I know you would," Neva said. *This is going to work. This has to work*, she thought. "I'll be back."

The door groaned as it swung open behind her, and Neva knew her time was up. Neva followed the guard out, looking forward to a time when she could put this place — all of it — behind her.

As they moved through the dark hallways, Neva and Miland noted intersections and cell doors. When Neva returned, she would need to know where to go without a guard to guide her. With one shot at memorizing the layout of the dungeon, Neva could only pray the gods would be on her side.

At Astiand's, Neva collected two swords — Lindzhi's former blade and another for Adam, which she took from Astiand's armory. It might not be much against Da'Valia, but it was better than leaving Adam unarmed. Neva gave Lindzhi's ivory chest to Miland to pack, handed over her sword for sharpening, and excused herself. She had one more stop to make.

Neva found Vivizhi at the north practice yards. The master at arms regularly made rounds, and Neva found her overseeing hand-to-hand combat. Neva caught Vivizhi's eye from near the grappling yard before making her way to the indoor training room where they had so often met. She knew the majila would find her.

She didn't have to wait long.

"You do realize that bright ball in the sky is the sun, don't you?" Vivizhi asked in an irritated tone.

"No one saw me," Neva said, not certain it was true. She had been so preoccupied, she had neglected to use her invisibility glamour.

"I saw you in the yard, which means someone else did as well," Vivizhi said bluntly.

"I apologize, but I didn't have a choice," Neva said. She sounded melodramatic, but she couldn't help it.

Vivizhi sighed.

"Well, what is it? I supposed you didn't risk exposure here for anything inconsequential."

"I'm leaving," Neva told her. "I'm leaving the Da'Voda. Tonight."

Vivizhi raised a brow at her.

"And what, pray tell, brought this about?" Vivizhi asked.

"It's complicated." Neva searched for the right way to explain. "I don't know all the details, but something ill has befallen my father. They need me back home."

"And the donazhi won't want you to go," Vivizhi said.

"I know," Neva said. "Her aliado doesn't even like it when I leave the house."

"It's a good thing you're a fighter, Nevazhi, because you're going to have to fight your way out. The donazhi doesn't let things go so easily." Vivizhi crossed her arms.

Neva smiled a little. Vivizhi didn't know the half of it.

"I don't expect her to," Neva said. "I just need one thing."

"What?" Vivizhi asked with a frown.

"I need to leave by the main gate." Neva knew she was asking a lot, and if she needed the favor from anyone else, she wouldn't have asked. But Vivizhi talked about the Da'Voda being supportive of Neva's fate, and Neva had a feeling it was more than idle chatter. Still, in Vivizhi's own words, she wasn't a traitor.

"You need to leave by the main gate?" Vivizhi repeated. Doubt laced her voice.

"Please, Vivizhi?" Neva asked. "But it must be done discreetly. No one can know you were involved."

No other escape would do. If Neva didn't leave by the main gate, she could never get Adam away in a hurry. The Da'Voda border patrol teams were keen sentinels. Neva knew that first-hand.

"I may be able to arrange it," Vivizhi said.

Neva let out a tense breath.

"You're a true friend," Neva told her.

"Your family needs you now," Vivizhi said. "Family is a luxury many of us don't have. Besides, I have a feeling one day you will make every effort to be there for the Da'Voda when we need you, too."

Chapter Twenty-Six

Twelfth Cravell, 1632

*I never imagined I would part from my people this way, and on the eve of
the summit no less.*

*I am determined to start a new life with Shaun and my child, who shall
never know of the Hand. Benjamand has made sure of that.*

*I am not quitting. This is my chance to make an unexpected play and to
change the outcome. If that outcome would otherwise have Trinizhi at the helm
of all clan politics, I know I am doing the right thing.*

*Dhianz has made his will clear to me, and I pledge to protect his Hand as
my own. Because now it is mine as well. My child.*

— Monazhi Da'Voda-Lira

Neva had always loved the thrill of thieving. Being a thief allowed
her to use her father's teachings and still conceal her natural gifts.
But the thrill. That was what kept her in the family trade. She never
felt as alive as when she was doing something forbidden.

That same rush livened her now, sending a heady energy through her as
she shoved her belongings into the sack she had brought with her from Glacier
Pass.

Neva and Vivizhi had quickly worked out the details for Neva's departure.

Her timeline was terribly tight, but she had no other options. She thanked the gods she had Miland on her side. He was busy buying food, healing tonic, and other supplies for her. He had also agreed to send an order to ready Astiand's carriage, which was undeniably the biggest risk he was taking for her.

Astiand, conveniently, had not yet returned, so Neva penned him a succinct note. She folded and placed it on her bed, where it was obscured by the pillows she had artfully arranged. If he looked in on her tonight, she hoped he would think she was sleeping.

> *"Astiand —*
>
> *You were right. My blood is tainted. I cannot stay where I am not accepted. To try to be a part of this clan would be a constant reminder I do not belong.*
>
> *There is nothing you or anyone else can do to change my thoughts on this. The human that came here today deserves his freedom, and so do I. I am taking the carriage to find somewhere no one will know what I am, if there is such a place."*

Looking at her handiwork, Neva added her signature with a flourish. It might have been a futile effort, but she hoped Astiand would take her message at face value. That if he or anyone else came after her, they wouldn't go first to Glacier Pass.

"I'll make sure everything is ready," Miland told her as she joined him downstairs at the servants' entrance. "Be careful."

"Miland, why do this for me?" Neva asked.

"I am doing this as much for myself as for you," Miland said. "You stood up for me after your firérite when I brought you too much food. It might have been a small thing, but I think it made an impression on Astiand. Otherwise, he likely would have sent me to Arroyand's residence."

"Would that have been so bad?" Neva frowned.

"When the donazhi decreed that my years of servitude be devoted to Astiand, I got the safest of her three aliados," Miland said. "He has sent me to Arroyand's in anger before, and it is something I would rather not relive."

"You mean Arroyand..." Neva was confused. "Does he hurt you?"

Neva thought back to when Trinizhi and Arroyand had visited to discuss alliad matters. She remembered the lingering caress Arroyand had bestowed upon Miland's cheek and the odd feeling it left in her stomach. She had heard the rumors and seen the way he treated other Da'Valia, too.

"Even when battles are not fought in the bedroom, they can be started there," Miland said, shaking his head. "Arroyand is a double-edged sword, and when you care for him to begin with, it only makes it worse."

The depth of his words hit Neva with force. It was apparent Miland cared for Arroyand, but it wasn't reciprocal. Arroyand would take advantage of Miland's body and mind given the chance, and with her plan, that opportunity might soon arise.

"So when Astiand realizes he no longer has my mother's journal, and when Trinizhi figures out I involved you in my escape? Won't they do something worse than sending you to Arroyand again? I mean, compare what we are doing now to serving me too much food!"

Neva's mind boggled at the implication. She was trusting Miland with her life and Adam's, but in doing so, was she also condemning him to death?

"I am aware of the consequences." Miland's steely resolve hinted at the Da'Valia he might have once been. "This is my choice."

"But you could come with us." Neva protested despite knowing better. "Come. Wherever I go, and I'll protect you. You know I have enough power to do it. Or take half the coin for yourself and go wherever you want."

"It's not a question of whether you or anyone else can protect me," Miland said. "When I needed to do that for myself, I failed, and now I pay the price. This is my home, whether or not I like it. Think of this, my helping you, as the one thing I have ever truly been responsible for in direct defiance to the donazhi. We're not even, she and I, but this I can live with or die for."

"You need to do exactly as I say," Neva spoke to Adam in hushed tones near the entrance of his cell. His shackles lay discarded on the rocky ground. It was so dark, she would have to be both their eyes.

"Not a problem," Adam promised. His brown eyes were wide and his breathing was quick.

"As soon as we get out the door, follow me closely but keep your back to the walls. Understand?"

Adam nodded.

Neva handed him the short sword she had commandeered from Astiand's armory. The weapon had been a pain to sneak in, but she had managed it, thanks to Uncle Morty's tutelage.

"Only use this if you have to," Neva warned Adam.

She didn't want him joining in any fights where he couldn't hold his own. Unfortunately, he would be outmatched in anything on Da'Voda land because their power tipped the scales. Adam's hands shook as he threaded the scabbard onto his belt.

Neva had been admitted to the dungeon as a visitor after shift change, which she hoped would allow their escape to go undiscovered for longer. They would have to travel as quickly as possible on the mountain roads before deviating to the main highway. Trinizhi, Neva was sure, would send someone after them. Adam's knowledge of their location was too important, and the donazhi considered Neva a prize.

But she wasn't anyone's prize, and Neva would do everything in her power to make sure Adam made it away from this mess. If they could make it to Glacier Pass and call upon the protective magic Flynn had paid for, Neva felt certain the Da'Voda would never find them.

First, she needed to earn a head start into the night.

Neva knocked to gain the guard's attention.

"I'm done," she said.

The guard pulled the door open, and she didn't waste time before sending a blast of power directly at his head. She must have been nervous, because she did so with more force than she intended, yanking her power back at the last moment.

The guard slammed into the wall behind him and crumpled to the ground. The smell of burnt hair mixed with the stench from the cell. He wasn't conscious, and Neva made sure he was breathing before motioning for Adam to join her in the hall. Relief washed through her. So far, so good.

After Neva dragged the guard into the cell and locked him inside, she and Adam moved quietly through the long, winding walkway. They passed by the lengthy series of cell doors before arriving at the front of the dungeon, where their exit was blocked by an iron portcullis and three guards on the opposite side of it. From behind cover of the tunnel wall, Neva spotted the closed side door and silently cursed her luck. The guard from earlier had left the side door open, but it seemed the gods weren't inclined to allow her an easy escape. She would need a distraction.

"Count to twenty and start for the door," Neva whispered to Adam.

She didn't wait for his response and instead called on her oh-so-familiar invisibility glamour. She had gone against Da'Voda troops when she helped Emiliand test the border. She had to take every advantage.

She inched forward until she was practically flush against the gate. She had to wait only a moment. Adam took no more than two steps outside the tunnel before the soldiers noticed him. Two hilans shouted to one another on the other side of the gate, rushing to pull it up and recapture their prisoner. A majila worked squeaky gears, causing the portcullis to rise with a groan.

As soon as the spikes on the bottom were far enough off the ground, Neva dropped and rolled to the other side, knocking one of the hilan's feet from under him. The majila stopped raising the gate, and the other hilan, who was missing several teeth, shot a blast of power toward Adam. Neva countered the shot and kept moving as she blasted the guards, one right after the other. One of her shots found its target and momentarily stunned the hilan with missing teeth. The other hit the majila's shoulder.

Neva rolled to her feet past the first guard. She spared a glance in Adam's direction, grateful he had the sense to duck back into the tunnel. Her next shot knocked the majila back, and the majila's shout was cut off at its start as her head slammed into the stone wall.

Immediately, Neva took another shot at the guard she had tripped. He blocked the shot so her power ricocheted and shattered a section of skulls in the dungeon wall. The guard cast a blanket of power at her with his sword drawn. She rolled beyond the burning edge of power before it evaporated and quickly took another shot at him. He fell, motionless.

The hilan she had stunned was protecting himself with a braided shield of midnight flame. He looked crazily at the air around him with his sword hacking in wide, random sweeps, seeking his invisible opponent.

She jumped on his back. He stumbled, and with one arm around his neck, Neva grabbed a horn and shoved out a paralyzing amount of power. Neva grunted as his weight landed on top of her. Luckily, her training with Vivizhi had taught her how to recover quickly.

"Adam?" Neva called as she rolled the soldier off her and rose to her feet.

"Neva?" Adam's voice shook.

The sword she'd given him lay discarded in the dirt, and a towering hilan held a blade to Adam's neck, digging into the skin the barest amount possible so Neva wasn't sure if she imagined the dewdrops of blood trickling where metal met flesh.

Neva stilled herself, glad she had not yet revoked her invisibility glamour. She had forgotten the fifth guard. Every team had five members. With the three out front, and the one who had led her back to Adam's cell, she should have anticipated the other nearby.

"Show yourself!" the soldier demanded.

He was large, at least a middel, and peppered with battle scars.

Neva didn't think. She shot a blast of power at the Da'Valia's head to knock him out — or it would have, if it had landed. Instead, the Da'Valia caught it with his own power, tore off a piece with a strained grunt, and flung it back at her. He repeated the action twice more. The attacks flew past her before exploding against the flagstone. Too close.

"I could do this until morning," the soldier spat angrily. "Show yourself or the human dies."

Neva wasn't willing to wager against the Da'Valia's threat. Adam's life meant too much to her, and if she tried anything bigger, someone in the village would notice their fight.

Neva spotted a gleam in Adam's eye as she was about to drop her invisibility spell. Intuition told her what he wanted her to do. Neva ripped the dagger from her boot and threw it at the soldier, letting her invisibility disappear. Adam dropped his weight at the same time, and the dagger found its mark in the soldier's throat.

The hilan fell, making labored sucking sounds as blood gushed out around him. Adam picked up his sword, raised it over the hilan, and brought it down with both hands, stabbing the soldier through the heart. Neva ignored the rock forming in the pit of her stomach. They had killed a Da'Voda soldier. If Trinizhi ever found them, she wouldn't let them live.

"It's time for clean-up," Neva said, forcing herself to keep moving. There was no going back now. "Get the dead one under cover of the tunnel, will you?"

She didn't want to look at the dead soldier, but getting him out of sight might win them precious time.

"On it," Adam said.

The other guards would need to be locked up before they stirred. Neva hooked her arms under the chins of two of the guards and dragged them into the dungeon, stopping at the first cell. She dropped the guards in the dirt, and she lifted the hand of the hilan with missing teeth. She pushed her power through his skin and watched as the door glowed softly.

The door swung in and she saw a scraggly majila around her own age huddled in the corner. It looked like it had been a long time since the majila's creamy hair had seen a washtub. Her skin, which should have been bright or pearlescent, was dull and streaked with dirt.

"Don't move," Neva ordered her.

The majila only stared back at her with empty eyes.

Neva lifted a guard by his uniform and tossed him inside the cell. He landed in a shallow puddle. The second guard followed, and then the majila, who Adam dragged in. Neva kept one eye on the majila, who was gazing at the guards more alertly now, as if she had ideas of what to do with them. Once all the bodies were inside, Neva slammed the door shut.

"Let's go," she said, trying to avoid looking directly at Adam.

She didn't want to know what he thought of this. Of her power. Her human glamour almost seemed silly now, when he had witnessed her knocking down Da'Valia and blasting apart stone. Still, she left it intact as they ran. She felt certain it was better this way.

As soon as Adam was through the portcullis, she hit the lever to drop it back in place and they fled into the night. Neva knew the layout of the clan well enough so they arrived at the stables without being seen. One or two Da'Valia might have heard something out of place as she and Adam sped by, ducking between buildings, but it could have been any number of nocturnal animals out scavenging.

Miland had done well, for they had been expecting her arrival, even so late. She gave her thanks to a majila who passed the reins after she climbed atop Astiand's carriage. The majila dipped her head in response, but avoided looking at her. Miland must have paid well, too, Neva mused. She hoped the coin had come from Astiand's coffers.

Neva yanked her hood up and set out at a leisurely pace, slowing briefly to allow Adam to climb aboard. When she heard the door snap shut and he pounded on the roof, she upped the speed.

Again, the majilas at the front gate were expecting her.

One of the uniform-clad authorities nodded to her as she passed. Neva copied the action and then stared straight ahead, her heart thumping. Vivizhi had come through for her. Neva whipped the horses into a frenzied pace the moment they were out of sight. Retracing the route she'd taken with Astiand, she kept the horses going well into the night, squinting to see and wiping away tears brought on by the relentless wind, grateful her stomach wasn't revolting now that she was in the driver's seat. She slowed only for the thick fog banks that wound around the middle of the mountains and made it impossible to tell where the road turned. She probably would have continued on, except Adam pounded on the roof late the following morning. They stopped so he could relieve himself.

They were still in the remote wilderness north of Livorna, so Neva didn't bother trying to leave the road clear where they stopped. Her shoes sank into the mud as she jumped down from the driver's bench. She groaned. Her fingers were sore from gripping the reins against the wind, her butt was numb, and now cold mud soaked her feet.

Neva watered the horses before unwrapping and shoving down some of the food from Miland. Excitement may have temporarily disabled her desire for food or sleep, but it would catch up with her eventually.

"You're allowed to chew, Neva," Adam told her as he walked back from behind some trees, looking at ease and handsome in the woods. She would have never guessed he'd been chained in a dungeon only hours earlier.

Neva gave him a dirty look out of habit, annoyed when it made him smile. She swallowed and asked, "are you ready?"

"I think we should talk." Adam said. His smile faltered.

She fought his gaze with a glance at the sky.

"First, we're getting farther away from the clan," Neva told him. "We have a decent start on them, but they have single riders and horses. They don't have to deal with the same bulk we do."

"I can ride," he said. "We should go on horseback."

"Well, I can't. Not well enough anyway," she told him. She hated admitting as much. "Besides, you wouldn't be able to ride these horses. Trust me."

"Fine. Let's go then. The faster we make it back home, the better."

They set off, driving through the day and into the night, stopping only so often. Neva took advantage of their short breaks to water the horses and check back along the road. She didn't see any indication they were being followed, but that didn't mean the Da'Valia weren't closing in on them. Many sections of the road were no worse off than the last time she had traveled it, but others were severely altered by the melting snow. Some turns and steep inclines made it impossible not to slow for fear of disaster.

Two days in, Neva felt surer of their lead. They stopped to cook a meal near a small stream in a snow-covered valley north of Stagg. Vestive showers wouldn't come to Glacier Pass for some time yet, so the more snow, the closer they were to their destination. She wanted to have some strength left when they made it back to Glacier Pass, so she needed to make eating a priority. Miland had sent more than enough food with them, but despite her best efforts, she hadn't been eating much of it.

"Tell me exactly what happened," Neva told Adam as she went about setting a fire.

Adam didn't react as he watched her spark the flame with her finger. They huddled around the flame to keep warm, and Neva wondered how long his composure would last.

"A lot changed after you left," Adam started. "After the tavern burned down, your aunt became ill, and it wasn't because of all the smoke she breathed."

Neva felt a growl rise in her throat but caught it before it unfurled.

"Will she recover?"

"It's more complicated. She was still alive when I headed out, but the healer warned that her condition was likely terminal," Adam said.

"When did you leave?" Neva asked.

"Soon after you," Adam responded. "A woman came to your father. She wanted you. When Shaun told her you'd left the Pass and he didn't know where you were, she became angry. Margret was there and, well, you know Margret. She told the woman to leave, and the woman said something to her in a different tongue. Margret became violently ill that night. We received a message by courier. The message said if you did not seek out the woman before the moon's waning, your aunt would die. I think — I think the woman was a witch, Neva. If you'd seen your aunt, the way she changed in a few hours. It was unnatural."

Neva pictured her cousins by Margret's bedside, wondering if she would still be there for them in the morning. Neva knew what it was like to grow up without a mother. How alone she had felt at times. She couldn't let that happen to James and Kendall.

Quickly, Neva turned her mind to practical matters and calculated exactly how long they had. She let out a heavy breath. They didn't have much time.

It took her and Astiand a little less than a week to travel from Glacier Pass to the clan. If she and Adam could continue at their neck-breaking pace, they might arrive in time. Maybe with less than a day to spare.

Adam seemed to know what she was thinking.

"It took me awhile to find you, Neva," he said. "No one knew where the clan was, and your trail wasn't easy to follow, but your father set me in the right direction."

Neva shook her head.

"You did fine," she said, holding back a flood of emotions. "You found me. That's what matters."

Chapter Twenty-Seven

First Auton, 1632

I am still unwell, but I am making my way back to Shaun in my human glamour. I cannot believe I snuck away from my people by moonlight. I wonder what they will think of me, or if they will think of me at all.

— *Monazhi Da'Voda-Lira*

Neva and Adam packed up and continued immediately after they finished their modest meal, traveling from the floor of the valley to the summit, where Neva checked back again. The sun was setting, draping a brilliant blanket of orange light over the snow and trees. It was still bright enough she could clearly see a great distance away.

"Gods." She cursed.

The carriage door squeaked as it swung open. Adam poked his head out.

"Why are we stopping?" Adam asked.

Neva ran her tongue along the backs of her teeth, trying to think before answering.

"I wanted to check back," she said.

"Well?" Adam looked out over the valley, inspecting the path they'd already traveled. The wind played with his hair. "We're alone out here, aren't we?"

Neva shook her head and jumped down from atop the carriage.

"No," she said. "They're here."

"Where?" Adam followed her from the carriage.

"On the ridge." Neva pointed to the top of a snow-covered mountain opposite them. "The donazhi — their queen — is relentless."

They were still at least a day from Glacier Pass, and the Da'Valia would be upon them by morning if Neva ignored their proximity.

She surveyed their surroundings with dismay. Trees, some rocks, and endless snow. Nothing she could use to attack their pursuers.

"We should leave the carriage here and go by horse," Adam suggested, squinting in the direction she had pointed. "We can ride double."

"That would only slow us down." Not for the first time, Neva wished she knew how to ride better.

What would Emiliand or Vivizhi do in this situation?

Then, it hit her. She didn't need to be rid of the Da'Valia completely. She just needed to slow them down.

"Well, then, what —?"

"I have an idea," Neva ignored his question, feeling pressure mounting. "Get back in the carriage and stay there."

She had never wanted Adam to know the truth of her ancestry, and she didn't want him to witness what she was about to attempt. However, what was the point of harboring a godly power if she didn't use it?

Neva rubbed her hands together and blew on them. The temperature was dropping. She shook her hands out at her sides and closed her eyes. Anticipation raced through her. She called on her power, pulling it from the reservoir in her mind. She went deeper than before, to the Hand. She gathered it so it filled every crevice and pore of her body until she thought she might burst with it. The Hand was part of who she was, and for the first time, she embraced it. Its essence stretched inside her, rising up.

She visualized the liquid fire pouring from her hands, materializing around her. When she opened her eyes again, she found a torrent of power dancing in giant circles, heating the air, singeing smaller plants and the bases of nearby trees, melting mounds of snow into puddles. The tips of her fingers were no longer icy. She was strong and full of heat.

She hadn't been sure what to expect, tapping into the Hand for the first time. It felt exhilarating.

In a single, brutal slash, she unleashed the Hand. It flew forth like a tidal wave, building, then becoming flat and elongated. It rolled over the valley like a burning sea of fog.

The sunlight luminescence called the attention of the Da'Valia. The group scrambled to get into a formation and attempt to block the oncoming tide. Streams of black and white power rose from their group, weaving in and out of each other to create a shield nothing short of masterful.

The shacklay around Neva's wrist sparked to life, but she ignored it.

Instead, she smiled at their pointless blockade. Although she was certain the Hand was capable of it, she didn't intend to kill them. She wasn't even aiming for them.

The Hand hit near the base of the mountain, and Neva pushed her power like a knife. It sliced under the snow, melting a thick layer beneath the packed white stuff. The mountain shivered, settled, and then broke. A flock of birds abandoned a section of pine trees, crying out as they took to the air. A river of snow and water roiled in a giant sheet, dragging down trees and rocks in its path. Shots of powder erupted into the air as the avalanche rumbled, leaving a sink of devastation in its wake.

The ground beneath Neva's feet shook as the avalanche obliterated the road through the valley. Then, silence took hold of the valley once again.

Neva gasped and bent over, catching herself on her knees, finally letting go of her hold on the flame. She sucked in air and coughed, a coppery taste flooding her mouth. She was unsurprised when she spit and a bright red spot of blood hit the ground. That wasn't good. She continued coughing until it turned into unstable laughter.

"Oh, Dhianz!" Neva said, awed, wiping her mouth on her sleeve. What had the god been thinking to create such power? What had her mother been thinking to call it into herself? The Hand was greater than anything Neva had ever imagined.

It stirred in the depths of her mind again, sensing her attention and calling to her. Using the Hand again didn't seem like such as bad idea, and she knew exactly what she wanted to do with it. Neva looked at Astiand's bracelet on her wrist and shoved a drop of the power directly into the shacklay. The metal shattered, and the pieces scattered into the mud. Neva grinned. Trinizhi and her aliados no longer had any influence over her. Neva pushed the Hand back, visualizing a vault in her mind, and locked the power away. She felt as though she had won the final throw of a tournament.

"Neva?" Adam was standing behind her. "What was that?"

That stopped her laughter. She gathered herself and stood, covering her mouth to stop a stray giggle as she looked over the valley. She hadn't wanted to believe the secrets in Monazhi's journal, but she couldn't deny any of it now. Neva looked down at the steam rising from her hands. Her human glamour flickered. This kind of power was intoxicating.

"I did what I needed to do," she told Adam.

The worst part was she felt like she wanted to do it all over again.

"That was amazing," Adam said, coming to stand by her side.

Neva froze and turned to him. He wasn't supposed to think that, was he?

"It will slow them down," Neva said. "But it won't stop them. We need to keep moving."

"Let's go, then," Adam said.

She considered his reaction as she climbed back to the driver's seat. Smoke wafted from where her hands touched the wood of the carriage. She was lucky she was wearing spelled Da'Valian clothing. Anything constructed by humans would have burned. She was practically cooking, a sensation that dissipated quickly as she flicked the reins and set into the night.

They were so close to home, she could feel it. Even the air felt right. Not too muggy or arid.

When they finally neared Grianch, Neva clutched the reins tighter and leaned in. Although danger lay ahead, she would be with the people she loved in a matter of hours. But she would need to be on guard, too, for the Vodou witches that Trinizhi's alliad had feared.

With Astiand on her trail — she had felt him invoke the shacklay in the mountains — and Bryand and Arroyand already in Glacier Pass, she couldn't bring the carriage within sight of the city. Word of a strange carriage and even stranger horses would spread quickly to interested parties.

Neva deviated from the road beyond sight of the city's wall. The forest was thick and the carriage lurched forward as she guided the horses into the snow and over tree roots. They didn't get far. She stopped as soon as she was certain no one on the road would see the carriage. Adam carried water for the horses from the Glacier Arm and assured Neva he would send Fletcher to tend to them once they were inside the city. Then, Neva and Adam went back to the road to cover their tracks and sprinkle the spelled powder Miland had promised would confuse her scent.

Once done, Neva slung their packs over her shoulder and eyed the city's wall. It was built with massive stones to protect from sieges and predators. The Watch locked and guarded the gates at all hours. For Neva alone it would require little effort to climb a nearby pine and slide over the top of the barrier. With Adam, they would need to go another way, and the quickest was her least favorite. Through the sewers.

They crawled out through an iron grate at the morgue, their boots soaked and smelling faintly of water waste. Adam went first, and Neva extinguished the power they had used to see by. He held the grate open so she could toss the packs and pulled herself through. The putrid scent of death put Neva on edge as she emerged. Holy servants devout to Riska had embalmed and stacked corpses under white sheets. Neva tried not to look at the shelves of bodies, which would be stored until the ground thawed enough for digging.

"About Flynn…" she started to say.

"What about him?" Adam asked.

"Was his body recovered?"

Adam stopped abruptly.

"Recovered? What do you mean recovered?"

Neva cursed quietly. Apparently, the Rings had not discovered Flynn's death before Adam left Glacier Pass.

"These people are after my family because of a commission he gave me.

They killed him." Neva didn't need to sugarcoat things for Adam.

"You're sure?" He glanced around, as if he would see Flynn's body on the shelf next to them.

She gave a nod, unable to do more.

"I'll need to find Roger as soon as possible, then," he murmured, half to her and half to himself.

"Just get me to my family first," Neva said.

Neva's family was staying in an apartment not far from the establishment where Amber worked — the building where Neva had last seen Flynn alive. Walking through Cul Corner, she shivered at the thought of him. Nothing in Cul Corner had visibly changed, but it wasn't the same to walk the streets without knowing for certain he and his men had her back. She hoped Roger was still running things.

Adam led Neva to an apartment building and left her on the second floor before a door showing signs of rot. Then, he went to gather his belongings from his sister's house. He would have to go into hiding and planned to head to Roger next. Neva gave Flynn's necklace to Adam, asking that he pass it to Amber, and thanked him. Alone, Neva knocked on the worn door, surprised to feel as nervous as she did.

They're living here? Neva supposed she should be glad her family had a roof over their heads after losing everything in the fire, but now she felt guiltier for leaving town in their time of need. She had been given everything, and had been waited on to boot, while living in Astiand's lavish home. Meanwhile, her father had been living in Cul Corner.

"Neva!" Shaun exclaimed when he opened the door. His frown softened upon seeing her, and Neva knew he had been worrying over whether she would make it back in time.

"It's so good to see you, Pa," Neva said, letting him wrap her in a bear hug. He smelled faintly of spirits and wood smoke. He smelled like home.

Over his shoulder, she saw the apartment was ramshackle at best. Water stains and black mold spores splattered the exterior wall. A modest stove warmed the space and someone had stuffed cloths in several of the larger gaps where termites had feasted around the windows, but daylight and cold air both poured into the room. James stared out a window at passersby with a sad expression, and Kendall was aggressively whittling in front of the warm stove. A grim determination settled over her.

"My girl," Shaun said, stepping back to look her over. "I'm so glad you're all right. We weren't sure if you would make it back in time."

"How's Margret?" Neva asked.

"Not well."

Neva dropped her packs by the door and hugged James and Kendall hello. They brightened considerably upon seeing her and were full of questions about whether she could help their mother and where she had been. Her father permitted them an answer each before he urged them away and took Neva to the rear of the apartment.

"After the fire, her lungs were damaged," Shaun said. "Now, it's worse."

Neva said nothing as he held open the door to Margret's bedroom. The walls were bare wood, gray from age, and the mattress was sloped in the middle where Margret lay. Margret's skin nearly matched the walls, and blue veins showed through her neck and cheeks. Even beneath the blankets, she looked slimmer by twenty pounds or more.

Neva's breath caught in her throat. She went to the woman's side and took her hand gently.

"Aunt Margret?" Neva spoke softly.

Margret's eyes fluttered open and then closed again.

"It was good of you to come." Her voice was hoarse.

"I'm going to make sure you get better, Aunt Margret," Neva whispered. She tried to ignore the tears stinging her eyes. "Just rest and you'll feel better in no time."

Neva left the room with her father and thought back to the night of the fire, when the healer had said her aunt might never recover from inhaling so much smoke. She didn't want to guess at how Margret might fare if they managed to get the curse removed.

"Where are they?" Neva asked Shaun as they returned to the living room. Neva needed to find the witch responsible and settle this immediately.

He looked perplexed.

"They have a camp in the woods, just past the northern wall along the Glacier Arm," he said.

"Good. I'll take care of it." Neva started toward the door.

"Neva, I don't want you going alone," her father said in a level tone, stepping in her path. "You need to think this through. Take someone with you. We can gather the Ring."

"Pa! She doesn't have any time left!" Neva lowered her voice quickly, casting a quick look at her cousins. Not to mention she didn't think her uncles would be too keen to confront witches and Da'Valia.

"At least wait until Adam returns," Shaun pleaded.

"You saw the same woman in there that I did," Neva said. "I will not let her die."

Shaun's eyes narrowed and he crossed his arms. She glared right back. They were both stubborn enough to get their way.

"You can come with me, if you want," she told him. "But I'm going now."

Chapter Twenty-Eight

Twelfth Auton, 1632

Never have I been so sure of making the right decision as I was when I saw the light in Shaun's eyes last night. It's been more than a full season since he's seen me, my belly is growing round, and still he looks at me like he did the night of our first kiss.

— Monazhi Da'Voda-Lira

"That's their camp," Shaun said, pointing to a faint line of smoke drifting from the pines on the other side of the river. They were crossing the great stone bridge at the Glacier Arm port, where barges were being loaded for shipment to auctions in Ashford.

"Then that's where we're going." Neva marched forward. She wouldn't waste energy by scouting the area. They were already at a disadvantage, because someone they both loved was in danger.

A strange calm washed over her. Her father had made her leave her weapons behind for fear of provoking another curse, so she should have been on edge. But she had survived her firérite, she had trained with Emiliand and Vivizhi, and she harbored the Hand. She *was* a weapon. She could protect herself and her father.

Neva made sure Shaun stayed behind her as they approached the camp. Three burly majilas emerged from the trees like ghosts, walking evenly with

Neva. They moved in a graceful synchronization for several steps. Two hilans came up on her other side. The Da'Valia were laden with scars and wore enough weapons to outfit twenty of the Order's soldiers. Unlike the Da'Voda, their uniforms were worn and brown, and their capes were twice as thick as Neva's, which made her think they must be unaccustomed to the glacial cold.

Neva passed several of the dozen deer-hide tents that dotted the camp and arrived at the center of the cluster. She stopped and glanced around. All she saw were Da'Valia. Where was the witch?

A moment later, Neva realized she hadn't needed to worry.

"Well, well, well," a woman's throaty voice came from the center tent. "Our elusive thief has finally arrived."

One of the most beautiful women Neva had ever seen stepped from the opening. She was green-eyed, curvy, and her chestnut hair was wavy and crimped as if recently released from a braid. Her face was one of such beauty that Neva was certain it could inspire the master painters at the House of Trescony. An elegant, dark corset cinched her around the middle, and embroidered silk skirts hung at a length that revealed fashionable heels laced to her ankles, indicating a level of elitism and wealth at odds with the militaristic camp.

Witch! Neva couldn't stop the growl that crawled from her throat.

The Da'Valia in her vicinity tensed, hands on their weapons, some already drawn.

"Margret cannot be the image of health by now." The witch ignored her growl. The witch's voice was like a thousand glass bells dancing in the wind.

"I'd like to change that," Neva said.

"Relax," the witch said, raising a hand to still the Da'Valia. "The thief won't cause any problems for us, will you, Neva?"

Few of the Da'Valia lowered their guard, and Neva fought the urge to rush the witch. She would feel a lot better if she landed even one good punch on that beautiful face.

"She's glamoured herself," a majila grumbled. "I'll not trust a thief bathed in magic."

"Perhaps you would lower your glamour to put our soldiers at ease?" the witch suggested, tilting her head as she scrutinized Neva.

"I prefer them uneasy," Neva said, lifting her chin. "Just as my aunt no doubt feels right now."

The witch gave a harsh laugh, and it tinkled, wracked with power.

"I must say, we expected you sooner," the witch said. "But you've come at last, so your aunt will live."

The witch held out a hand, and small black slugs wiggled on her palm. Even though the sight of the slimy creatures turned her stomach, Neva felt some relief. She strode forward to collect them. The witch dropped the three leech-like creatures into her outstretched hand. Deftly, Neva wrapped the worms in a handkerchief, passing the collection to her father when she was done.

"You must let her blood for three days," the witch said, looking at Shaun. "The creatures have been spelled. They will do the work."

Neva tore her eyes from the woman and looked at her father.

"Go," she told him. "I'll be fine."

He hesitated.

"Go," Neva said sharply. She needed him away from these people.

He gave her a warning look and backed away slowly, turning and rushing away in a half-run toward the city as soon as he was beyond reach of the Da'Valia. His limp slowed him, but Neva felt the tension in her shoulders release once he was out of sight. Margret would mend. Everything Neva had done up until now had been worth it.

"We are eager to learn what you know," the witch said. "Follow me."

The witch pulled back the flap of the tent. The inside of the shelter was small but far more ornate than was needed for a field tent. The rugs covering the ground would fetch decent coin on the black market, and colorful quilts hung on the walls of the tent, insulating it against the cold.

As Neva passed through the entryway, the witch followed, lightly bumping into her. The smell of manure overwhelmed Neva for a moment, and she almost shoved the witch away, but she stopped abruptly as she saw a toppel majila. A beautiful silver headpiece with hundreds of inlaid jet stones adorned the majila's head. The majila's face was long and her features sharp. She pushed her thick white hair over her shoulder as she came to her feet from where she was lounging on a plush stool.

The majila reminded Neva of Trinizhi, although there was no physical resemblance. A headpiece, a regal air, and a deadly look in her eyes... This had to be the Da'Foha's donazhi.

Neva's fingers twitched, itching to go for the blade strapped to her ankle, but it wasn't there.

The majila's silver-white eyes roiled with power, and so much confidence — too much confidence. She looked like Mikel after he won a knife-throwing tournament.

"Well done, Deidra," the majila said, giving Neva the name of the witch. "You must be Neva Roberts."

"And you are?" Neva asked. She maneuvered so she had the donazhi, Deidra, and the door all in her sights.

"Melanzhi Da'Foha," the majila said.

"You're a donazhi," Neva said, stating the obvious.

"Indeed, and you..." Melanzhi narrowed her eyes. She looked Neva over and sniffed. "What an adorable glamour. A majila in human skin. I must say, you aren't what I expected."

Out of the corner of her eye, Neva saw the witch move to a humble altar several feet from the door and set to work with a mortar and pestle, crushing herbs and insects. Four votive candles were alight and a large jagged amethyst stone glinted between them. Dried herbs tied to animal bones hung off the stand. Judging by the size of the bones, they were from rodents, Neva observed with relief. The Da'Foha were known for their cannibalistic ways, but at least she didn't see any obvious signs of human sacrifice.

"Take a seat, if you please," the donazhi said, gesturing to the wool rug decorating the center of the tent.

Neva folded to the floor gracefully, and Melanzhi retook her seat on the stool.

"Show me your neck," Melanzhi said.

Uncomfortable but seeing no alternative, Neva pulled her hair to the side and turned her head.

"Da'Voda," Melanzhi said, shooting Deidra a pointed look. "Are you aware, Nevazhi, that the Da'Voda have set up a camp beyond the south wall?"

"I know they traveled here," Neva answered.

"And you are one of them, but you are not working with them now?" Melanzhi asked.

"We've parted ways." Neva was careful to keep her answers truthful, even if it was an understatement.

"Good," Melanzhi said. "I confess, we did not expect you to be one of us — a Da'Valia by blood — what with your human family. Not at all."

"Do you want my life story, or is there a reason you cursed my aunt?" Neva asked bluntly.

Deidra sat on the rug across from Neva. In one hand, the witch held a black sack. In the other, she held a bowl of herbs and crushed insects laced with the tell-tale glow of magic.

Neva focused on the sack. She would recognize it anywhere.

"No, you're right," Melanzhi said as Deidra pulled the material away from the face of the goblet with gloved hands. "Obviously, whoever your mother was, she made some poor decisions. We want you to tell us about this goblet. What do you know?"

"It can..." Neva swallowed nervously. She had hoped to never see the goblet again. "It can show you the future."

"And?" The witch cocked her head to the side.

With a start, Neva realized they already knew that. They didn't need her to tell them what it could do. But then... Why did they need her?

"I suppose, then, the reason the donazhi — of the Da'Voda — wants it so badly is to predict battles?" Nevazhi's guess sounded weak to her own ears.

"And how would she do that?" Melanzhi asked, lifting the goblet, the material of the sack wrapped around the stem.

With surprise, Neva realized what they were truly trying to discern. They knew what the goblet did, but they didn't know how to control it. Neva frowned.

"I suppose she would simply have to touch it," Neva said, confused.

"What do you take us for?" Melanzhi's voice went livid. The majila leaned forward, looming over Neva.

Neva scooted back. She didn't doubt Deidra would recast the curse on her aunt if she didn't answer their questions.

"I don't know what you mean," Neva said tensely.

"You don't, do you?" Melanzhi asked. She pulled back, sweeping her hand at Deidra in a silent order.

Deidra murmured a string of ancient-sounding words and drew a series of symbols in the air. A soft wind entered the tent and swept back the quilt hanging at the rear. Neva had thought the tent ended at the cloth wall, but with it gone, a young girl on a low cot was revealed. She had luscious brown hair that matched Deidra's, and she was gaunt with gray circles under her open eyes. Eyes that stared at nothing. Neva could barely perceive a slight lifting of the girl's chest as she breathed, yet the girl mumbled incredibly fast, whispering words that made no sense.

"This is my sister, Gillian," Deidra spoke with a dangerous edge. "We share Vodou blood from our mother. Do you want to know how old she is? She has only seen fourteen Firesides, but she is already the strongest in our family."

Neva didn't speak. She didn't know what to say.

"Do you know what it is that makes us special, Nevazhi?" Deidra was in a different place as she spoke. Her eyes were unfocused. She addressed Neva, but Neva had to wonder if she knew where she was. "We can touch things and know them. We can glimpse into the past of any object with a touch, so it would make sense to you why we are so interested in working with the Da'Foha in this endeavor. The Dhianz's Eye can show us the future, if we know how to use it."

Oh gods, oh gods, oh gods. Neva's heart lurched as the witch spoke the true name of the goblet.

Dhianz's Eye. The first prong of his greatest weapon, the Trishula.

Neva's mind raced. The Da'Foha didn't appear to be focused on using the Eye to redeem the Da'Valia as Monazhi had once intended. And that was why Trinizhi wanted the piece. What Da'Valia would dare deny any of Trinizhi's orders when she might return the Trishula to Dhianz and break the Da'Valia's curse?

But Melanzhi had an entirely different objective. She and Deidra wanted the weapon for its prophetic ability.

"But as you can see…" Deidra drew another series of runes in the air, muttering more words Neva couldn't understand.

Another gust of ringing wind yanked down a series of curtains behind Gillian's cot. The tent doubled in size. The enclosure stretched on to house three more cots. A toppel hilan rested upon each. They appeared to be in conditions akin to Gillian, mindless and mumbling although they barely seemed to have the strength necessary. Neva shot a look at the altar. Four candles alight for four stricken allies. No, not allies. These, Neva realized with shock, must be Melanzhi's aliados.

Deidra and Melanzhi wanted to wield the Eye, but this was personal for them now. Neva's sense of danger heightened. She eyed the exits, quietly trying to map an escape.

"Our thief said you awoke the goblet, but you've not been afflicted," Deidra said. "We want to know how."

"I am afraid I have to disappoint you, but the Chameleon was wrong," Neva said. She didn't know why she had been spared the fate of those on the cots. Perhaps because of the spell her mother had used to bind her powers, or because the Hand and the Eye were meant to be wielded together. But she wasn't about to share her most valuable secrets.

"Was he?" Melanzhi challenged.

"I'm good at stealing things, but I'm a half-breed for gods' sakes," Neva said. "I've no training in magic. I can't tell you anything you do not already know."

"I am sorry to hear that," Melanzhi told her, not sounding sorry at all.

"What a waste," Deidra said with a disgusted scoff.

In deft and practiced movements, the witch tossed the contents of her spell bowl at Neva and bit off a rapid line of words that called magic around Neva's skin, electric and harsh.

Neva threw herself into motion, punching the witch. She heard a satisfying *crunch* as Deidra's nose broke. Neva didn't watch as the witch fell back with a cry, her hands moving to catch the blood running down her face.

Melanzhi grabbed Neva as she raised her hand to unleash her power at the donazhi. A heavy wave of fatigue hit Neva so hard that her hand dropped and her eyelids drooped. The witch's spell penetrated her mind, lulling it to sleep. All Neva had to do was call on her power, and she was sure she could break free of the hold.

Be strong, Neva thought. *Fight*. Somehow, it was Vivizhi's voice, echoing off the training room walls, that she heard.

Neva resisted the lethargy with all of her being, but it dragged her down, turning her into a rag doll. She struggled to stay alert as sleep washed over her.

"She'll pay for this," Deidra raged.

"She is but a pawn, nothing more than a common thief," Melanzhi said. "But let's not give her Da'Voda sisters and brothers a chance to bolster their ranks. Bind her power."

"Why not kill her now?" Deidra challenged.

"We must give our spy more time," Melanzhi insisted. "If we kill a Da'Voda, Trinizhi will use it as an excuse to turn the other clans against us. Do as I said and bind her."

Chapter Twenty-Nine

Fourth Fireside, 1632

Shaun's family has welcomed me as well as they are able. They're not the kind to trust easily, but the other night his father invited me to share some mead, and his sister seemed to like it when I braided her hair for Bridoona-al. Slowly, this place is beginning to feel like home.

— Monazhi Da'Voda-Lira

Her mind heavy, Neva slipped in and out of consciousness. Voices whirled around her. Majila, hilan, unintelligible. The sounds blended in a muffled symphony, repeating, rising, and falling. Vaguely, she recognized the tone of a muffled speaker. She knew that voice, but she struggled to place its origin. The voice was deep, like a shepherd's horn when it echoes through the mountains.

Bryand.

Neva sensed his nearness. Her thoughts wrapped around his presence, and she struggled to make out what he was saying. Did he know she was there? Would he be able to help her, or had Trinizhi sent him here to take her back to the Da'Voda? She focused on making out what he was saying.

"You should have warned me someone from my clan was here," Bryand said.

"She's unconscious. She couldn't possibly connect you to us." Neva

243

couldn't tell if it was Deidra or Melanzhi who spoke. Everything was muffled, as if she were listening to a conversation beside a rushing river.

"That's what I fear," Bryand said. "Since Nevazhi provided no insight, how much longer will that take? We're running out of time. I cannot deceive them forever."

"Deidra is going to try something new," Melanzhi said. "Buy us a few days' time before you poison Trinizhi. If this doesn't work, we'll need to see if we can extract the information from her by force."

"You had better hope it doesn't come to that," Bryand said. "The Da'Voda will go to war with you."

"It won't, I assure you," Melanzhi said. "In the meantime, dump the thief in the city, will you? We're done with her. Deidra has ensured she'll never be a threat to anyone ever again."

Neva wished she could see what was happening around her, but her ears allowed the truth to siphon through. Bryand was working with the Da'Foha. Bryand had betrayed Trinizhi and the Da'Voda.

Neva's fragile grasp on consciousness sputtered, Deidra's cursed magic pulling her down. The memory of Bryand's face formed in oily tar, following her down a spiral of fog and into a dream-less land.

Neva blinked at the strange gray ceiling with brown water spots staining it and two sets of matching blue eyes peering down at her.

"She's waking up!" Kendall shouted.

Neva winced, his voice stabbing through her head. The aftereffects of Deidra's magic lined her mind, making everything look fuzzy. Her stomach roiled. She closed her eyes again with a groan.

"Boys, step back," Margret hurried into the room, her skirt billowing behind her. She nudged the boys aside. "Here. Give her some room."

Neva cracked her eyes open a sliver to see her aunt scooch onto the edge of the small bed.

"Margret." Neva's voice emerged in a painful croak. She had no concept of how much time had passed since meeting with the Da'Foha, but her throat was dry. "You're alive."

Neva pushed herself up, and the room tilted as if it were affixed to a spinning top. Margret caught Neva around the middle and helped her prop herself up against the cold wall. Neva took a deep breath and then another, waiting for the nausea to pass.

"Are you all right?" Neva asked Margret when she felt like she could breathe again.

"Look at you, asking if I'm all right," Margret chided. "I'm fine, love. Thanks to you and Shaun."

Neva dropped her head into her hands, holding back tears of relief. She asked her cousins to bring her packs from the front room and downed a good portion of the healing tonic Miland had packed. As soon as she swallowed, she started to feel better. Her vision cleared, and she was able to sit up without assistance. She slowly took in her surroundings. At some point, Margret must have dressed Neva in a nightgown. She was cold, her toes practically numb. She felt drained and oddly empty, starving in fact.

Margret appeared to have recovered, so three days must have passed. *Three days!* Neva thought. Trinizhi's trackers surely must have made it to Glacier Pass by now. She hoped Adam had either smuggled himself far away or hidden himself where even his mother couldn't find him.

Neva reached for Emiliand's charm around her neck and rubbed the burning sun with her thumb as she tried to put her thoughts in order. The last thing she remembered was punching Deidra in the face, and then... Horror swept through her. *"Bind her."* The memory of Melanzhi's order jolted Neva, sending blood rushing through her head.

"Oh gods," she said aloud.

"What is it dear?" Margret asked, sounding alarmed.

Neva raised her hand and tried to call her power to life. Her palm remained empty. She closed her eyes and reached deep within herself, searching for her inner flame only to find the barest trace of it, not even enough to light a candle. Her stomach clenched. She went deeper, to the vault where she had trapped the Hand. All she found was a slick, solid stone wall. Impenetrable.

The witch had bound her powers.

Some things were innate, such as her sight, strength, and fluidness. But Deidra had blocked the strongest part of Neva from herself. Neva would now be useless if she went up against the Da'Foha, which she was sure had been their intent, but this binding would last well beyond any business with Deidra and Melanzhi.

"It's…" Neva trailed off, not sure how to explain any of this to her aunt. "It's nothing I can't solve. I'm just glad you're all right."

Neva swallowed hard, trying to rein in her emotions. The relief she felt at finding her aunt recovered was immense, but not as overwhelming as finding herself cut off from her power, and from the Hand. If Trinizhi's trackers found her now…

"Where's Pa?" Neva asked. If she could talk this over with him, maybe they could come up with a solution.

Margret looked down at her hands, which shook with a faint tremor. One of three leeches still sucked on her wrist.

"When you didn't come back, he —" Margret choked on a sob.

Fear unlike anything Neva had ever known washed through her.

"No," Neva said. "Tell me he didn't go back there."

"The young Brenner boy found you only hours later in an alley in Cul Corner. We've no idea how long you were there before he found you, but it was too late." Margret refused to look Neva in the face and failed to contain another sob. "James, go get the note."

James ran to the apartment's main room and returned a moment later, carrying Shaun's cane. It had been snapped in half. The sight of the strong wood reduced to jagged splinters turned Neva's vision red. If she had access to her power, she would have set the room ablaze. James handed her the cane so she could read the note nailed to the wood. When she was done, she ripped off the note, crumpled it into a ball, and threw it across the room.

Melanzhi was officially a thousand times worse than Trinizhi. The Da'Foha and their witch had bound Neva's powers, killed Flynn, cursed her aunt, and burned her home. As if that weren't enough to crush her spirit, now they were holding her father hostage. They could have turned him away. They could have told him to go search Cul Corner's dirtiest, darkest alleys for her. But they had snapped an old man's cane and kidnapped him instead. He probably still didn't know what had happened to her. He might not know she was alive.

It was no wonder Trinizhi and her aliados had been so cautious. Neva felt like a fool.

"I want to be alone," Neva told her aunt. "Can you give me time to clear my head?"

Margret nodded mutely and ushered the boys from the room. Neva turned and shoved her face into her pillow. She screamed her frustration into the feathers and stopped breathing, feeling the moist warmth of the residual wail against her face. She would not cry. She refused to cry. When she couldn't bear to hold her breath any longer, she tossed away the pillow and crawled out of bed. Her clothes had been washed and were folded neatly atop her packs. She rummaged around for more healing tonic and dressed herself with no particular plan in mind.

Neva walked out of Cul Corner feeling utterly lost despite knowing these streets as well as her own reflection. The stench of the district helped propel her forward. It was late afternoon, the light from the sun had turned harsh, and the wind had already started kicking up. And her father was out there, on the other side of the wall, held captive, likely suffering from neglect.

She wanted to blame this situation on not having formulated a plan together, but that wasn't the truth. The truth was that Neva hadn't wanted to feel any more guilt over having taken such a dangerous job in the first place. She'd wanted the weight lifted as soon as possible, and she hadn't asked for help because that would have meant sharing details about her connections to the Da'Valia. She had been selfish, and as a result, she had become even more deeply entangled in the rivalry between the Da'Foha and the Da'Voda.

Neva passed by the Watch headquarters, the shuttered Garin warehouse, and the busy day market, where merchants called out the merits of their wares with less gusto than they did in the morning. She eventually arrived at the blackened remains of the tavern. It had largely been reduced to a pile of rubble. Some bigger timber that had made up the frame of the building still stood, but none of it was salvageable.

Neva's hands curled into fists as she gazed unseeingly at the wreckage. Deidra had destroyed the tavern, trying to silence Neva before word of the Chameleon working in Glacier Pass spread, trying to sever the trail that could have led Trinizhi's alliad to the Da'Foha. Neva might not have access to her power anymore, but she had a piece of information for which Trinizhi would pay dearly and a network of thieves she could approach for help, if she could find the courage to be honest with them for the first time in her life. Neva spun on her heel and started running back to Cul Corner, a strategy taking shape in her mind.

Once Neva's aunt and cousins began spreading word that Shaun needed help, it didn't take long for people to arrive at their tiny apartment. Neva's family, Roger, and her Ring, including Adam, who hadn't left town yet, huddled in the main room by the time night had fallen. A lucky few had seats, and the rest stood shoulder-to-shoulder in the cramped space. The floorboards bowed in places with irksome creaks, and everyone was waiting to hear what Neva had to say.

Neva moved to stand in front of the door, scraping her bottom lip nervously between her teeth as the people closest to her peered at her expectantly. How was it, she wondered, that telling them the truth took more courage than infiltrating the House of Trescony to steal from the duke's own quarters? She was about to disappoint them, that was how. She had lied to them for years.

She cleared her throat loudly. James and Kendall stopped showing each other choke holds long enough to pay attention.

"I asked you to come here because I need your help to save Pa," Neva started. "But first, I have to tell you something."

She stopped, not sure how to proceed.

"Get on with it then!" Archibald encouraged her. His beard was recently trimmed, and he wore a fine new cravat, both which made Neva think he must have pulled off a well-paying job recently. That, or he had a new lady friend.

"Give the lass a moment, Archie," Neil admonished, elbowing the other thief in the side. "Can't you see she's a mite nervous?"

"It's all right, dear," Margret said from her chair near the fireplace. "Tell us what you need to tell us in your own time."

"Maybe…" Neva gathered her courage, and perspiration broke out along her forehead. "Maybe it's best if I show you."

Neva reached behind her neck to unclasp the glamour charm that made her appear human. She closed her eyes as she let her magical disguise fade away. When she opened her eyes again, her family and her Ring were staring at her open-mouthed and with stupefied expressions.

"Why does she have four horns?" Archibald asked, the first to speak. "They don't usually have four horns, do they?"

Neva frowned. *Usually?*

"You look just like your mother when I first saw her," Morty said, a tear in his eye.

"Just like her," Neil agreed. "Before she started wearing her glamour."

Wait, what? Neva was startled by their responses. She didn't think they were trying to present a brave front, but not one of them was looking at her with the fear or trepidation she had expected.

"You're beautiful, dear," Margret added. Neva thought she detected a ring of pride in the older woman's voice.

"Captivating," Adam said. A second later, he crossed his arms over his chest and adjusted his stance as if realizing he'd spoken aloud.

"You…" Neva looked around at her Ring. "You knew?"

"Lass, Morty and me met your mother before Shaun did," Neil bragged.

"But none of you ever said anything," Neva told them.

They looked at each other, and Archibald shrugged. "Didn't seem like our place."

"So all of you knew, er, know I'm half Da'Valia?" she asked.

Her uncles nodded or voiced their agreement. Roger remained stoic in the corner as he usually preferred. Neva reached out to steady herself against the wall, but found Adam there instead. He took her hand.

"We do now," Adam said, nodding at Fletcher, whose piercing blue eyes shifted nervously from the floor to her face. Fletcher was younger than the other men. He wouldn't have been around when Neva's mother hired Shaun all those years ago, but he was dependable. They'd worked a couple low-profile jobs together, and he wasn't greedy.

Well, not too greedy, she thought.

"Fletcher, I couldn't tell you before," Neva said, needing to explain. "I was too frightened of the truth getting out."

"It's all right," he said gruffly, appearing to muster himself to look at her squarely. "You're doing so now. You're honorable, lass."

Roger nodded slowly in agreement. Warmth swelled in Neva's chest at the compliment. Out of the reactions she had envisioned, she had never expected this. She would never have thought her Ring would embrace her, and with praise to boot, when she told them the truth.

Margret took her other hand.

"Was this what you were so nervous about showing us?" her aunt asked kindly. "Neva, you know we love you no matter what."

"I do now," Neva said, trying not to cry.

"Neva, just what kind of trouble is Shaun in?" Morty asked. "And more importantly, how can we help?"

"The worst kind," she admitted. She took a deep breath and told them exactly what she needed them to do.

Neva had made a mistake when she took on the Da'Foha and their witch the first time. She wouldn't make that mistake again. She needed more experience and firepower to go up against them, and she didn't have many options. Her allies among the Da'Voda were far away, and they had already risked their own safety in aiding her escape. Only those acting under Trinizhi's orders were nearby, and Trinizhi either wanted Neva locked away, or dead. The irony of the situation was not lost on Neva.

But if there was one Da'Voda in their camp who Neva might sway, it would be Astiand.

The Da'Voda's camp wasn't hard to find. It was exactly where Melanzhi had said it would be, beyond the southern wall. Neva watched the Da'Voda from afar as they moved about. She was perched in a tree well away from the wall to determine which tent was Astiand's. The Da'Voda soldiers who had chased her joined up with the original group Trinizhi sent to strike a deal with the Da'Foha. A mission that had been doomed from the start because Bryand had betrayed them all.

Neva recalled her chats with Bryand during his recovery. He had often used a disgruntled tone explaining the way things used to be when the clans worked together during the Great War. She hadn't realized how deep that malcontent went inside him. There had been times when she had thought a friendship was growing between them. But friends didn't leave unconscious friends in dark alleys.

Neva adjusted her headscarf as steam rose around her, the morning sun warming snow that sat precariously piled upon the branches of the tree. Finally, she saw him. Astiand marched out of the largest tent in the camp, arguing with Trinizhi and Arroyand. They used hushed tones amid the curious ears of other Da'Voda, but Neva knew it was a fight because she recognized the look on his face.

Dhianz, save me! Neva prayed upon seeing the donazhi and her aliados. Trinizhi was here. In Glacier Pass. Neva still needed the Da'Voda, but now she would have to be even more persuasive.

Astiand threw up his hands, ending whatever discussion he had been having with Trinizhi, and stormed into another tent near the center of the encampment. Neva had seen no one else enter that tent. She bided her time for an hour before calling on her invisibility glamour to sneak past the soldiers on watch and into the camp. Only her mission to rescue her father kept her from fleeing back into the city.

With a practiced ease, Neva slipped inside Astiand's tent to find him asleep atop a thin mat, garbed in his practical soldier's uniform. She was hit with a flurry of emotions. Mostly, anger. The past month had been a game to him, and he somehow justified his actions — not telling her about her mother's journal and reporting Neva's activities — by considering it necessary for his alliad.

But Neva was also shocked by her longing. She had missed him, she realized with some surprise. Her Da'Valia side desired to be near him despite his attempts to govern her life. That side of her argued he had always tried to protect her — with the shacklay and with warnings. It was ridiculous and infuriating to feel both ways at once, but his strength and power called to her, often against her better judgment. She wanted to believe her blood didn't matter. She wanted to believe in him. She crept nearer and couldn't stop herself from reaching out an invisible hand to caress the side of his face with a feather touch.

His eyelids twitched, but his breathing remained even. His non-reaction prompted a peculiar boldness. This was what she came here for — approaching him alone was the only way she would have a chance of securing the Da'Voda's help against the Da'Foha.

Neva leaned down to his sleeping form, feeling her heart jump in her chest. She hesitated for the slightest moment before lightly brushing her lips across his. Once, then twice.

After a moment, a sound between a purr and a growl climbed from Astiand's throat, and he moved his mouth in response, still between the land of dreams and consciousness. His reaction made her breath catch in her throat as a familiar warmth radiated from where their skin met. She had been so cold since the witch bound her powers, but being near Astiand stirred a passionate heat within her.

Neva was about to turn her attention to slowly disarming him when he caught her hand in his and yanked her down, pinning her between him and the sleeping mat. He crushed her mouth under his own with a heated domination. One of his hands caressed her horn so streaks of his power assailed her senses and she nearly forgot where she was. He opened his eyes to look at her and abruptly pulled back, fierce and fully alert.

"Show yourself," he demanded. A hint of confusion clouded his eyes, and Neva realized belatedly that while she had felt his power, he wouldn't have been able to feel hers.

Neva hesitated only a moment before letting her invisibility fade away.

"I didn't know you could do that," he said.

Neva could practically see him connecting her invisibility with her presence in his house, near Trinizhi's alliad and its dealings. His voice was steely with displeasure, but he hadn't blasted her with his power or shouted to alert the camp — and she had his attention.

"I have a proposition for you," she blurted out.

"Do you really?" Astiand's eyes glinted with an interest, making her realize he could take what she had said one of two ways, and considering their current position... He ran a warm finger over her bottom lip, and she had to focus to stifle the desire that shot through her.

"Aye." Neva licked her lips, forcing herself to collect her thoughts.

"Well? What is it?" Astiand asked. He moved his hands to where her wrap exposed her flesh.

His touch was exquisite, and she wanted more of it, but it was his tone that strengthened her resolve. She couldn't afford for him not to take her seriously right now. She needed a level address, which was rather difficult with him on top of her.

"Don't let her kill me." Neva caught his eyes with hers, imploring him to protect her.

"And?" Astiand raised an eyebrow.

"That's it," Neva said. "That's all I want from you."

"That's not a proposition," he said.

"I'll owe you a favor," Neva said, not liking owing anyone, but willing to strike such a deal to save her father.

Astiand glowered at her.

"What makes you think I would want a favor from you?" he asked.

Exasperation choked her. She didn't know which she wanted more — to kiss him, or hit him.

"If I know anything about you, it's that you possess some wisdom, despite appearances," Neva told him sharply. "No matter how much you hate me, I don't think you'll pass this up."

"You don't, do you?"

Did she detect amusement in his tone?

"No. You won't." Neva said confidently. Right now, he still thought she was the most powerful Da'Valia he'd ever met. That would change, but until it did, there was no way he would turn down the chance to have her owe him a favor.

"You're probably right." He didn't sound happy about it. "And I don't hate you, Neva, but you do realize how dangerous it is for you to come here, don't you? A Da'Voda soldier died during your escape. Trinizhi might not kill you, but don't think she'll hesitate to lock you away for the rest of your days. Trust me. I've seen her do it."

"Trust *me*," Neva told him. "If there was any other path open to me, I would have followed it."

"You should have stayed away," Astiand said, but he rolled to his side next to her as if he was ready to listen.

"I couldn't," Neva said. "I need to speak with Trinizhi."

"You don't know her. That is no simple thing. Not for you."

"I know her better than you think." Neva insisted. She had learned a lot listening through walls and reading her mother's journal. They stared each other down, with steadfast determination on her part and smooth calculation on his.

"I'll keep you alive for a meeting," he agreed. "You will owe me according to my terms. Whenever, wherever."

"Agreed." Neva started to rise, but he stopped her. Pulling her toward him by her belt, he claimed her mouth with a gentle finesse. It was a moment before he released her, but when he did, she gulped down air. He needed no magic to cast a spell over her.

"I will hold you to your promise," he said, still pulling her in with his enthralling gaze.

"I'm counting on it." Her heart was pounding in her chest. She didn't even realize she managed to have the last word.

Chapter Thirty

Ninth Fireside, 1632

*Shaun has asked for my hand. Of course, I accepted. We will be wed before
the baby arrives if all goes according to plan. Me. A wife.*

— *Monazhi Da'Voda-Lira*

Astiand lured Trinizhi to his tent under the pretense of continuing their
earlier conversation. Neva waited, trying not to bite her nails, at the rear
flap. She hoped to make a quick getaway should the need arise. Neva's
bound powers were a serious disadvantage and at the forefront of her thoughts.

Trinizhi stilled with an eerie immobility as soon as she saw Neva. The donazhi
looked like a draped alabaster statue, dressed in a dark green like her soldiers. Her
headpiece was the only adornment that would identify her as anything more.

"I should put you under the lash right now." Trinizhi's voice was calm, so
Neva was shocked when the donazhi spun and backhanded Astiand. The skin
over his cheekbone split and blood trickled down his face.

"Was that necessary?" Astiand asked, his voice drenched in disdain.

"I don't know, was it?" Trinizhi challenged. "Is there a reason she isn't
bound and gagged? Was her power too much for you to resist?"

Astiand slowly looked at Neva, massaging his jaw.

"Did you help her escape, too?" Trinizhi threw the accusation at Astiand,
lashing out a shot of power at him.

He stepped to the side, easily avoiding it.

"Don't be ridiculous," he told Trinizhi, ignoring the tent as it burst into flames behind him. "I brought you so you can hear what Nevazhi has to say."

"You." Trinizhi locked her silver-white eyes on Neva. "I should lock you up for the rest of your days. I'm down a soldier because of you, our stronghold is no longer protected as it once was, and you've undermined my authority."

"What if I told you I know something you don't?" Neva asked, sensing the time to share information was fast evaporating.

"Unlikely," Trinizhi said.

Neva prayed to Dhianz what she said next would make a difference.

"I know which of your aliados has betrayed you." Neva spoke quietly in case anyone outside the tent was listening.

"Who?" Trinizhi asked, her voice taking on a deadly edge.

Astiand growled. The smell of smoke and burned hide traveled to Neva as the wind played with what was left of the tent behind him, but he seemed not to notice. His attention, and Trinizhi's attention, was trained solely on Neva.

"He doesn't know that I know, but Bryand is with the Da'Foha," Neva said. "Who can say for how long, but he is. They have the goblet, and they don't intend to give it up, ever. They know what it can do. They just can't control it."

Trinizhi relaxed her stance. She was still on the defensive, but she hadn't tried to capture or kill Neva, which made Neva think the donazhi now wanted to hear what she had to say. Astiand continued to watch Neva with the same level of interest.

"If you want the goblet, we need to attack now, before Bryand discovers I've spoken with you about *this*," Neva stressed the last word to indicate the Da'Foha might expect something else. If Bryand had the slightest suspicion that she had discovered his treachery and revealed it to Trinizhi, Neva's plan would be over before it had begun.

"What else would he assume?" Trinizhi questioned coolly, picking up on the distinction.

"They want me to convince you to leave the Pass," Neva said, knowing how ridiculous it sounded.

"That isn't going to happen," Astiand said. The last trails of smoke dissipated behind him.

"I know it's not," Neva replied.

"What proof do you have Bryand has betrayed us?" Trinizhi challenged her.

Neva had expected this, and she worried it was the weakest link in her argument. She remembered Trinizhi snapping at Bryand when they met at Astiand's home, touchy about the possibility of her alliad having faults. Neva hoped that sensitivity stemmed from deep-seeded doubt.

"You know it's true," Neva said. "How else would the Da'Foha know they possess Dhianz's Eye when they can't even touch it?"

"Gods curse it! I warned you." Astiand raised his voice at Trinizhi. "He still remembers when the clans worked together during the Great War. You shouldn't have shut them out for something this important."

"We're not going into that now." Trinizhi turned her powerful gaze on Astiand. "Not with *her* here. That decision was strictly between our alliad."

Astiand quieted, but his expression said their conversation was far from finished.

"What do you mean they cannot touch it?" Trinizhi turned to Neva.

"They can't." Neva shook her head. "It's too much for them. One witch and all Melanzhi's aliados have been incapacitated."

Trinizhi tapped a manicured finger on the hilt of the sword at her waist.

"Give me one reason to keep you alive," the donazhi said.

"I'll give you three," Neva said. "I'm here to help you, and I've been in their camp." She described the tent Deidra and Melanzhi shared with the sickbay in the back.

Trinizhi's gaze was trained on her as she spoke, but Neva could tell the donazhi's thoughts were on the other side of the city with the Da'Foha, and Bryand.

"And I've found the goblet before, so I'm confident I can find it again," Neva finished.

"Exactly when did you 'find' the goblet before?" Astiand asked, sounding confused.

Neva swallowed hard. She had protected her Lynx identity for as long as she could, but she had to count on that small piece of information elevating her worth to the Da'Voda. Otherwise, it would be too easy for Trinizhi to get rid of her. A part of Neva wondered how things might have gone differently if she had been honest earlier, when they had found Flynn with his throat slit, but she couldn't go back in time.

"When I was commissioned to steal it from the House of Trescony," Neva said. She waited for their reactions.

"You're the thief we hired through Flynn?" Astiand's features smoothed as realization dawned. "You're the Lynx?"

"A lass has got to earn a living." Neva tried to keep her tone light, but she couldn't play this off with a cheeky comment like she could while waiting tables. She cleared her throat. "I've worked for Flynn for years."

"And you didn't think to share this information earlier?" Astiand asked.

"You've never been open either," Neva said, her temper flaring. "I think it's safe to say I learned from the best."

"Enough." Trinizhi cut in. "You've convinced me that you're more valuable to us if you're not in chains. For now. What else did the Da'Foha tell you?"

Neva walked them through what happened when she arrived, leaving her father and aunt out of the story. She reluctantly told them about the witch binding her powers. If Neva had learned anything from Vivizhi, it was that Trinizhi would interpret Neva as less of a threat if she didn't have her power anymore. She revealed that Bryand and Melanzhi had discussed poisoning Trinizhi — and Neva made sure to include how they had thought her asleep, so the Da'Voda were sure to have an advantage if they attacked now.

"It's a shame we won't have your power in the fight," the donazhi mused, but she didn't sound particularly disappointed. Silence fell as Trinizhi contemplated the situation, her brow tight with concentration. "You say they planned to poison me?"

"That or torture you," Neva replied.

"Bryand is still in the city with Hanazhi, purchasing supplies supposedly," Trinizhi said bitterly. "We'll gather everyone to attack. I want to see their blood run. We're not waiting on this, not if they have Bryand on their side."

"They do," Neva assured her.

"You had better not be lying," Trinizhi said. "You'll be coming with us, and I'll kill you myself if you are. Dhianz would thank me for the favor."

Astiand gave a curt nod. "I'll round everyone up."

"Take her with you." Trinizhi motioned at Neva. "If she's out of your sight, you're not doing your job."

Neva exchanged a look with Astiand.

"Don't think this means I've forgiven your blatant disrespect of our laws, Nevazhi," Trinizhi said before heading back to her own tent. "Know I will find your human."

"You heard her," Astiand told Neva. "You leave my side and things will not end well for you."

Or me, his tone implied.

"I won't." Neva's jaw clenched. She wished he would stop looking at her in quite that way, as if she were doomed whether or not she followed Trinizhi's orders.

"We are going into battle and you have no power," Astiand told her. "You're practically human. Your chances of survival are not good if you stray from me."

"You won't be able to get rid of me," Neva replied, annoyed he didn't believe her.

He held her gaze until she finally looked down.

Damn it, she thought. She was certain he knew she was lying. She would stay near him while it suited her and not a moment longer. Thankfully, she had been trained by the Da'Voda's own master at arms.

"What happens after?" she dared to ask.

"If I had to guess?" Astiand led the way to the edge of the camp. "She'll make an example of you."

The image of Miland's horns flashed through her mind.

"You have to help me get my power back," Neva said to him as she hurried to catch up.

Astiand didn't respond, instead informing a majila on the perimeter that Trinizhi wanted to see everyone in her tent. He ordered the soldier to gather their forces, but Neva knew there weren't many more Da'Voda to fight with them. Trinizhi had sent her aliados to Glacier Pass incognito originally, and the rest of their forces consisted only of those sent to apprehend Neva and Adam.

"Shouldn't she be in chains?" the majila challenged Astiand with a ferocious glare in Neva's direction.

"I've got it handled," Astiand told her dismissively. "Our orders have changed."

"Astiand, how can I undo this spell?" Neva said as soon as the majila moved out of earshot.

"I don't know much about their magic, but Vodou witches like to work with effigies," Astiand told her. "She would have had to procure some piece of you and use it to create a likeness. A cut of skin, a drop of blood, a strand of hair. It doesn't matter. You have to burn it. If you don't and Trinizhi is still breathing at the end of this, be prepared to suffer. You might have been an indulgence once, but you quickly became a threat and you are at your weakest now."

Neva grew quiet, thinking. Deidra had bumped into her as they had entered Melanzhi's tent. Neva would have noticed if the witch had tried to pickpocket her, but a strand of hair? She hadn't known what the witch could do with such a small thing. Neva studied Astiand out of the corner of her eye. He was looking out for her, and right now that meant everything.

The Da'Voda convened at Trinizhi's tent. Five soldiers gathered inside with Trinizhi, and Arroyand trickled in behind Neva and Astiand. The tent was spacious enough so they all stood with room to spare. The team the donazhi had brought with her included three toppel majilas and two toppel hilans. Trinizhi, obviously, did not take Neva's and Adam's departure lightly. After reading about the majila in her mother's journal, Neva would not have expected less.

Neva saw malice in some of their eyes as they watched her. The largest hilan and one of the majilas, who growled and fingered the hilt of her knife upon seeing Neva, refused to look away from her.

"Why hasn't she been secured?" the hilan tracker asked. His voice was gruff, and Neva could tell it wouldn't take much for him to attack. She recoiled a little, shadowing herself between Astiand and Arroyand.

"A change of plans," Trinizhi said sharply. "For the moment, anyway. I trust you're all ready for a fight."

That got their attention, and Neva breathed more easily as they looked away from her. While Trinizhi relayed information about the Da'Foha and outlined a plan of attack, Arroyand appeared to listen half-heartedly. He snagged a lock of Neva's hair and played with it.

"You put on an impressive show in that valley," he murmured to her, overly friendly. "What say you go for a repeat and wash away the Da'Foha for us?"

Neva frowned. Even if she could create another natural disaster, she wouldn't do it here. Glacier Pass had been her home her entire life.

Astiand reached around Neva and knocked Arroyand's arm away, but the donazhi's consort had already drawn her attention.

Trinizhi stopped talking to the group and glared at Arroyand.

"As I said, the Da'Foha have at least one Vodou witch at their disposal," Trinizhi said. "It so happens we cannot rely on Nevazhi's power in our fight, since this witch has bound her powers."

The large hilan grinned at Neva in a way that made her think if they did live through this, he would be the first to come after her.

"So, if you wouldn't mind paying attention?" Trinizhi arched an eyebrow at Arroyand.

"Ah, too bad." Arroyand shrugged. "But, of course, I am sure we'll prevail under your leadership."

Trinizhi finished detailing their approach, handling military terminology and answering her soldiers' questions with an expertise that made Neva think maybe they *could* prevail against the Da'Foha. Once Trinizhi concluded the conference, her soldiers rushed around the camp, saddling their war horses and strapping on armor. Only Neva, Trinizhi, and her aliados remained in the tent.

"Bryand?" Arroyand cursed at Trinizhi's confirmation. "That bastard."

"I'll deal with him when the time comes." Trinizhi said with such bitterness that the temperature drop was nearly tangible.

"Donazhi," a majila's voice came from the door flap.

Neva spied a familiar Da'Voda standing in the doorway. Hanazhi, who used to work the boundary patrol with Kelizhi, Roland, and Jorand, hesitated and ducked her head in respect before stepping inside.

"Quand told me there's been a change of orders," Hanazhi said.

"Bryand didn't return with you?" Trinizhi asked.

"No, Donazhi," Hanazhi said. "Do you want me to go back for him? He said he had a few more items to buy and he would be back before dark."

"Darrand will fill you in on your new orders." Trinizhi dismissed the soldier.

As soon as Hanazhi left, Trinizhi faced what remained of her alliad.

"It's just as well if he's with them," Trinizhi said. "He can try to hide behind Melanzhi, but he will not live past today."

Before long, another soldier arrived and announced the horses were ready.

"Let's go," Arroyand said.

"Die with honor." Trinizhi's voice came quietly after them as they exited the canvas covering. "Bryand certainly won't."

Chapter Thirty-One

First Vestive, 1633

*She made a screaming entrance into the world. I couldn't be more proud. I
named her Nevazhi after my mother.*

— *Monazhi Roberts*

Neva mounted behind Astiand and wrapped her arms around his
midsection, certain his steed could sense her nervousness. The
beast was huge, and the saddle was not made for more than one
rider, so she felt awkward and uncomfortable. The Da'Voda squad, ten in all,
followed the wall around the city, crossing the Glacier Arm's downriver bridge
and then traveling back up it. They came to a stop not far from the Da'Foha's
camp, and Neva filled them in on how it was situated.

"They are just ahead," Neva started her report, steadying herself against
Astiand's back as their horse jittered with nervous energy. "When I was there,
three Da'Foha came from the east and two came from the west. I think they
were monitoring the perimeter. Another three came from within the camp, but
there were a dozen tents in all. One witch and the donazhi came from the fourth
— the fifth tent from the right. Inside are her three aliados and the other witch,
who were incapacitated at the time. That is where the goblet will be."

"Are we killing the indisposed as well?" asked the gruff Da'Voda soldier
named Quand.

"All of them," Trinizhi said grimly.

"Is there anything else we can use to our advantage?" Hanazhi questioned.

Neva started to shake her head but then stopped.

"I don't know," she said slowly. "Maybe. Their capes are thicker. That might come in handy. But whatever you do, if you see the goblet, don't let it touch your skin."

Neva's eyes slid to Trinizhi.

"I know you want it," she told the donazhi. "But it's trapped four of them in a trance-like state, so if anyone sees it, don't let it touch you."

"You heard her," Trinizhi said. "Quand, take your team and Hanazhi to see if you can't quietly neutralize the watch. We'll wait for a count of five-hundred before coming in, unless you give us a sign we should do otherwise."

Quand and his team set off with Hanazhi trailing.

"Feels like old times, doesn't it?" Arroyand asked Astiand.

"You weren't there in the old times," Astiand said after a moment.

Neva could tell he was thinking about Bryand, who had fought alongside him during the Great War. They were brothers in arms, friends, and aliados of the same ruthless donazhi. This siege put Astiand in an unenviable position. Instinctively, Neva tightened her arms around him.

"Can you hear anything?" Neva asked after a moment, not directing her question to anyone in particular.

"Not yet," Arroyand replied. He was scanning the horizon, his head tilted, listening.

"Is that good or bad?" Neva asked.

"It's good," Astiand replied. "It means the Da'Foha likely haven't heard anything, either."

They all fell quiet, and Neva felt as if an eternity passed before Trinizhi motioned them forward.

"The count's almost five-hundred," Trinizhi said.

They kicked their horses into gallops, thundering through the woods and bursting into the Da'Foha's camp. Trinizhi blasted two tents out of their way with a massive show of power. The donazhi let out a shrill battle cry, a warrior queen — with her sword raised, jet stone adornment atop her head, charging in atop an armored warhorse. The sound of her battle cry bounced off nearby trees as their horses jumped over the burning tents and into the center of the camp. Neva's bones jarred as they landed. More cries sounded around the camp, seeming to ricochet like banshee screams.

The Da'Foha immediately engaged their attackers. Neva scanned the camp, looking for her father. She jerked in surprise when a majila sprung herself on Arroyand from behind a tree, latching onto him and going for his eyes. The fight between the other Da'Foha soldiers and Quand's team at the far end of the camp came into Neva's view as the majila yanked Arroyand out of his saddle and to the ground. His horse turned and bucked, knocking the majila in the head with a hoof before prancing away. Blood gushed from the majila's head and she fell back into the snow, stunned. Arroyand went in for the kill.

A strange glowing power that smelled like manure and reminded Neva of lightning radiated from Melanzhi's tent. Neva realized her count had been off. It was the fourth tent, not the fifth. That didn't matter, though, because Trinizhi had figured it out and was facing down a triad of Da'Foha that had braided a shield as the first line of defense. Warlocks. Neva cursed in her mind. She hadn't seen this group in her earlier visit. Another team meant the Da'Voda were outnumbered.

Where was her father? Neva's head whipped around, but there was no sign of him. Astiand headed straight for Trinizhi, his black flame joining hers against the triad's shield. It took Neva a split second to capitalize on the distraction. She called on her invisibility glamour as she awkwardly launched herself off the back of Astiand's steed. Neva landed in a roll and regained her footing as Astiand and Trinizhi combined their power in a stunning barrage that seemed to come at the triad from all directions.

From around the camp, Da'Voda warriors targeted blasts as they were able, but to no avail. A barrier seemed to deflect their power how the training rooms absorbed wayward shots.

Neva took a chance, squeezing her eyes shut and diving between the main tent and its neighbor. An airless feeling bombarded her as she passed the intangible wall of defense. Had her powers been unbound, she didn't know what would have happened, but she was instead able to shimmy under the edge of the hide and into the makeshift sickbay.

Neva stilled once she was in the tent, barely breathing as she assessed her surroundings. Melanzhi and Bryand stood together near the front, awaiting the moment Trinizhi would break through. Melanzhi had the goblet affixed to her belt. Although it was covered, the shape was telling. Neva's honed thieving skills told her the best chance of finding the source of the witch's binding spell was at the altar next to Bryand and Melanzhi. Deidra, her face bruised from her broken nose, was sitting cross-legged on the center rug surrounded by a circle of small black rocks. Her skin practically glowed with the electric power coursing over it, and her eyes were rolled back in her head. Her long hair flew about her, controlled by unseen currents as she rocked back and forth.

Shaun was gagged and bound to a sturdy pole in the back corner on the other side of the tent.

Pa! Neva hurried over to him, furious to see her father victimized this way. She would get him out of here if it was the last thing she ever did.

Neva started loosening the bindings on his wrists and feet.

"I'm going to release you," Neva whispered in her father's ear. "The Ring is just outside in the trees. They'll help you get away."

Her father twitched, but her voice calmed him. He was familiar with her methods and he could hear the battle raging outside. He nodded slowly so as not to alert his captors. Neva pulled her daggers and slid one into Shaun's hand. She was ready to usher him out of the tent through the rear flap, but he resisted her as she pulled on his arm.

"Go," she told him. "I'll follow."

"My legs," Shaun whispered to her. "The witch. I can't move them."

Neva gripped her blade so tight her knuckles turned powder white. *Curse it all,* Neva thought, her gaze narrowing on her father's cheek, where a fresh cut of flesh was missing. Astiand's suggestion that the witch might have spelled an effigy had Neva looking again to the witch's altar.

"As soon as you can move, get out of here," Neva whispered. "Don't look back."

With that, she rose and strode to the front of the tent, skirting Deidra's foul-smelling circle. Neva approached Melanzhi slowly, judging how close she would have to get to the donazhi to access the altar.

A slight shift in Bryand's stance was the only warning Neva had before he delivered a sharp backwards kick toward her middle. Neva fell in a graceful drop to stay out of his reach, but doing so meant she failed to avoid the end of Melanzhi's blade as the donazhi hacked the air blindly. Melanzhi's sword drew a bloody line down Neva's side, deep enough that the metal scraped against one of her ribs. Neva forgot how to breathe as pain burst through her. Blood splattered onto the rug.

Neva locked onto the pain, channeling her strength to retaliate. In a smooth twist of her body, Neva leveraged Melanzhi under her and slammed the hilt of her dagger against the majila's fingers so she released her sword. Neva dropped her own dagger and took hold of the sword. She lifted the blade, and rammed it down with both hands, staking Melanzhi's arm into the hard earth with all of her might.

Melanzhi screamed and convulsed. Trinizhi's fight broke through the Da'Foha's barrier and into the tent, sending Bryand staggering back. Deidra stopped rocking and began drawing runes in the air with crackling magic. Before she could complete her spell, Astiand was on her. Trinizhi, radiating power, dove straight for Bryand, not sparing Melanzhi a second glance.

"You should have known better," Trinizhi told Bryand, raising her sword.

Bryand's blade crashed against Trinizhi's and power erupted out of both of them, ripping the front of the tent off at the seams so their quarrel spilled into the middle of the camp.

Deidra was fighting off Astiand like a wildcat, scratching with her nails whenever she wasn't combating his attacks with her strange magic. Astiand was slowed significantly by her spells. He was moving no faster than a human and Deidra kept dousing his power as it manifested.

Neva blocked out everything around her as she struggled with Melanzhi. Though one arm was staked into the ground, the majila didn't shy from using her power. Neva avoided the first blast but failed to evade the second while pinning the donazhi. It singed her lacerated side in a burning so severe, she knew it would leave permanent scars.

Neva needed to gain an advantage quickly, so she did the first thing of which she could think. She went for one of Melanzhi's horns and yanked. She could feel Melanzhi's power shored there, spiked and tingling. Neva had opened a channel between them, now she willed the donazhi's power into herself. Melanzhi fought her for control, screaming again, this time with rage. Melanzhi yanked the goblet from her belt, the silk bag sagging away from the top of it, and slammed the metal into Neva's throat.

A wave of tar gushed from the goblet, pouring over Neva's face and ensnaring her so she failed to move for the briefest moment. The next thing Neva knew, Arroyand was there, delivering a kick to Melanzhi's head, severing the goblet's connection to Neva and Neva's connection to Melanzhi. The oil cascaded back into the goblet and sent a shock wave out, slamming into Neva and tossing her into the air.

Neva went flying and landed on one of Melanzhi's incapacitated aliados with a grunt, the wind knocked from her. She could only watch as Arroyand flipped back to his feet and went for Melanzhi. He staked Melanzhi's free arm into the ground and sliced her throat in a clean stroke. He ripped her headdress free and raised it toward the heavens with a victorious battle cry.

Power leaped inside Neva, free again. The Fye had ripped through her body and mind, and as a result, the binding Deidra had placed on Neva shattered much like how Monazhi's spell had fractured in the duke's study. Neva had immediate access to the reservoir of power inside of her. Relief, then fear washed through her.

She had to get her father out of here.

Neva regained her footing to find Astiand struggling against magical rope Deidra had wrapped around his throat, lifting him from the ground. Neva fought the urge to go to his aid. Arroyand was several steps ahead of her, so she ran to the witch's altar instead. Neva could already sense the difference within her. Her power felt stronger than it had a few days earlier, as if the short dormancy had allowed it to gather and pool. But that wasn't all. The Eye had awoken the Hand, and it clawed at her from the depths of her mind, wanting to show itself. *Demanding* it show itself.

Neva closed her eyes, breathing deep, calling on her memories of the firérite and Astiand's shacklay, fighting to keep the Hand reined. She looked at the altar helplessly, then kicked it over in a perhaps reckless decision. Candles rolled and the fabric draping it fluttered away. A small door in the wooden stand popped open. Neva fumbled with a leather bag she found inside, praying it contained the figurine Astiand had described and the one imprisoning her father.

The Hand was fighting to climb out of her, demanding freedom. It seeped through her pores and she was having trouble holding it back. She needed to get some distance before Dhianz's Hand materialized and she destroyed everything and everyone around her, including her father.

Neva stopped fumbling with the bag. She grabbed a Da'Foha-style cloak Melanzhi had hanging along the side of the tent and wrapped it around herself, trying to keep her power contained a moment longer with the thick flame-retardant material. She pulled the hood over her head and steadied herself, dizzy from the influence of the goblet. The urge to let the Hand out was becoming unbearable. She felt as if it would burn her up from the inside if she didn't release it.

Focus. Neva dug her nails into the wounds in her side. The pain was excruciating, but she used it to gain back a modicum of control. Spots danced in front of her eyes and obscured her vision as she pulled out her bloody fingers. Tears slid down her face. She grabbed the bag again and ripped it open. She caught the figurines and engulfed them in flame.

Free from the magic, her father struggled to his feet, using the pole he'd been tied to for support.

"Run!" Neva shouted at him, drops of power falling from her like a light rain.

Shaun fled. He didn't bother to check his surroundings, limping into the trees as quickly as he could.

Neva looked over and witnessed Deidra stunning Arroyand into unconsciousness. He landed in a lump. It appeared to be the distraction Astiand was waiting for. He punched through Deidra's spells, and Neva knew he had used some of Trinizhi's power because his black flame was tinted white. He grabbed the Vodou witch by the throat and lifted her. Her magic crackled around her, growing a brighter blue as he held her suspended, choking the life from her.

Neva moved past them, past Melanzhi's corpse staked into the earth, and to the center of the camp. As she walked, fire and weapons and warriors created a tempest around her.

Neva saw Trinizhi and Bryand locked together, their hands on each other's horns, their skin fading darker and lighter as they fought to destroy each other. Few bodies had fallen. The clans were well-matched. Neva forced herself to keep walking, and she didn't stop until she passed the edge of the camp, where she climbed a small knoll, certain she could pinpoint where in the woods her Ring and, hopefully by now, her father were waiting for her.

The hill gave her an amazing view of the battle raging below. She wondered at the familiarity of this scene. Then, with horror, she realized why she recognized it, and with that thought, her mind had wandered from the pain restraining the Hand. The Hand had been testing her fragile hold on it, now it broke free.

Chapter Thirty-Two

Second Cravell, 1634

Alizhi, I am sending this journal to you because war is upon us and who knows how long each of us has left? When I saw Calland on the street the other day, I decided it. You were the best mentor a majila could ask for, and you deserve to know the whole story of what happened. I used the trick you showed me to hide what I've written from prying eyes. I trust you've figured that out.

Please know I am happy even though I am not among our people. Shaun challenges me in all the right ways, and Nevazhi made it through her first Fireside. She is strong, this little one. I am proud that even when I failed at collecting the prongs of the Trishula, I did this one thing right.

Should you live longer than I, I hope you'll keep Nevazhi in your thoughts and lend her your protection should she need it. Know I miss your friendship every day.

— Monazhi Roberts

The final prophecy materialized before Neva. Unable to contain the Hand, she flung out her arms to release it. A wave of fire washed over the field, enveloping everyone in its path. Da'Voda and Da'Foha alike fell to the ground, their meager shields failing under the godly power. The Hand leveled tents and uprooted nearby trees.

It was exactly the image Neva had seen in liquid tar when she stole the goblet, but it was so much more potent in its size, in that she could see the expression on Hanazhi's face as she cried out, falling to the ground. Unable to bring her braided shield up in time, Hanazhi was consumed by flame.

Only Trinizhi had the strength to throw up a shield. The donazhi ripped away from Bryand at the last possible second, surrounding herself, Arroyand, and Astiand under screens of raw power that deflected the wave so the Hand crashed and spurted up upon impact like the ocean upon rocks. Trinizhi's defenses buckled slightly but held under the force.

Neva somehow knew, if she had intended this attack, even the donazhi's power would not have been able to withstand it. If Neva wanted to, she could force the Hand through the shields and claim their lives.

But she didn't want any of this to happen.

She could see a red flag atop a tree not too far away. Roger had promised to raise the marker so she would know where to reunite with her father. The sea of flame was quickly approaching their location.

Neva grit her teeth and focused all of the pain, all of her will to rein it back in. This was *her* power, *her* burden. She *was* the Hand. She could control it.

Neva latched onto the inexorable truth of that and screamed her effort as if she were lifting an ox, calling the power she had released to an abrupt stop. The Hand halted and hovered. She sent it down in an almost-perfect circle. The liquid flame plunged to the floor of the forest, slamming harmlessly into the snow and dirt below. Slush splattered from where the power collided with the terrain and created deep trenches. Smoke rose from the charred trees all around the camp.

Neva meant to lower her arms, but as she surveyed the damage, her hands moved to cover her mouth instead. Horror constricted her stomach. Nearly nothing from the camp was left, except charred remains she would be hard-pressed to identify. It wasn't a bona fide hecatomb, but it was plenty close enough. Neva turned and grabbed a tree as she vomited into the mud. She wiped her mouth on her cape and rushed down the hill to what remained of Trinizhi's alliad.

Arroyand lay unconscious in a pile of ash that had once been the Da'Foha's sickbay. Astiand was leaning over Trinizhi's unmoving form looking like he might collapse atop her at any moment. Everyone else had burned into piles of ash.

Neva approached Astiand and Trinizhi cautiously, afraid of what she would find.

"Is she...?" Neva couldn't bring herself to say the word.

Neva didn't believe in or approve of Trinizhi's methods, but she also didn't want to be the cause of so much death and destruction. Maybe that was what Dhianz had created the Hand for, but that didn't mean she had to like it. The Da'Voda's way of life worked because of the structure the donazhi enforced. Without that structure, Neva didn't know what would happen to the clan, or to the friends she had made there.

Astiand raised his eyes to meet hers. He had no cuts or apparent wounds from his fight with Deidra, but he was swaying as he tried to remain standing.

"She will live," his voice was coarse. "She drained our alliad for the shield, but she will mend."

The donazhi's skin was a crystalline alabaster, but Neva had seen the donazhi and her aliados nurse Bryand from the edge of death, so she didn't doubt Astiand's words.

"What was Dhianz thinking, creating this power?" Neva murmured. Guilt was slowly seeping into her limbs.

"It is not our place to know his mind," Astiand said. He straightened and grabbed her by the arm. "You have to listen to me, now. It won't take Trinizhi long to revive, and she won't rest until you and your human are locked away."

"So?" Neva asked, shaking her head to clear it. Her side was burning, her head was pounding, and she wasn't sure she was breathing properly anymore. What had she done?

"You have to run." Astiand's hold tightened with urgency. "Get as far away from here as you can."

"Astiand, look around," Neva said. "I did this. I killed all of them, without even meaning to. Maybe the best place for me is inside the donazhi's dungeon, where I won't be able to hurt anyone."

Neva recalled the majila whose cell she had tossed the unconscious guards in during Adam's escape. The majila with the dead eyes. Neva didn't think it would take long for her own spirit to fade in captivity. But maybe it would be for the best.

"You think if Trinizhi has you that you wouldn't do this again and again, whenever she decides?" Astiand asked, sounding incredulous. "She would use your power for her own. Don't fool yourself."

Neva shook her head but stopped, afraid she might pass out. She wasn't sure if it was an aftereffect of the goblet, or the blood loss that made her vision spin.

"Go south," he ordered. "Beyond Cirandrel, to the desert. Hundreds of years ago, when the mages started persecuting the Da'Valia, our people abandoned it. None of the five clans goes there anymore. You'll be safer there."

"What good would my escape do? I can't run forever." Neva spoke in hushed tones. Everything seemed incredibly quiet compared to the battle that had been raging a moment before.

"Not forever," he continued in a pressing manner. "I promised someone a long time ago, if I ever stumbled upon you, I would protect you. Your leaving is the only way I can do that now."

Neva squinted at him, seeing double.

"Who did you promise?" Neva asked. What he was saying didn't make any sense to her.

"My mother, Alizhi. She was a close friend of your mother's. Committed to restoring the Trishula as much as Monazhi was." Astiand spoke as if the memory of his mother pained him. "Their intent to find the Trishula was just and good, but Trinizhi has gone about it in the worst way."

All the puzzle pieces fell into place. Alizhi had passed on this duty to Astiand. This was why he had Monazhi's journal in his safe. This was why he had quizzed Neva about her mother. This was why he had helped Neva in the kilstroke, against Deidra, and why he had tried to protect her from Trinizhi. Neva had never known Alizhi's last name, nor the name of Astiand's mother. She would have needed one or the other to connect the dots.

Neva tried to poke holes in what he told her, but she suspected he was finally being forthright. If she remained within Trinizhi's domain, she would be discovered as Dhianz's Hand and the donazhi would take advantage of her. It was only a matter of time, if this display of destructive power had not already revealed her secret.

"Bryand was right about one thing," Astiand's eyes locked on the cooling pile of charred flesh and bone that had once been his friend and fellow soldier. "Redeeming the Da'Valia to the great Dhianz will take our entire race. It was wrong for Trinizhi to go after that much power alone — but I can understand why she did."

"I'm sorry," Neva told him. She didn't know if it was her fault or if Trinizhi had killed Bryand before the Hand incinerated him, but the result was the same. Astiand had lost a dear friend today.

"Just go," Astiand nearly whispered the directive, and Neva realized something she hadn't before. The donazhi endeavored to obtain the Trishula because it would mean total dominion. That was her temptation. But Astiand was also drawn to the power of the Trishula, and Neva might well be the epitome of that lure. Even though he might not know she was the Hand, he recognized her potential.

Neva swallowed hard. Why did he have to be Trinizhi's aliado? She could feel the palpable connection between them flare to life. It danced on her skin, bringing gooseflesh to the surface. There was something between them, but if she left now, it wouldn't ever have the chance to grow.

"You're truly noble, Astiand," Neva told him. She stood on her toes and wrapped her arms around his neck, kissing him hard and fast before breaking away. Not that she was counting, but that was number four.

Their eyes met, and she gave him no warning before slamming her power-backed fist into his head. He hit the ground with a dull thud, and she crumpled to her knees beside his unconscious body with a sob.

She couldn't fathom how things had come to this, but she had no other choice. She couldn't fight his reasoning, and, if she was running, she wasn't going to provide the donazhi with any reason to doubt his commitment.

Neva was afraid of how much blood she had lost, and she was exhausted from all that had transpired in the past week. Pain radiated from the cut in her side. The desire to lay next to Astiand's body and let Trinizhi do with her what she would was tempting.

"Neva!" Adam called out to her from where he and her father stood at the edge of the trench. Behind them was Morty with his crooked eye patch, Neil with his bushy eyebrows scrunched together, and the rest of her Ring. Adam had supplied them with numerous weapons, and they appeared ready to use them, but the fight was over.

Their arrival pulled her from her wallow. Neva hadn't come this far to give up. She pooled her determination and forced herself to stand.

"Didn't I tell you to keep a distance?" Neva called out to them, holding back tears. Honor did exist among thieves. It was hard to find sometimes, but they had come through for her.

"Get over there and help her, lad!" Morty gave Adam a push.

The thieves followed Adam's lead across the trench and came to stand around her in an uneven formation.

"Pa!" Neva hugged her father, not wanting to let go. "You're all right?"

"I'm fine, my girl," Shaun said. His voice was thick with emotion. She wasn't the only one trying not to cry. "Thanks to you."

"What happened?" Adam rested a hand on her shoulder, an angry expression on his face as he looked at Astiand on the ground next to her.

"I — it was terrible. A terrible battle." Neva tried to focus as her father released her from his embrace. Dizziness tugged at her knees.

"I'll say." Archibald kicked a pile of ash that was once a Da'Foha soldier.

Neva's vision swam, and she reached out to Adam to hold herself up.

"Neva, my girl, you've been hurt." Her father sounded horrified, and given what they'd both just lived through, it made her love him even more. "Get that healer over here quick!"

"We'd best make away before the Order comes out in force," Neil interjected, looking around nervously.

Neva glanced down to find blood had soaked through her clothing and was now dripping onto the ground. She could fix it herself, but she needed to wash the wound first.

"I'll be fine." Her words were unconvincing, even to her own ears.

"We have a carriage packed and ready to go," Adam said. "The healer will tend to your wounds there and then we'll be off."

"Wait," Neva pulled away. "Wait, I — I need to…"

Neva pushed past her Ring and made her way to Arroyand, calling on her Da'Valian vision. The shining aura of the goblet beckoned her, and she swept it up, wrapping it in the edge of her cape. Trinizhi would know who'd taken it — of that there was no doubt — but she couldn't allow the donazhi to have the Eye, not when Neva might keep other Da'Valia clans free from Trinizhi's ruthlessness.

"Lass, it is time to go," Morty's gentle reminder brought her to her senses. "The Order and the Watch will be here any moment, and we'll all want to be long gone when they arrive."

"Aye." Neva took a step toward the group and faltered. The strength drained from her legs, and she lost her balance. Adam and Roger were there in an instant, supporting her under her arms.

"Don't worry, Neva." Adam adjusted his stance to accept more of her weight. "We'll be far away before they track us."

"Why not dispose of them before they can follow?" Archibald asked, leaning over Trinizhi's still form.

"No!" Neva shouted with as much energy as she could muster. "That would cause more — more of them to come."

"Let's get you away from here, lassie," Neil said again, shuffling his feet. "I have a nasty feeling coming on."

With that, the Ring headed back into the forest. No one questioned it when Neil had one of his 'feelings.' The carriage Neva had stolen from Astiand was not far, and Neva noticed with relief her Ring had managed to find two horses to replace the ones with glowing red eyes. The healer cleaned Neva's wound and let her cauterize it herself before adding an extra bandage as a precaution. He gave her a sickeningly sweet tonic to thicken her blood, another bitter one to dull the pain, which he warned would make her sleepy, and a jar of salve to discourage infection in smaller cuts.

Margret and the boys were already in the carriage with their meager belongings stowed. One by one, her uncles, Fletcher, and Roger hugged Neva and her family goodbye. The medicine the healer helped her swallow worked its way through her system, lulling her into a slumber. Her eyes closed as

Adam flicked the reins and they rolled out onto the road that would lead them away from Glacier Pass forever.

"You're safe now, Neva," Margret whispered, stroking her hair. "Everything will be all right."

Epilogue

Neva looked out the window of the uppermost suite in the House of Amaryll. A gentle wind caught her hair, drawing the darkened locks away from her face as her gaze flitted over the hundreds of merrymakers who took to the city streets. The warm sunset bathed a crosshatch of buildings in a brilliant orange and cast a looming shadow from the mountains over the fields, which stretched as far as the eye could see in every direction beyond the urban expanse. Vestive was a busy time for trading crops, not as lively as mid-Cravell celebrations perhaps, but this was a high holiday that brought all into the streets. Today, Cirandrel honored the gods of prosperity and mercantile and bounty, Odonus and Ceris. Neva appreciated the distraction.

The city of Farleigh had provided Neva and her family a perfect place to escape. Shortly after their departure from Glacier Pass, they had sold Astiand's carriage for an impressive amount of coin, which they in turn had used to purchase a wagon and disguises as they traveled. Neva was now Alys and had a glamoured face in case anyone might recognize her. Shaun, Margret, and the boys wanted for naught thanks to the gold and silver of Lindzhi's holdings — not to mention the money to be made when nobles were too preoccupied with the harvest festival to monitor their own belongings. Of course, the sleeping guards in the hallway had been put in charge of that, but they had been easy enough to subdue with the mysterious gift of a special brandy her father had brewed for the occasion.

"We're packed." Adam inched up behind her. The sack he carried was full of their loot. "You have the scroll?"

"It's secure," Neva confirmed.

The scroll was the one item for which they had been promised payment, and she had it tucked safely into the bag at her waist. It was time to leave her mark — or it would have been. Neva was mourning the demise of the Lynx, since it wasn't safe to use now Trinizhi knew the moniker. Her thoughts skipped to Astiand, and she smiled faintly, thinking of life among the Da'Voda. She often missed training with Emiliand and having Astiand around to fight with when she was in a bad mood. At the same time, she felt more complete than she had in her entire life. Neva knew what was harbored inside her now, and she was learning to use the Hand bit by bit.

The Hand pushed against her mind, sensing her attention, but Neva shoved it back. She would release a drop to create a distraction so that Adam could make a clean getaway, but only when the time was right.

Now that Adam had learned the truth about her mixed blood, they were developing a dependable partnership. Once, something as dangerous as infiltrating the House of Amaryll would have deterred him, but not any longer. Being thrown in the Da'Voda's dungeon had helped Adam move past his fear of the Order. "They're just men," he liked to say.

"I'll meet you at the rendezvous point," Neva told Adam. She grabbed hold of the smooth river stones framing the window and swung a leg out. The ground was a long way down.

"You're mad. You know that, don't you?" Adam asked her, shaking his head.

"Not mad," Neva said. "I'm Da'Valian."

She flashed him a grin and dropped out of sight.

Glossary

Abel Kittle – Aunt Margret's deceased husband, father of James and Kendall.

Adam Tate – A thief in Neva's ring who dabbles in trading weapons and is a skilled tracker and hunter.

Aliado (al-E-odd-O) – A hilan member of a majila's alliad.

Alizhi Da'Voda-Cuchilla– A majila friend and mentor of Monazhi.

Alliad (al-E-ad) – A group of Da'Valia that agree to work together and share their power following a private bonding ceremony performed by an otima.

Alys (al-ice) – An alias of Neva's.

Amber McCaine – A prostitute who helps run the Geary Brothel, and the long-time girlfriend of Flynn Abernathy.

Archibald – One of the thieves in Neva's Ring that she calls her "uncle."

Arroyand Da'Voda-Esava (a-roy-and) – A toppel aliado of Trinizhi, the donazhi of the Da'Voda clan. A sexual sadist, and ruthless fighter.

Ashford – The premier trading hub of Cirandrel, a city of prosperity and waterways that connect to other parts of the kingdom.

Astiand Da'Voda-Cuchilla (as-T-and) – A bitter and handsome toppel aliado aligned with Trinizhi, the donazhi of the Da'Voda clan. Son of Alizhi Da'Voda-Cuchilla.

Auton (ah-ton) – The season after Cravell and before Fireside. When the weather is crisp and leaves turn to orange.

Battle of Olgor – A long-ago battle in which the last troll died in the Dark Wood forest.

Benjamand (ben-ja-mand) – A topple scholar among the Da'Xana and old friend of Monazhi's.

Beastie – A slang term for unaligned hilans.

Brakane Desert (bray-cane) – The desert region where the Da'Foha reside.

Bridoona-al (bry-doon-a-al) – A high holiday, celebrating the arrival of Fireside.

Bryand Da'Voda Solatta (bry-and) – A toppel aliado of Trinizhi, the Da'Voda's donazhi, and longtime friend of Astiand Da'Voda-Cuchilla.

Calland (cal-land) – A trustworthy hilan of Monazhi's era.

Cashcar Ports – The primary shipping hub on Cirandrel's western coastline.

Casting – 1. Usually a public action in which a majila uses a lure of power to declare her interest in forming a casual or formal relationship with a hilan. 2. Among magic workers, the use of spells to mold power into magic.

Ceris (C-ris) – The goddess of bounty and the hunt.

Chameleon, the – An alias of Thatcher Sullivan, an unscrupulous and notorious thief from the west.

Chaunzhi (ch-a-un-zee) – A majila who dallies with Arroyand.

Cirandrel (ser-an-drel) – The country in which Neva grew up. It is governed by a King Stephan and his Order of Cirandrel, twelve dukes who run Houses across the realm.

Colavalia (col-ah-vall-E-ah) – A race of supernatural guardians Dhianz created as a gift to Riska to protect the gates to the Underworld.

Conviction marks – This is how the Order of Cirandrel keeps track of who has been convicted of a major crime. Those with three marks are shipped off to Lithlorian Island for life.

Cravell (craw-vell)– The season after Vestive and before Auton. When the weather is warm.

Cul Corner – A rundown, poorer side of town full of prostitution, drug use, and slums in Glacier Pass.

Da'Bruna (da-broo-na) – The most brutal Da'Valia clan remaining. The Da'Bruna reside in the Grasslands on the edge of the desert. They have kept many old traditions going and are cannibalistic.

Da'Foha (da-foe-ha) – Another Da'Valia clan that keeps with the old ways and eats its dead, the Da'Foha reside in the Brakane Desert.

Dand District – An upper-class section of Glacier Pass adjacent to the House of Trescony.

Darrand (dare-and) – A toppel Da'Voda soldier.

Da'Roha (da-row-ha) – A nomadic Da'Valia clan led by a donazhi and consisting of hilan warriors who sign on for service with the desire to find majilas to align with from other clans.

Da'Valia (da-vall-E-a) – Fierce creatures created by Dhianz, the god of war, for battle. They're strong, fast, cunning, and they have exceptional eyesight that allows them to see when something has been spelled. They were forced out of Ramanaji hundreds of years ago by the Obsidian Brotherhood and Djinn. Only five clans remain, and each is commanded by a toppel majila, who is called a donazhi. The hilans, the males of the race, were brought into being at midnight, and the majilas, the females of the race, were brought into being at dawn, which is reflected in their coloring and power. They value skilled fighters, power, and honor. After their creation, they were subsequently cursed by Dhianz with an imbalance of power that is more punishing to all the majilas.

Da'Voda (da-vo-da) – The most remote Da'Valia clan remaining. They're extremely wealthy and reclusive, and reside in the northern mountains of Cirandrel.

Da'Xana (da-zan-a) – The most prestigious Da'Valia clan remaining. They have many scholars and warlocks and reside in the coastal fortress known as Picquereau in Cirandrel.

Dhianz (diane-zz) – The god of war.

Deidra – A Vodou witch for hire and the older sister of Gillian.

Djinn (gin) – Creatures demonic in essence who specialize in possession, created by Goj.

Donazhi (doe-na-zee) – A toppel majila, who is favored by Dhianz and who rules a Da'Valian clan. This is not an inherited position, and a majila must win her place as ruler. Her reign ends only when she dies.

Ellazhi Da'Voda-Ostra (ella-zee) – A young Da'Voda who goes through her rite of passage at the same time Neva does.

Elzhi (el-zee) – A majila who dallies with Arroyand.

Emiliand Da'Voda-Riga (E-me-lee-and) – A handsome and humble half-breed hilan soldier who is the Da'Voda's best fighter. Orphaned at birth, he never met his mother, a former Da'Bruna, nor his father, a Colavalia. He's a toppel who can secretly also read minds.

Eye, the – A powerful tool of prognostication and the first prong of the Trishula.

Farleigh (far-lee) – A large urban expanse and agricultural mecca at the base of the mountains and above the flood plains of Cirandrel.

Ferand (fair-and) – The demigod son of Dhianz and S'donzhi who was killed by Dhianz's brother Goj when S'donzhi betrayed Dhianz.

Firérite (fee-ray-rite) – An incredibly painful, sometimes debilitating, and sometimes deadly, rite of passage among the Da'Valia. Hilans are quite young when they go through the process, and majilas do so when they reach adolescence. After the rite of passage, a Da'Valia has immediate controlled access to their power.

Fireside – The coldest season of the year, Fireside follows Auton and comes before Vestive.

Flynn Abernathy – The cunning and charming crime lord of Glacier Pass, also Neva's longtime boss.

Fletcher – A younger thief in Neva's Ring who likes to guzzle his booze and isn't too greedy.

Gaband (gah-band) – One of Vivizhi's weapons masters who specializes in daggers.

Garin – A family in Glacier Pass that sells firewood to Neva and others who mark it up and sell it to clients around the city.

Geary Brothel – A famous brothel in Glacier Pass, located on Geary Street in the Cul Corner district. The base for Flynn Abernathy's operations.

Geary Street – A popular street in Cul Corner where anything is for sale.

Gillian – The younger sister of Deidra, a Vodou witch.

Glacier Arm – The river that runs from the glacier along Glacier Pass and through the mountains, eventually connecting to another river that flows to Ashford. It's incredibly dangerous, impossible to travel down during Fireside, but effective for moving cargo during the warm seasons.

Glacier Pass – The northernmost city in Cirandrel, originally established by those who were seeking riches mining in the mountains and now a thriving metropolis and the top exporter of both base and precious metals. Home to the House of Trescony.

Glamour – A usually cheap spell attached to a charm of some sort that imbues the wearer physical attributes they think are advantageous or attractive. Usually created and sold by hedge witches.

Goj (gah-j) – The vengeful god of trickery, Dhianz's half-brother.

Grasslands – The harsh bog-ridden plains that are the de facto boundary separating Cirandrel and the deserts. This is where the Da'Bruna reside.

Great War – A civil war resulting from the Order of Cirandrel's eventually successful attempt at a coup, which lasted from 1633 to 1644 as King Stephan stole the throne from his cousin, King Charles.

Grianch (gree-anch) – A small town in the mountains not far from Glacier Pass where travelers frequently stop on their way to and from the city.

Guard, the – A military force led by the Order of Cirandrel. In times of peace, their primary objective is to protect the Houses and the King. In times of war, they protect the realm.

Hanazhi Da'Voda-Gnerre (hana-zee) – A Da'Voda soldier and single mother.

Hand, the – The second prong of Dhianz's greatest weapon, the Trishula. It can be wielded to level a fiery destruction upon one's foes.

Hagave (ha-ga-vay) – A spicy alcoholic beverage, which unlike many other spirits does have an effect on the Da'Valia.

Hedge witch – A human blessed with a sprinkle of power from no god in particular, a hedge witch usually lives off making glamour charms, tinctures, and telling the future.

Hilan (hee-lan) – A male Da'Valia.

House of Amaryll (ama-rill) – The House of Amaryll is one of the twelve houses of the Order of Cirandrel and is located in Farleigh.

House of Trescony – The House of Trescony is one of the twelve houses of the Order of Cirandrel and is located in Glacier Pass.

Illuminator – A globe that is spelled so when it is activated, it reveals all – casting light in the dark and disarming spells.

James Kittle – Neva's eldest cousin on her father's side, a twin to Kendall and son of Aunt Margret.

Jasand (ja-sand) – A Da'Voda solider.

Jorand Da'Voda-Lira (jor-and) – A lowel hilan and Neva's cousin, he works the Da'Voda boundary patrol and was Lindzhi's brother.

Junipero (hoo-nee-peer-O) – A tasty, minty alcoholic beverage that, unlike many spirits, has an effect on the Da'Valia.

Kamash Islands (ka-mash) – A cluster of six rich islands where silk originates off the western coast of Cirandrel.

Kelizhi Da'Voda-Gamonda (kell-E-zee) – A middel majila who is aligned to Roland and is a soldier for the Da'Voda usually working the boundary patrol.

Kendall Kittle – Neva's youngest cousin on her father's side, a twin to James and son of Aunt Margret.

Kilstroke – A fight to the death among the Da'Valia. It must be sanctioned by a donazhi and the rites conducted by a prima otima. The kilstroke is considered the catalyst for Dhianz's judgment.

King Charles – The previous ruler of Cirandrel who was usurped by King Stephan and the Order of Cirandrel in a decade-long war for the realm.

King Stephan – The ruler of Cirandrel, who colluded with the Order of Cirandrel to steal his position from his cousin, King Charles.

Landscape – A term for the plane of existence between the realm of the living and the Underworld, where those favored by Dhianz may pull another's spirit with them for a private conversation.

Laurand Da'Voda-Steila (la-rand) – A toppel hilan, he is the second best fighter among the Da'Voda.

Lindzhi Da'Voda-Lira (lind-see) – A middel majila and Neva's cousin who works as a mercenary, taking high-risk, high-paying jobs.

Lithlorian – A dragon with a legendary treasure trove who struck a deal with the Order of Cirandrel to act as the warden of Lithlorian Island in exchange for a steady supply of convicts to eat.

Lowel (low-el) – The lowest level of power among the Da'Valia.

Lure – The string of fog-like power a majila casts to a hilan when she wants to establish a relationship, either casual or formal.

Magic – God-given power that has been worked through a spell.

Majila (ma-hee-la) – A female Da'Valia.

Margret Kittle – Neva's aunt and Shaun's sister, Margret is also James and Kendall's mother.

Master at arms – The highest military position among a Da'Valian clan. The person holding this position reports to the donazhi directly. The master at arms oversees all military training, strategies, and assignments, and their direct subordinates are commanders.

Mazhi (ma-zee) – An older soldier in the Da'Voda forces who works the border patrol for the enclave.

Melanzhi Da'Foha (mel-an-zee) – The donazhi of the Da'Foha.

Middel (mid-el) – The second level of power among the Da'Valia.

Mikel (me-kel) – A friend of Neva's who also delivers firewood around Glacier Pass to make end's meat. His wife is expecting, and he frequents knife-throwing tournaments.

Miland (me-land) – A disgraced Da'Voda hilan whose punishment included cutting off his horns to sever him from his power and servitude for the rest of his life.

Monazhi Roberts (m-O-na-zee) – Formerly Monazhi Da'Voda-Lira, she was a former frontrunner for the position of the Da'Voda's donazhi and a talented warlock. She is the mother of Nevazhi Roberts.

Morty – One of the thieves in Neva's Ring who she grew up calling "uncle," he has a jovial outlook and one eye.

Mouth, the – The third prong of the Trishula. It's power has not been seen in centuries.

Neil – One of the thieves in Neva's Ring who she grew up calling "uncle," he has an uncanny gut instinct that has helped keep him alive.

Nevazhi Roberts (ne-va-zee) – A half-human, half-Da'Valian thief who grew up in Glacier Pass. She's the daughter of Shaun Roberts and Monazhi Roberts.

Obsidian Brotherhood – The order of mages who rule Ramanaji Desert with Djinn.

Odonus (O-don-us) – The god of prosperity and mercantile.

Old King's Highway – A network of roads maintained by the Order that connect all the Houses in Cirandrel.

Oliand Da'Voda-Dejada (O-lee-and) – An elder warlock among the Da'Voda whose occupation is to evaluate majilas before they go through their firérites to help determine their place within the clan.

Order of Cirandrel – A group of twelve dukes who conspired against the former king of Cirandrel to put King Stephan on the throne, now the ruling order.

Otima (O-tee-ma) – A holy servant of Dhianz who is androgynous and adept at magic.

Perzhi Da'Xana (per-zee) – The donazhi of the Da'Xana clan.

Power – Power is god-gifted to people, places, and things in Cirandrel. It can be molded and directed by those who know how to use it, either in its raw form or in spells.

Prima otima (pree-ma O-tee-ma) – The lead otima of a clan, they are an expert in rituals and casting magic in honor of Dhianz. Their specialities include healing, kilstrokes, alliad ceremonies, geldings, death rites, and similar events.

Quand (kw-and) – A toppel hilan soldier with a talent for tracking in the Da'Voda ranks.

Ramanaji Desert (ra-man-a-G) – The harsh desert country the Da'Valia were driven out of by the Obsidian Brotherhood and Djinn.

Rings, the – Gangs of career criminals in Glacier Pass who answer to Flynn Abernathy.

Riska (risk-a) – The goddess of death and ruler of the Underworld.

Roberts' Tavern – The tavern in Glacier Pass owned by Shaun Roberts.

Roger – Flynn's right-hand man.

Roland Da'Voda-Punya (row-land) – A middel hilan and aliado of Kelizhi, he works the boundary patrol in the Da'Voda's ranks.

Rule of Rhianzhi (r-I-an-zee) – The Da'Valian rule requiring anyone who finds a majila about to come into her power to do everything they are capable of to bring that majila before an otima in time for a firérite when the majila says she is invoking the Rule. The Rule was established after a majila did not make it to her firérite before her power lashed out and humans hunted down Da'Valia as a result.

Scry – A magical process of locating something, usually with a map and a crystal or other powerful object.

S'donzhi (s-don-zee) – An extremely beautiful and powerful warlock. This toppel majila caught Dhianz's interest when the clans were still unified in Ramanaji Desert. She fell in love with him and his brother when they walked the realm in the form of hilans. S'donzhi gave birth to a son, who she named Ferand.

Shacklay – A magical bracelet used by the Da'Valia to subdue a majilas' uncontrolled power before her firérite and to constrain those in custody.

Shaundrazhi Da'Bruna (shaun-dra-zee) – The donazhi of the Da'Bruna clan.

Shaun Roberts – Neva's father, a retired thief, brewer, and bartender.

Summit – A meeting of the clans that occurs once per year at Picquereau.

Thatcher Sullivan – Alias: Chameleon, a notorious thief.

Thieves' Code, the – The Thieves' Code in Glacier Pass is a set of rules all who operate under Flynn Abernathy abide by. The First Rule: Thou shall not snitch. The Second Rule: Thou shall answer to Flynn Abernathy. The Third Rule: Thou shall not lead authorities to thy brothers and sisters. The Fourth Rule: Thou shall give tithe to thy crime lord.

Tiger's Eye – A Da'Voda pub with an auditorium and fighting ring in the basement.

Toppel (top-el) – The highest level of power among the Da'Valia.

Trinizhi Da'Voda (trin-E-zee) – The donazhi of the Da'Voda. She is aligned with Arroyand, Astiand, and Bryand.

Trishula (tri-shoo-la) – The greatest weapon ever created by Dhianz. The tridents' three prongs are the Eye, the Hand, and the Mouth.

Tyvse Sea (tie-vees) – The ocean separating Cirandrel from Amania.

Vestive (vest-ive) – A rainy and sunny season following Fireside and preceding Cravell.

Vivizhi Da'Voda-Mourda (viv-E-zee) – A toppel majila, the master at arms for the Da'Voda is a mentor to Emiliand and was once involved with Astiand romantically.

Vodou witch (voo-doo) – A powerful witch from the Vodou line, known to be deadly and dangerous to Da'Valia.

Warlock – A Da'Valia trained in magic with an emphasis on battle magic.

Watch, the – Glacier City's Watch is a government force that protects its citizens according to the laws of Cirandrel and guards the wall around the city.

Acknowledgments

Thank you to my #1 alpha reader, Joyanna, who was the first to read this book when it didn't resemble a book. Your enthusiasm and feedback kept me going over the many years it took me to put it together properly. And to my writing partners — your friendship and support helps me show up and stay sane. Moana and Kelsey, I love you ladies. To my husband, Brian, who doesn't like to read but who read this book multiple times and challenged me to be a better writer. He supports my writing because he knows I love it. He steps up and "dads" so I have time to write, and does so much more. I couldn't have done this without you.

Shout-out to all my beta readers but especially Heather Derocher, Ella Cooper, Allegra Pescatori, and Stephanie Anne. Your feedback made me think twice more than once (pun intended) and inspired me. Ruxandra of Methyss Art, you are an artistic goddess. Thank you for the amazing job you did bringing Neva to life on such a beautiful cover.

Thanks also to my parents, Joy and Steve, for raising me with a healthy imagination and enough self-confidence to think I could write a book. And last, but certainly not least, to Laurie Mallet, who taught me how to write a sentence seven different ways with workbooks from the junior college at the long wooden table in the upstairs of the Odd Fellows building in Boulder Creek. I'll always miss you.

About the Author

CHRISTINA DAVIS was born and raised in Santa Cruz, California, where she was home-schooled in the mountains and read every book she could get her hands on at the local library. She graduated *summa cum laude* with a Bachelor's degree from San Jose State University and enjoyed a career in sports and digital journalism before moving into financial services marketing. She is now a stay-at-home mom who writes every chance she gets. She lives in beautiful Monterey County with her husband and daughter.

If you enjoyed this book, please join The Kilstroke Circle newsletter at ChristinaDavisWrites.com for book updates, giveaways, secret scenes, and more!